LITTLE OF DROPS OF WATER . . .

A fugitive draft blew over Margaret's wet skin, and she shivered, pulling the towel closer around her.

"Dry yourself," Philip said, suddenly appearing in her doorway, "before you catch an inflammation of the lungs."

"I will . . . as soon as you leave my room."

"This is my house," Philip said, "and everything in it awaits my pleasure . . . including you!" He strode across the room and, jerking the towel out of her fingers, began to briskly rub it over her wet body.

Margaret could feel his hard fingers pressing into her soft flesh. Her skin felt tight and tingling. She had to get him out of her room, quickly, or she'd be fighting both him and herself . . . with no hope of winning either battle.

"I'm dry," she whispered.

"You're wrong," he murmured, running his fingertips over her shoulder, dipping into the hollow of her collarbone. Lowering his head, he pressed his lips against her flesh. "There's a tiny bit of moisture right about here."

Margaret tried to retreat, but Philip was too quick for her. His arms encircled . . . and the burning heat of his body scorched her, from chest to thigh. . . .

YOUR PLACE ON OUR WEBSITE
AND MAKE THE
READING CONNECTION!

We've created a customized website just for our very special readers, where you can get the inside scoop on everything that's going on with Zebra, Pinnacle and Kensington books.

When you come online, you'll have the exciting opportunity to:

- View covers of upcoming books
- Read sample chapters
- Learn about our future publishing schedule (listed by publication month *and author*)
- Find out when your favorite authors will be visiting a city near you
- Search for and order backlist books from our online catalog
- Check out author bios and background information
- Send e-mail to your favorite authors
- Meet the Kensington staff online
- Join us in weekly chats with authors, readers and other guests
- Get writing guidelines
- AND MUCH MORE!

Visit our website at
http://www.zebrabooks.com

DECEPTION

Judith McWilliams

Zebra Books
Kensington Publishing Corp.

http://www.zebrabooks.com

ZEBRA BOOKS are published by

Kensington Publishing Corp.
850 Third Avenue
New York, NY 10022

First Printing: January, 1999
10 9 8 7 6 5 4 3 2 1

Printed in the United States of America

Prologue

Philip Moresby, eighth Earl of Chadwick, stalked into his club and shoved his high-crowned beaver hat and leather gloves at the waiting butler.

"Good morning, my lord. Mr. Raeburn is waiting for you in the gaming room."

The earl nodded curtly and went in search of his friend. He found him sitting beside the fire reading the *Post*.

Lucien glanced up, studied Philip's rigid expression for a long moment and then reached for the bottle of port on the table beside him. After refilling his own empty glass, he handed a drink to Philip.

Philip drained the wine in one long swallow, then glared at the empty goblet as if he wanted to smash it.

"Consider the dignity of Brookes," Lucien warned as he rescued the glass and set it back down on the table.

Philip dropped down in the chair beside him and scowled at the floor.

"The House of Lords didn't receive your speech well?" Lucien hazarded a guess.

"They didn't receive it at all! I was speaking to an all-but-empty chamber. Something as important as the plight of the returning soldiers, and those codheads . . .

"Demmit, Lucien, there has to be a way to make them see sense!"

"The House of Lords, see sense?" Lucien gave him a pitying look. "You might as well pin your hopes on divine intervention, like Fields over there." He gestured across the room to where a pale young man was staring blankly at the card the faro dealer had just turned up.

Philip snorted. "And probably be as successful as he is. He'll have gambled away everything he owns by morning."

"Maybe you ought to set up a gambling establishment. Since men like Fields seem determined to lose their patrimony anyway, they might as well do it for the benefit of England."

"Tempting, but too chancy a method of finance. Besides," Philip said, "the soldiers have earned a pension, not alms. They fought and a great many of them died so that sapskulls like Fields there, could continue their aimless existences."

"True," Lucien readily agreed, "but then how many of us get what we deserve in this life?"

Philip winced, his brown eyes darkening almost to black beneath the flood of bitter memories that Lucien's chance comment had jarred loose. Determinedly, he shoved them aside and concentrated instead on the problem that was consuming his days and disturbing his nights.

"You do have a few members of Parliament firmly on your side," Lucien offered a crumb of comfort.

"True, but to get my bill through Parliament, I have to have wider support and so far, no argument I've tried has made any impression on the older, more influential peers. As far as they're concerned, the soldiers were paid to defeat Napoleon and what happens to them now that they've managed to do it, is no concern of Parliament's."

"And since you're just a sprig of thirty-five, they aren't going to listen to you," Lucien said.

"I hadn't thought of it that way before, Lucien, but you could well be right. Maybe I should be attacking the problem from another angle."

"I was never much good at geometry, old boy. Explain the angle."

"If the older peers won't listen to me because they think I'm too young, then the obvious solution is to find someone older they *will* listen to. But who could influence enough of them to make a difference?" Philip stared blankly at a painting of a pack of hounds dismembering a fox.

"Hendricks!" Philip suddenly announced. "He's one of the most respected men in England. If he were to champion the soldiers' cause, it might swing enough votes to carry the bill."

"It might," Lucien agreed. "But from what I hear, the only cause Hendricks is interested in is finding his daughter."

Philip frowned, remembering snippets of gossip. "He does have a daughter, doesn't he?"

"More likely *had,*" Lucien corrected. "It's been almost twenty-five years since his wife took the child and all the jewels she could lay her hands on and ran off to the Continent with her lover. The chances of their having survived all these years with the war raging are not good."

"Women always find a way to survive," Philip said. "Usually at the expense of some fool of a man."

"Maybe, but Sally Jersey said that Hendricks's agents have been scouring the Continent for signs of his daughter ever since the war ended and they haven't found a single clue."

"Maybe they aren't asking the right people. I wonder . . ."

Lucien studied his friend's absorbed expression, remembering Philip's disconcerting habit of dropping out of sight for weeks on end. Rumor had it that he had operated a highly effective spy ring during the war, but not even Lucien, who considered himself to be Philip's oldest and closest friend, knew if there was any truth to those rumors.

"Perhaps your contacts in France would be able to run Hendricks's daughter to ground?" Lucien dared encroach on the invisible barrier Philip seemed to maintain around himself.

Philip studied him for a long moment. "Perhaps."

"Although even if you did somehow manage to find the chit, that might not help you," Lucien pointed out. "Hendricks would probably want to take her home to his estate."

Philip laughed cynically. "Hendricks may want that, but I'll guarantee you that his daughter will choose the glitter of London society."

"Possibly," Lucien conceded. "And if she does come to London, Hendricks will accompany her."

"Which will allow me to subtly pressure him to repay me for finding his daughter by supporting my bill."

"You haven't a subtle bone in your body," Lucien scoffed.

"I'll have you know that the ministry sees me as a budding diplomat. They've asked me to deliver a diplomatic pouch to Castlereagh in Vienna. I could easily stop in France first and put an investigation in place. With luck, I might be able to retrieve Hendricks's daughter on my way home."

"But she's no longer a child. She might not want to be retrieved."

"I'll make sure she does." He gave his friend a smile that was totally devoid of humor. "I'll do whatever I have to."

Lucien felt a sudden chill of foreboding at Philip's grim expression. He poured himself a glass of port as he weighed his chances of talking Philip out of trying to locate Hendricks's daughter. Nil, he decided, and that being so, there was no sense in angering his friend by trying. All he could do was to wait and hope that nothing disastrous occurred as a result of his chance comment.

One

Margaret Abney shivered as a blast of wind-driven rain slammed against the room's one window. Its poorly fitting pane did little to keep out the icy air, and she inched closer to the sluggish fire sputtering fitfully in the fireplace.

She squinted down at the dog-eared copy of Xenophon's *Polity of the Lacedaemonians,* but the tiny print was becoming harder and harder to see as the deepening dusk filled the small room with shadows. Briefly she considered lighting a candle and then decided to wait until her cousin George came home. There were so few candles left and when they were gone . . .

She shuddered at the thought of her pitiful hoard of coins, which was all that stood between them and disaster.

Common sense had told her that Vienna would be expensive with most of the aristocracy of Europe converging on it, but the prices they had encountered here had little to do with common sense. Even the two minuscule rooms they'd found in the attic of a house on the outskirts of town cost them more than ten times what she'd expected to pay.

Nevertheless, Margaret couldn't regret George's insistence that they come to Vienna. It had been exciting to watch some of the most powerful men of the world come and go in the streets—men who previously had been only names in newspapers. It was an experience she would always remember.

Where was George? Margaret shifted uneasily in the hard wooden chair. He'd specifically said that he would be home early this evening to change for a ball at the English embassy to which he had somehow managed to wangle a single invitation. She knew he was looking forward to the event, hoping to make contacts there that would gain him entrance into the homes of the aristocracy.

Getting to her feet, she wandered over to the window and pushed back the gray, tattered curtain, peering down at the cobbled street four stories below. Except for a small figure scurrying through the driving rain, it was deserted. She rubbed away the mist on the pane and checked the winding street in both directions, but there was still no sign of George.

Maybe he had found a card game and forgotten the time. At the sight of a deck of cards, George lost all track of such commonplace things as dinners and promises.

Half an hour later, she heard the sound of footsteps echoing on the bare wooden stairs, followed a moment later by a single, tentative rap on the thin paneling.

Margaret frowned, wondering who it could be. George wouldn't knock and their landlord, Frau Gruber, didn't do anything tentatively. She would have beaten on the door with all the assurance of ownership.

Margaret tiptoed across the small room and pressed her ear against the door, but there was nothing to be heard on the other side.

Carefully unlocking the door, she opened it a crack and peered out into the dark hall. Her unease instantly dissolved as she recognized the man standing there. George's friend Henry Armand was well into his sixties, inches shorter than her own five-foot-three, and stick-thin. He was not a figure to inspire fear in anyone's breast.

"Come in, Armand." Margaret swung the door open.

"George isn't back yet, but I expect him momentarily. Would you care to wait for him?"

Armand tugged his sodden black hat off his balding head and inched into the room where he stood dripping onto the threadbare carpet.

"Why don't you warm yourself at the fire?" Margaret suggested. "George shouldn't be long."

Armand shook his head. "Won't, you know," he muttered.

"What won't?" Margaret asked.

"Be long. George, I mean." Armand heaved a mournful sigh. "I promised to come and tell you."

A premonition of disaster sliced through her, raising goosebumps on her arms. "Tell me what?" she demanded.

"What happened," Armand said, and then lapsed into silence.

"And that being—?" Margaret prodded.

"It weren't poor George's fault. Leastwise, not exactly. The devil was in the cards this afternoon and when he came in . . ."

"George lost at cards?" Margaret tried to hurry him up.

"Badly dipped," Armand confirmed. "Was giving his vowels to everyone. That's why he was so glad to see him, don't you see?"

Margaret bit back her raging sense of impatience, knowing that there was no way to hurry Armand. His thought processes—such as they were—were slow and ponderous.

"I'm afraid I don't know who *'he'* is," she said.

"Chadwick," Henry whispered hoarsely, almost as if he were afraid of being overheard.

Margaret tried to place the name. It sounded English, but she couldn't remember anyone named Chadwick being mentioned in the English papers.

"The Earl of Chadwick," Armand elaborated. "He's not . . . an easy man."

"Name me one member of the aristocracy who is," Margaret said tartly.

"Yes, well, some are easier than others, and George should have known. If he just hadn't lost so much before, he never would have done it."

"Done what?" Margaret kept her voice level with a monumental effort.

Armand furtively glanced around the dim room and then muttered, "Cheated."

Margaret blinked in surprise. As far as she knew, George had never stooped to cheating before. "I take it George was found out?"

Armand nodded unhappily. "Chadwick caught him trying to use a marked deck. No question about it."

Margaret winced at the thought of the embarrassment and shame George must have felt at having been publicly branded a cheat. But maybe it was for the best, she tried to tell herself. Maybe this would finally convince George that he didn't have the ability to make a living playing cards. And he certainly wouldn't want to stay in Vienna now that everyone would know of his disgrace. He'd undoubtedly agree to go back to Paris where the living expenses were more manageable. The thought momentarily lifted her spirits.

"I guess I'd better start packing our trunks." She glanced around the sparsely furnished room. "George will probably want to leave at first light."

"Wants to leave now," Armand muttered, "not that it'll do him much good."

Margaret studied Armand's downcast face for a moment and then asked, "Why not?"

" 'Cause he can't. Can't go nowhere, locked up the way he is."

"Locked up!" Margaret repeated in shock. "What do you mean, locked up?"

"I mean they took him away."

Margaret frowned. "Chadwick?"

"No, some general who was there at the club when it happened. He said that he wasn't having no Captain Sharps preying on Vienna's guests, and he told his soldiers to take George to the military jail. Said George could stay there until the Congress was over and there weren't no one to fleece."

"Over! Why it could be months."

"Years," Henry amended gloomily. "You know how politicians are once they get to talking."

"Exactly where have they taken George?" Margaret demanded.

"To a prison on the western edge of the city. Nasty damp place with stone walls and water running off them."

Margaret felt a clutch of fear at Henry's description. George couldn't stay in a place like that. The doctor who'd attended him during his last frightening illness had been very specific about the dangers of cold and damp on weak lungs. She had to get George out of that place before he took sick.

"What about an appeal to the British ambassador?" she said.

"Tried that first thing." Armand dashed her hopes. "Blasted man said he wasn't going to risk upsetting Chadwick for someone who was no better than he should be."

Of course he wouldn't help, Margaret thought bitterly. The aristocracy stuck together and anyone outside their closed ranks could be damned for all they cared. Even so, there had to be some way to get George free— She suddenly remembered her precious hoard of coins.

"Armand, can we bribe someone to let him go?"

He shook his head. "Tried that already. No one is willing to risk making the general or Chadwick angry. But they are willing to look the other way if I was to bring in some warm blankets and food. That is, they would if we were to slip them a few coins."

Margaret hurried over to her reticule, and poured most of her coins into Armand's outstretched hand. "Would you see that he has everything that he needs?"

"What he needs is to be out of that place," Armand muttered as he left.

No, what George needs is some common sense, Margaret thought, rubbing her forehead which was beginning to ache. She sank down on the chair and, leaning her head back, tried to plan, but her fears made it difficult. The thought of poor George locked in a damp cell terrified her. And underlying her terror was an impotent anger. There had been no need for Chadwick to lock him up. George wasn't a threat to anyone. He wasn't even a very adept cheat. He was just a nice old man with a rather obliging sense of right and wrong.

Too agitated to sit still, she began to pace across the small room. She had to do something, but what? Breaking him out of jail was totally beyond her capabilities, which meant that she had to get him released. But how? Armand had already appealed to the British ambassador and been turned down. And the general wouldn't help because he wanted to placate Chadwick.

Margaret paused as an idea occurred to her. If the general had put George in jail because Chadwick requested it, presumably he would also *release* George if Chadwick requested it.

She let her breath out in a long, uncertain sigh. Her hypothesis seemed reasonable, but was it feasible? What argument could she use to convince Chadwick to have George released? Compassion for an old man? If she were to promise to remove George from Vienna the minute he was released . . . Maybe, just maybe, it would work. If it didn't . . .

Margaret tried to swallow her rising sense of panic. She couldn't abandon George to his fate. Not only did she love the old man, but she owed him far more than she could ever repay. Somehow she had to find a way to win his freedom.

"Damnation!" Philip stalked across his host's exquisite Oriental carpet, the pressure from the heels of his gleaming Hessians leaving faint marks in its nap. He quickly reached the other side of the study and swung around to face the man standing beside the desk.

"Could your information be wrong?" Philip demanded.

Monsieur Dupree shook his head, clearly unhappy to be the bearer of bad news. "Unfortunately not, milord. I have checked out all the facts myself and they are inescapable. Lady Hendricks's lover left her and the child at the Convent of the Immaculate Heart of Mary ten months after they left England. He told the good sisters he would return for them when she delivered the child she was carrying. Unfortunately, Lady Hendricks died in childbirth and the babe along with her. The little girl succumbed to a fever a few months later."

Philip absently rubbed his jaw as he searched Monsieur Dupree's recital for flaws. "Could your informant be lying to you?"

"My informant was the Mother Superior herself. I very much doubt that she considered me worth lying to. She also sent along this to be returned to the child's father." He handed Philip the packet he'd been carrying.

Philip emptied it on the desktop. It didn't contain much, just a few folded sheets of paper and a gold locket. He picked the necklace up and studied it in the candles' warm light. A sense of defeat pressed down on him as he recognized Hendricks's coat-of-arms.

"The Mother Superior said that the child was wearing

it around her neck when she came. They saved it to give to the man they assumed was her father when he returned."

"It's never safe to make an assumption when one is dealing with women's loyalty," Philip said. "I take it Lady Hendricks's lover never returned?"

Monsieur Dupree shook his head. "According to the Mother Superior, no one has ever inquired about either Lady Hendricks or the girl. Which is hardly to be wondered at. The convent is a small one outside Cluny. If it had not been for a few inspired guesses on the part of one of my operatives, I never would have tumbled to the truth. I am only sorry that I was not able to give you better news, milord."

"That you managed to trace them at all is something of a miracle," Philip said. Opening the top desk drawer, he extracted a heavy leather bag which he handed to the Frenchman. "For your efforts and your forgetfulness."

The man nodded. "But of course, milord. I have already forgotten."

"I will remember your resourcefulness as well as your discretion. Feel free to call on me if I can be of service to you."

"You are too kind," Monsieur Dupree replied. "Will you be staying in Vienna for the Congress?"

Philip shook his head. "No. I intend to leave as soon as possible. Vienna reminds me of Vauxhall Gardens on public night. Too many people with too little purpose, fueled by too much liquor."

"And too much intrigue," Monsieur Dupree added. "Myself, I leave immediately." He tossed the bag in his hand, judging its weight with satisfaction. "The prices are ruinous. This Congress will be the making of every merchant in Vienna."

"So I've been told. I was fortunate that Lord Castlereagh was able to arrange for me to stay here as a guest of Mr. Kettering," Philip said as he escorted Monsieur Dupree to the front door.

Philip watched Dupree sprint down the steps through the driving rain and jump into his waiting carriage, then returned to the study. The lustrous gleam of the medallion caught his eye, and he stared at it in frustration. All of his hopes had come to nothing. Mary Hendricks was long dead, and all because her mother had chosen to ignore her marriage vows.

He scowled. Lady Hendricks had gotten no more than she deserved when her lover abandoned her, but the child hadn't deserved to be wrenched from her home and her doting father and carried off to a foreign country. And all in the name of love.

Philip stalked over to the fireplace, too upset to stand still. He stared blankly down into the bluish depths of the dancing flames as he considered his options. If he told Hendricks what he'd discovered, the old man would be bound to associate him with the bad news, virtually guaranteeing that Hendricks wouldn't lend his support to a soldiers' relief bill.

Suppose he *didn't* tell Hendricks what he'd discovered. Since Hendricks had no idea that he'd been looking for his daughter, he could simply remain silent. But if he chose that option, Hendricks would continue to waste what was left of his life in a doomed search.

Philip turned at the sudden rap on the study door.

"Come in," he said, assuming that it was the butler with the message that he'd been expecting from Lord Castlereagh.

It was indeed the butler, but the message he bore was not from Lord Castlereagh.

"Milord, there is a woman who desires to see you."

Philip's brows lifted at the butler's use of the word "woman" rather than "lady."

"She was most insistent, milord," the butler added. "She says that it is a matter of grave importance."

Only to *her,* Philip thought cynically. "Very well, show our visitor in. We don't want her standing about the hallway and disturbing Mr. Kettering."

"She would be far more likely to disturb Mrs. Kettering, milord," the butler observed. Turning, he gestured the woman into the room and then left, closing the door behind him.

Philip's eyes widened as he got a good look at his unexpected visitor. She wouldn't just disturb Mrs. Kettering, he thought wryly. His visitor would send that self-centered young woman into hysterics.

Philip watched as the woman walked farther into the room, stopping about ten feet from him, almost as if she were loath to get too close to him. For some reason the thought annoyed him.

In retaliation, he deliberately studied her, allowing his gaze to linger on the swell of her breasts beneath her damp woolen gown. The sudden involuntary tightening of his body caught him by surprise, making him vaguely uneasy. It was unlike him to react so strongly to a woman, even one as beautiful as this one. And she was beautiful. He tried to find a flaw in the exquisite perfection of her elegantly carved features, but there wasn't one. Her ash-blond hair framed a perfect complexion and her eyes . . .

Philip's attention was caught by her huge blue eyes, which dominated her face. They seemed filled with a poignancy that he instantly mistrusted. He, better than most, knew the folly of believing the promise of a woman's eyes. Determinedly, he forced his gaze down, only to find himself staring at her perfectly formed lips. They were a luscious rose-pink. Unbidden, his mind began to consider what her lips would feel like beneath his own.

"Who are you?" he snapped, his uncertainty at his reaction to her making his voice harsh.

A fool, Margaret thought in despair as she stared into Chadwick's hard brown eyes. There was no softness in them, no compassion. Not in his eyes, nor in the sharply chiseled lines of his face. He looked totally impervious to the softer emotions. How could George ever have thought he could cheat this man and get away with it?

But then what had she expected? she thought, with a suffocating sense of hopelessness. Chadwick was of English aristocracy, and compassion or even fairness was not among their chosen virtues.

Her gaze returned to his eyes and a frisson of nervousness coursed through her at the glitter of interest she could see sparkling in their depths. She'd seen the greedy, covetous reaction men had to her beauty far too many times not to recognize it for what it was.

"I presume you have a name." Philip's impatient voice broke into her confused thoughts.

"Margaret Abney," she forced out, when what she really wanted was to turn and run back to the dubious safety of her rented rooms. Chadwick's very presence made her feel threatened in a way she never had before.

Margaret tried to prop up her dwindling courage. She'd hated the aristocracy for so long that she endowed them with powers they didn't have. Chadwick was just a man, she assured herself. The only difference between him and George was that fate had favored Chadwick with a title and a fortune.

"Margaret Abney." His deep voice seemed to taste her name, and Margaret felt a strange, fluttery sensation in her chest. "Tell me, Margaret Abney, exactly why have you sought me out?"

"I've come to ask you to release George Gilroy," she blurted out.

Philip frowned, trying to place the name and failing.

Margaret stared at his blank face in disbelief. He'd condemned George to prison and he didn't even remember his name! "George is the man you were playing cards with yesterday afternoon when he tried to—"

"Cheat," Philip supplied, on a sense of disappointment the depth of which surprised him. So this Incomparable was connected to that inept fool who'd been stupid enough to assume that he was ripe for the plucking.

"Please ask to have him released," Margaret asked. "They've put him in prison."

"Where he'll stay until the Congress is over," Philip said flatly. "A few months with nothing to do but to contemplate the error of his chosen way of life will do him a world of good."

"He didn't choose his life, chance did!" Margaret's frustration spilled out. "The same chance that made you an earl. It certainly wasn't a position you earned or even deserved."

Philip blinked as emotion lent a silver sparkle to her eyes and painted an alluring flush on her pale cheeks. He had thought she was beautiful when he'd first seen her, but he was fast coming to the conclusion that she was more than merely beautiful. She was a diamond of the first water.

The mystery was why was she wasting her time with a penniless Captain Sharp. With her looks she could surely find a protector with much deeper pockets. Unless she had used Gilroy as a ticket to get to Vienna where most of the rich and powerful men of Europe were congregated. But if that were the case, then why try to get him out of prison? Why not simply forget about him and find another protector?

Unless . . . A stifling surge of desire clogged his throat. Could she be using her supposed concern for Gilroy as an excuse to try to capture his interest? Probably not. He reluctantly discarded the idea. Women trying to attract men didn't visit them wearing threadbare dresses his servants would disdain to wear. Nor did they insult their prospective protector. No, Margaret Abney didn't want to attach him. She wanted Gilroy free. And from the looks of her tense features she wanted it very badly.

But why? he wondered, his curiosity well and truly caught. What advantage accorded to her with George's release? His eyes narrowed as a glimmer of an idea flittered through his mind.

Slowly he walked over to the desk and picked up the letter that the doctor who had attended Mary Hendricks in her fatal illness had written. The doctor had described the child as having light golden hair and blue eyes.

Philip looked back at Margaret. Her eyes were blue, but her hair was darker. But then, blond hair normally darkened with age. With how much age? Philip riffled through his notes and found the information he wanted. If Mary Hendricks had lived, she would be twenty-seven.

"How old are you?" Philip shot at Margaret.

Taken by surprise at the seemingly irrelevant question, Margaret answered it. "Twenty-nine last July."

Close enough. Philip absently rubbed his jawline as he considered the plan taking shape in his mind. Only desperation and the conviction that time was running out for thousands of soldiers and their families ever would have made him seriously consider it.

"Tell me," he said slowly. "Do you have family here in Vienna?"

"I have no family left anywhere except George, who is a distant cousin of my mother's," she said, rejecting her natural father as he had rejected her so long ago. She felt a shiver of apprehension at the smile that lifted his lips at her answer. She didn't like the looks of that smile. It seemed to hint at things that boded no good for her.

"Sit down." Philip gestured toward one of the leather

chairs beside the fireplace. "I want to think about something."

Margaret cautiously skirted him as she headed for the chair. She preferred her spot by the door, but she didn't want to anger him if she could possibly avoid it. Not with George in his clutches. Sinking down into the chair, she absently held her numb fingers out to the roaring flames as she surreptitiously watched Chadwick out of the corner of her eye.

Philip picked up the golden locket and stared at it, trying to evaluate his chances of success. Not good, he decided. But not impossible, either.

It was a desperate gamble, but what other choice did he have? He needed Hendricks's help to get his relief bill passed, and he was never going to get it while Hendricks's only ambition was to locate his daughter. A daughter Philip knew was long dead.

Speculatively he studied Margaret's slender figure, noting her erect carriage and the patrician cast of her features. Despite her unfashionable clothes, she looked more like a daughter of the aristocracy than what she really was—an old man's fancy piece. Her speech was impeccable and any lapses in her manners could be put down to having spent her life in foreign parts.

But would she cooperate with him? Once he put his plan into operation, she might decide to change the rules to suit herself. It was an all-too-familiar feminine tactic. Promise one thing and, when the man was irrevocably committed, do something entirely different. And not only that, but he didn't know what real motivation was behind her desire to free Gilroy. Even though he didn't believe that gammon about him being a cousin of hers, there clearly was some tie between them. Since he didn't know what it was, he didn't know how much it would influence her actions.

No, Philip decided, he would be a fool to trust Margaret

Abney any farther than he could see her. That being the case, he would have to be very careful to keep her close. To keep her very close.

Margaret blanched at his expression. He was looking at her as if she were a mouse and he a very hungry cat. She tried to look more confident than she felt. Bitter experience had taught her that cowering never worked. Aristocrats seemed able to sense fear and to use it to their own advantage. And Chadwick already had enough advantage in this miserable situation.

"About George—" she began.

"Yes, George. I'll make you a trade."

"A trade? What is it you want?" Margaret asked, even though she didn't really want to hear the answer.

"Nothing too arduous. Simply marry me."

TWO

Chadwick's words echoed eerily through Margaret's stunned mind. She closed her eyes and took a deep breath. It didn't help. She could still hear his improbable words. She didn't for one moment believe that he actually meant to marry her, so why had he said it? She didn't know. The only thing she did know was that whatever his motivation was, it would be to his advantage and most emphatically not hers.

Opening her eyes, Margaret slowly raised them, up past his buff-and-blue striped waistcoat, over the complicated arrangement of his starched white neckcloth, to his face. And found him studying her with remoteness that somehow made her feel less than human. As if she were a thing to be used and not a person with feelings to be considered.

"Well?" Chadwick chopped the word off, and it seemed to hang in the air between them.

No, not well at all! Margaret gulped back the hysterical laughter that clogged her throat. Nothing in her world was well at the moment. And from the looks of it, things weren't likely to improve anytime soon.

Information—the word suddenly surfaced through her chaotic thoughts. The more facts she could glean, the better chance she had of fighting him. Her gaze collided with his watchful eyes and her stomach lurched nervously. No, not fighting him. Simply surviving her encounter with him would be enough.

"Why?" Margaret did her best not to make the word sound demanding.

"Why?" he repeated the word as if he didn't recognize it. As perhaps he didn't, Margaret thought on a flash of black humor. There probably weren't many people in Chadwick's world who would dare to question his motivation.

"It seems a fair question, all things considered."

"Fair! What would the likes of you know about fairness?"

Margaret fought to keep her face expressionless, when what she wanted to do was to yell at him, but righteous indignation was an indulgence she couldn't afford. Not while poor George was so firmly in Chadwick's clutches.

"The question seems even more pertinent given your opinion of me. Why would a man in your position propose marriage with a woman in mine?"

"Have you never heard of a man falling victim to a lasting attachment in an instant?" Chadwick's sneer hurt her in some way that she couldn't quite understand.

"Yes, and I've also heard of the fairies and the basic goodness of mankind!"

Philip blinked, clearly taken aback at her retort and Margaret felt a momentary easing of the tension that was slowly strangling her. If she could just keep Chadwick the slightest bit off balance . . .

Then what? She mocked her sudden flare of hope. She very much doubted that a loaded dueling pistol would give her an advantage in dealing with this man.

"Because, my dear Miss Abney, I have a problem that marriage to you would go a long way toward solving."

Margaret studied the tightly corded muscles of his jawline uncertainly. She found it hard to believe that he had

a problem in the first place, let alone one that would benefit from her help.

"I require you to influence a man named Hendricks."

Margaret stared down at the faded green material of
her dress as if looking for some enlightenment there. She
understood each of his words individually, but taken as a
whole they didn't make any sense. But then, why should
they? Nothing else about this interview had made sense
so far.

Latching on to the name he'd used, Margaret pursued
it in the hopes of understanding something. "Why would
someone named Hendricks care what I thought about anything?"

"Because he'll think you're his long-lost daughter come
home to brighten his old age."

Margaret frowned uncomprehendingly. The aristocracy
might be monumentally selfish, but they weren't normally
careless with their children. "Why long-lost?"

"Hendricks's wife ran off to the Continent with his secretary over twenty-five years ago. She took their only
child with her. A chit of two. I managed to trace them to
the convent where her lover abandoned them. They both
died there, but Hendricks doesn't know that. Nor does he
have the ability to find out. I intend to tell him that you
are his daughter."

It took Margaret a second to realize that the ragged
laughter she could hear echoing around the room was
coming from her. Desperately she pressed her lips together, but the laughter didn't stop. It merely became muffled, bubbling out of her throat. It really was hilarious, in
a macabre sort of way. She had left England years ago
because one member of the aristocracy had denied the
legitimacy of her birth, and now Chadwick was proposing
to take her back to England as the daughter of yet another
member of the aristocracy.

"Stop that! I will not countenance the vapors."

"No, just lies." The words slipped out before she could stop them.

To her surprise, a dull red flush washed over his face, highlighting his lean cheekbones.

"This charade is necessary," he muttered.

"Strange how many of the aristocracy are admirers of Machiavelli."

"I don't need a lecture on ethics from the likes of you!"

You could use a lecture on ethics from someone, Margaret thought as she bit the inside of her cheek to keep back the sharp retort. The longer she was in his company, the harder she found it to repress her normal personality. To remember that her role was to appease him. That George's health depended on it.

Margaret looked up, her attention caught by the movement of his hands as he toyed with a pen. He had nice hands; the irrelevant thought momentarily distracted her. His fingers were long and slender, with clean, well-kept nails. The only ring he wore was a simple gold signet which, from it's well worn edges, looked very old.

She jumped as the quill suddenly snapped from the pressure he was exerting. He also looked very strong. Uneasily her eyes lingered on the breadth of his shoulders beneath his light blue coat. Quite clearly he didn't need the extra padding that so many of his contemporaries did.

Margaret ran her tongue over her dry lips. He looked physically capable of snapping far more than a pen. Such as a person. Her?

"You are simply wasting time!" Chadwick said. "You have my terms for freeing your . . . cousin. You will marry me and accompany me back to England where you will tell Hendricks exactly what I want you to."

"But . . ." Margaret began and then fell silent when she realized she had nothing to say. Nothing that would make the slightest difference to Chadwick.

"There is nothing more to discuss." Chadwick had apparently reached the same conclusion. "You have until tomorrow to accept my terms, or Gilroy remains in jail until the Congress is over."

Opening the study door, he pointedly waited for her to leave.

Forcing her trembling legs to carry her across the room, Margaret stopped in front of Chadwick, raised her eyes as far as the deep-blue sapphire nestled in his neckcloth, and said, "I will call with my answer in the morning."

Ignoring the obvious curiosity of the butler, she escaped through the outer door the footman opened for her, into the relative safety of the night.

Philip instinctively took half a step toward her when he saw her brace her thin shoulders against the wind-driven rain before he realized what he was doing and stopped himself. *Start as you mean to go on,* he told himself. Margaret Abney had arrived in the rain and could just as easily leave in it. No doubt she had a man waiting around the corner to drive her home. He felt a surge of impotent anger at the thought of some faceless man pulling her into his carriage and into his arms. He couldn't do anything about her wanton behavior now, but within a few days she'd be firmly under his control. And there she'd stay. An unexpected feeling of satisfaction filled him at the thought of having her in his power, and he turned back to the study with a feeling that was almost anticipation.

The long trip across Vienna quickly assumed the proportions of a nightmare for Margaret. A wet, frozen nightmare. Unable to pay the exorbitant cost of hiring a carriage, she had no option but to walk the miles between Chadwick's fashionable address and the anonymity of her own.

Finally reaching Frau Gruber's, she unlocked the front door and let herself in.

"Ah, Fraulein Abney, it is you," her landlady called to her through the open salon door. "I see it is still raining." She clicked her tongue in sympathy. "Would you like to come in and warm yourself?" She gestured toward the closed stove that was emitting a cozy warmth that Margaret could feel even in the hall.

Not even the luxury of getting warm tempted Margaret. She only wanted to escape to her rooms where she could be alone and try to think. To try to understand what rig Chadwick was running and exactly where she fitted into it.

"You are most kind, Frau Grubber, but I must change my wet clothes."

Frau Gruber shrugged her plump shoulders. "As you wish, fraulein. I have not seen your cousin today." Her dark eyes gleamed with curiosity. "He is well?"

"Yes, the Earl of Chadwick most kindly offered him accommodations," Margaret twisted the truth.

"Indeed?" Frau Gruber looked frankly skeptical, but to Margaret's relief she didn't ask any more questions.

Margaret quickly made her escape up the steep stairs before Frau Gruber remembered that the rent was due for the following week and tried to collect it. The only way Margaret could pay the rent would be to use all of her remaining coins, and if she did that . . . Margaret closed her eyes against the feeling of panic that flooded her at the thought of being stranded alone in Vienna with neither funds nor lodgings. It was a panic that she knew she couldn't give in to. Bitter experience had taught her that fear was not only a waste of time and energy, but it dulled your mind, leaving you more vulnerable.

Once inside her rooms, Margaret quickly stripped her soaking clothes off and dried herself with one of the threadbare towels Frau Gruber had provided. Wrapping herself in a faded blanket, she huddled in front of the smoldering ashes in the fireplace and tried to make sense of the interview she'd had with Chadwick. She couldn't. Nothing about it made any sense to her, but she'd bet her last coin that it made perfect sense to him. And she'd also bet that his motive was the acquisition of power or money or both. It always was, when the aristocracy was involved.

Her distracted gaze swung around the room, landing on the thin volume of several of Plato's more obscure essays she'd discovered in the open market the day they'd arrived in Vienna. *Use logic.* She reminded herself of a basic tenet of Greek philosophy. *Gather the facts you do know and extrapolate possibilities from them.*

Margaret made a valiant effort to force her shocked mind to function with its usual efficiency.

"I know that George is locked up and if I don't gain his release soon he'll likely suffer an inflammation of the lungs," she muttered aloud, drawing comfort from the sound of a voice, even her own. "I also know that Chadwick is willing to let him go free for a price."

Marry him, he'd said—not that she believed for a moment that he actually meant it. Wealthy earls of sound mind didn't marry penniless spinsters of uncertain origins.

Margaret idly watched a tiny puff of smoke drift upward from the dying fire. Could that be the answer? Could Chadwick be all about in his head? She shivered as she remembered the purposeful gleam in his night-dark eyes. No, Chadwick wasn't insane. For some reason he wanted a man named Hendricks to believe that he'd married her.

A sudden gust of scalding anger shook her as she remembered how her father had tricked her mother into believing that he'd married her. No doubt that was what Chadwick had in mind. A conveniently hired actor to play the part of the minister with herself cast in the role of the naive, gullible bride.

The fact that she was neither naive nor gullible didn't give her any more control over events than her mother had had. To save George she was going to have to go along with Chadwick's plan. But how far did Chadwick expect her cooperation to extend? The unnerving thought suddenly occurred to her.

She wrapped her arms around her chest in an instinctively defensive gesture. How far did Chadwick intend to carry his pretense of theirs being a real marriage? Could he be intending to carry it as far as her bed?

Margaret's breath caught in her throat and goosebumps danced over her skin as she remembered the hard line of his mouth. Slowly she rubbed her fingertips across her own mouth. What would it feel like to have him press his lips against hers? A fluttery sensation twisted through her stomach, and she hastily banished the errant thought. She'd worry about how to fend off Chadwick if and when it became necessary. At the moment she had far too many other things to worry about.

She was so tired, so incredibly tired of trying to cope with a world that lately seemed to have been created expressly to bedevil her. She rubbed her aching forehead. No, that wasn't exactly true. It wasn't the world that was causing her so many problems. It was George's refusal to face the reality of that world. Not that she could find it in her heart to blame him. Reality left a lot to be desired.

Reality dictated that tomorrow morning she was going to retrace her footsteps to Chadwick's residence and meekly agree to fall in with his plans.

Margaret gnawed uncertainly on her lower lip. It wasn't going to be easy to play the part of Chadwick's pawn. In the ten years since her mother had died, she had become accustomed to ordering her own life, at least as far as circumstances allowed her. She wasn't used to guarding her tongue or toadying to her so-called betters. But perhaps it wouldn't be as bad as she feared; she tried to boost her flagging spirits. Perhaps she wouldn't see much of Chadwick once they were in London. He'd undoubtedly be busy with his own interests. Surely she could manage to rub along with him for the short times they'd be together.

Margaret felt a spurt of excitement tighten her skin as she suddenly realized something: Her natural father would be in London, too, since the Fall Season would be under way by the time they returned. As Chadwick's supposed wife, she would have access to London society where she could reasonably expect to meet her father. Even better, it would be anonymous access since Chadwick was intending to pass her off as Hendricks's daughter. Her natural father certainly wouldn't recognize her. It had been twenty years since that never-to-be-forgotten day when he'd callously informed her mother that she wasn't really his wife, just his mistress, and then walked out of their lives, leaving her mother penniless and heartbroken. Even before that, he'd been away with his regiment for months and sometimes years on end. When he had come home on leave, Margaret had been ushered into his presence where he'd pat her on the head, mutter that she'd certainly grown and promptly dismiss her.

No, the Baron Mainwaring would not recognize his bastard daughter, but she would never forget him. A wave of hopeless loss washed over her and for a moment Margaret could smell the cloying scent of the flowers that had covered her mother's coffin. His treachery had murdered her mother just as surely as if he had driven a knife through her heart.

Long ago, she'd sworn vengeance for what he'd done. A vengeance she'd never really expected to be able to exact, but now, unexpectedly, it seemed a tantalizing possibility.

She would allow Chadwick to use her to further his own schemes because she had no real choice in the matter. But once in England she would somehow find a way to make her father pay for his villainy.

* * *

"A clergyman?" Wells, one of Castlereagh's young diplomatic aides, stared at Philip as if he'd just expressed a desire for him to locate a dragon.

"An English clergyman," Philip qualified. "Not German."

"Can't say as I blame you, milord. Them Lutherans are demmed dour. Always ranting about hell and eternal damnation. Best to leave the Church alone. Always getting after a man to do something he don't want to."

"Nonetheless, I still wish to locate an English clergyman."

Wells scratched the side of his nose and stared blankly around the embassy reception room as he considered the problem. Chadwick was not a man a rising young diplomat wanted to offend, and if Chadwick wanted a clergyman, however improbable that might sound, then he'd just have to find him one. But where was he supposed to find an English clergyman in Vienna?

Wells's face lit up as he suddenly remembered something he'd heard at a reception several evenings ago. "I believe that Mr. Carrington's wife brought her chaplain to Vienna with her. Carrington is renting a mansion two houses north of where Tsar Alexander is staying."

"Thank you for your assistance."

"Yes, milord," Wells said as Philip turned to leave. He still wanted to know what Chadwick was up to, but not so badly as to come right out and ask. Chadwick was not a man one took liberties with.

Philip accepted his hat and gloves from Castlereagh's butler and left, well aware of Wells's curiosity, even if he had no intention of satisfying it. He wasn't sure even in his own mind why he felt compelled to find an English clergyman. It wasn't as if a German one wouldn't do for a marriage that was little more than a mockery of the sacra-

ment. But then, weren't all marriages? Marriage was a
fool's game played for the benefit of women. A game most
men would never indulge in if they didn't feel the need of
an heir.

He jammed his hands into his tan leather gloves. Even
then, they couldn't be sure the brat was theirs. Like as
not, it belonged to his wife's latest lover.

Philip had no trouble locating Carrington's ornate mansion. As he jumped down from the carriage without waiting for the footman to let the steps down, a wind-driven
blast of rain slapped him in the face and he frowned, wondering how far Margaret had had to walk last night before
her accomplice picked her up. That she had one he never
doubted for a moment. Women who looked like she did
and lived with reprobates like Gilroy always had another
man waiting in the wings.

Giving in to the sudden gust of anger he felt, he
pounded the door knocker. As of tomorrow Margaret
wasn't going to have any more lovers. This time he wasn't
going to make the mistake of assuming that a beautiful
face also meant a beautiful character. This time he was
going to keep his wife so close to him that she'd never
have the opportunity to cuckold him. And if she found
she missed her male companionship . . .

"Ah, good morning, milord." The Carringtons' butler,
like most good butlers, knew virtually all the aristocracy
by sight. "Come in out of the rain. Mr. Carrington isn't
receiving yet, but I'm sure—"

"No, don't disturb Mr. Carrington. I actually came to
see his chaplain."

"Chaplain!" For a split second the butler's professional
calm cracked.

Philip's lips twitched in wry amusement. "I really must
do something about mending my ways if the very thought
of my talking to a clergyman astonishes people so much."

"No, no, milord." The butler scrambled to recover himself. "It isn't you. It's just that in the normal way . . ." He lowered his voice conspiratorially. "One doesn't talk to Mr. Preston. One listens to him."

"Nonetheless, I wish to see him."

"Certainly, milord. Come into the bookroom. No one is using it at this time of the morning, and I'm sure Mr. Carrington would want us to aid you in any manner that we could." The butler threw open the door and ushered Chadwick inside. "Just you warm yourself at the fire while I locate Mr. Preston."

The sound of the butler's receding footsteps echoing through the vast entranceway gave Philip a feeling of impending doom—a feeling which, he told himself, was not only irrational, it was irrelevant. He had no choice. He had to have Hendricks's support to pass the bill and this was the only way he could think of to get it.

Much as he disliked tricking Hendricks into believing he'd found his daughter, the one thing his years of fighting had taught him was that battles weren't nice, neat affairs where everyone followed a gentlemanly code of conduct. They were bloody messes where everything and everyone was expendable in the need to achieve the greater good.

He had to do it; he repeated the words like a litany. The alternative was to let thousands of soldiers and their families starve. Once the bill was passed . . . He stared blindly down into the blazing fire as, for the first time, he looked beyond the immediate problem. Once he got his bill passed, *then* what was he to do with his hastily acquired wife? Or himself, for that matter?

No ready answer came to mind.

"Ah, my lord." A thin, elderly man rushed into the room. The crumbs on his crumpled neckcloth gave mute testimony to the fact that Chadwick had interrupted his tea. "You wished to speak to me?" Preston managed to sound both doubtful and gratified in the same breath.

"Yes, I require a minister of the Church of England."

Preston rubbed his gnarled fingers together and chuckled richly. "I am that. Tell me, my lord, how may I be of service to you?"

"I want you to perform a wedding service tomorrow morning."

"A wedding, eh? Well, it's been forty years since I've officiated at a wedding, but I'm sure I can find a copy of the ceremony. What happened? Did one of your footmen forget himself with one of the parlormaids?"

Philip eyed the smirking man in distaste. "I was referring to my own nuptials."

"You, my lord!"

"I assure you; I am completely eligible for marriage."

"Oh, indeed, my lord, why I remember when . . ." Preston caught himself at Philip's bleak expression. "Now, my lord, I hope you won't take my advice amiss, but—"

"I don't intend to take it at all. I have asked you to perform the duties of your calling. Are you refusing?"

Preston shuddered at the expression in Philip's dark eyes. "No, my lord, of course I am not refusing you. If . . ." He paused as if steeling himself, and said, "If you wish to marry the woman—"

"Lady!" Philip corrected. He might know what Margaret Abney was, but as far as the world was concerned, she was Hendricks's long-lost daughter whose virtue had been guarded by the nuns.

"Lady," Preston hastily agreed. "I shall officiate." He brightened as he suddenly realized something. "I know nothing about the local laws governing marriages."

"I have already obtained a special license from the proper authorities."

Preston shrugged as if disclaiming all responsibility. "In that case, I am at your disposal, my lord."

"I'll send a carriage for you tomorrow morning at ten. Till then, I'd appreciate it if you were to hold your tongue about this."

Preston looked genuinely affronted. "I can assure you, my lord, this piece of work is not something I'm likely to be bragging about." Giving Chadwick a jerky bow, he left the room, his back stiff with frustrated disapproval.

Philip followed him, nodding to the waiting butler as he left the house. Dashing through the driving rain, he vaulted into his waiting carriage. By this time tomorrow, Margaret Abney would be his wife and firmly under his control. He frowned as something suddenly occurred to him: He'd promised her he'd release Gilroy from prison after the marriage. But if he did that, he would lose his main lever guaranteeing her cooperation. He was almost certain that Margaret would do as he wished because of the financial rewards she could get from him, but in case he was wrong . . .

He shifted uneasily as he remembered the expression in her eyes when she'd begged him to release Gilroy. There was something about her relationship with that old humbug that he didn't quite understand and until he did, he intended to make absolutely sure that Margaret didn't bolt once Gilroy was free. But how . . . ?

A smile that owed nothing to humor curved his lips. He'd remove Gilroy from prison as he'd promised, but instead of turning him loose as Margaret no doubt expected, he'd install him in a villa he owned in the north of France, under guard. Then, if Margaret didn't play her part exactly as he directed, he could threaten to have George returned to prison to serve out the remainder of his sentence.

Yes, Chadwick thought in satisfaction as he leaned back against the carriage's soft leather squabs. The stage was now set and the players were all waiting in the wings. All that remained was for events to unfold as he'd planned them.

Three

"He's in the front salon. You may have five minutes, no more," Chadwick said. "The minister is waiting in the study."

Margaret struggled to contain her growing panic. Everything was happening too quickly. She needed time to adjust. And yet time was exactly what Chadwick was denying her.

But at least she'd won this battle, small though it was. She had flatly refused to leave Vienna until she saw George. Even Chadwick's obvious anger hadn't deterred her. She had to see for herself that George had suffered no ill effects from his stay in that damp prison.

Mentally rehearsing the lies she'd decided to tell George, she followed Philip to the front of the house. Telling him the truth was out of the question. George might be surprisingly lax about some of the social conventions, but she knew he would cut up rough at the thought of her masquerading as Philip's wife.

Pasting what she hoped was a convincing smile on her face, Margaret slipped through the salon door Philip held open for her.

"Maggie!" George jumped out of the wing chair he'd been perched on and rushed across the room to her, enveloping her in a hug. "Oh, Maggie, my dear. I've been that worried about you!"

Margaret winced as Chadwick shut the door on them with a decided snap, then completely forgot about him as George began to cough.

"Sit down." Margaret gently pushed him into a chair. She glanced around the room, looking for something for him to drink and saw a silver tray holding several crystal containers on the breakfront.

Grabbing what looked like a decanter of port, she picked up a glass to pour him some.

"The brandy, m'dear," George gasped between coughs. "If we're going to help ourselves, we might as well take the good stuff."

Margaret reached for the decanter filled with amber-colored liquid. If George wanted brandy, then brandy he would have.

George drained the liquid in one swallow and looked expectantly at the decanter. Margaret silently handed it to him and then sat down on the sofa beside him.

"Excellent stuff." George filled his glass again. "Just the thing to put heart in a man."

Margaret eyed him wryly. "Would that I knew a way to put some common sense in a man."

George hung his head. "I deserve your censure, m'dear. It was a very silly thing to have done."

"It was a very *stupid* thing to have done! The Earl of Chadwick is not a man to cross lightly."

George shuddered. "He isn't a man to cross at all! What I can't understand is why he brought me here. Unless—"

George's eyes suddenly widened. "Maggie!" He grabbed for her hand and in his agitation spilled some of the brandy on her skirt. "You didn't . . ." He gestured impotently.

Margaret used the excuse of sopping up the brandy with her handkerchief to avoid meeting his eyes. She hated lying to George, but telling him the truth would only agitate him more. And it wasn't as if he could do anything to help.

"If you are trying to find a delicate way to ask me if he was so smitten by my charms that he was willing to forgive you, the answer is no. "It seems that Mrs. Barton, the wife of a friend of Chadwick's, is tired of Vienna and wants to return home. Unfortunately, her daughter's governess has become enamored of some man and left her service."

"Ha! Good for the governess!" George chortled. "Time those demmed aristocrats realize that the rest of us are people, too."

"Anyway, Mrs. Barton is desperate to find an English-woman to accompany her. Her husband appealed to Chadwick and, when I came to ask him to release you, he offered me the job in exchange."

Margaret took a deep breath as she got to the tricky part. "Chadwick doesn't want to let you go free because everybody heard him say he wouldn't, and he's too proud to back down. So he's going to keep you in a villa he owns in the north of France until after the Congress is over."

George's eyes narrowed suspiciously. "Seems like a lot of trouble for him to go to just to acquire a governess. I know what a pearl beyond price you are, Maggie, but Chadwick hardly can."

"Perhaps he wants something from the Bartons and this is his way of putting them in his debt."

"Perhaps, but I still don't like it. Maybe it would be better if I went back to prison and you told him no?"

Margaret gave him a quick hug, warmed by his concern. "I don't have the means to pay next week's rent and still eat," she said bluntly.

George's shoulders hunched at the reminder of their precarious finances. "To think that it would come to this."

"Nonsense," Margaret said. "This time we've landed

on our feet. I have a genteel position that will take me back to England—"

"Taking care of some other woman's brat? A beautiful woman like you should be taking care of her own."

Margaret blinked, as for one mad moment a vision of a small boy with Philip's dark hair and eyes and her features floated through her mind. Truly horrified at the direction of her thoughts, she hurriedly banished the image.

"I don't want a husband."

"You're too stubborn by half. That's what comes of all that reading you do. Ain't natural. You think too much, Maggie. It makes a man demmed uncomfortable."

"Not *you*."

"Oh, I just ignore it. But a husband now . . ." George shook his head. "Husbands are a horse of another color. They'll be wanting their own way."

Margaret's eyes involuntarily swung to the door. Even pretend husbands wanted their own way. And one of the things Philip wanted was for her to hurry.

Quickly opening her reticule, she pulled out the last of her precious hoard of coins which she had tied up in a handkerchief. "Take this and use it to get to England when Chadwick lets you go."

"No!" George vehemently shook his head. "You might need it."

"Mrs. Barton has agreed to pay me a salary." Margaret stuffed the money into his waistcoat pocket. "I've been thinking about how you can find me, since I don't know how long I'll be with Mrs. Barton once we get to London. I think the best plan would be for me to leave a message with the butler at Lord Chadwick's London house, giving you my direction."

George heaved a huge sigh and immediately burst into a coughing spasm. When he'd managed to tame it with another swallow of brandy, he muttered, "I don't like this."

"George . . ." Margaret scrambled for something to say to ease his mind.

Before she could think of anything, there was a sharp rap on the door, and immediately it opened to reveal Philip's dark visage. For once, Margaret was glad to see him. If her meeting with George lasted much longer, he was liable to see through her lies and flatly refuse to go along with the charade.

"Your transportation is here, Gilroy," Philip said.

With one last, worried look at Margaret, George got to his feet. Belatedly remembering his still half-full glass of brandy, he drained it.

"Why not take the decanter with you?"

Margaret winced at Philip's caustic tone, but George only heard the words.

"Thank you, milord, that's right civil of you." George snatched up the bottle.

Margaret glanced worriedly at Chadwick, praying he wouldn't demolish poor George. To her shock, Chadwick's eyes gleamed with humor and a fugitive smile was tugging at one corner of his hard lips. He looked like someone else entirely. Someone . . .

His expression suddenly vanished as if it never had been. And maybe it hadn't, Margaret thought in confusion. Maybe in her tiredness and fear she was imagining things, such as a sense of humor in her captor.

Turning to George, Margaret hugged him, refusing to be intimidated by Chadwick's glacial stare.

George kissed her cheek and whispered, "As soon as I can, I'll come for you. Take care."

"I shall," Margaret whispered back. It took all her considerable willpower not to burst into tears as the last familiar face disappeared out the door, leaving her alone with Chadwick.

"The minister is waiting for us in the study," Chadwick said.

Margaret didn't bother to respond; nothing she could say would make any difference. She swept past him, wanting to get this farce over with. She knew full well that whoever was waiting in the study was no man of God. More likely a cohort of the devil, to lend himself to such a sacrilege.

As Margaret entered the study, she noticed a pair of somberly-dressed men standing in front of the window. They didn't look any happier to be there than she did.

"Ah, yes," a reedy voice greeted her with a forced joviality. "I'm the Reverend Mr. Preston and you must be . . ."

Margaret turned toward the fireplace where an elderly man dressed in rusty black was standing.

"The bride," Margaret said, wondering where Chadwick had found him. Whatever his normal profession, if indeed he had one, he was clearly ill at ease in the guise of minister.

"Ah, yes, yes, just so." The man's Adam's apple bobbed nervously. "If you would just stand here, miss . . ." His long nose twitched as she approached him, and he stared at her in horror.

For a moment, Margaret didn't realize what was bothering him and then she remembered the brandy George had spilled on her. Did this charlatan think she was addicted to strong drink? A nervous giggle bubbled up in her throat which she tried to turn into a cough, without much success.

Focusing her gaze on a truly ugly portrait of someone's late—and from the look of him, probably unlamented—ancestor, Margaret struggled to get control of herself. It wasn't easy. This entire situation had all the elements of a badly written farce. Here was Chadwick pretending to marry her, a down-at-the-heels charlatan pretending to be outraged at finding the scent of brandy on the woman he was pretending to be marrying, while *she* was pretending to believe the whole thing was real.

"Get on with it, man!"

Margaret jumped as the rough material of Chadwick's deep-blue coat scraped against her arm when he stepped beside her. She could feel the heat of his body crowding against her, making her uncomfortably aware of him.

Mr. Preston gulped, twitched his none-too-clean neck-cloth, and muttered, "Milord, if I could just speak to you alone for a moment?"

Very well done, Margaret mentally applauded his performance. A seeming reluctance to marry an earl to a woman who smelled of brandy added a nice touch of authenticity to his role.

"The only words I want from you are the marriage vows." Chadwick's words left no room for discussion, and with a martyred sigh, Mr. Preston opened the thin black book he was holding.

Margaret listened to him stumble over the obviously unfamiliar words. He could have practiced the ceremony a little, just enough to convince her that he'd done it a few times in his life. Ah well, perhaps Vienna didn't boast that many English-speaking, out-of-work actors with no sense of morality.

". . . and wife." Mr. Preston finally stumbled to a halt. Taking a grayish handkerchief out of his pocket, he rubbed his shiny forehead and looked at Chadwick as if seeking a cue for his next step.

Chadwick gave it to him. "The license is on the desk. You and the witnesses need to sign it."

The two witnesses, who hadn't budged from their spot by the window, immediately scurried over to the desk, scrawled their signatures on the lone sheet of white paper sitting in the middle of it, and escaped from the room with an almost palpable sense of relief.

Chadwick turned to Margaret. "You can write your name, can't you?"

Mr. Preston gave a strangled gasp and began to mutter something that sounded suspiciously like a prayer.

Margaret bit back the childish impulse to tell Chadwick that she was not only literate in English but French, Spanish, Latin, and Greek as well. One thing she had learned in her study of the ancient Greek philosophers, was that knowledge was power and at the moment she needed every scrape of power she could muster.

Walking over to the desk, she reluctantly picked up the pen, dipped it in the silver inkpot, and stared down at the ornate lettering on the cream vellum. She knew the license was no more authentic than the inept Mr. Preston, but even so, she didn't want to sign it. Telling herself that she was being irrational, Margaret hurriedly scrawled her name. Chadwick took the pen out of her clenched fingers, scribbled, *Philip Moresby,* and shoved the pen at the minister.

As if loath to take the final step, Mr. Preston slowly approached the desk. He accepted the pen and then turned to look at Chadwick. With a mournful sigh, he finally signed. "I wish you happy, to be sure, my lord, even though . . ."

With yet another sigh, he gave an awkward bow, accepted the thick envelope the earl handed him, and hurried out.

Philip turned and stared down into the deep blue eyes of the woman he had just married. For a moment, panic at the irrevocability of the step he'd taken, shook him. This was necessary, he reminded himself for at least the hundredth time. Men had given their lives to win this war. Nor was this marriage going to change his life permanently. Once he managed to get his bill passed, he would give his chance-gotten wife an allowance, and install her on one of his remoter estates, and not see her from one year to the next. He could live his own life far away from her. The sudden thought sent a chill of foreboding through him. How might she choose to enjoy herself if he weren't there to keep a tight rein on her?

His eyes lingered on the creamy perfection of her skin, so soft and velvety, like the roses his mother had delighted in growing. Would her skin feel like those rose petals?

Why shouldn't he touch her and find out? He tried to rationalize his impulse. She had been living with that old roué, Gilroy, and who knew how many men before that. Although . . . He studied her uncertainly. She really didn't look like any man's mistress. There was a curiously self-contained air about her that seemed entirely out of character with her chosen profession.

Slowly raising his hand, Chadwick brushed his knuckles across her cheek, watching intently as her eyes widened. He could see a pulse beating in her throat, but whether it was beating in fear or in anticipation, he couldn't tell.

"Milord, your carriage has arrived." The butler's voice broke into Philip's thoughts.

"After you, madam wife." Philip gestured toward the door and then fell into step behind her. Of their own volition, his eyes wandered down the straight line of her slender back to linger on the slight sway of her hips beneath her threadbare woolen gown. What did her legs look like? he wondered as he watched her accept her cloak from the butler. The chill breeze which slapped him when the footman opened the door, helped to cool his ardor.

Margaret scrambled into the closed black carriage with more haste than finesse. She could still feel the touch of Chadwick's knuckles on her cheeks and it unnerved her. *Fear,* she tried to tell herself. *You're afraid of the man.*

She stole a quick glance at him as he climbed into the seat opposite her. No, that wasn't quite true; she refused to allow herself to hide behind a facile lie. She wasn't precisely afraid of Chadwick; she was afraid of what he might do. Surviving her encounter with him with no lasting damage was going to require a great deal of finesse on her part, as well as luck—something that had been in short supply in her life recently.

Margaret braced her feet against the floor as the carriage began to move, and peered out at the bustling city. Somehow it looked different from inside Chadwick's luxurious coach than it had when she'd been trudging its dirty streets.

She shot a furtive glance at Chadwick, but he was busily perusing a sheaf of papers he'd taken out of the case on the seat beside him. Philip Moresby—Margaret remembered the name he'd written on the marriage certificate.

Her eyes narrowed as her active imagination supplied an image of Philip seated astride a large black horse. The leather reins were wrapped around the long, tanned fingers of one hand and in the other he held a silver sword aloft. The muscles of his forearm rippled as he waved it and—

"Is the motion of the carriage making you ill?" Philip's voice jarred her out of her daydream.

"No, I never get sick. Thank you for your concern, though," she added with an attempt at politeness.

"I was concerned that you might delay us." He turned back to his papers.

Margaret grimaced. Apparently common courtesy wasn't the way to deal with him, but what was? She stared blankly out the window as she considered the untenable situation she found herself in. *Think of this as a military campaign,* she told herself. *Philip is the enemy* . . . She stole another quick glance at him. A stray beam of sunlight was caressing his left cheek, softening his sharply chiseled features. Philip might be her enemy, but she had the disheartening feeling that she wasn't important enough to him to be classified as his such. She was merely a tool that he had acquired to do a job for him. A tool that he would discard as soon as he was through with it.

Which made it all the more imperative that she develop some kind of plan for dealing with him, she told herself; but her mind remained a discouraging blank. So much had happened to her in such a short time that she felt mentally as well as physically exhausted. And cold. Shivering, she snuggled deeper into her thin cloak. She felt as if she'd never be warm again.

Margaret closed her eyes to try to shut out the distractions of the teeming city and promptly fell asleep.

Philip looked up from his notes, frowning when he saw her limp figure. Her cloak wasn't warm enough for this weather. He eyed it with disgust. Nor was it what his wife should be wearing. Once they reached Paris, he'd see about having a wardrobe made for her. One more befitting the role she was going to be playing.

Philip stared out at the passing landscape as he considered what she would need. Definitely evening gowns. It was imperative that they become socially active as soon as possible, since that was the only way he would ever see some of the more indolent members of the House of Lords.

His eyes were drawn back to her face. She was too pale. Far too pale. Probably from the cold. Opening the compartment under his seat, he pulled out a thick woolen blanket which he gingerly tucked around her. It would never do if she were to become ill; he rationalized his actions. He needed her to be healthy, and he was willing to do whatever it took to keep her that way.

He watched as she snuggled deeper into the warm blanket and a faint smile curved her lips. Fascinated, he studied the full line of her lower lip. It looked so soft. What would it taste like if he were to run his tongue over it?

His breath caught as she shifted slightly and the soft mounds of her breasts were outlined beneath the blanket. What would they feel like in his hand? He clenched his fingers into fists as a tingling danced across his palms. Would her breasts be as soft and velvety as the skin on her face? A tight band of longing wrapped itself around his chest, constricting his breathing. He was becoming far too interested in her, but while his mind could see the danger of adding sex to the explosive blend of lies that bound them together, his body didn't care.

Though this time he wasn't a naive, lovesick fool willing to believe every lie that tripped off his lover's honeyed lips. This time he knew precisely how treacherous women were, the lies they told. How they could weave a sexual spell to blind a man to reality. This time he had the whiphand, and he didn't intend to relinquish it. As long as he recognized his urges for what they were—a craving for physical release in the body of a beautiful woman—he was in no danger of losing his head over her, he assured himself.

And that being so, there was no reason why he shouldn't quench his desire in her arms. But not just yet. He'd do better to wait awhile so that she wouldn't think he was too eager for her body. Perhaps, when the Little Season was over and his bill had been voted on, he could take her to his seat in Kent and discover the delights of her body at his leisure.

Feeling slightly better, Philip turned back to his papers.

They finally reached Paris in the midst of a driving rainstorm. Margaret glanced across the carriage at Philip, who was deep in the seemingly inexhaustible supply of papers he'd brought from Vienna. It was almost as if he were using them to establish a barrier between them so that she couldn't encroach on his privacy.

She almost giggled at the thought of trying to capture Chadwick's attention. The very idea strained even her ready imagination. Brief though her acquaintance with him was, she would be willing to bet that he was impervious to all feminine wiles.

"We will shortly reach the hotel where I have engaged a suite for the next week," Philip said. "I have had my agent in Paris engage Madame St. Denis to make you a wardrobe." Philip waited for her squeals of pleasure at the thought of new clothes. To his surprise, they didn't come. She merely grimaced.

"You object to new gowns?" There was a definite edge to his voice.

"No, I would like a new dress," Margaret said. "I merely find it tedious to stand motionless in a chilly room while a sadistic seamstress sticks pins in me."

Philip frowned, wondering why she was lying to him. She had to be. Every woman he'd ever met had flown into ecstasy at the thought of a new gown, let alone a whole new wardrobe. For some reason she was trying to portray herself as different. But whatever rig she was running, he had no intention of being taken in.

"You will cooperate with the seamstress," he ordered.

"Yes, milord," Margaret muttered, biting back the impulse to tell him that if he didn't want to know what she thought, he shouldn't ask.

"And that brings me to something else. . . ." He paused, and Margaret glanced up at the odd note she could hear in his voice. In someone else she would have thought he was embarrassed, but she didn't think Chadwick knew the meaning the word.

"The tale that I am putting about is that we were so overcome with—" A deep flush stained his cheeks and he fidgeted with his neckcloth.

Margaret's eyes widened with disbelief. He really was embarrassed. The mighty Earl of Chadwick actually felt a few of the inconvenient emotions that lesser mortals felt. The idea cheered her immensely. She gave him a limpid look and left him to struggle for words.

"—with emotion, that we couldn't contain ourselves and married immediately. And no one is going to believe it if you persist in referring to me as 'milord!' " he added with a snap, rather as if he blamed her for his embarrassment. "You'll have to do better."

Better? Uncertainly Margaret stared at him. What did he consider better? Could he actually want her to touch him? Her eyes lingered on the very faint darkness of the emerging beard on his jawline. What would his skin feel like? Certainly not smooth like hers. Would it be rough? A totally unexpected surge of warmth engulfed her.

"Since you are supposed to be my beloved wife, you will call me Philip."

Supposed to be his wife indeed! The reminder of their fake marriage ripped through her thoughts like a dull knife.

"Yes, of course I shall call you Philip, milord."

Philip glared at her in frustration, feeling that he'd lost that exchange without having been aware that he was competing. Frustrated, he subsided against the soft leather carriage seat.

Could she be testing him in some way? Women usually did try to discover the limits of their influence early in a relationship, but if that was her game she was about to find out that her influence was nil. She would do exactly as she was told, or he'd know the reason why not!

Four

"We'll be at the house in a few minutes," Philip's clipped voice interrupted Margaret's absorbed study of the darkening London streets.

Margaret looked at him curiously as she considered his choice of words. *"The house,"* he'd said. Not "my home," or even the name of his house. Just *"the house."* As if they were coming to a place that held no importance beyond providing shelter.

An involuntary shiver twisted through her. Was there nothing that he cherished? Nothing that meant something to him?

Even after two weeks, she was no closer to answering that question than when she'd first met him. Except for the brief sessions when he'd drilled her in her role as Hendricks's daughter, Philip had remained entirely aloof from her—both mentally and physically. Where he'd spent his time in Paris had been a total mystery to her. All she knew was that he hadn't spent it with her. Virtually all of her time had been spent being fitted for a wardrobe which seemed excessive to Margaret, by anyone's standards, even the aristocracy's.

"If I might have your attention?" Philip's impatient voice pulled her out of her thoughts, and she blinked, refocusing on him.

"Yes, milord."

"Yes, *Philip!*"

"Yes, Philip." Margaret corrected herself. Somehow she found it hard to remember that she was supposed to know this man well enough to be using his first name. And she found it impossible to believe that she was supposed to be in love with him. Fascinated by him, yes. In much the same way she found a thunderstorm fascinating—unpredictable, elemental, and very, very powerful. But love certainly played no part in it.

"I must remind you that it is imperative that we convince Hendricks that ours is a love match." He sounded long-suffering.

"No, you mustn't," Margaret snapped in a flash of annoyance. Did the man think her wits were addled that he had to keep repeating himself?

"Nevertheless, we shall review what you have been studying in Paris."

Margaret stifled a sigh. She was beginning to have a great deal of sympathy for soldiers who had to put up with having orders barked at them all day.

"Your name is . . . ?"

"Mary Frances Georgina Hendricks, but my mother changed my name to Margaret when we reached France, and I am used to it and would prefer to continue to use it."

"Early upbringing?"

"My mother sought refuge at a convent in rural France when her lover abandoned us. The nuns nursed her through her final illness and provided me with a home afterward. They hoped that someone would make inquiries about me after the war and they would be able to return me to my family," Margaret rattled off.

"And why didn't they make inquiries themselves?"

"My mother had refused to give them my name, and I was too young to do so."

"Very good. Now, if you can just remember to give me languishing looks from time to time . . ."

Margaret was unable to stop the gurgle of laughter that bubbled up.

"You find the idea humorous?" Philip looked down his nose at her.

"I am not the type of female who is in the habit of giving anyone languishing looks," she tried to explain.

"I'm not 'anyone.' I'm your husband. Flirt with me."

Margaret stared at him for a long moment. "How?" she finally asked.

"How? What do you mean, how? All women know how to cozen a man."

Margaret closed her eyes and tried to remember some of the feminine behavior she'd seen at the very few social events she'd attended with George. It had all seemed so silly. Peeking at men over fans and giggling at nothing. But if that was what it took . . .

Taking a deep breath, she opened her eyes wide, blinked several times, and said, "La, sir, I vow you are the most amusing man."

"Is that the best you can do?"

"I haven't got a fan," she mumbled, strangely hurt at his words. "Nor, since I'm not a member of the aristocracy, am I trained in the art of duplicity."

"All women are duplicitous. They learn it in their cradles."

" 'Generalizations are the mark of an uneducated mind too lazy to learn the facts necessary to support a considered opinion'!"

Philip blinked. His tutor at Oxford had been wont to say something very similar and, if he remembered correctly, the quote was from one of the Greek philosophers. So where had a woman who frequented the backstreets of Europe learned it?

Margaret felt her stomach lurch as the carriage suddenly stopped in front of a huge house. It rose four stories above the flagstones. There were eight windows on either side of the gleaming black door. She'd never even been inside a house this grand, and now she was supposed to masquerade as its mistress?

Not waiting for the groom to put down the carriage steps, Philip jumped down onto the flagway and turned back to the carriage, holding out his hands for Margaret.

Reluctantly she moved toward him, trying not to react as his hard hands closed around her waist and he swung her to the ground.

Tiny pinpricks of awareness flowed from his touch, seeping into her flesh and making her feel strangely disoriented.

Margaret stole a quick glance at Philip. But it appeared that whatever had caused her strange reaction was not something he shared. He was staring at his front door as if he'd forgotten her presence.

"That shouldn't be there," he murmured.

Margaret followed his gaze, but couldn't see anything amiss.

"What shouldn't be there?"

"The knocker. I've been out of the country, so why is it up?"

"Anticipation by your staff?" Margaret suggested as she followed him up the five gray marble steps to the door.

Either that, or . . . A feeling of dread suddenly enshrouded Philip as a second reason occurred to him. Surely Estelle wouldn't have . . . A sense of impotent anger filled him. Of course she would have. There was little any woman wouldn't do.

Hoping that Margaret was right and the knocker was nothing more than the sign of an overeager staff, he grabbed the brass lion's-head and gave it a sharp rap.

The heavy thud echoed through Margaret's body, escalating her fears. She was so far out of her natural element—although, if her father had been an honorable man, she wouldn't be. Then mansions like Philip's would be commonplace in her life. In fact, she probably would have married into one of them as the only daughter of the Baron Mainwaring.

When the door didn't open immediately, Philip muttered something under his breath and shoved it open himself.

Obedient to the tug of his hand on her arm, Margaret entered, trying not to gawk as she surveyed her surroundings. The entrance hall was enormous, with a pattern of black-and-white marble tiles stretching in all directions. Sunlight streamed into the area from the huge fanlight above the door illuminating the exquisite workmanship of an ivory- and jade-inlaid table, and bounced off the ornately carved, gilded mirror above it. A twelve-foot white marble statue of what Margaret thought was a representation of Cupid stood beside the wide, curving staircase.

"Where is . . ." Philip began, and then paused as the green baize door at the end of the hall opened and an elderly man emerged.

The man stopped dead when he saw Philip, then hurried toward them. "My lord, forgive me. I did not hear the bell and the footman is away."

Philip was about to demand an explanation for the knocker being up in his absence when he suddenly remembered that he was supposed to be an adoring bridegroom.

Putting his arm around Margaret, he pulled her rigid body closer to him.

"My dear, this is Compton, the mainstay of my household. He's been with the family longer than I have. Compton, this is your new mistress, my countess, Lady Chadwick."

Margaret watched as the august butler forgot himself

so far as to gape at her. Why was he shocked? she wondered. Because Philip had married, or because he'd married *her?* Probably the latter. George always said that servants could tell an imposter far faster than their masters.

"Con—" Compton's voice cracked. He firmed it and hurried on. "Congratulations, my lord. And please allow me to extend the best wishes of the staff to you, my lady."

"Thank you," Margaret muttered, wondering just how many people the staff encompassed, and just how soon she was expected to cope with them.

"Serve tea in the small salon at once, Compton," Philip said.

Compton opened his mouth as if to say something, clearly thought better of the impulse, and hurried back through the green baize door.

Margaret watched him go.

"What's the matter?" Philip glanced from her thoughtful face toward Compton's retreating back.

"I have the strangest feeling that he's escaping," she said.

"Do you think I beat my servants, madam wife?" Philip took her arm and headed down the broad hallway.

"It's not that. It's—"

She gasped as Philip's fingers suddenly tightened around her forearm with bruising force. A second later she heard the shrill titter of a woman's laughter.

"Damn it to hell!" Philip bit out.

Margaret shivered, wondering, Who was the woman laughing and why did Philip look so furious?

Dropping her arm, he stalked toward an open doorway halfway down the hall.

Margaret hurried after him, not knowing what else to do.

"Philip!" The shocked word was uttered by a very fat woman of indeterminate middle-age who was sitting beside the ornately carved, white marble fireplace. Across from her, on a pale blue sofa, was another middle-aged woman and an elderly man wearing an old-fashioned wig.

Margaret watched in fascination as the fat woman's teacup slowly tilted sideways and spilled its contents over her purple silk skirt and onto the beautiful cream-and-rose Aubuson carpet.

"Estelle, your tea!" the other woman shrieked, and Estelle hastily set the now-empty cup down.

"Really, Chadwick, you ought to show better manners than to come bursting in here like that," the elderly man said.

"Forgive me, Sir William." Philip made a stiff bow. "I didn't realize that I was entertaining visitors in my absence."

"Well, Philip, I didn't . . . I thought . . . What with the Little Season starting and . . ."

Margaret winced in sympathy at Estelle's stammering. Philip tended to affect her that way, too. But who was Estelle, that she felt free to take up residence in his home while he was away? And why had Philip's servants allowed it?

"Visitors!" Sir William glared at Philip from underneath his bushy gray brows. "That's a fine way to talk about your mama-in-law, Chadwick."

Margaret stared at Estelle in shock. How could Estelle be Philip's mother-in-law if he was supposed to be married to her?

"And who is that ravishing creature behind you?" Sir William gave Margaret a leer that she never even noticed.

"Is she one of Daddy's ladybirds, Grandmama?" A thin voice from the corner asked.

Surprised, Margaret turned to see who had spoken and discovered a small girl of about seven, half hidden by the drapes in the window alcove.

"Annabelle!" Philip's outraged tone bleached the child's pallid cheeks to parchment.

Instinctively responding to the fear in the child's face, Margaret tried to defuse the situation. "It would appear that my nanny was right when she used to say that little pitchers have big ears."

Philip took a deep breath, reining in his anger with an almost visible effort. "Allow me to make known to you my late wife's mother, Estelle, her friends, Mrs. Wooster and Sir William."

Margaret dropped a polite curtsy, using the motion to regain her composure. Why hadn't Philip told her he'd been married before? Because she wasn't important enough for him to bother. The obvious truth did nothing for her already-shaky self-confidence.

"And this is my new countess, Lady Chadwick," Philip announced boldly. There was a second of appalled silence while Estelle stared at her in horror, and then Annabelle shrieked, "No! I don't want a stepmother! She'll beat me!"

"She won't be the one beating you, if you don't remember your manners," Philip snapped in frustration, feeling as if he'd completely lost control of the situation. Instead of being able to pick the time and place to introduce Margaret to the ton, his hand had been forced.

"I won't—" Annabelle began.

"Get up to the nursery where you belong!" Philip cut her off.

Helplessly Margaret watched the child scurry out of the room. She wanted to comfort Annabelle. To tell her not to worry. That she wasn't really her stepmother; she was merely a temporary player in an elaborate play that her father was staging. But she couldn't.

"I'd better go to her," Estelle muttered, heaving her considerable bulk to her feet.

"And I must be going," Mrs. Wooster bounced up and, accompanied by Sir William, hurried out after Estelle.

Margaret watched as Philip closed his eyes and pressed the bridge of his nose between his thumb and forefinger as if he were trying to ease some pain. He looked so tired. Tired and worried and just plain angry. And he had a certain right, Margaret conceded. Mother-in-law or not, Estelle should not have invaded his home while he'd been away.

"My apologies." Philip's words sounded stiff, as if they weren't words he used very often. "I certainly didn't intend—"

He broke off as Compton suddenly appeared in the doorway with the tea tray. "Bring that along to the library, Compton. We can be private in there," he told Margaret.

Margaret followed Philip into a large room which had two walls entirely filled with books. Despite her worries, a feeling of anticipation shot through her at the thought of exploring the many volumes.

Margaret sank into the brown leather chair beside the crackling fire Philip gestured to, and waited while Compton set the tea tray on the desk.

When Compton had left, Philip began to pace across the dark blue oriental carpet. Margaret studied the rigid line of his back and waited for him to say something.

Finally he stopped and turned to her.

"The truth," she said.

He blinked. "What?"

"You're obviously trying to decide what to tell me, and I was suggesting that the truth would be most expedient. As you keep reminding me, we're supposed to be married."

"And what do truth and marriage have to do with each other?"

"Very little, from what I've seen." Her mother's bitter experience made Margaret's voice sharp. "Try thinking of it as arming a fellow combatant with the weapons necessary to fight a battle."

How very apt an analogy, Philip thought. Marriage was indeed like a war with the husband constantly fighting a rearguard action against his wife's excesses. No, not constantly, he amended. Sometimes wives tried to sidetrack their husbands with lovemaking. He studied the soft contours of Margaret's cheek, which the blazing fire had warmed to a delicate rose-pink. His eyes followed the line of her cheek down over her lips, and he felt a coil of desire grip him. He wanted to press his lips against hers. He wanted to taste them. To run his tongue over them and force them open so he could explore her mouth.

What kind of lover would she be? he wondered. His eyes narrowed as he focused on how her small breasts rose and fell beneath the thin material of her bodice. Would their tips be a dusky brown, or a soft pink like her alluring lips?

He stalked over to the window, twitched aside the heavy damask drapes, and stared blindly outside. He didn't want to think about Margaret's other lovers. It made him feel strangely violent, and he didn't understand why. He had never cared before who had warmed his lovers' beds before.

He turned as Margaret got to her feet and walked over to the tea tray to pour herself a cup. The sway of her hips added to his inner turmoil. He wanted to yank the material away, toss her down on the sofa and bury his manhood deep in her body.

He reminded himself of his decision to wait before he bedded her. But if it was too soon to bed her, it certainly wasn't too soon to kiss her.

He sat down and as Margaret passed him to return to her seat, he grabbed her arm. Taking the teacup out of her fingers, he set it down on the table beside his chair.

Taken unawares, Margaret let out a startled squeak as

Philip suddenly exerted pressure, tumbling her into his lap. She landed across his hard thighs, and her forehead bumped against his chest. Tensing her muscles, she took a deep breath. It was a mistake. This close to him she could smell the scent of the sandalwood soap that he used, and underlying that was the faint, elusive male scent of the man himself. She gulped, trying to ignore the way his hard thighs were pushing into her soft hips.

The air in her lungs felt heavy, too heavy to breathe, and her mind seemed to be slowing down under the onslaught of sensation pouring through her.

Margaret briefly considered trying to get off his lap, but she knew that if he didn't want her to go, he could easily stop her. She had no illusions about how much stronger than her he was. Not only that, but struggling to escape would let him know exactly how disconcerting she found their contact. And if he knew that, he could use the knowledge against her anytime he chose to. It was better to let Philip think that she was impervious to his physical presence. She prepared to endure the subtle torture.

Her resolve suffered a major setback when he put his arm around her rigid body and inexorably drew her back against his chest.

"You need to feel comfortable around me." He uttered the first excuse that occurred to him. "Like a wife would." His warm fingers began to rub slowly over her back. Back and forth.

There was something hypnotic in his movement. It held her motionless as a cascade of shivers poured over her. It was the buzzing in her ears that finally alerted her to the fact that she wasn't breathing, and she took a hasty gulp of air.

"I'm feeling more comfortable." She managed to choke out the lie.

"You're tense as a bowstring. Anyone would think you're afraid of me."

Anyone would be right. Or, more precisely, she was afraid of how he made her feel. Was it him, personally, she wondered, or could any man make her feel this strange, shivery sense of excitement? Was that why women flitted from lover to lover in Philip's world? Because there wasn't any difference in how they felt when a man embraced them? It was a strangely lowering thought, and one that she didn't want to explore. It seemed to devalue her as a rational being.

"Look at me." Philip's voice sounded deeper to her.

Cautiously tipping her head back, Margaret peered up at him. Her gaze was caught and held by the tiny lights glimmering deep in his dark eyes. What was he feeling? she wondered. Did men feel a sensation similar to the emotions tormenting her?

"I'm going to kiss you," he said.

Margaret stared at his lips and tried to contain the mixture of fear and anticipation that curled through her. She had long been curious about what it felt like to be kissed by a man, but even so, she knew that kissing this particular man was a very bad idea.

"Why?" she forced the word out, thinking that as long as she kept him talking, he couldn't do anything. "It's not likely anyone is ever going to see us kissing."

"No," Philip muttered, his eyes never wavering from her mouth. "But lovers impart their intimate knowledge of each other to onlookers in a hundred unconscious gestures and moves. At the moment the only information you're giving an onlooker is that you're nervous of me. Hendricks may be old, but he's not a fool. He'll notice, and once he notices, he'll begin to wonder."

Philip's hand captured her chin and, holding her still, he lowered his head.

Margaret waited with a sense of inevitability. Try as she might, she couldn't think of a single objection that might sway him.

Instead of immediately pressing his mouth against hers as she'd been expecting him to, he turned her face slightly and lightly ran his lips over her cheek. Her breathing developed an uneven cadence, and she could feel the skin on her face contracting beneath the heated warmth of his breath.

Slowly, as if he had all the time in the world, Philip traced over her brow. Her eyelids closed as shivers raced over her skin. She could hear him saying something, but the words seemed to be coming from a great distance and they made no sense. The only reality for her at the moment was the way she felt, and her compulsion to get closer to him. To feed the growing spark of desire burning in her abdomen.

At last Philip's mouth closed over hers, and Margaret froze at the unexpected sensation. Roughly his fingers speared through her curls, holding her head motionless as he exerted pressure. His tongue darted out to lick her bottom lip.

Margaret gasped, and the sound was swallowed up by the devouring cavern of Philip's mouth.

She wasn't sure even in her own mind if she was pleased or not when Philip suddenly pulled back. She felt as if she were floating up through a thick, heavy fog that made it hard to see and hear, and even harder to think. She shook her head to dispel the lingering tendrils of sensation that bound her to Philip. The abrupt movement brought reality rushing back, and on its heels came a sense of shame at her wanton behavior.

Confused and embarrassed, she scrambled out of Philip's lap with more haste than dignity.

The knock on the bookroom door told her why Philip had broken off their kiss, and she hurriedly retreated to the chair on the other side of the fireplace.

"Come in," Philip said, and the door instantly opened to reveal Compton's impassive features.

"Mr. Hendricks just arrived, my lord, and even though I told him that you had just this moment come home from foreign parts, he insisted on seeing you."

Margaret mentally braced herself, aware that her part in this farce was about to begin.

"Show Mr. Hendricks in, Compton," Philip said.

The minute Compton withdrew, Philip turned to Margaret, his face hard and determined, all traces of the man who'd been kissing her gone. "You remember what you're supposed to say?"

Margaret merely nodded. She would have to be a dolt not to have learned the lessons he'd been conning her on since they'd left Vienna.

She tensed as she heard the sound of Compton's measured tread in the hallway. There was a second pair of steps behind him, lighter and more hesitant.

She took a deep breath as Compton announced, "Mr. Hendricks."

A short, thin man with a wispy white fringe around his bald head paused on the threshold. His faded blue eyes quickly located Margaret. Slowly, as if unsure of his welcome, he inched into the room, not noticing when Compton closed the door behind him.

"Mary?" Hendricks stared at Margaret as if looking for some sign of recognition.

Margaret forced a smile even as an entirely unexpected feeling of disgust at her own duplicity filled her—a reaction that caught her off guard. She hadn't expected to feel anything but satisfaction at duping one of her despised aristocrats. But despite her hatred of Hendricks's class, she still felt guilty. Forcing the crippling emotion to the back of her mind, she tried to concentrate instead on what had to be done.

"As I mentioned in my letter, your wife changed your daughter's name to Margaret and that's what she's used to now," Philip offered to the growing silence.

Hendricks sighed. "It doesn't surprise me. We named her for my mother, and my wife always disliked my mother."

Philip shot Margaret a warning look over the top of Hendricks's downcast head, and she desperately scrambled for something to say. Anything.

"Mary is a lovely name, but I am rather used to being called Margaret," she tried.

To her dismay, Hendricks's eyes filled with tears, and his lips trembled. "Oh, my dear, it doesn't matter what you're called. You're my own precious daughter come home to me." He opened his arms and, seeing no way to avoid it, Margaret walked into his frail embrace.

He gave her a quick hug and then released her. Stepping back, he took out a large white handkerchief and vigorously blew his nose. "I fear I'm becoming maudlin in my old age. You probably don't even remember me," he said, but the hopeful look in his eyes belied his words.

Margaret had a sudden urge to assure him that she did. That no daughter could forget him, but she bit back the impulse. The fewer lies she told, the better. There were already far too many for her to remember.

"I'm sorry," she murmured. "I don't even remember my mother."

"What!" Hendricks looked appalled.

"She became ill and took refuge in the convent where she died when I was very young . . ." Margaret rattled off the story Philip had supplied her, but for the first time it meant something more than a recital of facts about long-dead people. To Hendricks, those long-dead people were real—real and very much loved.

"What about . . . ?" Hendricks turned to Philip as if unwilling to ask his daughter about his wife's paramour.

"According the records of the convent, they were brought there by a man who said he was your wife's husband. He claimed sanctuary for her and the child, and then left. He never returned."

"He probably only stayed until they'd spent the funds she brought," Hendricks said.

"He didn't take this, though." Philip pulled the thin gold heart out of his pocket and handed it to Hendricks. "Your daughter was wearing this when she was brought to the convent."

Hendricks took the necklace with fingers that trembled visibly. He stared down at his coat-of-arms engraved on one side before opening it. His face went stark white as he stared at the two miniatures inside.

Margaret, afraid he was going to collapse, put her arms around him and helped him into a chair.

"Here, sir, drink this." Philip shoved a glass of brandy into Hendricks's fingers.

Hendricks swallowed the brandy in one gulp. "Sorry, my dear." He gave Margaret a wan smile. "It was just such a shock to see it again. I remember when the miniatures were painted. I was so happy and then . . ." He seemed to make a tremendous effort to regain his composure. "But it's all right. You've been returned to me."

Margaret smiled weakly back.

Hendricks turned to Philip. "I can't thank you enough for finding Mary—Margaret," he corrected himself.

"Ah, but it is I who owes you the debt." Philip walked over to Margaret and put his arm around her thin shoulders.

Margaret resisted the impulse to try to shrug them away. His arm felt so heavy, like the wages of sin. The echo of a long-ago Sunday sermon danced through her mind.

"Without you, I never would have found the perfect wife."

"Wife!" The word exploded from Hendricks.

"Yes, sir." Margaret sank to her knees at Hendricks's feet and took his trembling hands into hers, fearful that her impersonation was going to drive him into a seizure. He looked so frail. "Please don't disapprove."

"No, no, dear. It isn't that I disapprove. I may live retired, but I am fully cognizant of what a matrimonial prize the Earl of Chadwick is."

Margaret shot a quick glance at Philip and felt like smacking him at his smug expression. How like the aristocracy to consider only rank and fortune when deciding who was a matrimonial prize!

"It's just that I selfishly wanted to spend a little time with you before you entered society and became so busy with parties and the like."

"I'm not all that interested in parties," Margaret said.

"Then will you and Philip visit me at my estate for a few months?"

Margaret hated to dash the hopes she'd inadvertently raised, but she knew she had no choice in the matter. Philip would never agree.

"Philip can't leave London now," Margaret said. "He's working on a bill to help the returning soldiers and I don't want to . . ." She allowed her voice to trail off, hoping that Hendricks would assume that she was reluctant to leave her new bridegroom, and spare her telling yet one more lie.

"Yes, my dear." Hendricks patted her hand gently. "I quite understand."

"But I'd also like to spend some time with you," Margaret said, wanting to banish the sadness in his eyes. "Why don't you be our guest for the Season?" she offered, hoping Philip wouldn't be upset at her invitation. Even though she knew Philip wanted Hendricks in London, that didn't mean that Philip wanted him as a houseguest.

It was just too bad if he didn't, Margaret thought on a flash of militancy. Philip was using this poor old man for his own ends; surely he owed him something in return. Not that it would occur to Philip to pay. From her observations, the only thing the ton ever repaid were gaming debts.

"Yes indeed, sir." Philip promptly echoed her invitation. "We would be pleased to have you."

"I . . ." Hendricks eyes widened as the penetrating sound of Estelle's voice echoed through the thick door.

"What's wrong?" Margaret asked.

"Nothing. I . . . Is Mrs. Arbuthnot visiting you?" he asked Philip.

"So it would seem," Philip said. "She was here when we arrived, and I haven't had a chance to find out what her plans are."

"What a nice surprise that must have been for you," Hendricks said, with a patent insincerity that made Margaret want to laugh. "I think it would be better if I were to open my own house for the season. That way we'll still be able to visit whenever we want and . . ." His gaze strayed to the door.

And what? Margaret wondered. It was clear Hendricks didn't want to stay in the same house as Estelle, but why? Margaret felt a dull throbbing spark to life behind her eyes at all the currents swirling around her that she didn't understand.

"Quite so," Philip said, and the two men exchanged a glance that effectively shut her out.

Hendricks got to his feet. "Now that that is settled, I'll go back to my hotel and set things in motion." He gave Margaret a warm smile. "I'll call on you tomorrow, if I may?" He looked uncertain for a moment.

"I'll look forward to it." Margaret reassured him.

"Bless you, my dear. I can't tell you what finding you has meant to me."

"And to me," Margaret forced the lie out.

"Till tomorrow, then. Chadwick." He shook Philip's hand and with one last glance at Margaret, left.

Margaret closed her eyes as the door shut behind him.

She felt unclean, contaminated by what she'd just done. It didn't matter that Hendricks was a member of the ton or that she'd really had no choice, she still felt like a villain.

"A promising beginning," Philip said.

Suddenly Margaret couldn't stand any more. She had to get away. To escape from the knowledge of what her impersonation might do to Hendricks and all her worries over George, but most of all she wanted to escape from Philip and the power that he held over her. Even if it was only for a moment.

"I have a headache." Margaret blurted out. "I want to rest."

Philip frowned at her and said finally, "Very well, I'll show you to your room. But I would advise you not to make a habit out of hiding."

If only she had the option, Margaret thought tiredly as she trailed along behind Philip. But it was only the wealthy who had the luxury of running from their problems. People like her had to stand and deal with them or be crushed beneath their weight. And she wouldn't be crushed. Her lips set in determination. She might not be able to stop Philip from using her, but she didn't have to crumble beneath that usage. She would survive. No matter what, she would survive.

Five

"Set the tea tray on the table by the fireplace, Daisy," Margaret said.

"Will there be anything else, my lady?" The young maid did as she'd been directed, then dropped a nervous curtsy.

"No, thank you. If I should need anything else, I'll ring."

"Yes, my lady. Thank you, my lady." The girl bobbed yet one more curtsy before scuttling out of Margaret's bedroom.

Margaret watched her go, wishing she could escape as easily.

Climbing out of the huge bed, she poured herself a cup of tea and then wandered over to the window.

Parting the faded damask drapes, she peered outside to see what kind of day the fates had gifted her with. For the first time since she'd arrived in England, the skies were clear, and she yanked the dark curtains aside to allow the golden light to spill inside.

It didn't help much, Margaret decided as she looked around critically. She'd been so tired and upset last evening that she hadn't noticed much about her surroundings beyond the fact that the room contained a large bed which she had immediately fallen on. Five minutes later she'd been deeply asleep.

But now that she was rested, it was impossible not to

notice the room's oppressive atmosphere. Margaret frowned, trying to decide just why it was so unwelcoming. It could be the oversized, dark mahogany furniture that seemed to loom over her slight frame, or maybe it was the extensive use of dark maroon and Egyptian brown. Whatever the reason, it was not a room that encouraged its occupant to linger.

Not that she wanted to. Margaret took another sip of her tea. She wanted to get this charade over with as quickly as possible so that she could go back to her normal life with George. George might not be able to provide much beyond the bare necessities of life, but at least he valued her for the person she was and not for the use he could make of her.

A tremor shuddered through her as she remembered what it had felt like to sit in Philip's lap. How his swollen manhood had burned against her hips and how his lips felt as they had moved over hers.

She had no idea why Philip's kiss had made her feel so disoriented—so . . . She couldn't even think of words adequate to describe the sensation. Worse, she had the disheartening suspicion that it was not a sensation decent women were supposed to feel, probably accounting for the fact that polite society didn't have words to describe it.

Was it possible she'd responded to Philip's kiss as she had because she was a bastard and something had been left out of her moral makeup? An icy tendril of fear wrapped itself around her mind. As a child, she'd over-heard enough gossip by her mother and her friends to know that women weren't supposed to take any pleasure in doing their wifely duty; women were supposed to en-dure it as a punishment for Eve's leading Adam astray. Margaret scowled. Not that she'd ever subscribed to the Church's theory that Adam was just a hapless victim of Eve's machinations.

"And what are you looking so ferocious about?"

Margaret jumped in shocked surprise, spilling tea down the front of her nightgown. She whirled around to find Philip standing in an open doorway beside a huge armoire she hadn't noticed before.

A fully-dressed Philip. Margaret's eyes skimmed over his dark blue coat with its shining gilt buttons. The sight of his broad chest raised memories she was trying to forget and she resolutely yanked her gaze down. It landed on his cream-colored breeches and a sudden warmth surged through her, doing nothing for her self-possession.

"Why were you looking so pensive?" Philip repeated.

"I was just thinking that Adam was a clodpole." She gave him the literal truth.

Philip's dark brows arched questioningly. "Adam who?"

"The Adam. The paperskull from the Bible."

"You've read the Bible?"

Margaret's nervousness at having him in her bedroom promptly sank in the depths of her outrage. "It may come as a shock to you, sir, but the lower classes have been reading the Bible for a long time. And from what I've observed, they pay a lot more attention to its teachings than the ton."

Philip barely heard the words her lips were forming. He was far too absorbed in the lips themselves. They looked even more delectable than he remembered. He wanted to run his thumb over them and explore their exact texture. He wanted to force them apart and taste her mouth. To run his lips down over her soft neck and nuzzle the delicate hollow at the base of her throat. The urge to bury himself in the promised delights of her slender body was fast becoming a compulsion, and he wasn't sure if his self-control would last another day, let alone until the end of the Little Season.

Margaret watched him warily, uneasy at the way he was

staring at her. His expression reminded her an urchin she'd once seen in a bakery shop. The boy had been staring at the dazzling array of pastries on display, and his face held that same mixture of greed and anticipation.

"What was it you wished, milord?" she ventured.

"For you to call me Philip!"

Margaret tensed as he strode across the room toward her. As he passed in front of the window, the sunlight splintered over his dark head and for one brief second he seemed engulfed in a rainbow. Margaret blinked and the illusion faded. Unfortunately, Philip didn't. He kept coming.

It took all of Margaret's considerable resolve not to retreat. Not only was there no place to retreat to, but she knew it would be fatal to allow him to know how much he frightened her.

Nervously her bare toes curled into the carpet as she waited for him to say whatever it was that he'd come to say. To her shock, he didn't say anything. Instead, stopping scant inches from her, he reached out and lightly traced over the tea stain on her bodice. His finger felt hot, seeming to burn through the thin muslin of her nightgown to the bare skin beneath.

Desperately Margaret locked her muscles in a vain attempt to control her reaction as his finger passed over the slight swell of her breast. A tingling sensation shot through her, and she could feel her nipples hardening. Even worse, she was afraid that he could see it.

"Take off your nightgown before you become ill." Philip's voice dropped several levels, developing a husky overtone that scraped seductively over her nerve endings.

"I never get sick. I'll change as soon as you've given me my orders for the day." Margaret fought to keep her tone level.

"You've just had your first one. Take off that wet nightgown."

Margaret stared into his face, wary of the sparks she could see dancing in his eyes, but even more wary of the strange effect his touch was having on her. It was hard enough fighting him. It would be impossible if she were also fighting herself. What was wrong with her? The question echoed and reechoed through her confused mind.

Frozen by uncertainty, she stared at his lean fingers which were busily opening the tiny pearl buttons that held her nightgown together. Slowly, as if he were savoring the action, he released first one and then another until her bodice was open almost to her waist.

Margaret's gaze swung around the room, seeking a way to stop him, but none presented itself. *Words,* she told herself. *Fight him with words.*

"What are you doing?" she blurted out, and then winced at the inanity of the remark. A blind man could see what he was doing. And it didn't take much imagination to figure out why.

Philip gave her a slow smile that unexpectedly tugged at her heart. He looked like a small, mischievous boy, but there was nothing childish in his actions.

"Playing lady's maid, since you don't have one yet." He ran the tip of his finger along her collarbone, and Margaret jumped as a cascade of sparks poured through her skin.

"I don't need a lady's maid." She searched frantically for the outrage she should be feeling, instead of the growing excitement.

"And what do you need, madam wife?" He suddenly pushed aside her nightgown and cupped her breast in his large hand.

Margaret gritted her teeth against the tide of urgency that poured through her at his shocking liberty. She felt brittle with tension, and underlying that sensation was anticipation.

"You're so very beautiful." Philip's voice deepened perceptibly. "I want to . . ." He rubbed the pad of his thumb over her nipple and a shaft of pure sensation shot through her breast, forcing out a small moan before she clamped her lips together.

"So very beautiful."

Margaret found the sound of his voice hypnotic. It seemed to fill her ears the same way that the feel of his hand on her breasts was filling her mind, deafening reason and common sense.

Philip slowly lowered his head and kissed the soft swell of her breast.

Margaret's mouth dried, and a shiver raced down her arms, raising goosebumps. She wanted . . . Her thoughts scattered as he touched the tip of her breast with his tongue, and she trembled violently. It felt as if her flesh were burning, fueled by a growing need, the depth of which terrified her. She shouldn't be allowing him to do this—the panicked thought surfaced through her muddled fears. She had to stop him. Now, while she still had some control over her reactions.

Frantically jerking herself out of Philip's arms, she stared fearfully into his face. There was a dark flush on his cheekbones and his eyes had a curious blankness to them. As if he were looking deeply within himself and not at the outside world at all.

"No!" she gasped as he reached for her again. "Don't!"

She watched as awareness seeped slowly back into his eyes, praying that he would listen to her. If he didn't . . . She shuddered. There was no one to stop him if he decided to bed her. Even if she were to scream, no one in this house would dare to interfere between a man and the woman who was supposed to be his wife.

"Why not?" His words were slurred, but even so they sent a wave of relief through Margaret.

If he had intended to rape her, he wouldn't have answered her. He'd have simply done it. Clutching the gaping front of her nightgown together, she muttered, "Because I don't want you to."

"Don't lie to me! I felt your body trembling with desire." He pushed her fingers away, jerked open her nightgown and covered her breast with his hand. His palm felt warm and rough against her much-softer skin. The sensation was almost more than she could bear.

"I can feel your heart beating like a trapped bird." He dropped his hand and stared at her in disgust. "It isn't the act that you don't want. So what's the matter? Did I forget to mention that I was willing to pay for the pleasure of your body?" The sneer that marred his features hurt her in some indefinable way.

He turned on his heel and stalked toward the hall door. "Be downstairs in fifteen minutes."

Margaret watched as the door slammed behind him and then collapsed into the bed. She felt breathless and light-headed, as if she'd just run a long distance in the burning summer sun. She gulped in air in a vain effort to regain her composure. It didn't help.

Why? The question beat into her mind, causing physical pain as it hammered at her sense of self-worth. Why had she reacted to him like that? What was there about Philip Moresby that made her body suddenly seem like a stranger to her?—a stranger with an agenda of its own, an agenda that defied common sense or even self-preservation. Was it that Philip possessed some strange quality that she'd never discovered in a man before? Or was it that she possessed some hitherto unsuspected trait that made her susceptible to him?

Was something missing from her moral makeup? she thought with a chill. Because no matter how much she tried to rationalize her response to him, it just didn't seem decent. Margaret squarely faced the appalling fact. It was not the kind of reaction that a respectable woman should have to any man, let alone one she didn't know all that well. It was too deep, too uncontrolled, too . . . emotional, she thought in despair—and she'd never been an emotional person. Her entire adult life she'd prided herself on her logic and her intelligence and yet suddenly she found herself caught in a situation which owed nothing to logic.

All she could state with any certainty was that no matter how good it felt when Philip kissed her, it was a very bad idea. It added complications to a situation that was already so tangled as to make the Gordian knot look like a child's puzzle.

Somehow she had to find a way to defuse her reaction to Philip. But how? Nervously she chewed on her lower lip. How could she control what she couldn't even understand? She didn't know. She just knew that she had to accomplish it somehow. Because if she didn't . . . A shudder wracked her at the thought of what might happen if she allowed him to continue to make love to her whenever the urge took him.

The clock on the mantel striking the quarter hour jerked her out of her half-formed thoughts, and she jumped to her feet, suddenly remembering what Philip had said about hurrying. She rushed across the room to the armoire, yanked out one of her new dresses at random and scrambled into it, fastening it with clumsy fingers. Under no circumstances did she want Philip coming back into her room to see why she was late.

Grabbing her brush, she raked it through her tousled curls, stopping when she suddenly remembered that while Philip had left through the hall door, he hadn't entered that way.

Impatiently pushing aside the annoying ringlets which the Parisian hairstylist had insisted on, she cautiously approached the door through which Philip had entered. Pressing her ear against it, Margaret listened but could hear nothing. She carefully grasped the silver knob and slowly inched it open. Pressing her eye to the tiny opening, she peered through and discovered a large sitting room. Encouraged by the fact that it was empty, she opened the door and took a good look. The room was decorated in the same depressing maroon and Egyptian brown as her bedroom.

Was it meant to be a sitting room for her bedroom? Or . . . Her stomach twisted nervously. Could this sitting room be meant to serve both the earl and his countess? Did the door she could see on the opposite wall, lead to Philip's bedroom?

Margaret hurriedly closed the door. She had no intention of opening the door on the other side of the sitting room and finding out. In fact, if she had the means to do it, she'd nail the door shut permanently.

The small ormolu clock on the marble mantel emitted a sudden chime, and Margaret jumped. Much as she dreaded facing Philip again, with the memory of his touch still fresh in her mind, she had no choice. Philip had said "fifteen minutes" and, while she didn't think he'd hold her to it exactly, she wasn't willing to take the risk. There was no sense in inviting trouble. She already had more than she could handle.

Tucking a lawn handkerchief into her sleeve, she hurried out of her room.

Margaret paused at the top of the broad front staircase and looked down at the entrance hall below. For a moment she allowed herself to simply enjoy the beauty of the ornately carved paneling and the gleam of the highly polished marble, delaying the moment when she'd have to face Philip.

"What are you doing?" A childish voice from behind her demanded.

Margaret jumped and then grimaced. If she survived the Moresby family without suffering a permanent agitation of the nerves, it would be a miracle.

"I'm admiring the foyer." Margaret ignored the scowl on Annabelle's thin face.

"It doesn't belong to you. It belongs to my papa."

"True, but that doesn't mean other people can't admire his possessions."

Annabelle glared at her. "Grandmama says all you want is his money. She says that you're nothing but a scheming baggage who trapped him into marriage!"

Grandmama says entirely too much, Margaret thought, and then her momentary annoyance faded when she saw the unhappiness in the child's light-blue eyes. She wanted to ease it, not add to it, but she didn't know how. She could hardly tell Annabelle not to worry. That she wasn't really married to her father. That he was simply blackmailing her and when her usefulness was over she'd be gone.

"Annabelle . . ."

"I'm *Lady* Annabelle!" the child yelled at her. "Don't you—"

"That's enough!" Philip's harsh voice from the foyer below cut through whatever it was the child was going to say.

Margaret watched in sympathy as Annabelle's sallow cheeks flushed and a sudden sparkle of tears coated her eyes.

"It's all right," Margaret said.

"It is not all right!" Philip said. "I won't have her being rude."

"I hate you! It's all your fault!" Annabelle shrieked at Margaret, and then turned and raced off toward the back of the house.

Margaret stifled a sigh as she started down the stairs. Philip should have foreseen Annabelle's antipathy. Suddenly acquiring a stepmother would be a shock to any child, especially one who appeared to be as indulged and petted by her grandmother as Annabelle was.

"I apologize for Annabelle's rudeness," Philip said stiffly when Margaret reached him. "She has gotten completely out of control."

Margaret paled as, for an eerie moment, her mind replayed the memory of her father using almost those same words about her when she had screamed at him not to leave her mother. *"An ill-bred bastard who is completely out of control,"* he'd said, and then turned and stalked out of their lives.

"What she needs is a strict governess."

"No!" Margaret instinctively protested. Harshness was not the answer to the child's confusion and anger over events she was powerless to control.

"No?" Philip looked at her in surprise. "You heard the child. She needs to be controlled."

"She doesn't need to *be* controlled. She needs to learn *self*-control. What kind of routine does she follow?"

Philip shrugged. "I have no idea. Ask Estelle. She can tell you."

But he couldn't? Margaret wondered. She had always assumed her own father had never shown any interest in her because he saw no point in becoming involved with a bastard. But that wasn't true in Annabelle's case, and yet Philip still seemed to have no tender feelings for the child at all. Was there something about the aristocracy that prevented them from being good fathers?

Margaret obediently sat in the chair in the breakfast room which Philip held for her, and the footman standing by the door jumped to fill her coffee cup. Margaret accepted it with a smile, shaking her head when he offered to get her whatever she liked from the crowded sideboard.

Philip impatiently motioned him out of the room and then turned to Margaret. "Eat something," he ordered.

"I'm not hungry," she said. Reaction from her earlier unsettling encounter with him in her room, and nervousness over Hendricks's impending visit, had destroyed her appetite.

"Eat anyway," he insisted. As if to emphasis his order, he picked up a thin porcelain plate from the sideboard, piled it with an assortment of food, and placed it down in front of her.

Margaret swallowed uneasily as the smell of some kind of fish assaulted her nostrils. "I feel like the sword of Damocles is hanging over my head," she muttered.

"What?"

Margaret looked up. "The sword of Damocles. You remember, it's from——"

"I know where it's from," he said. "I'm simply surprised that you do."

"Education is not the sole prerogative of the aristocracy!"

"No, but it does tend to be the province of men."

"Why do you say that?" Margaret asked, only too happy to discuss something with no emotional overtones.

"It's obvious."

Margaret merely looked at him and waited.

"Women don't go to school. Not real schools," he finally said.

"Schools are not necessary to obtain an education. In fact, from what I've seen, they seem to be a positive hindrance to it."

"Are you an admirer of Mary Wollstonecraft and that group of Bedlamites she consorts with?" Philip asked.

"I admire her for having the courage to speak her mind."

"Of all the——"

"Excuse me, my lord." Compton appeared in the doorway. "This message just came for you." He handed a thick cream-colored note to Philip.

Philip hastily broke the seal and read it.

"One of the members that I've been trying to talk to

about my bill has finally arrived in London and will be at Westminster this morning." He frowned uncertainly at her. "I don't like leaving you alone with Hendricks," Philip murmured, almost as if he were voicing his thoughts aloud.

Margaret didn't say anything, knowing that nothing she said would make any difference.

He glanced back down at the letter. "But talking to Fooley is too good an opportunity to miss."

Getting to his feet, he said, "If Hendricks comes while I'm gone, do your best."

He headed toward the door and then turned. "I almost forgot. We'll be attending a ball this evening. Wear the deep-blue gown. And eat your breakfast." He threw one final order at her.

Margaret waited until she heard the front door close behind him, and then shoved the offending plate out of the way. It gave her a great deal of satisfaction to thwart him even in so small a thing.

"Oh!"

Margaret turned to find Estelle hovering in the doorway.

"If you're looking for Philip, he has gone to Westminster," Margaret said.

Estelle eyed her as if she were mad. "Looking for Philip! Whyever would I do that?"

Because he's your son-in-law? Because he's your host? Because you'd like to talk to him about his daughter? Margaret could come up with several excellent reasons on the spur of the moment, but her manners were far too good to give voice to any of them. Besides, she didn't want to alienate Estelle unless it was unavoidable. Estelle might be willing to tell her some of the things she wanted to know.

Estelle might even be acquainted with Margaret's natural father! She'd have to be very careful how she phrased her questions, though. Margaret hurriedly reined in her sudden excitement. She didn't want Estelle to begin wondering why Margaret was curious about Baron Mainwaring.

Estelle came into the room and headed straight for the sideboard. "I had breakfast in the nursery with dear Annabelle, but that was an hour ago. I think I could have just a bit more."

Taking a plate, Estelle piled it high with food then, sitting down across from Margaret, fell to with an appetite.

Margaret barely suppressed a shudder at the rate with which the food disappeared. It was no wonder Estelle was plump as a Christmas goose.

"Annabelle is such a lovely child." Margaret tried a compliment as an opening gambit.

Estelle swallowed it along with her food. "Yes, although she is bran-faced, as you must have noticed, but I tell her not to worry. That if she doesn't improve, we can try rice powder. Do you use rice powder?" Estelle stared at Margaret's flawless complexion.

"No. One needs a deft hand to use artificial beauty aids and remain natural-looking," Margaret quoted her mother.

Estelle stopped eating long enough to nod emphatically. "How right you are. Why, when you see what some of the women who call themselves leaders of society look like!" Estelle leaned closer to Margaret. "Painted hussies, that's what!"

"Really?" Margaret muttered, pretending not to see the two spots of rouge which shone on Estelle's full cheeks.

Estelle nodded. "Yes, indeed. Now, my daughter Roxanne was a dab hand at the rouge pot. She—"

Estelle suddenly broke off. "But you won't be wanting to hear about Chadwick's first wife. Second wives always try to pretend the first one didn't exist.

"I've seen it so many times before." Estelle's words were slightly muffled by the gammon she was chewing.

"It's only natural for the second wife to want her own children to inherit."

Margaret looked around the elegant room and her blonde eyebrows rose expressively. "I would say that any child of Chadwick's will be more than amply provided for."

Estelle heaved a sigh. "But men can be so easy to manage when they're in love."

Margaret blinked, tried to imagine Chadwick being manipulated or even being in love, and failed utterly.

"Why, I remember when Chadwick was presented to Roxanne," Estelle continued. "He took one look at her and nothing would do but that he marry her out of hand. She was so beautiful with her black hair and her milk-white skin. Chadwick gave her an emerald necklace with huge stones in it for a bride gift. He said the emeralds matched her eyes. Roxanne had the most beautiful green eyes. All the young bucks were writing odes about them."

"I don't think I've ever seen anyone with green eyes," Margaret said, feeling some comment was called for.

"Not like my Roxanne had," Estelle said. "Everyone else just has common blue or brown."

Margaret briefly closed her own common blue eyes and reminded herself that it was normal for Estelle to be partial to her daughter. That it wasn't important because she wasn't going to be playing the part of Philip's wife long enough for Estelle to wear on her nerves.

Estelle dumped three heaping spoonfuls of sugar into her tea, stirred it vigorously and, after a hefty swallow, asked with seeming casualness, "Did Chadwick give Roxanne's necklace to you?"

Margaret firmly suppressed the urge to say that the only thing her precious Chadwick had given her was a great deal of bother, and said, "Of course not. It would hardly be the thing, would it?"

"Much Chadwick would care about that. But if he didn't give it to you, then where is it?" Her voice hardened noticeably.

"Perhaps he put it away to give to Annabelle when she marries."

"Do you really think so?" Estelle asked, and Margaret felt a flash of pity. Estelle might be a silly, vain woman, but she clearly loved her granddaughter and was worried about her future now that she thought Chadwick had remarried.

"Could you ask him what he intends to do with the necklace?"

"Ask him?" Margaret repeated, mentally shuddering at the interpretation Chadwick would put on it if she were to inquire into the whereabouts of a valuable necklace.

Estelle nodded vigorously. "Ask him when— It's like I told my Roxanne when she married Chadwick. Wait until he wants you to do your duty, and then ask him for what you want. Men will promise anything to get their way."

Margaret felt a shimmer of distaste at employing such a strategy, along with an unwilling sympathy for Philip. As far as she could see there was no difference between using Estelle's plan and being a man's mistress. In fact, being a mistress seemed more honest. At least mistresses weren't trying to disguise the fact that they were trading their favors for financial gain.

"You mind my words. You haven't had a mother to offer you counsel, and what would a bunch of nuns know about the marriage bed? Yes indeed." Estelle nodded vigorously, and Margaret watched, fascinated, as her heavy jowls shook. "I'll be more than happy to tell you how to go on."

"Thank you. As fashionable as you are, you must know everyone." Margaret tried her best to sound admiring. It was becoming increasingly clear that Estelle responded to flattery.

Estelle beamed, restored to good humor by Margaret's acknowledgment of her social acumen. "Indeed, I do. Every one of the ton worth knowing. Every peer and matron and sprig and bud."

Bud? The word caught Margaret's attention. One of the last things she remembered her father saying was that he intended to marry a woman of his own class. If he had done that immediately, he well could have a daughter old enough to be out.

"Are any of the peers presenting daughters this season?" Margaret tried to make the question sound casual.

"Not too many. Most prefer to wait until the Spring Season, but there are a few. Let me see." Estelle tugged her fleshy lower lip between her thumb and forefinger. "There's Wolford's second daughter. She has twenty thousand pounds, but she also has spots. Lady Wolford probably thinks the competition will be less now. Then there's Mainwaring's chit."

Margaret felt a sudden clutch of excitement. "Mainwaring? I think Philip mentioned him."

Estelle sniffed disparagingly. "I can't imagine why. Mainwaring is a common-enough sort. Never would have had the title in the normal way. Why, I remember when—"

"Excuse me, my lady."

To Margaret's dismay, Compton interrupted Estelle's memories.

"Mr. Hendricks has just arrived, my lady. He is in the morning room."

"Oh, how nice." Estelle clapped her hands together in a parody of a child's gesture. "Tell him we'll be right there, Compton."

"He asked for Lady Chadwick," Compton tried, but Estelle ignored him as she headed toward the salon.

Margaret was beginning to suspect Estelle ignored anything she didn't want to hear.

Reluctantly Margaret got to her feet and trailed after Estelle. She was not looking forward to telling more lies to that poor old man.

Six

"If it isn't the doting bridegroom. Allow me to wish you happy."

Philip turned at the sound of the mocking voice, grimacing when he saw Lucien Raeburn's sardonic smile.

"I must say, Philip, you look a little pale. Too many late nights?" Lucien fell into step with Philip as he crossed St. James Street.

"Repressed temper," Philip gritted out. "I swear, Lucien, one day I'm going to simply explode from the force of all the words I've had to swallow."

"From that I take it you're still trying to get your bill passed? I would have thought that a new bridegroom would have other things on his mind. Especially when rumor has it that your bride is a diamond of the first water."

"Rumor, for once, doesn't lie." Philip's voice unconsciously deepened as the memory of Margaret's soft skin and the very faint fragrance of roses that clung to it, drifted through his mind, momentarily soothing his anger.

"And even more fortuitously, she happens to be Hendricks's daughter."

Philip eyed his friend for a long moment, but he had absolutely no impulse to tell him the truth. "Just so," Philip said.

"And when do I get to meet this paragon?"

"Tonight at the Templetons' ball."

"Rather a daunting affair for someone who has spent her life in a convent."

"Margaret will manage." Philip said, trying to still his own doubts about the wisdom of pitchforking her into the ton at something as public as the Templetons' ball. But he simply didn't have the luxury of waiting for a more sedate event. He had to increase his lobbying for his bill, and he could best do that at the social events which would attract the most influential members of the ton.

"Margaret? I thought Hendricks's daughter's name was Mary."

"Hendricks named the child after his mother, and his wife hated her mother-in-law. Once she got to France she changed it to Margaret," Philip recited the agreed-upon lie.

"Am I to conclude that Hendricks's erring wife is safely dead?"

"Yes, and from what I've learned, it was the only obliging thing the woman ever did in her life!"

"But then, women are so seldom obliging," Lucien said. "For example, I hear your mother-in-law has taken up residence in your home."

"Yes," Philip said as he dodged a street vendor selling pies.

"You know, Philip, I am most grateful to you." Lucien followed Philip up the steps to Brookes. "What with Napoleon defeated, this had promised to be such a boring season. And, instead I have you providing so much amusement."

"Don't interfere." Philip handed his hat and gloves to the footman who opened the door, and headed toward the reading room where he hoped to find at least one of the older peers that he could talk to about the discharged soldiers' plight.

Lucien gave him a wide-eyed look of innocence that

didn't fool Philip for a moment. "Me! Acquit me of meddling. This is no bread-and-butter of mine. I merely intend to watch from the sidelines. Rather as one watches a play."

"As long as it doesn't turn into a Greek tragedy," Philip said, pausing in the doorway to survey the dimly lit room. Seeing Lord Jersey in the corner, he nodded at Lucien and headed toward his quarry.

"My dear Mr. Hendricks!" Estelle sailed into the salon, leaving Margaret to bring up the rear.

Margaret felt a twinge of compassion at the hunted expression on Hendricks's face.

"Good morning, sir." Margaret hurriedly stepped around Estelle. "I've been waiting for you to arrive."

"Naughty girl." Estelle playfully shook a finger at Margaret. "You never told me that we were to have such a treat this morning."

"Good morning, Mrs. Arbuthnot." Hendricks bowed stiffly to Estelle. "Mar—Margaret," he hurriedly corrected himself, "I have something that I want to show you at my house and—"

"Oh, how exciting!" Estelle clasped her hands together. "Whatever can it be, Margaret? Maybe he's going to give you some of your grandmother's jewels. I can hardly wait to see."

Margaret waited for Hendricks to tell Estelle that she would be decidedly de trop, but to her surprise he didn't. He merely gave another jerky bow and muttered something that sounded like, "Charmed."

Charmed was hardly the word she would have chosen, Margaret thought tartly.

Turning to Estelle, she said, "It's very kind of you to offer to come along, Estelle, but I can't put you to the trouble of rearranging your schedule."

"Oh, but—" Estelle began.

"I'm sure you understand my desire to become reacquainted with my father," Margaret interrupted her. "Perhaps another time."

"Yes, another time," Hendricks hurriedly threw in.

Margaret accepted the cloak Compton was holding out for her and, taking Hendricks's arm, allowed him to rush her out of her house. Bundling her into his closed carriage, he threw one last glance over his shoulder at Estelle who was standing in the open doorway looking after them with impotent frustration.

"Thank you, my dear," he said when the carriage pulled into the road.

"Why didn't you just tell her no when she invited herself along?"

Hendricks looked faintly shocked. "A gentleman never contradicts a lady, my dear. It simply isn't done."

Margaret frowned. It would appear that there were some disadvantages associated with being an aristocrat that she'd never considered before.

"Perhaps not," she said, "but it seems to me that a lady wouldn't invite herself somewhere where she clearly wasn't wanted."

"She shouldn't, of course, but, nonetheless, my code of conduct isn't dependent upon her lapses."

"An interesting ethical consideration," Margaret said. "But tell me, why did she want to come with us and why don't you like her?"

Mr. Hendricks winced. "Was I that obvious?"

Margaret chuckled.

"Normally I abhor gossip but . . . Tell me, my dear, what has Chadwick told you about Estelle and Roxanne?"

"Virtually nothing," Margaret conceded.

"Well, once you go out into society all kinds of malicious people will try to insinuate things, and you should know the truth."

Margaret couldn't agree with him more. Any information she could glean from any source, would help her.

"Ideally Philip should be the one to tell you, but . . ." Hendricks sighed. "It was such a tragedy when Roxanne died."

He paused as if trying to decide what to say.

"To truly understand what happened, you must also understand Roxanne's background. Her father was a ne'er-do-well younger son. He inherited a competence which he proceeded to gamble away. Roxanne was still a child when he died in a hunting accident, forcing her and Mrs. Arbuthnot to live on the charity of relatives. Fortunately, Roxanne grew into a spectacularly beautiful woman. Inky black curls, bright green eyes, and a perfect complexion. She was a joy to look at." A reminiscent smile tugged at the corners of Hendricks's lips.

Margaret bit back the impulse to say something rude about the perfect Roxanne, and waited for him to continue.

"Chadwick took one look at Roxanne and was caught."

"What about her?" Margaret asked. For some reason, the thought of Philip playing the part of besotted suitor to Roxanne bothered her.

Hendricks shook his head. "Who could tell? For one thing she was young, only seventeen, and it was clear that all the adulation she had received had gone to her head. Chadwick proposed, Roxanne accepted, and they were married immediately. Little Annabelle was born the following year, and a year after that, Roxanne died. Chadwick withdrew from the social scene and was rarely seen in London."

"And Estelle?"

"She took charge of Annabelle, and Chadwick pays her bills. She is also trying to find a more secure source of income in the form of a second husband."

"And she's got you in her eye?" Margaret suddenly understood Hendricks's reactions.

"Yes." Hendricks shuddered. "But don't you worry, my dear. I may be a gentleman, but I am not a fool. I would never propose to her.

"Here we are." He changed the subject as the carriage pulled up in front of a narrow three-story home.

Margaret studied it curiously as the groom helped her out of the carriage. It was significantly smaller than Philip's home, but still larger than any house she'd ever lived in.

"Come in and see what I want to show you."

Margaret took his arm and followed him up the two red-brick steps and through the open door the elderly butler was holding open.

"You really do have something to show me? I thought that was just a ploy to get us away from Estelle."

"Not at all. Margaret, this is Lorton. Without him, I'd sink into disarray."

"Good morning, my lady." Lorton bowed majestically.

"Good morning." Margaret smiled at the old man.

"Would you serve us tea in the study?" Hendricks took Margaret's hand and urged her down the hall.

Apprehensively Margaret went, hoping that Estelle had been wrong and Hendricks wasn't going to give her some of his mother's jewelry. Under the circumstances, it would be little better than theft to accept them. But if she refused, he'd undoubtedly be hurt. And she didn't want to hurt him. He'd already been hurt far too much.

Eagerly Hendricks shoved open the door to his study and gestured above the white marble fireplace. "There. It took me most of last evening to locate that portrait, but I finally found it in the attic."

Assuming that he wanted to show her a portrait of his late wife, Margaret walked toward it, only to come to an abrupt halt when she got a good look. She stared at the portrait in confused shock. How could Hendricks's wife look so much like her, when she wasn't her daughter?

An eerie tremor chased over her skin, raising goose-bumps. It was almost like peering into a slightly foggy looking glass.

Hendricks smiled happily at her obvious amazement. "I thought you'd be surprised. I had the strangest feeling when I first saw you yesterday that I'd seen you before. At first, I thought it was just because you were my daughter, but last night it finally came to me. You are the spit of that portrait."

"There are a few differences." Margaret tried to distance herself from what she didn't understand.

He nodded. "A few. Your eyes are bigger and their color is darker and your chin is stronger, but, even so, the resemblance is remarkable."

"It's uncanny."

"You don't like it?" Hendricks looked disappointed.

"No, it's not that," Margaret lied, not wanting to spoil his pleasure. "It's just that . . . Have you ever read any of the Eastern philosophers who say that when you die you don't go to heaven, you get reborn?"

Hendricks blinked in shock. "No, can't say that I ever have. Where did you read about things like that in a convent?"

"There were a great many books." Margaret skirted the truth. "And no one ever minded if I read."

"And so they shouldn't have. But I can't say as I like that particular bit of knowledge. Why, it's as if your body isn't really yours. Like you're only a joint tenant.

"Although I feel I should warn you, my dear, not to . . . I mean, among the ton . . ." He gestured, at a loss.

"Thoughts in women's heads are unacceptable?" Margaret said.

Hendricks nodded unhappily. "I fear that's the way it

is in society, my dear. And while that may be lamentable, since you're going to be making your home here . . ."

"It would never do to offend convention," Margaret finished, grateful that she was only going to have to guard her tongue for a few weeks at most. Once Philip managed to get his bill passed, she would be free to be herself again.

Hendricks patted her hand comfortingly. "Anytime you want to talk about ideas, you come and see me, my dear. In fact, I'd very much like to explore this idea of past lives." He looked thoughtful. "I studied the Greek philosophers when I was a young man at Oxford, but I don't remember anything anywhere near that interesting."

"Probably because the Greeks spent all their time debating very esoteric questions."

"Really?" Hendricks said weakly. "Maybe the book you read was a bad translation?"

"Oh, I read the philosophers in the original Greek," Margaret assured him, and then realized her mistake when he choked. *Dash it all,* she thought. Talking to Hendricks was dangerous. He seemed so harmless that she forgot to watch her every word. If she were to make Hendricks suspicious . . . She barely repressed a shudder at the thought of the revenge Philip would exact if she were to ruin his carefully-laid plans.

"The nuns taught you Greek?" Hendricks asked incredulously.

"So that I'd be able to read the scriptures in the original Greek," she improvised.

Hendricks swallowed. "Of course, and was it interesting?"

"More frustrating," Margaret said truthfully. "A great many of the more interesting books got left out of the Bible. I liked Thomas's gospel far more than any of the four they included."

Hendricks beamed at her. "So did I my dear, so did I.

But when I tried to talk to the bishop about it, he refused to discuss it."

Margaret laughed. "Being a woman, I had better sense than to mention my preferences to a member of the clergy."

"Umm, my dear, are you . . . I mean, did you . . ."

Margaret stared at him blankly, wondering what he was trying to say. Whatever it was, it was clearly bothering him.

"Are you Papist?" he finally blurted out.

"No, I'm Church of England, although I must admit that the depth of my piety is open to question."

"Which hardly distinguishes you from the rest of the ton," he said. "People go to church to be seen, not to nourish their souls."

"My lord—"

"I would consider it a great honor if you would call me Papa." He looked wistfully at her, and Margaret felt a jab of shame at what she and Philip were doing to him.

"I'd be honored." Margaret gave the only response possible. Given the lie in which she was so firmly enmeshed, there was no way she could refuse.

"Papa." Margaret choked the word out of a throat closed tight with bitter memories. The last time she'd uttered that word had been when she'd stood in the hallway and begged her father not to leave them.

"Who is that lady in the portrait?" Margaret asked.

"Her name was Jane Hendricks. She was the wife of an ancestor of ours. I looked her up in the family Bible, but all it gives is her name and the fact that she died in childbed in 1713 at age twenty-nine."

Margaret swallowed nervously. Jane Hendricks had been the same age as she was now when she died. But that still didn't answer the perplexing question of why the woman bore such an uncanny resemblance to her. There had to be a logical explanation for it but at the moment she couldn't think what it could be.

"I'm going to leave it hanging there until I can arrange for you to be painted. You don't mind sitting for a portrait, do you?"

"No, of course not." Margaret couldn't bring herself to quench the anticipation in his eyes. It didn't matter, she told herself, because by the time sittings could be scheduled, she'd be gone and Hendricks would know the truth about her. She found the knowledge cold comfort.

"Ah, here's Lorton with our tea." Hendricks rubbed his hands together in pleasure as the door opened. "Sit down, dear, and pour."

Margaret obediently sat down on the deep-rose damask sofa. Picking up the pot, she poured a cup of tea and handed it to Hendricks.

Hendricks beamed at her. "You do that exactly as my mother used to do. The nuns did an excellent job of teaching you social skills." He looked faintly uncertain at the idea.

"Most nuns in France are members of wealthy families." Margaret gave him a fact and allowed him to draw his own conclusions.

"I am indebted to them. I'd also like to do something for them to express my gratitude for caring for you all these years. If you could give me their direction?"

Margaret stared down into her teacup as she frantically tried to decide what would be the best thing to say. She saw nothing wrong with Hendricks giving money to a convent in France, even under false pretenses. He clearly had more than he would ever need, and the nuns would put it to good use. The problem was that Philip hadn't told her exactly which convent had supposedly sheltered her all those years.

"I've never been very good with exact directions," she

finally said. "But Philip would know. Perhaps you could ask him?"

To her relief, Hendricks accepted her explanation. "Certainly. Where is he, by the by?"

"He went to talk to someone about his bill," Margaret said.

Hendricks blinked in surprise. "I don't remember young Chadwick being interested in government."

"He's very concerned about the plight of the discharged soldiers who are being left to starve."

"Surely it isn't as bad as that?"

Margaret felt a flash of anger at Hendricks' failure to have noticed the disabled soldiers begging on street corners. How like the aristocracy to sit in their snug homes and ignore anything that wasn't directly related to their own comfort!

"I'm sorry, my dear," he went on, "but I have been living retired in Suffolk for almost twenty years. I'm afraid that I'm sadly out of touch with what has been happening in the world."

Margaret stared down at the steam rising off her tea as an idea slowly formed in her mind.

"Papa, you said you wanted to repay the nuns for their care of me?"

"Certainly. A gentleman always pays his debts."

Margaret almost choked. Some of her earliest memories were of her mother lamenting the fact that Mainwaring hadn't paid the merchants in so long that they would no longer extend credit unless they were paid something on account.

Shoving her memories of her father to the back of her mind, she said, "I remember reading once—Saint Thomas Aquinas, I think it was—that one should take a kindness shown you and pass it along to another person," Margaret said.

"You read Latin, too?"

"I have a decided affinity for languages, and since I was fortunate enough to have the opportunity to indulge it . . ."

"Quite." Hendricks nodded as if reassuring himself.

"Why don't you repay the nuns' kindness to me by helping Philip pass his soldiers' relief bill?"

"Me?" Hendricks looked nonplussed. "But, my dear, I haven't had anything to do with politics for longer than I care to remember. I've been tending my estate."

"You can be just like Cincinnatus. You remember," she added at his blank look. "He was the Roman who left his plow in the field and rode off to lead the army against an invader, and when the threat was over he went back to his plowing."

Hendricks smiled ruefully. "Somehow, I can't see myself as a hero."

"The real heroes in this world are those who do their very best for what they believe in, no matter what the odds against them are," Margaret said with utter conviction, remembering George's efforts on her mother's behalf.

Hendricks sighed. "My dear, you make me ashamed of myself."

"I don't mean to. It's simply that without the soldiers' defeating Bonaparte, I wouldn't have been able to come back to London. And I know how frightening it is to not have anything to eat."

"You'll never know that feeling again!" Hendricks's fierce expression startled her. "I am a very wealthy man. It will all come to you when I'm gone and, in the meantime, I'll see that you never want for anything."

Margaret felt a strange feeling of warmth curl through her at his words. Her own father had barely seemed to notice that she was alive during his infrequent leaves from his regiment, and her mother had been a frail woman who wasn't able even to take care of herself, let alone Margaret. And as for George . . . George meant well, but he always seemed to be tumbling into one scrape after another from which she had to rescue him.

"I hope I don't inherit for a long time yet," she finally said.

"Don't you worry, my dear. I still have a few years to go before I reach my fourscore. And if you want me to try to influence members of the House of Lords . . ." Hendricks took a deep breath. ". . . then I'll do it, but I'll need to think very carefully how to go about it. Most men think their taxes are already too high."

"Thank you." Margaret felt almost limp with relief. She'd made a start on fulfilling Philip's demands. With Hendricks's help, it shouldn't be long before she was free to rejoin George.

Her relief ebbed, and a feeling of uncertainty replaced it as she studied Hendricks's elderly face. What would happen to him once she'd left? How much worse off would he be for her having come into his life?

It isn't your responsibility, she tried to quiet her squirming conscience. She was as much a victim of Philip's machinations as Hendricks was. She'd *had* to agree to the impersonation. George's life could well have depended on it, and much as she was coming to like Hendricks, she loved George—loved him and owed him a debt she could never fully repay.

All she could do was to try to make Hendricks as happy as she could in the time she was impersonating his daughter, she finally decided.

"Tell me about the Hendricks family," she said, seeking a neutral topic.

Hendricks smiled at what he thought was her interest and launched into a humorous account of his many relatives, all of whom seemed to be long dead.

Margaret settled back to listen, allowing his soothing flow of words to ease her tensions.

* * *

Her sense of inner peace lasted through the rest of the visit and sustained her during a dreary afternoon spent hiding in the library to escape the inane chatter Estelle used to fill every second of silence.

Of Philip, there was no sign. A fact Margaret told herself was good, because as long as he wasn't there, he couldn't torment her.

She had just finished dressing for the Templetons' ball when Philip suddenly appeared in the connecting door between their rooms.

Startled, Margaret swung around to face him. All she could think of was the last time he'd been in her bedroom, and the kiss they'd shared. She was still shaken by her mindless reaction to him, but the thing that appalled her most was that in some deep recess of her mind, she wanted him to do it again.

She tensed as he slowly walked toward her, an imposing figure in his stark black evening coat. There was a huge sapphire nestled in the snowy folds of his elaborately tied neckcloth. He looked a very powerful, very wealthy, very pampered member of the aristocracy—exactly what he was.

But he was still only a man. She tried to bolster her dwindling courage as he stopped a few feet in front of her. Only a man, like George. The problem was, she didn't believe it. The difference between this man and George was so great as to be unbridgeable.

Margaret forced herself to meet Philip's dark gaze, almost flinching when she saw the gleam in his eyes. A gleam that deepened as he studied her gown.

Tiny pinpricks of feeling danced over her skin as his eyes slowly wandered over the creamy swell of her breasts exposed by the gown's deep décolleté.

To her dismay, Philip moved closer still, and Margaret

could feel the warmth from his lean frame crowding against her, making her uncomfortably aware of both him and her own body.

Margaret watched, mesmerized, as he raised his hand and lightly ran the tip of his forefinger along the cut of her bodice. Heat seemed to pour from his wandering finger, seeping into her flesh and undermining her determination to remain aloof from him.

A stifled gasp escaped her as his finger dipped under the material and rubbed over her nipple. Instinctively Margaret jerked backward.

"What are you doing?" She blurted out the first words that occurred to her.

His dark brows shot up in mock surprise. "What is it that you don't understand?"

Margaret winced at the bite in his voice. The honors were about even in that exchange.

"What exactly do you want?" she tried again.

"You," he said bluntly. "I have a lot more money than Gilroy."

"But I love George," she muttered desperately.

Philip jerked back as if he'd been struck, and he glared at her in anger, an anger she was at a loss to understand. He clearly believed she was George's mistress, so why shouldn't she be in love with him?

"I find that hard to believe!"

"I'm not asking you to believe it. And you still haven't told me why you have invaded my privacy." She launched an offensive.

"You have no privacy where I'm concerned." His voice hardened. "Until I've finished with you, you will do exactly as you're told."

"Yes, sir." Margaret gritted the words out when what she wanted to do was to smack him. Hard. To grab him by the elaborate folds of his pristine neckcloth and shake him until his teeth rattled. To somehow make him see that simply because she was a bastard didn't mean that she wasn't a person, too. A person who had every bit as much right to privacy as he did.

"Yes, *Philip,*" he corrected her.

"Yes, Philip!"

"That's better. Always remember that a woman should ever be conciliating."

Had his precious Roxanne been a softly-spoken, conciliating type of person? Had she spoiled him for all other women? Not that it mattered to her personally, Margaret assured herself. She didn't intend to stay around Philip one minute longer than she had to.

"You have the most annoying habit of going off into airdreams," he complained.

"Would that that were the only annoying habit I had!"

"I didn't say it was your only bad habit. But enough of this. I came to inspect you before we left."

"I feel like I should be wearing a uniform and carrying a musket," she muttered.

"That dress is a uniform and a woman is far more deadly than any musket ever was."

Margaret watched the bleakness settle in his eyes and wondered what he was remembering.

"The deep blue of that gown sets off your eyes just as I expected it would," he said with an impersonal air that chilled her. "But I think it needs a necklace to complete the image. "Diamonds, I think," he said. "Go downstairs and tell Compton to have the carriage brought round. I'll meet you in the salon."

He turned on his heel and left abruptly.

Margaret let her breath out on a long whoosh. She didn't know why, but every encounter with Philip left her feeling emotionally drained.

Picking up her silver lace stole, she hurried downstairs to find Compton. It would never do to delay and give Philip an excuse to come back into her room.

"Ah, there you are, Margaret," Estelle greeted her as she walked into the salon.

Margaret's eyes widened when she saw Estelle's gown. Row upon row of flounces decorated the skirt of purple satin and the neckline . . . Estelle preened happily under Margaret's wide-eyed stare, obviously believing that Margaret was overcome with admiration.

"How fashionable you look." Margaret groped for a believable tone.

Estelle shrugged her shoulders, and Margaret held her breath, afraid she would spill out of her scant bodice. To her relief, Estelle remained mostly covered. "I had it made just last week by Madam Burset, London's most fashionable modiste. Your own gown was made in France, wasn't it?"

"Mais oui."

Estelle peered suspiciously at her. "What did you say? Speak English. Only heathens speak French."

"What a particularly English attitude," Margaret said.

"What is?" Philip walked into the room. He was carrying a flat black leather case. He glanced toward Estelle, and Margaret watched in reluctant sympathy as a tremor passed over his features.

"Margaret was spouting that monster's language," Estelle said.

"French is also the language of Descartes and Moliére," Margaret pointed out.

Estelle sniffed disparagingly. "As I said, a pack of heathens."

For a brief moment, Margaret's eyes met Philip's, and she was entranced by the humor she saw dancing in them. She quickly looked away, not wanting to share the moment with him. She didn't want to share anything with him. Philip was the enemy, she reminded herself. She couldn't afford to forget it for a moment, because Philip wouldn't.

Estelle's sharply-indrawn breath caught Margaret's attention, and she followed the direction of Estelle's gaze. Margaret blinked at the glittering strands of diamonds that trailed from Philip's fingers as he walked toward her. The stones caught the flickering candlelight and broke it into hundreds of tiny rainbows which were reflected on the cream damask wallpaper.

Margaret couldn't quite suppress the shudder that trembled through her when Philip put the necklace around her neck and its cold weight settled around her neck. Like a shackle, she thought in panic. Something to bind her even closer to him. She could feel his fingers as he fumbled to fasten the clasp. They felt burningly hot against her chilled skin. As if he were leaving an imprint of his ownership on her flesh.

Philip turned her around and studied the necklace critically for a long moment. Frowning slightly, he readjusted the central stone. His fingers brushed against the swell of her breasts, and her soft flesh contracted with almost painful intensity.

Margaret swallowed uneasily. It seemed as if every time he touched her, she became more susceptible to him.

"Oh my, how lovely! I think I remember when Roxanne wore it." Estelle's voice sounded high and tight.

"You are mistaken," Philip said curtly. "That necklace belonged to my mother."

"But your mother died some months before my own dear Roxanne."

"Roxanne never wore any of my mother's jewels." Philip's flat denial did not invite further discussion.

Estelle shrugged, giving Margaret a glance that clearly conveyed the impression that Philip was lying.

But despite Estelle's insinuations, Margaret believed Philip. For one thing, she didn't think he cared enough what either she or Estelle thought to bother to lie to them. Which led to another, far more interesting question. Why hadn't Philip given Roxanne his mother's jewels? Both

Estelle and Hendricks had told her how besotted he was with his first wife, how he could deny her nothing.

"The carriage is waiting, my lord." Compton's measured tones broke into Margaret's thoughts, and she allowed them to slide away.

Estelle quickly appropriated Philip's arm and Margaret trailed along behind them as they left the house. Despite her almost sick dread of the evening, there was a tiny spark of anticipation. With luck she might see her natural father again after all these years. And maybe, if she were to meet him, an idea of how to exact revenge for her poor mother would occur to her. She was determined that for once in his misbegotten life, her father would pay for his sins.

Seven

None of this mattered. Margaret tried to still her growing nervousness as she made her way thorough the crush of people streaming into the Templetons' brilliantly lit mansion. Not the ball itself or the overdressed, overfed people who were eyeing her so covertly. This artificial world wasn't hers. She didn't belong here, and she wouldn't be staying. Just as soon as Philip was through using her, she would be returning to the real world. A world whose rules and mores she understood and felt comfortable with.

Margaret dipped a polite curtsy to the Templetons when she finally reached them, thankful that the crush of people behind her prevented her hostess from asking any of the questions Margaret could see in her avid gaze.

Philip took her arm and led her through the packed hallway toward the ballroom at the back of the house. Margaret's skin tightened as people jostled past her, and a faintly panicky feeling of not being able to breathe engulfed her.

"What's the matter?" Philip looked down at her pale face.

"I don't like crowds," she whispered. "They always make me feel faintly claustrophobic."

Instead of saying something cutting as she'd expected, Philip sped up, hurrying her toward the huge ballroom.

Margaret breathed a sigh of relief once they reached it. The ballroom was still too crowded for comfort, but at least no one was physically touching her.

She glanced around curiously, watching the brilliantly clad women moving gracefully in the steps of a quadrille.

"If anyone should ask you to dance . . . You can dance, can't you?" Philip suddenly thought to ask.

About to say no, Margaret thought better of it. If she did, he'd undoubtedly arrange dancing lessons, and she didn't want any more demands made on her. She needed as much free time as possible to work out her own plans for revenge against her natural father.

"I can dance," Margaret said, "although . . ." Her eyes widened as the movements of the dance suddenly gave her an unobstructed view of a young woman.

"What's the matter?" Philip followed her gaze, but could see nothing amiss.

"That lady's gown is stuck to her!" Margaret whispered in shock. "You can see . . ."

Philip wondered at her prudish reaction. Could her outrage be real or was it assumed for his benefit? But why would she do that? He already knew her for what she was—another man's mistress. But then, who could fathom the workings of a woman's mind? The only certainty was that whatever she was planning would be for her benefit and not his.

"Dampened gowns are the latest fashion," he said.

"Really?" Margaret looked closer.

Philip felt a tremor of foreboding at her speculative expression. "Don't you dare even consider it!" his voice hardened at the thought of her parading her body for every lecher in London to gawk at.

"Come on. There's Lord Hawlings. I want to talk to him." Philip's fingers closed around her wrist like a shackle, and he pulled her toward the portly man standing beside the pillar on the other side of the room.

"Lord Hawlings," Philip greeted the man. "Allow me to make known to you my wife, Lady Chadwick."

Hawlings gave her a warm smile which deepened appreciatively as she dipped a graceful curtsy and he noticed her cleavage.

Philip frowned, finding Hawlings's open admiration of Margaret's charms offensive. A fact which confused him because he'd never minded when men had stared in admiration at Roxanne. Far from it. He'd been pleased that she had elicited such universal admiration. But he was older now. Older and wiser. Now he knew how that kind of admiration could turn a woman's head.

"Welcome to London, my lady." Hawlings beamed at her.

"Thank you." Margaret smiled back, feeling some of her tension fade.

The orchestra began another tune before Philip could bring up the subject of his relief bill, and Hawlings turned to Margaret.

"Will you do me the honor, Lady Chadwick?"

Margaret nodded politely and, taking his hand, followed him onto the dance floor, leaving Philip standing on the side of the floor.

"How are you finding London, my lady?" Hawlings asked.

"I'm very impressed with the city."

Hawlings nodded happily. "Yes, indeed, hub of the universe and all that. Nothing in the world to compare with it."

Margaret gave him a limpid smile, finding irresistible the impulse to poke fun at his insularity. "I take it you are an admirer of Ptolemy's theories?"

Hawlings blinked in obvious confusion. "Don't think I am. That is to say, I can't remember having talked to him."

"You would have remembered if you had," Margaret said. "He's been dead for over two thousand years."

"Ah, that would account for it." Hawlings nodded sagely. "Pretty gals like you shouldn't be thinking about dead people."

"You're quite right." Margaret seized the opening he gave her. "I ought to be more like you and my husband and worry about the living. Such as those poor returning soldiers and their families who are starving!" Margaret was careful not to let her gaze stray to his prominent stomach.

"Umm, yes," Hawlings mumbled, clearly uncomfortable with the unexpected turn the conversation had taken.

Margaret peered up at him from beneath her thick, golden lashes and tried for an adoring expression. She felt ridiculous, but his smile widened, so she persisted.

"Can you actually believe, Lord Hawlings, that there are members of the House of Lords who oppose my husband's bill to help the returning soldiers?"

Hawlings glanced around as if looking for help. When none materialized, he muttered, "Taxes are already too high."

Margaret nodded. "Yes, but you and my husband know how shortsighted that argument is. Why, think of what happened to the French."

Hawlings looked confused. Obviously thinking wasn't his strong point. "We beat Boney."

"I meant the Revolution." Margaret lowered her voice in simulated horror. "It was frightful what the lower classes did to the aristocracy and all, because they felt that they had nothing more to lose."

Hawlings swallowed uneasily. "I do remember hearing something about it."

"It's too bad that more peers aren't as wise as you are." Margaret tried blatant flattery.

Hawlings brightened slightly at her praise, and Margaret dropped the subject, deciding that she'd said enough for the moment. Hopefully her words would linger in his mind.

When the dance ended, Margaret looked around uncertainly, not sure if she was supposed to leave Lord Hawlings and go sit on the sidelines, or if he was supposed to escort her there. To her relief, she saw Philip making his way toward them.

"Thank you so much for the dance, Lord Hawlings," Margaret said when Philip reached them.

"Pleasure, I'm sure." He gave Philip an uncertain glance and hurried away.

"What did you say to him?" Philip asked.

"I tipped the butterboat over his head," Margaret said.

"But then why—"

"Good evening, my dear, Chadwick." Hendricks seemed to materialize out of the crowd. "How are you finding your first ball, Margaret?"

"Crowded." Margaret inched backward as a woman elbowed past them.

"Yes, it is a sad squeeze. Mrs. Templeton will be so pleased." Estelle's voice came from immediately behind them.

Margaret watched Hendricks's eyes glaze over as Estelle pushed her way between him and Philip.

Estelle had the instincts of a hunting hound for finding its quarry, Margaret thought.

When neither of the men said anything, Margaret decided it was up to her to maintain the social pretense of good manners. "Why would a hostess want to have too many people for her rooms to hold comfortably?"

Estelle looked at Margaret as if she suspected her of being deliberately obtuse. "Why, a sad squeeze is the goal of every hostess."

"With the idea of paying back all your social obligations at one time?" Margaret guessed.

"If you are trying to apply logic to social events, it's hopeless," Philip said.

"Now, now." Estelle playfully tapped Philip on the forearm with her elaborate ivory fan. "Remember the wonderful parties that Roxanne used to give? I doubt they'll ever be equalled."

"Certainly not by me," Margaret promptly agreed. "I prefer my guests in more manageable portions."

"Ah, the ideas these youngsters have!" Estelle gave Hendricks a coquettish look that sat oddly on her chubby face. "Shall we leave them and enjoy a dance?"

"Papa is promised to me." Margaret instinctively responded to the look of mute appeal in Hendricks's eyes. "We're going to sit, and he's going to tell me who everyone is."

Estelle clapped her hands together in the childish gesture which was starting to grate on Margaret's nerves. "What a capital notion. I shall accompany you."

Margaret mentally scrambled for an excuse. Having Estelle with them would make it hard to get a word in edgewise and impossible to direct the conversation around to finding out what Hendricks knew about her natural father.

To Margaret's surprise, Philip came to her rescue. "Why don't we leave Margaret and her father alone to get better acquainted?" Philip's voice phrased it like a question, but his tone of voice left no doubt that it was really an order. An order he softened slightly by offering his arm to Estelle and saying, "If you will join me in the set forming?"

Estelle, partially mollified by Philip's offer to dance, gave him a tight smile and muttered, "Of course."

Hendricks took Margaret's arm and hurried her away.

"I think we've made a successful retreat," Margaret said when they reached two empty chairs against the wall.

"That woman is a ninnyhammer! Philip should send her back to Kent where she belongs."

And Margaret back to France where she belonged, but strangely enough, the idea didn't seem as attractive as it should have. It was just that she didn't want to leave England until she had somehow managed to avenge her mother's death, Margaret assured herself.

"Papa, I really would appreciate it if you would tell me who all these people are." Margaret said, deciding to slip inquiries about her natural father among questions about others so as not to make Hendricks suspicious. "For example, who is that man?" Margaret gestured at a thin man wearing a none-too-clean neckcloth and a supercilious expression, who was leaning against a white marble column, watching the dancers.

Hendricks's features momentarily hardened—for an eerie moment reminding Margaret of Philip. "Not someone you should know!"

Margaret looked closer at the man. "Why not?"

"Because, my dear, to give you the word with no bark on it, he is a rake."

Margaret blinked in surprise. "Really? He must have a great deal of money because his person wouldn't serve to fascinate anyone."

Hendricks choked.

"From a woman's perspective, that is."

Hendricks gave her a grin that made him look twenty years younger. "I begin to think that I have never properly appreciated nuns before. They did an interesting job of raising you."

"Thank you." Margaret decided to take his comment as a compliment even though she had her doubts. "But you will tell me who everyone is?"

"Certainly, I simply won't introduce you to all of them." Hendricks began to identify their fellow partygoers, adding whispered warnings about the majority of men and a great many of the women he identified.

Margaret was incensed with the injustice of it. Poor George's transgressions were mere peccadilloes beside some of the things Hendricks told her about these people and yet they were accepted into polite society, and George was an outcast.

Hard as it was, Margaret didn't say anything scathing, concentrating instead on gleaning as much information as she could in as short a time as possible.

It was almost time for the supper dance when Margaret looked up and saw her natural father standing not ten feet from her. An icy feeling of shock drenched her, chilling her skin and squeezing the blood from her face, leaving her pale.

He had changed since that never-to-be-forgotten afternoon when he'd stalked out of her life, but despite the fact that his wavy brown hair had thinned to a gray wispiness and his athletic body had thickened, Margaret had no trouble recognizing him.

Her eyes suddenly caught his, and for a moment she was catapulted back in time, to the frightened, angry child she'd been. She wanted to confront him and demand to know if he had any idea what had happened to the poor woman who for ten long years had believed that she was his wife.

Margaret bit the inside of her cheek hard enough to draw blood as she fought for control. Yelling hadn't worked then and it wouldn't accomplish anything now. This time she'd use guile and patience. And the first step would be to maintain the fiction of being a stranger while she probed his defenses for weaknesses. For a way to inflict even a fraction of the pain on him that his callousness had inflicted on her mother.

"Lord Hendricks!" Mainwaring's jovial tones jabbed at Margaret's shaky composure. "All of London is talking about your good fortune in having your daughter restored to you."

"Mainwaring." Hendricks nodded civilly, but Margaret could hear no particular warmth in his voice. "Lady Chadwick, allow me to make known to you Baron Mainwaring.

"No need to be so formal," the Baron said. "After all, we're related."

Margaret froze, as for one heart-stopping moment she thought Mainwaring had recognized her.

"Your father and my father had the same grandmother," Mainwaring said.

Margaret's heart began to beat again in heavy, thudding strokes as she realized that it wasn't she he was claiming kinship with; it was Hendricks. Although . . . She caught her lower lip between her teeth and tried to force her muddled mind to think. If Mainwaring was related to Hendricks, then she was, too. By blood if not by law. Very slightly, from the sound of it, but there was still some connection. Enough to explain that eerie portrait?

"I see you find it hard to believe, Lady Chadwick." Mainwaring drew his own interpretation of her silence. His voice had a slightly peevish note that loosened a flood of memories from Margaret's childhood. How many times had she heard that aggrieved note in his voice? And always her mother had rushed to placate him.

"Not at all." Margaret hurried to disarm his suspicions. "I was simply trying to work out the relationship."

"Slight," Hendricks said, and Mainwaring flushed an unbecoming shade of red.

"My wife said that I must be sure to make myself known to you when she saw you were here. Why, she doesn't even hold your marrying Chadwick against you."

"Why should she mind?" Margaret asked, when she

realized that Mainwaring was waiting for her to say something. "She's already married to you."

Mainwaring patted his pudgy belly in smug self-satisfaction. "To be sure, and very content she is, too. But she had hopes of Chadwick making a match of it with our daughter, who is making her bows this season, don't you know. Not but what Drusilla won't form a brilliant connection. Why, the young men swarm round her like honeybees."

Margaret felt a corrosive surge of anger at the pride in his voice, and then it seeped away, leaving an aching sense of loss—a feeling she ruthlessly quashed. She'd long since given up caring that he'd rejected her, she reminded herself.

"Ah, here they are now." Mainwaring turned as a middle-aged woman and a teenage girl joined them.

"This is my wife, Lady Mainwaring, and my daughter, Drusilla."

Margaret hoped the smile she managed didn't look as artificial as it felt. She studied Lady Mainwaring, trying to find some resemblance to her mother, and failed. This woman appeared composed of nondescript shades of neutrals—totally unlike her own vividly beautiful mother had been.

Margaret forced herself to look at the daughter who had supplanted her. She saw a young, moderately pretty girl wearing an exquisitely-cut gown of white glacé silk decorated with pale pink silk rosebuds sewn along the hemline. Her light brown hair was arranged in a profusion of curls held back by a circlet of the palest pink rosebuds. A shy smile lit the girl's light-blue eyes, and she blushed a becoming shade of pink when Margaret acknowledged her.

"Lord Hendricks, you and your daughter must join us for supper," Mainwaring said.

"Thank you, but no," Hendricks said. "We're joining Chadwick's party."

Despite the necessity of fostering Mainwaring's acquaintance if her plans for revenge were to have any hope of success, Margaret felt nothing but relief at Hendricks's refusal. She needed time to conquer the violent emotions her natural father had raised in her. Time to rebury all the pain that seeing him had brought to the surface. In her present unsettled state of mind, she might accidently say something that would give everything away.

"He is, of course, welcome to join us." Lady Mainwaring's thin nose twitched, reminding Margaret of a cat contemplating a particularly plump mouse.

"We are his guests," Hendricks said. "And I could hardly take it upon myself to upset his arrangements."

"I see." Lady Mainwaring looked annoyed, but to Margaret's relief, she didn't further push the invitation.

"Until later, then." Mainwaring nodded to Hendricks, smiled expansively at Margaret and, taking his wife's arm, left.

With a softly muttered "Good-bye," Drusilla scurried after them.

Margaret watched them disappear into the crowd and then turned to Hendricks.

"Why don't you like him?" Margaret acted on her instincts.

"Mainwaring is a self-indulgent fool."

"Which hardly makes him unique among the ton."

Hendricks sighed. "No, it doesn't. And in all fairness he's no worse than a great many others. But unlike most of the ton, I have the misfortune to be related to Mainwaring and the even greater misfortune to have had to serve as the trustee of the estate that he inherited.

"Charles, the cousin from whom Mainwaring inherited the title, and I, were lifelong friends. Such good friends that Charles named me as executor of his will. Of course, when I agreed to do it, we both thought that it would be one of his sons who would inherit."

Hendricks looked sad.

" 'Man proposes, but God disposes,' " Margaret quoted in sympathy.

Hendricks sighed. "Quite true. At any rate, when Charles and his sons were drowned, I found to my dismay that I was saddled with the thankless task of turning William Mainwaring into a credible replacement for Charles. Given Mainwaring's history of irresponsible gambling and his propensity for low company, I very much feared that he'd game away all that Charles had worked so hard to accumulate."

"He seems unexceptional," Margaret lied when Hendricks fell silent.

"Yes, but he wasn't always unexceptional. He capped a singularly dissolute career at Oxford by eloping with an heiress."

"Eloping!" Margaret gasped.

"Oh, nothing came of it. The girl's guardian caught up with them before nightfall. Charles bought Mainwaring a commission in the army and washed his hands of him. Mainwaring made everyone happy by disappearing so thoroughly that it took my agents almost a year to track him down after Charles's death.

"I was determined not to make the mistake Charles had made, of trying to reason with Mainwaring. I told him that the title was his no matter what I did, but that if he wished to ever see a shilling of Charles's money, he was going to have to marry Miss Wilcox and take his rightful place in society."

"Marry?" Margaret whispered as a sense of sickness twisted through her. This quiet, gentle old man had been the instigator behind her father casting her mother aside?

Hendricks, deep in his memories, didn't notice Margaret's reaction. "Miss Wilcox was a stable, sensible woman from an excellent old Devonshire family, with a respectable dowry. I hoped that marriage to her would be the making of him, and I was right. She did have a very settling affect on Mainwaring and, of course, he dotes on his children."

"He has more than just Drusilla?" Margaret was having a great deal of trouble containing her rioting emotions.

"Mmm." Hendricks nodded. "A young son who is very delicate. One rarely sees him in company.

"Ah, here's Chadwick come to join us."

Margaret tensed as she looked up to see Philip approaching. He nodded to Hendricks and then held out his hand to her. "This is the last dance before supper. Will you honor me?"

For a brief moment Margaret wondered what he'd do if she simply said no: No, she didn't want to dance with him. That she already felt confused and uncertain and just plain angry after having first seen her natural father and then discovering Hendricks's role in her father's rejection of her mother. That at this moment she most emphatically didn't want to have to cope with the strange reactions being close to Philip always engendered. But tempting as the thought was, she knew it would be foolhardy in the extreme. Even though Philip wouldn't retaliate while Hendricks was smiling so benignly on them, Hendricks wouldn't always be there. Later this evening she'd have to go home with Philip. Go home to a bedroom with a connecting door. There would be no one to protect her then from anything Philip might choose to do.

"Go ahead, my dear." Hendricks assumed that her hesitation was caused by her reluctance to leave him alone. "Enjoy yourself, and I'll see you at supper."

Margaret gave Hendricks a weak smile and, bracing herself, took Philip's hand. She felt his warm fingers close over hers, the roughened texture of his skin scraping slightly.

Margaret tensed as the orchestra began to play a waltz.

Philip put his arms around her, frowning at her body's rigidity. "What's wrong? You said you could dance."

"But I didn't say I could dance well." She scrambled for an excuse to avoid being in his arms. She didn't really expect him to listen to her, since he hadn't done so so far in their acquaintance, and she was right. He didn't.

"Practice makes perfect."

No, Margaret thought. In this case, practice makes for shattered nerves. If only she could understand why being close to Philip affected her so. Why the feel of his arm around her waist seemed to burn through the thin silk of her gown.

She took a deep, steadying breath, forcing the scent of the sandalwood soap he used deep into her lungs where it seemed to heat the air trapped there.

Philip executed a turn and peered down into her abstracted features. "Don't try to concentrate on the dance steps so much. Let yourself move with the music."

To her embarrassment Margaret tripped over his foot and pitched forward. His arms closed around her slight frame, crushing her against his chest. Margaret shivered as her breasts brushed against the rough texture of his coat. She could feel her sensitive flesh tightening, her nipples hardening with a longing for something that she couldn't put a name to, and feared to even try.

Philip stared down into her deep blue eyes, watching the emotions swirling through them and wondered what she was thinking. Did she have any idea just how much he wanted to carry her off? How much he wanted to yank down that bit of silk that almost concealed her breasts, and explore every inch of them?

Philip swallowed as his body began to react to his thoughts. He focused grimly on the top of her head, trying to quench his desire before it became clear to everyone else in the room. He watched the way her soft curls seemed to catch the reflected gleam of the candlelight, trapping it deep in its golden depths. He took a deep breath of the tantalizing scent of roses that clung to her. She smelled so good. So mysterious. Not blatant like most of the women he knew. As if she kept most of herself hidden.

He turned them to the left to avoid a particularly inept pair of dancers, and Margaret stumbled again in her attempt to follow him. He almost groaned at the feel of her soft breasts pushing against his chest. He couldn't stand much more of this! He had to have her. He had to sate himself in her soft body so that he could dilute whatever fascination she exerted on him.

To hell with his timetable! Once this interminable affair was over, he'd impress the feel of his body on her flesh so thoroughly that she wouldn't be able to remember the other men she'd had in her bed. The thought gave him a savage sense of satisfaction.

Eight

"Botheration!" Margaret muttered as she struggled to reach the last few pins holding her gown together.

"Where's Daisy?"

Startled, she whirled around to find Philip standing just inside the door that led to their mutual sitting room.

Margaret hastily clutched her bodice to her breasts and eyed him nervously, wondering what he wanted at this hour of the night. If he had any orders for her, surely he would have given them to her on their silent ride back from the Templetons' ball.

"Well?" Philip walked farther into the room, and it was all Margaret could do to keep from retreating.

"I . . ." Margaret winced at the breathless sound of her voice. Firmly, she went on. "I told her not to wait up for me."

Margaret ran her tongue over her bottom lip as she struggled to get a firm grip on her skittering emotions. *Don't let him see that you're nervous,* she told herself. *Act as if finding a man dressed in a brocade dressing gown . . .*

Her eyes strayed downward, and she swallowed uneasily as she noticed the expanse of bare leg between the hem of his dressing gown and his slippers and realized that he was probably naked beneath it. The knowledge sent a burst of confused emotion swirling through her, mocking her efforts at self-control.

She had to get rid of him, and she had to do it now before her already shaky self-control fell apart.

"What do you want?" Margaret demanded, her voice sounding hard from the effort she was making to hold it steady.

She watched Philip's lips thin in displeasure, and she felt like bursting into tears of frustration. The last thing she needed was to make him mad with an ill-chosen word.

She felt like a minor actress who had suddenly been thrust into the lead role without a script and told to improvise. Her lips twitched nervously at the idea.

"You find me amusing, madam?"

Margaret barely repressed a shudder at Philip's silky tone. "I find nothing amusing at this hour of the morning." She tried to placate him. "All I want is my bed."

"Then allow me to help you achieve your desire." He closed the last few steps between them.

What was he playing at? she wondered frantically, and then shivered at the hard, determined lines of his face. He wasn't playing—she answered her own question. He was serious. But serious about what? Bedding her?

He couldn't! She hastily beat back both the fear and the totally unexpected surge of excitement that engulfed her.

"I don't need any help," she said.

"No?" Philip's dark eyebrows lifted. "How do you intend to unfasten your gown?"

"I can do it," Margaret lied, preferring to sleep in the dress to running the risk of letting Philip undress her.

"Turn around." He barked the order at her.

Not knowing what else to do, she slowly turned, feeling as if she were committing an irrevocable act which would haunt her for the rest of her days.

Her breath caught in her throat as she felt his hard fingers brushing against her back. Their warmth seeped into her bare flesh, making her feel strangely disoriented.

Hurry up, Margaret mentally urged him as he slowly—far too slowly—removed the pins she'd been unable to reach.

"You're too thin," Philip said.

Margaret jumped in shock when he ran a finger down along her spinal column.

"Don't do that!" She spun around to face him.

"Why not? I'm your husband."

Margaret raised her chin, about to tell him that she knew full well that the disreputable Mr. Preston was no more a man of the Church than was George. But the memory of George stilled the hasty words on her tongue. Philip could return George to that damp prison if she made him angry enough.

"We have an agreement." She tried to sound calm and rational.

"We have a marriage, although I am aware that even wives expect to be paid for the use of their bodies. Tell me, madam, what price do you put on your charms?"

"You are insulting!"

"The truth is always insulting to the likes of you." Frustration lent a razor's edge to his words.

"You don't have the vaguest idea what I'm really like." Margaret edged backward, trying to put some distance between them. Distance she hoped would allow her agitated nerves to cool.

"But I'm trying to improve my knowledge of you."

The totally unexpected thread of humor in his voice caught her by surprise. He sounded almost . . .

Stop it, she jerked her imagination up short. The situation was complicated enough without her imbuing him with the qualities she wanted him to have.

"Go away!" Margaret tried to put every ounce of resolution she had in her voice.

She couldn't really expect him to calmly turn around and leave, could she? No. She had far too much experience not to know exactly how enticing a man would find her present state of dishabillé. She was probably just trying to make him pay more for the privilege of bedding her. His eyes narrowed as he remembered Roxanne pouting and telling him that if he really loved her he'd give her a diamond necklace like the one Lady Jersey had worn to their ball.

And he'd promptly agreed to her demands in his eagerness to make love to her. The memory sent a spurt of self-disgust swirling through him. He might have been a gullible fool with Roxanne, but he was older now, and infinitely wiser in the way of women. Margaret would take what he was willing to give her and give him what he wanted when he wanted it.

Margaret watched his eyes narrow with a feeling of impending disaster. He wasn't going to listen to her. Fear twisted through her making her shake.

"No!" she gasped. "I don't want to."

He ignored her. Grabbing the bodice of her gown, he pulled it down, ripping it out of her tense grip. Philip never even heard the sound of the fragile fabric tearing. His entire focus was on Margaret. On the way her exposed breasts gleamed like old ivory in the candlelight.

Philip swallowed hard as he stared at their dusky pink tips. She was so beautiful, so exquisitely beautiful, and she was all his. His to do with as he pleased.

He took a deep breath, feeling his body harden to almost painful rigidity. He wanted her so much—had wanted her from the very first moment he'd seen her, and now he was finally going to have her.

Reaching out, Philip cupped her breast, watching in fascination as the tip convulsed. He rubbed his thumb along the slope of her breast, feeling the frantic beat of her heart. For all her show of reluctance, she was as excited as he was. She was certainly experienced enough to know the pleasures to be found in sex. The thought brought him no satisfaction, and he swallowed on a bitter taste of anger at the thought of all the men who'd given her that knowledge.

He yanked her to him, feeling a quick surge of pleasure as her body collided with his. He closed his eyes, the better to concentrate on the feel of her.

Margaret gasped when she realized that the tie around his robe had slipped, allowing the front of his gown to gape open. Her bare breasts scraped over his chest, sending a series of shivers coursing through her. She couldn't let him do this. She tried frantically to concentrate. She had to find a way to stop him, but how?

Her thoughts became hopelessly jumbled as his arm encircled her slender waist and bound her even tighter to him. Margaret gasped as she felt something hard and very hot pushing against her thigh.

Panicked, she tried to strain her lower body away from him, but he merely tightened his hold on her until it seemed she was a part of him.

Margaret gulped in air, and the faint scent of sandalwood that always seemed to cling to him poured into her lungs in a thick, suffocating tide.

His intriguing scent flowed over her fears, reshaping them into a single bright flame of longing that was as inexplicable as it was unexpected.

Her eyelids were becoming increasingly heavy, and it was an effort to keep them open. Even more disturbing, it was becoming harder and harder for her to remember why she had to do so. Margaret jerked in surprise as his hands slid down her back to cup her bare buttocks. His fingers seemed to burn her skin as he lifted her more fully against his manhood.

She shuddered as hitherto-unknown sensations rocked her. How could this feel so good? Every one of her mother's friends had been unanimous in their disgust with what went on in the marriage bed. But then, this wasn't the marriage bed. The thought served as a break on her growing excitement. This was what a man would do with a mistress.

Was she reacting so wantonly because she was a bastard? The appalling thought exploded into her mind like breaking shards of glass.

Desperately she tried to conquer her growing sense of disorientation as he swung her up in his arms so she could think. She wasn't given time. Philip kicked her dress out of the way and tossed her onto the bed.

Margaret's breath whooshed out of her lungs as she landed on the thick mattress, but before she could scoot off the other side, Philip followed her down. His heavy body pinned her much-smaller one to the bed. Frantically she wiggled, in a vain attempt to escape. All her struggles seemed to do was to increase her awareness of him.

"Stop it!" Philip's warm, brandy-scented breath wafted across her cheek.

Margaret tried to ignore both him and the odd sense of urgency growing in her. It became impossible when his mouth suddenly captured hers.

She could taste the brandy he must have drunk before he'd come into her room. But it tasted different from any brandy she'd ever had, she thought in confusion. Not really like brandy at all. It tasted of heat and pleasure and Philip and . . .

A strangled moan bubbled up out of her throat as he shoved his tongue into her mouth. Its movement sent shivers coursing over her skin and raised goosebumps in their wake. She felt so hot. Hot and disoriented, as if . . .

He gasped as he began to nibble on her lips, first lightly biting them and then running the tip of his tongue over them.

A trembling started deep within her as Philip rubbed

his palm over her bare breast, and the strange sense of urgency deepened, becoming a force that would not be denied. Instinctively she arched her body, pushing against his hand in a mindless attempt to intensify the delicious sensation.

"Do you like that?" Philip's voice sounded almost smug, but she didn't care. She didn't care about anything at the moment but that he not stop. She began to shake uncontrollably as his lips followed where his hands had been, and he captured her taut nipple in the warm cavern of his mouth.

"Philip!" Her shocked gasp echoed wildly around the room.

Instinctively she grabbed his head to push him away from her, but the feel of his mouth suckling on her breast defeated her. A throbbing began to pulsate deep in her abdomen, making her feel frantic. Her fingers tightened around the hardness of his skull, and she clutched him closer still, reveling in the sensations she'd never even suspected existed.

Dimly she was aware when he slipped his knee between her thighs to nudge them apart, but only dimly.

The first feeling of disquiet to nibble at the edges of her intense pleasure came when she felt the strangeness of his hot, seeking manhood brushing against her inner thigh. Her disquiet abruptly became panic as Philip suddenly surged forward, forcing himself into her.

"No!" Margaret gasped, trying to twist away. "Please don't!" She shoved against his chest, but it was like pushing on a wall. He didn't even seem to notice. His eyes were curiously blank as if he were looking inward at some unseen vision.

Margaret bit her lip to keep from crying, but a muffled sob escaped from between her tightly clenched teeth as he drove deeper and deeper into her. Finally, with what she thought was a shout of pleasure, he collapsed on her rigid body.

She didn't understand how he could find pleasure in what he'd just done when it had been only painful for her. It didn't make any sense. But what finally did make sense was all the veiled hints her mother's friends had made about the horrors of the marriage bed. But they were wrong about one thing. There couldn't be enough benefits in marriage to make enduring this pain night after night for the rest of one's life worth it. Thank God she wouldn't have to. The thought helped steady her. As soon as Philip had passed his bill she would be free to go back to Paris and George and normalcy.

To Margaret's relief, Philip rolled off her, and she instinctively curled herself in a protective ball.

Philip shook his head, trying to clear his pleasure-drugged senses so he could think. Levering himself up on his forearm, he stared down at her huddled body, for once in his life completely at a loss. What the hell was going on? His gaze dropped to the stain on the white sheet beneath her hips. How could she be virgin? It didn't make any sense. She'd been living with that old roué. If she hadn't been his mistress, then what had been the relationship between them?

He climbed out of bed and stood looking down at her huddled figure as guilt and frustration drowned the last lingering remnants of satisfaction he'd felt in her body. An angry flush burned across his lean cheeks. If he had known, he could have been gentler.

"Why didn't you tell me?" He voiced his frustration.

Margaret trembled violently at the anger she could hear pulsating in his voice. She had no idea what he was talking about. What could she have told him that would have stopped him? An appeal to his basic good nature? The very idea struck her as so outrageously funny, she began to giggle. Desperately she pushed the back of her hand against her mouth, trying to hold back the ragged sound. She had the frightening feeling that if she began to laugh she wouldn't be able to stop.

"Damn it, woman!" Philip touched her shoulder, and she flinched away from him. He dropped his hand as if her silken flesh had scorched him, and stalked naked back to his bedroom. He vented some of his frustration by slamming his door and then dropped into one of the chairs in front of the fireplace. He stared down into the glowing coals of the dying fire and tried to make sense of what had just happened.

He'd made love to his wife and found that she was a virgin. It seemed impossible, but the evidence was unmistakable. Margaret hadn't been Gilroy's mistress. Or any other man's.

Despite his confusion, he was aware of a deep sense of satisfaction even though he knew it didn't really make any difference. Just because Margaret hadn't as yet had an affair didn't mean she wouldn't take a lover when the first opportunity presented itself.

The memory of Roxanne's amatory exploits burned like fire through his mind. Within a month of their marriage she had embarked on her first affair. Margaret would be the same.

He grabbed the half-full decanter of brandy from the table beside his bed and poured himself a glass, downing the fiery liquid in one long gulp. *What can't be cured must be endured.* He reminded himself of one of his nanny's favorite sayings. It brought him no more comfort now than it had then.

"You look a fair treat in that dress, milady," Daisy said. "Blue certainly does suit you."

"Thank you." Margaret dredged up a smile for the

young maid. It was a distinct effort. She felt confused and uncertain and very sore.

"Will there be anything else, milady?"

"No, thank you. You may go."

Margaret watched the hall door close behind Daisy, and her eyes swung to the door through which Philip had disappeared last night. Not that his absence brought her any peace. She'd spent what was left of the night tossing and turning and replaying their disastrous encounter in her mind until she'd finally drifted into an exhausted sleep shortly after dawn. Only to awake a few hours later with a pounding headache as well as an overpowering dread of having to face Philip again.

Her face flamed as she remembered how, initially, she'd responded to his kisses. He probably thought her response was ample proof that she was immoral.

But what did it matter what Philip Moresby thought? She tried to rally her courage. He certainly didn't care what she thought. She very much doubted if he even saw her as a real person with feelings of her own. There was no need for her to worry about meeting him this morning, she tried to reassured herself. He probably hadn't given her or what had happened another thought after he'd left her room.

A fugitive spark of warmth curled through her at the memory of his bare chest and the long length of his legs as he'd stormed out.

Stop that! Margaret ordered herself, truly horrified at the wayward direction of her thoughts. Decent women didn't even know what a naked man looked like, let alone dwelt on the memory. But then, she was a bastard. As far as most of society was concerned she wasn't decent at all.

She shivered as she remembered a treatise by a Spanish bishop she'd once read that had justified society's brutal treatment of bastard children by claiming that they were incapable of behaving morally.

At the time she'd dismissed the idea as self-righteousness on the Church's part, but now she wasn't so sure. The sure knowledge that allowing Philip to make love to her was wrong had been buried beneath the blaze of unexpected feeling he'd so effortlessly aroused in her.

This wasn't the time to worry about it, Margaret told herself as she left the room. Now she had to go downstairs and try to pretend that last night had never happened. Maybe if the gods were smiling on her, Philip already would have left the house and she would be able to postpone their meeting until this evening.

As she hurried down the front steps, she heard a strange sound by the ornate table in the front entranceway. Curious, Margaret looked beneath it and found Annabelle huddled there. The child's face was smudged with dirt and one of the numerous ruffles decorating the front of her pale pink silk dress had been ripped loose.

"Good morning," Margaret said.

"Go away!" Annabelle hissed at her. "Go away or I'll . . . I'll murder you!"

"Really?" Margaret repressed an urge to smile, knowing that Annabelle wouldn't appreciate being laughed at. "How?"

"How?" Annabelle repeated uncertainly.

"Yes, how do you intend to murder me? You could shoot me, but I understand that guns are hard to aim. You might only wound me, and then where would you be?"

Annabelle stared at Margaret, clearly caught off balance by the unexpected turn the conversation had taken.

"You could stab me, but it would make a frightful mess. I'd probably bleed all over your father's carpets, and he wouldn't like that."

"No," Annabelle muttered.

"So I suppose we'll have to rule out stabbing. And I

doubt you're strong enough to strangle me." Margaret appeared to give the matter some consideration. "About all that leaves is poison which does have history on its side. It was a favorite with Lucrezia Borgia. Rumor has it that she disposed of hundreds of enemies with poison."

"Really?" Annabelle looked intrigued. "Do you know her?"

"Only by repute. She's been dead for hundreds of years."

"Oh." Annabelle momentarily looked crestfallen, but she quickly rallied. "Where do I get a poison?"

"I'm not sure. I suppose an apothecary shop, but they might become suspicious if you asked for one strong enough to kill a person."

Annabelle's blue eyes narrowed speculatively. "I could send the nursery maid."

Margaret emphatically shook her head. "Absolutely never involve a third party in murder. You will spend a lifetime being blackmailed."

"I'd not mind being blackmailed, if I could kill you," Annabelle insisted.

"That is enough!" Philip's outraged voice caught both Margaret and Annabelle by surprise. "You will apologize this instant."

"I won't!" Annabelle screamed at him. "I hate her." Scooting around her father, she pounded up the front stairs. At the top she turned and screamed, "I hate you, too," before she fled down the hallway.

Margaret, who had caught the glint of tears on Annabelle's thin cheeks, felt nothing but pity for her.

"I'm going to send her back to the country, and she can damn well stay there until she learns to be seen and not heard."

"What a thoroughly depressing philosophy of child-rearing," Margaret said.

Philip stared at her in surprise. "How can you defend her after what she said?"

"I have far better sense than to take anything a child of that age says seriously." Margaret followed Philip into the breakfast room and sank down on the chair the footman hurried to pull out for her.

"That will be all." Philip dismissed him once he had served Margaret with a plate of food she didn't want.

It was all Margaret could do not to ask the footman to stay. As long as he was in the room Philip couldn't say anything personal, such as refer to what had happened last night. She stared down at the coddled egg sitting like a disembodied eye in the middle of her plate.

To her infinite relief, when Philip spoke, it was not about her response to his lovemaking.

"I will be spending the morning at the House of Lords. When Hendricks comes by this morning . . ."

"I don't want to see him," Margaret instinctively protested, remembering Hendricks's startling revelation that he had been the prime mover behind her natural father's decision to abandon she and her mother.

"I didn't ask what you wanted, madam wife. You were recruited to play a part and if you think last night changed how I view you—"

"I don't. I just . . ." Margaret stumbled to a halt, knowing she could hardly tell Philip the truth. And she was far too agitated to come up with a believable lie on the spur of the moment.

"Then you will do as you are told."

"Yes, Philip."

"Good." He got to his feet. "Since we're agreed, I'll go." He stared at her down-bent head.

When she didn't say anything more, he stalked out.

She had fifteen minutes of peace to drink her coffee before Compton appeared in the doorway.

"Lord Hendricks has arrived, my lady. He is in the morning room."

Margaret bit back her instinctive protestation. She could see no way out of allowing him to take her sight-seeing as she'd agreed to do last night, without making Philip angry—something to be avoided if at all possible.

"Thank you, Compton." Margaret slowly got to her feet, dreading the coming hours.

Nine

"Good afternoon, my lady, Lord Hendricks." Compton opened the door for them when they returned from their sightseeing trip.

"Good afternoon." Margaret mouthed the polite words even though she couldn't see a single good thing about it. She felt utterly exhausted with the effort it had taken her to behave normally toward Hendricks.

"Will you stay for tea, Papa?" Margaret forced herself to ask.

"No, my dear. I've made arrangements to spend the rest of the afternoon with several old friends from the days when I was active in government circles. I have hopes of convincing them to lend their support to Chadwick's bill.

"Now, I want you to promise me something, my dear. After you have had your tea, will you rest? You've been distracted all afternoon. You aren't yet used to the frantic pace of life during the Season."

"Yes," Margaret said, willing to promise anything to get rid of Hendricks. She needed time. Time alone to come to terms with her anger over what he'd done.

Hendricks dropped an awkward kiss on her cheek before he turned and left.

Freed for a few minutes from the necessity of playing a role, Margaret felt her shoulders sag with relief. Unless . . . She tensed slightly as she remembered Philip. He'd said that he intended to spend the day at Whitehall, but if he'd changed his mind and come home early . . .

Her head began to throb at the thought of facing him again with the memory of last night between them—although he hadn't said anything about it earlier, she reminded herself. Maybe because in his mind there was nothing to say. To Philip, last night was probably no different from what he'd experienced many other times with many other women.

She frowned, annoyed at the thought that she was nothing more than one of a long line of anonymous women warming his bed.

"Is anything the matter, my lady?"

Margaret jumped at the sound of Compton's voice. She had totally forgotten his presence.

"No! No," she moderated her tone. "Is the Earl at home?"

"No, my lady. Mrs. Arbuthnot is, however."

Lovely, Margaret thought. Just what her tattered nerves needed. To be talked to death.

"And a letter came for you."

"A letter?" Margaret felt a sudden surge of anticipation. Could George have written to her?

"Where is it?"

Compton stared at a point over Margaret's right shoulder and said, "Mrs. Arbuthnot took it. She is in the small salon."

Why would Estelle take a letter that was addressed to her? Handing her pelisse and bonnet to the hovering footman, Margaret went to the small salon to find out.

"Ah, Margaret, there you are." Estelle patted down a cluster of curls that seemed to be making a determined bid to escape from her head. "Is your dear father with you?"

"No. Compton said that you took a letter addressed to me?"

"La, but you are eager to read it." Estelle gave her a sly smile. "Does Philip know that you are receiving letters from France?"

George! It had to be. Pleasure warred with worry over what might have happened to him that would have caused him to spend some of his small store of coins for postage.

"And that you go off into a daze when you think about it?" Estelle's voice sharpened.

Margaret studied Estelle's pudgy features, wondering whether she was fearing or hoping that the letter portended a scandal. Probably hoping, Margaret decided. Estelle's class thrived on gossip and discord.

"My letter?" Margaret ignored the question and held out her hand.

With a dissatisfied sniff, Estelle rummaged through the mound of social invitations on the table beside the sofa and extracted a battered letter, pausing to peruse the handwriting before handing it over to Margaret.

Margaret was hard-pressed not to snatch it out of Estelle's plump fingers. Taking her precious letter, she hurriedly left the salon.

Gaining the dubious sanctuary of her bedroom, she broke the greenish seal on the letter and unfolded the single sheet. Her gaze slipped to the bottom of the page to check the signature. It was from George! Holding the thin sheet up to the light, she struggled to make sense of his atrocious handwriting. Dear George, she thought—even his handwriting was undisciplined.

Margaret felt her tension dissolve as she managed to decipher the cross-hatching. George appeared to be not only healthy, but happy. He raved about the housekeeper's cooking and expounded at length on the gullibility of the head gardener from whom he had won ten francs in a card game. Part of which, he informed her, he had used to send her the letter.

Margaret shook her head ruefully. George would never

change. At the sight of a deck of cards he totally forgot what past events should have taught him.

Wearily she sank down on the bed and leaned back against the pile of plump pillows. She was immediately engulfed in the fragrance of sandalwood which still clung to them.

Philip! Her stomach clutched nervously, and she jerked upright as graphic memories of what had happened the last time she'd laid on that bed flooded her mind—memories of the feel of his hard body pushing her into the soft mattress, and the intoxicating sense of pleasure that had filled her as he'd caressed her. As well as the sudden pain that had shattered that pleasure.

She rubbed her hands over her forearms, as for the first time she thought in terms of the future. Would Philip want to do that again, or would once have been sufficient for him? And if he did want to repeat the act, what could she do about it?

Too agitated to sit still, she jumped to her feet and walked over to the window, peering blindly down at the street below.

"You need to think," she told herself, leaning her forehead against the cold glass pane. "So far all you've done is react. Now you need to plan."

Margaret moved away from the window and sank down on a tobacco-brown chair, wiggling slightly to try to find a comfortable spot on its hard surface. It was hopeless. Comfort and the chair did not go together.

She chewed thoughtfully on her lower lip as she tried to weigh the situation she was in objectively. For the moment, at least, George was safe and well, so she didn't have to worry about him.

Which left the problem of how to deal with Philip. Her gaze instinctively swung back to the bed, and she shivered. No, she corrected herself. One didn't "deal with" Philip. One survived Philip, rather like one survived a force of nature. Her best course of action where Philip was concerned, would be to try to keep out of his sight as much as possible. That, and do everything she could to help him pass his bill so that she could go back to George.

And to help him pass his bill, she was going to have to be in Hendricks's company a great deal, even if she didn't want to be.

Margaret sighed. For all his wealth and power Hendricks was every bit as much a victim of Philip as she was. And if she truly wanted revenge for the part Hendricks had played in her father's desertion of her mother, she'd have it when Hendricks found out that his beloved daughter really was dead.

The idea brought her no satisfaction.

Maybe because Hendricks hadn't knowingly condemned her mother. In fact, from what he'd said last night, it didn't sound as if he had even been aware she and her mother had existed. She doubted very much if her natural father would have given Hendricks any information which might have hurt his chances of inheriting a fortune.

No, the responsibility for what had happened to her mother rested squarely with Baron Mainwaring. Somehow she had to find a way to make him pay for his duplicity, but how? She squinted at the mud-colored woodwork, trying to utilize the Greek principles of logic.

What she needed was to identify what Mainwaring valued. Money immediately came to mind, and was just as quickly dismissed. There was nothing she could do to endanger his fortune.

What else did Mainwaring value? Her eyes narrowed as she remembered the tone of his voice as he'd introduced his daughter last night. He appeared to dote on her. Could she extract her revenge through his daughter? The daughter who had replaced her?

Margaret's speculation was interrupted by the unexpected thud of running feet in the hallway outside her door. They were immediately followed by Estelle's voice calling for Annabelle to stop.

Margaret sighed. Poor, unhappy Annabelle, yet one more complication in an already overly complicated situation. The child should be playing happily with her toys, not worrying how her new stepmother was going to make her life miserable. She also should have a doting father to love her. So why didn't she?

Could Philip blame the child for being alive when his Roxanne was dead? Margaret frowned thoughtfully. It seemed rather far-fetched, but both Estelle and Hendricks had been at pains to tell her how besotted Philip had been with the incomparable Roxanne. And emotional excesses rarely had anything to do with logic.

"Annabelle, I'm warning you. If you don't behave I'm going to whip you." Estelle's angry voice was clearly audible through Margaret's closed door.

Margaret's lips tightened in annoyance. Beating the child wasn't going to make her behave. Annabelle needed reassurance and guidance, and there didn't seem to be anyone in this household willing to give it to her.

Margaret listened to the sound of Estelle's footsteps as they passed her door and retreated down the front stairs.

She could do it, Margaret encouraged herself. Even if her motivation was guilt instead of love, Annabelle would still benefit from her help.

Margaret cautiously opened her bedroom door and checked to make sure that Estelle really had gone. The hallway was empty, and Margaret ran lightly up the back stairs to the nursery.

Cautiously sticking her head around the half-open door, Margaret looked inside. Annabelle was sitting in the middle of the floor, beating the head of a very expensive doll on the thick Aubusson carpet. The nursery was luxurious to the point of oppression. Whatever Philip's personal feelings for the child, it was clear that he begrudged no expense in her care.

Uncertain of what to say, Margaret decided to wait for a clue from Annabelle. Entering the nursery, she sat down in a pink plush chair that was far more comfortable than anything in her own room. Other than Annabelle, the room was deserted. Where was the governess? Margaret wondered, realizing that she hadn't been introduced to one.

"Go away!" Annabelle glared furiously at her.

"Why?"

Annabelle blinked as if taken aback at the question. "Because if you don't, I'll crack my doll's head open."

Margaret shrugged. "It's your doll, not mine. Why should I care if you break it?"

"Grandmama does."

"I am not your grandmama."

"You're not my mama neither!" Annabelle screamed.

"Of course I'm not," Margaret promptly agreed, wondering how much of Annabelle's behavior was inspired by fear and how much was the result of being appallingly indulged by Estelle.

"My mother's name was Roxanne, and she was beautiful!" Annabelle hurled the words at Margaret like weapons.

Margaret nodded. "A diamond of the first water. Everyone says so."

Annabelle's belligerent expression faded somewhat at Margaret's ready agreement. "I don't look like my mama."

The matter-of-fact comment tore at Margaret's soft heart. "You're more like your father."

"If I look like my papa, then why doesn't he like me?" Annabelle's question caught Margaret off guard. "Grandmama says that he can't help himself." Annabelle suddenly threw the doll against the bed where it collapsed in a piteous pile of silken skirts. "But I don't care. I don't like him. And you don't like me neither."

"You haven't given me any reason to."

"What?"

"People usually like or dislike you based on how you treat them. You haven't made any secret of your dislike of me, so why would you expect that I would return friendship for anger?"

"Because I'm Lady Annabelle." For a moment she sounded uncannily like her arrogant father. "My papa is an earl, and he has pots of money."

"And I'm married to an earl—the same one, in fact—but it doesn't seem to have made you like me."

Annabelle scowled at her. "That's different."

"Possibly. Tell me, is your governess below stairs at the moment?"

"I haven't got one. She left. She said I was completely out of control," Annabelle related with a great deal of relish.

"How sad for you."

"Huh?"

"To have to put up with a succession of governesses."

"Succession? You mean like the kings? You don't talk like Grandmama."

"Perhaps your grandmama hasn't had the benefit of the education I have had."

"Grandmama says that I don't need to be educated to catch a husband. That my title and dowry will get me a good one."

"Any man who marries a woman for her money and social position is by definition not a good anything!"

"Grandmama says—"

"But what do *you* say?"

Annabelle stared at Margaret as if she were speaking an unknown language.

"You have a title, and titles were originally given out

to men who distinguished themselves in some way, and people like that were leaders, not repeaters of what others say. Leaders form their own opinions."

Annabelle pushed out her lower lip and glared at Margaret. "I don't have to think. I have money. Lots of money."

For a brief moment Margaret felt a great deal of sympathy for Estelle's threat to beat Annabelle. But what had she expected? For Annabelle to suddenly realize the good sense of what she was saying and become a model child? And what was a model child anyway? Margaret seemed to hear the echo of her old nanny's exasperated voice telling her that if she didn't mend her ways she was going to go to Hell.

"Go away!" Annabelle demanded.

"All right." Margaret got to her feet, hastily suppressing a smile at the child's surprised expression. "Good afternoon, Lady Annabelle."

Annabelle pointedly turned her back on Margaret.

Ah well, Margaret told herself. Rome wasn't built in a day. Maybe she ought to ask Estelle if what Annabelle had said about the governess was true, because if it was, someone should be seeing about hiring a replacement. And she had the disheartening feeling that the someone was going to be her.

The quarrelsome sound of Estelle's voice floated up from the entrance hall, interrupting Margaret's thoughts.

Estelle seemed to be complaining about typhus fever. Curious, Margaret hurried down the front stairs only to regret that curiosity a moment later when she saw who else was in the hallway.

Philip! A shudder slashed through her at the sight of him staring so disdainfully at his mother-in-law.

"Margaret!" Estelle looked up and caught sight of her. "Come down here and tell him. Maybe he'll listen to you."

And maybe the Second Coming will occur tomorrow and none of this will matter, Margaret thought, bracing herself as Philip transferred his glare from Estelle to her.

With an effort Margaret stiffened her legs, which suddenly felt boneless, and forced herself to descend.

"Tell him." Estelle ordered when Margaret reached the bottom step. "Tell him they can't stay."

They? Margaret blinked for the first time, realizing that there was someone standing behind Philip in the shadow of the long-case clock. She looked closer. Two someones.

Margaret wondered who the couple was. Certainly no one she would have expected Philip to even acknowledge, let alone bring into his home. The woman was thin to the point of emaciation, making the fact that she was increasing all the more obvious. The gaunt man beside her was leaning heavily on a crutch. His skin had an unhealthy grayish tinge, probably as a result of having lost his leg. Margaret's heart went out to the unlikely-looking pair.

The strange tableau was suddenly broken when the woman uttered a barely audible moan and seemed to collapse. The man grabbed frantically for her, lost his balance, and fell to the floor.

Philip also grabbed for the woman and swept her up in his arms.

"Put her down! She might be contagious!" Estelle wailed.

Margaret was unable to suppress the giggle that bubbled up in her throat at the thought of pregnancy being catching.

"Margaret, this is no time for levity!" Estelle said.

Margaret's eyes met Philip's dark ones, and she almost giggled again at the wry humor she encountered there. Could he have had the same ridiculous thought? Margaret wondered, and then dismissed her curiosity as irrelevant.

"Sorry," Margaret said. "You're right, of course. This is a time for common sense." She hurried to help the man who was struggling to his one remaining foot. His entire attention was focused on the pale young woman.

What would it be like to have a man look at you as if you were his one hope of eternal salvation? Margaret wondered.

According to what everyone had told her, Philip had looked at the incomparable Roxanne like that.

The woman moaned, and Margaret hurriedly brushed away the thought.

"She needs to rest," Margaret said. "And she needs to see a doctor."

"Ain't got no money." The young man forced the words out as if they might choke him.

"I will take care of it," Philip said.

"Carry her up . . ." Margaret paused when she realized she didn't have the vaguest idea how many guest rooms there were in the house, or even where they were located.

"No!" Estelle yelled. "Think of Annabelle."

"If I might suggest, my lady?" Compton spoke.

Margaret looked up to find him standing just inside the open green baize door. Behind him seemed to be most of the staff eagerly peering into the hallway for a glimpse of the unexpected drama.

"Yes?" Margaret said.

"There are several empty rooms in the staff's quarters. Perhaps the young couple would like to rest there?"

"Yes, please, milady. We'd be more comfortable with our own kind," the young man said.

"Now, what's all this about?" The housekeeper's voice carried over the servants' muffled chatter. "Get back to work, the lot of you." Mrs. Smith shooed them away.

"Why, Ned Walkins! Whatever has happened to you, lad?" Mrs. Smith said. "And who is that his lordship is holding?"

"M'wife," he muttered. "And as for what happened to me, I's a cripple. No good for nuthin' now."

"Compton." Margaret turned to the butler. "If you would show his lordship where they can stay and then send someone for the doctor."

"Certainly, my lady." Compton lead the way through the green baize door followed by Philip carrying Lorraine and Ned hobbling behind them.

"Mrs. Smith," Margaret stopped the housekeeper when she would have followed them. "You know the man?"

"Most his life. I come from his lordship's principle estate in Kent, so I know most of the local people. Ned's ma and me were girls together." She shook her head. "Ned was always a hey-go-mad boy. Nothing would please him but he had to join the army and go fighting in foreign places, and see what's came of it! Him a cripple, and half starved by the look of it."

"And now Chadwick's brought him into the house and who knows what plague he's brought with him!" Estelle said

"That will be all, Mrs. Smith," Margaret said hurriedly, afraid from the expression on the housekeeper's face that Mrs. Smith was about to jeopardize her position by telling Estelle what she thought of the idea of her friend's son being a plague carrier.

"This is all your fault!" Estelle didn't even wait until Mrs. Smith had closed the green baize door behind her before she began to yell at Margaret.

"We are all called upon to help those less fortunate than ourselves," Margaret said.

"By who?" Estelle followed Margaret into the front saloon.

"By the Lord." Margaret sank down onto the Nile green-and-yellow-striped sofa, and poured herself a much-needed cup of tepid tea from the half-empty pot sitting on the tea table.

"The Lord didn't mean that we were to allow the raff

and scaff of London into our house," Estelle said. "He meant we were to give a few coins to the less fortunate."

And I'd be willing to bet a considerable sum that Estelle doesn't even do that much, Margaret thought.

"And what about my poor Annabelle?" Estelle continued.

"Yes, Annabelle. I've been meaning to ask you. Does she have a governess?"

"No." Estelle seemed thrown off balance by the change of subject.

"Have you made arrangements to interview new ones?"

Estelle shrugged. "After the Little Season is soon enough to be thinking of it. Not that it does much good. She has no head for lessons, just like my dear Roxanne. Not that it ever mattered. Look at the fine match she made."

Unanswerable, Margaret conceded. As far as society was concerned, making a good match was the pinnacle of every girl's existence. And not just the ton, either. Her own mother's dearest wish had been to see Margaret married.

"I shall be out this evening." Philip's unexpected announcement from the doorway caused Margaret to jump.

"Don't come in here after you've been carrying that woman!" Estelle said.

"Madam, if you fear that my house is unsafe, I will be more than happy to call the carriage and have you conveyed back to Kent."

Margaret glanced down at her teacup to hide the smile she couldn't suppress. Trust Philip to find Estelle's vulnerable point.

"Kent?" Estelle's hand went to the front of her chest as if warding off a blow. "Now, Philip." Estelle tried a laugh that rang false. "I was as much concerned for Annabelle as for myself. And for Margaret," she hurriedly added when she realized that he might send Annabelle with her.

"As you wish," Philip said, as if bored by the whole thing. "If you should change your mind, let me know."

Without another word he turned and left the house.

"Well, I never!" Estelle vigorously fanned herself with her lawn handkerchief. "I must say that marriage doesn't seem to have mellowed Chadwick any. Why, when he was married to my Roxanne, I'm sure he was the most amiable man alive."

And the streets of London were paved with gold, Margaret thought, beginning to hate the very name Roxanne.

"Where are you going?" Estelle demanded when Margaret got to her feet.

"To my room to rest."

But despite her intention of losing herself in an hitherto unseen volume of Plato that she'd found in Philip's library, Margaret was unable to concentrate. Her thoughts kept returning to Philip. To the memory of him bending over her, his dark eyes alight with passion. To the memory of his warm lips moving on her body. To the fear and pain she'd felt when he'd possessed her, destroying the fragile fabric of her pleasure. She shifted restlessly. Try as she might, she couldn't banish the thought of him from her mind.

Ten

Philip stared at the ivory knob on the door to Margaret's bedchamber, fighting his desire to turn it, to walk in on her and perhaps find her dressing for the day.

Grimly he forced his hand back to his side. He would not go into her room for at least another week. He reminded himself of the decision he'd reached late last night. A decision spurred by the very depths of his compulsion to bed her again. He knew that he had to establish distance between them and, since physical distance was impossible at the moment, it would have to be emotional.

He'd only lost control because it had been so long since he'd had a woman. He repeated the rationalization that almost half a bottle of brandy had given birth to. Now that his initial desire for her body had been sated, his desire would quickly fade, provided he didn't continue to feed it.

With a mental effort that was almost physical, he forced himself to step away from her door. He took a deep breath, rather pleased with himself. He still had control of himself. Every time he refused his traitorous body's desire to bed her, his own strength of purpose would grow stronger.

The sudden flurry of sound echoing through her closed bedroom door jerked him out of his thoughts. He didn't want to be caught standing outside her door, even if he did have an unexceptional reason to see her. He needed to make sure she understood what he expected her to do today. Left to her own devices, she would undoubtedly spend the day either shopping or gossiping with the other empty-headed women of the ton.

Although . . . Philip frowned uncertainly as he retreated back through their shared sitting room to his own bedroom. Margaret wasn't empty-headed. In fact, sometimes he had the unsettling feeling she was better educated than he. Which was ridiculous—he scoffed at the idea. She couldn't possibly be.

Margaret softly closed her bedroom door behind her and surreptitiously glanced around the hallway. To her relief it was empty. There was no sign of Philip. She felt the tension in her shoulders ease slightly.

She headed toward the nursery stairs, intending to look in on Annabelle before she went down to breakfast. Margaret wasn't sure just how one went about making a friend of a child, but common sense told her that accustoming Annabelle to her presence would be a good place to start.

Philip heard Margaret's bedroom door close and hurriedly left his own room, intending to intercept her. To his surprise, she wasn't on the front stairs. She was climbing the back stairs to the nursery. Why was she going up there? he wondered.

Philip felt the increasingly familiar pressure begin to grow in his loins as he watched the gentle sway of her hips beneath the thin green wool of her morning dress. His hands instinctively clenched as he remembered how those hips had felt when he'd cupped them in his hands and lifted them to meet his hard thrusts.

For one brief moment Philip was tempted to leave the house without even seeing her this morning, but his pride wouldn't let him take the coward's way out. He could control his growing fascination with her.

Margaret paused in front of the half-open nursery door when she heard Annabelle's shrill voice.

"I won't!" Annabelle shrieked. "And you can't make me!"

Stifling a sigh, Margaret stepped inside. Annabelle was standing in the middle of a huge pile of toys. As Margaret watched, Annabelle lifted her foot and deliberately kicked a box from which spilled an assortment of brightly colored game pieces.

"Don't be naughty, Annabelle." Estelle spoke from a chair beside the fireplace.

"I will if I want to!" Annabelle yelled at her. "I hate these toys. They're for babies. And I'm not a baby."

"One would never know it from your childish temper tantrum," Margaret said. "Good morning, Estelle." Margaret nodded at the discomposed-looking woman. "What seems to be the problem?"

"It's all her fault!" Annabelle pointed to the young maid cowering by the night-nursery door.

"I thought your name was Annabelle," Margaret said.

"Huh?" Annabelle looked confused.

"I asked your grandmother what the problem was, not you."

Annabelle glared at her, but Margaret ignored her, turning back to Estelle.

"It's all that silly girl's fault," Estelle pointed to the trembling maid. "She told Annabelle to get dressed, and she wasn't ready to do so yet."

Margaret allowed her glance to pass from the maid to the glowering Annabelle, taking note of the thin muslin nightgown the child wore.

"If you are still in your nightgown, then it must be because you are ill," Margaret said. "And that would account for your shocking lack of control in flinging your toys about. And the best place for anyone who is ill, is in bed."

Margaret smiled at the young maid, unable to recall having seen her about the house. "What is your name?"

"Annie, miss," she gasped. "I mean, milady."

"Annie, has Lady Annabelle's breakfast been served yet?"

"No, milady. Mrs. Smith, she said I was to help Lady Annabelle get dressed before I served it."

"Excellent. Please go downstairs and tell Cook that Lady Annabelle is feeling poorly today and to make her some thin gruel for breakfast."

"I hate gruel!" Annabelle screamed.

"Then it is to be hoped that you are feeling better by luncheon," Margaret said, having no idea if what she was doing was right or had any hope of success. All she knew for certain was that she had to try to teach Annabelle some self-control, because no one else seemed to care enough to make the effort.

"I won't and you can't make me!" Annabelle screamed at Margaret.

"What the hell is going on in here?" Philip's unexpected appearance in the doorway caught Margaret by surprise, as did the way her stomach suddenly twisted at the sound of his dark velvet voice.

"Well?" Philip walked into the room and stood surveying the mess. "Who is responsible for this?"

"That stupid girl." Estelle pointed to the nurserymaid who was trembling so badly that Margaret could hear her teeth chattering from across the room.

Of course, blame the poor servants, Margaret thought angrily. *Never accept responsibility for your own acts.*

Philip's dark brows rose in disbelief. "You were the one who threw these things all over the place?" he asked the maid.

The girl didn't answer. She simply stood there, trembling violently.

"She made me do it," Annabelle said.

"No one can make you do anything you don't want to do," Philip said.

Ha! Margaret thought. Maybe in the monied world Philip lived in that was true, but in the lesser levels that the maid and Margaret herself inhabited, one quite often found oneself doing things one didn't want to do. Such as pretending to be Philip's wife.

"Now, Philip," Estelle began placatingly, "there's no need for you to get involved in nursery doings."

Philip turned and gave her a look that silenced her. "Madam, I begin to wonder if you are equal to the task I have given you."

Despite her own belief that Estelle wasn't fit to raise a kitten, never mind a child, Margaret felt Philip's stricture was unjust. Estelle couldn't do it all herself. Philip was Annabelle's father. He should be actively involved in the child's upbringing.

"You," Philip pointed to Annie, "go about your business."

Annie almost ran from the room in her eagerness to escape.

"And you, Annabelle, pick this mess up." Philip's cold voice was chilling.

"No! No one can make me do what I don't want to do." Annabelle flung his words back at him, and Margaret held her breath when she saw his hands clench in anger. Surely he wouldn't strike the child, would he?

To her infinite relief, Philip didn't.

"If you don't care enough to pick them up, then perhaps they should be given to a foundling hospital where the children will appreciate them," he said.

"You can't! They're mine."

"I can, and I will." Philip's voice was hard. Hard enough to break one's heart on—the fanciful thought struck Margaret. Not that she was in any danger, she assured herself. A woman would have to be all about in her head to cherish any tender feelings for Philip Moresby. And she most emphatically wasn't addled, even if she wasn't showing her usual common sense lately.

Margaret stifled a sigh as she studied the two intransigent faces in front of her. Somehow Philip had to be made to take an interest in the development of Annabelle's character before it was too late and her willfulness became fixed.

No, not "made," Margaret amended, doubting that anyone short of the Almighty could make Philip Moresby do something he didn't want to do. But if he couldn't be forced into developing a relationship with his daughter, maybe he could be subtly maneuvered into it. And the best way to accomplish that would be to get him to spend some time with the child. Margaret hastily swallowed a giggle as an image of Annabelle lobbying for Philip's bill crossed her mind. Since it was clearly ineligible for Annabelle to enter Philip's world, he would have to enter hers.

Margaret watched as Annabelle began to pick up her scattered toys. Perhaps they could play a game together? Annabelle certainly had enough of them.

"When you're done, you may pick out a game, and we'll all play it." Margaret tried to sound more confident of her idea than she felt.

"Play a game!" Three voices simultaneously parroted her words.

"Surely it is not such a bizarre idea as all that?" Margaret said.

"Papa doesn't play with me," Annabelle said, and Margaret's lips tightened, remembering her own childhood and the total disinterest of her natural father.

"Of course Chadwick doesn't," Estelle said. "What possible interest could he find in a children's game?"

Philip found his gaze caught and held by the emotion he could see swirling in Margaret's eyes. Despite the fact that he knew it was impossible, he could almost see sparks flying off them. Sparks of anger and disgust. He straightened his shoulders in automatic negation of her unspoken condemnation. She had no right to look at him like that. He did his duty by the child. He provided her with every luxury money could buy, and even put up with that fool Estelle so that the child would have a grandparent to take care of her.

Estelle caught the annoyance in Chadwick's eyes and decided it was time to retreat. "I am going to breakfast," she said. "I trust I shall see you both there shortly." Without waiting for an answer, she hurried out of the room.

"What game would you like to play, Annabelle?" Margaret asked.

"I have a new chess set," Annabelle said, with a doubtful look at Philip.

"Chess is a man's game which requires logical thought." Philip automatically quoted his tutor.

Margaret clenched her teeth to hold back her opinion of that statement. This might be one of those cases when actions really did speak louder than words.

"Your father will play a game of chess with me to show you what he means when you have picked up your toys, Annabelle."

"All right." Annabelle hurriedly flung her toys into a windowseat and then got out her chess set which she held out to Margaret.

"This is pointless," Philip said.

"Children learn best by example." Margaret sat down at a small table.

Philip impatiently pulled his pocket watch out of his waistcoat and checked the time. "I have a few minutes before I have to leave for Westminster."

Margaret smiled blandly at him as she began to unpack the chess pieces. It was a beautiful set of jade and ivory. Far fancier than any she had ever played with.

"Do you want white or dark, Philip?"

"Dark. You do know what the individual pieces can do, don't you?"

Margaret nodded innocently. "Oh yes. My play is about average. For a woman, that is."

Philip frowned, suddenly uneasy at her expression. He had the disquieting feeling that he was missing something.

Margaret moved one of her pawns, and Philip casually countered, his attention centered on the slight line between her eyebrows. He wanted to smooth it out with his mouth. To kiss every inch of her flawless complexion. And then he'd move on to her neck, he planned, as he absently moved his own pieces. He'd press his mouth against the pulse that beat in her neck while—

"Checkmate."

"What?" Philip tore himself out of his erotic dreams to stare down at the board. To his shock, he found she was right. Somehow she'd stumbled onto a way to win, and in an embarrassingly short time.

"Does that mean you beat Papa?" Annabelle inched closer to the table and peered down at the board. "But you haven't got very many of his pieces at all."

"The object of the game isn't to take the most pieces, Annabelle. It's to make it impossible for your opponent to move his king," Margaret said, watching Philip's confusion with intense satisfaction. She felt as if she'd just struck a blow, not only for herself, but for all women.

"I wasn't paying attention," Philip said, not able to figure out how she'd done it. He was a good chess player. She shouldn't be able to beat him.

Philip replaced the chess pieces, determined not to fall in the trap of watching her instead of the board again.

The only difference it made in the outcome of the second game was that it took longer for her to win. But not that much longer. She cut through his defenses with embarrassing ease.

"Once more," Philip said, determined to win. No

woman was going to beat him at a masculine pastime. Especially not his own wife.

The third game was also gratifyingly short. At least, from Margaret's viewpoint.

"I just don't understand it," Philip muttered.

"Can you teach me to play chess?" Annabelle asked.

"I don't have time," Philip said.

"Not you, her." Annabelle pointed at Margaret.

Margaret hastily ducked her head to hide her sudden grin which was fueled equally by Philip's outraged expression and her satisfaction at Annabelle's words. Maybe teaching the child chess would provide a way to make friends with her.

As if Annabelle's words had been the last straw, Philip shot to his feet. "I'm going to be late," he accused Margaret.

"I'm sorry. Next time I'll be faster."

Philip's lips tightened, and he stalked to the door, pausing only to throw another order at Margaret.

"Make sure that you are in the morning room to receive callers and if Hendricks comes—"

"I know," Margaret cut him off, not wanting to listen to yet another lecture on what she was supposed to be doing with Hendricks. She already knew. She simply didn't want to do it.

"Will you teach me to beat Papa?" Annabelle demanded.

Margaret shrugged, trying to keep her voice casual so as not to trigger the child's seemingly endless anger.

"I can show you the basic moves of the game, and we can look for a book for you to study."

"But I can't read."

"Can't read!" How could the daughter of an earl—even as uncaring a one as Philip seemed to be—not have learned to read?

"Not good enough to read real books," Annabelle said.

"Why not?"

Annabelle shrugged. "My last governess said I was impossible, and Grandmama said that it wasn't important."

And it probably wasn't to Estelle. Margaret tried not to let her anger show.

"Perhaps not, but it could be a real problem when you're old enough to go to dances and you can't read who has signed your dance card. And you won't be able to read the reports in the papers about all the parties and who attended and what they wore and all about the latest fashions from Paris. But as you say, it isn't important," Margaret finished, well satisfied with Annabelle's thoughtful expression. She'd let her think that over for a few days and then she'd broach the subject of reading again.

"I have time to give you a chess lesson now, if you wish," Margaret said.

To her relief, Annabelle slid into the chair Philip had vacated.

Annabelle proved to be an apt pupil, listening closely to Margaret's instruction. Almost an hour passed before a footman appeared in the doorway to tell Margaret that her first morning callers had arrived.

"Don't go," Annabelle ordered imperiously. "I haven't finished learning yet."

"One never finishes learning the game of chess." Margaret quoted the old schoolmaster in Paris who'd taught her to play.

"I don't want—"

"What you want or what I want, for that matter, is not the issue. It is my duty to go downstairs and welcome my callers."

Ignoring the signs of Annabelle's anger, Margaret got to her feet, and with what she hoped was a neutrally friendly smile, left the room.

A most promising start, Margaret told herself as she hurried down to the salon.

Margaret's sense of satisfaction increased when she entered the salon and discovered that the callers were Lady Mainwaring and Drusilla.

"Ah, Cousin Margaret—you don't mind that I refer to our relationship, do you?" Lady Mainwaring asked, and then continued without waiting for an answer. "We were just asking Mrs. Arbuthnot if you were at home and here you are."

"Good morning." Margaret glanced at the window where Drusilla was sitting by herself watching the traffic on the square outside.

"Why don't you visit with Drusilla while I talk to Mrs. Arbuthnot?" Lady Mainwaring said.

Drusilla would be far easier to get information out of than Lady Mainwaring herself, Margaret thought, and immediately felt a twinge of guilt when Drusilla gave her a shy smile.

"You have such a lovely home, Cousin Margaret," Drusilla said as Margaret sat down beside her. "It quite takes my breath away."

"Thank you."

"It's so big. And the ceiling . . ." She gestured toward it.

"Yes," Margaret said absently. "The room is an interesting amalgam of Cipriani's painted roundels and the Collins overmantel panel on the chimney of a pagan sacrifice. There's another panel in the library that depicts bacchic revelers."

Drusilla's small pink mouth fell open.

Botheration! Margaret thought in vexation. When was she going to learn to guard her tongue? The last thing she wanted to do was to put Drusilla on her guard, and if she continued sounding like she knew anything other than the latest fashions, she most definitely would.

"Chadwick is very proud of his home. He has told me all about it and even though I don't understand it all, I learned it to please him." Margaret tried to repair the damage.

"Oh, I see." Drusilla relaxed visibly, apparently believing that parroting what some man had told her was perfectly acceptable, while having learned it for herself was not.

Margaret found it hard to believe that this young woman was in any way related to her. Drusilla's thought processes were so different from hers that there seemed to be no common ground. Which seemed strange to Margaret. She would have thought that siblings would have at least some characteristics in common, even if they had different mothers. It was an unsettling question for which she didn't have an answer. And she didn't need one, Margaret told herself. Her relationship to Drusilla was important only because it could point a way to avenge her mother's death.

"You must be very fond of Chadwick to have learned all that."

"My feelings for Chadwick are indeed very strong," Margaret said, allowing Drusilla to draw her own conclusions.

Drusilla blushed a rosy shade of pink and glanced toward her mother who was still gossiping with Estelle. Leaning toward Margaret, she whispered, "I know just how you feel. I, too, have an all-consuming interest."

"Oh?" Margaret felt a sudden surge of excitement. Unless she missed her guess, this interest was not one approved by her parents or Drusilla wouldn't be so careful to check if her mother was listening before imparting the news.

Not needing much encouragement, Drusilla launched into a glowing description of a Mr. Daniels.

"He sounds like the answer to every maiden's prayers," Margaret said.

"Oh, he is." Drusilla's eyes shone with pleasure at the thought that someone else appreciated Mr. Daniels's worth.

"And when will the formal announcement of your betrothal be made?"

Drusilla's lower lip quivered and her large brown eyes filled with tears. "Oh, Cousin Margaret, my parents are determined to tear us apart!"

"How Gothic."

Drusilla nodded vigorously. "Exactly what my special friend Emily says."

"But why?"

"My parents are so worldly. All that matters to them is social position and wealth, and Mr. Daniels has neither. Much that I care."

And there speaks someone who has spent her whole life surrounded by every creature comfort her doting parents could provide, Margaret thought. And probably always would, even if she were to marry an impecunious man.

Margaret remembered the look on Mainwaring's face when he'd spoken of his daughter. Mainwaring would never cast her off. The only thing that would be affected if Drusilla married to disoblige Mainwaring, would be his pride. He wanted Drusilla to achieve a brilliant match to enhance his own social standing. So if Drusilla married beneath her it would be a tremendous blow to his pride. A public blow. And it was probably the best revenge she could hope for in the circumstances, Margaret thought.

"What are you finding so engrossing, Drusilla?" Lady Mainwaring said as she stood up to take her leave.

"I was just telling Cousin Drusilla about the latest fashions in Paris," Margaret lied.

"Come for a walk tomorrow in the park with me, and I'll tell you all about Mr. Daniels," Drusilla whispered as she got to her feet.

Margaret nodded agreement. It was too bad she didn't

gamble, because luck was really with her today. First she'd beaten Philip at chess, then she'd made a fragile beginning of friendship with Annabelle, and lastly Drusilla had given her an idea for revenge against Mainwaring.

"Would you like tea?" Estelle asked Margaret once Drusilla and Lady Mainwaring had left.

"No, thank you. I'm going to inquire how the Walkinses passed the night."

Ignoring Estelle's disdainful sniff, Margaret went in search of Compton.

Eleven

"How is Ned this morning, Compton?" Margaret asked.

"The poor young man is still abed, my lady."

"And Lorraine?"

"She is in the kitchen shelling peas for Cook."

Margaret frowned. "Surely she should be resting also. I would like to see her."

"Certainly, my lady. I will send her to you."

"That isn't necessary. I can go to her."

"To the kitchen?"

"I sincerely doubt that anything in Chadwick's kitchens will shock me," Margaret said, taken aback at his reaction.

"As you wish, my lady." Compton led the way through the green baize door, his body rigid with disapproval.

Margaret found Lorraine sitting at a large, scrubbed wooden table with a copper bowl full of peas in front of her. She glanced up as Compton entered, caught sight of Margaret, and jumped to her feet, spilling the peas across the slate floor.

"Oh!" Lorraine muttered, her lower lip beginning to quiver. "I'm that sorry, milady. I didn't . . ." Her voice became suspended in tears.

"Never mind. It was an accident," Margaret said. "I'll help you."

"I will." The scullery maid hastily began to scoop up the peas.

"Did you want to see me, milady?" Cook emerged from the pantry, wiping her hands on her spotless apron.

"No," Margaret said. "I came to inquire after Lorraine. I certainly didn't mean for her to work."

Cook seemed to swell with outrage. "It wasn't my idea, milady."

"Please, milady, I asked to help," Lorraine's soft voice was barely audible.

"Not but what I don't think she's right," Cook said. "Busy hands make for a light heart."

Margaret looked around the kitchen in dismay. It seemed to her that everyone who worked in the house was there. And they were all staring at her. As if she were an interloper whose presence they didn't know how to cope with.

Compton was right. She should have had Lorraine come to her. Then she would have been able to talk to her without an audience.

"Please sit down," Margaret said when the young woman seemed to grow paler. "Has the doctor been?"

"Yes, milady." Lorraine dropped into the chair. "He says my Ned will get better with rest and nourishing food."

"That's good," Margaret said.

"Good!" For a moment Lorraine's respectful attitude slipped, and her eyes blazed with anger and grief. "How is he to eat anything at all, let alone nourishing food, when he can't do nothing to earn it?"

Margaret ignored Compton's scandalized murmur.

"He'll rest and eat here until he is well enough to travel back to the earl's estate," Margaret said, assuming that was what Philip intended to do.

"But he won't go! Ned said he won't take nobody's charity." Lorraine choked on the tears that were clogging her throat.

Margaret felt her heart twist in sympathy. She was probably the only one of all the people in this cheerful kitchen who knew the panicky feeling of not having food or shelter.

"Perhaps I should speak to him," Margaret said.

"You, milady?" Lorraine twisted her thin fingers together uncertainly.

"It sounds as if someone should. Will you take me to him?"

"Yes, milady." Lorraine slowly got to her feet, reluctance in the line of her body.

Margaret followed her up three flights of stairs to the fourth floor where the servants were quartered.

"We're in the last room, milady." Lorraine led the way down the long, central corridor. Curiously Margaret glanced through several of the open doors to see comfortably furnished rooms. Much more comfortably furnished than the majority of rooms she and George usually were able to afford.

Lorraine pushed open the door and addressed the lump beneath the covers. "It's the earl's lady come to see you, Ned."

Margaret watched as a tousled black head emerged and looked up at her. A sudden surge of pity engulfed her at the hopeless expression in his eyes.

"Milady," Ned mumbled.

"Did the doctor say when you would be well enough to make the trip to . . . the earl's estate?" Margaret finished when she realized that she didn't know the name of Philip's estate or even where it was in Kent. And she could hardly ask. Even the most featherbrained of brides would know that.

"Don't matter none. Nothing I can do. I was a farmer a'fore I ran away to enlist." His face twisted in bitter lines. "Can't farm with only one leg."

"Quite true." Margaret saw no sense in uttering polite lies; he'd simply see through them.

"And I won't take no charity!"

"Ned!" Lorraine shot Margaret a fearful glance, but both Margaret and Ned ignored her.

"Charity is for those who can't help themselves. I see no evidence that you are helpless," Margaret said.

"I told you—"

"That you can't farm. There are other jobs besides farming."

"For a cripple!"

"How you do dwell on your limitations." Margaret ruthlessly stifled her natural sympathy. Pity would only reinforce his feelings of helplessness. "Don't you think it's time you climbed out of that well of self-pity you're wallowing in, and started to think of your wife and the baby?"

Margaret ignored both Lorraine's gasp and Ned's scowl. Something was needed to shake him out of his present mood and, if hard facts were what it took, then hard facts it would be. She knew better than most that one had to face one's problems if one was to have any hope of conquering them.

Margaret turned, and with a smile for the trembling Lorraine, left, hoping she'd done the right thing. Slowly she made her way back to the earl's part of the house.

When she reached the bottom of the front staircase, she found Compton waiting for her.

"Lord Hendricks has arrived, my lady. He is in the front salon."

Margaret tried not to let her sudden tension show. Hendricks hadn't even known about her and her mother's existence, she reminded herself, but even knowing it was true, couldn't entirely erase her bitterness.

"Thank you, Compton. Is Mrs. Arbuthnot entertaining him?"

"No, my lady. Mrs. Arbuthnot has already left the house."

At least she wouldn't have to deal with Estelle, Margaret thought as she went into the salon.

"Have I come at an inopportune time, my dear?" Hendricks asked with a glance at her tense features.

"No, no," Margaret repeated more strongly, knowing she didn't dare take advantage of his offer and ask him to leave. If Philip found out, he'd be furious and there was no telling what he might do to punish her.

Hendricks smiled at her, his pale blue eyes twinkling engagingly.

"Are you airdreaming about your bridegroom? I just left him trying to talk to Ashton about his relief bill." Hendricks chuckled. "I can't decide if Chadwick is an optimist or a fool, but one thing I do know is that Ashton cares for nothing that won't realize an immediate profit for himself."

Just like the rest of the aristocracy, Margaret thought, and then remembered that wasn't quite true. Philip cared passionately about the returning soldiers. And so far she had found no evidence that his concern was tied either to money or power, as she'd originally thought.

"However, you may tell Chadwick when you next see him that I have managed to convince both Warwick and Ludlum to support his bill."

Margaret forced a smile. "That is good news. Philip will be so pleased. Won't you have a seat? Mrs. Arbuthnot is out," she added when she saw him glance toward the door.

Hendricks's quick grin sparked an answering smile from Margaret, and that bothered her. She didn't want to share a sense of humor or anything else with him. She only wanted to fulfill her contract with Philip and leave, without becoming personally involved with anyone.

"I have a trifle for you. I found this at a bookstore

which handles rare books," Hendricks handed her the slim
volume he'd been carrying.

Margaret automatically took it, glancing down at the
cover. It was a book of Greek plays by Aristophanes. Carefully she opened the fragile volume, her eyes widening
as she read the inscription.

"Molière? Was it really his?"

"According to the bookmonger."

"Thank you!" Margaret didn't have to feign enthusiasm. She was enchanted with the volume. "It was kind
of you to give it to me."

"I want to give you everything!" his voice was unexpectedly hard. "When I think of all the years . . ."

"Don't!" Margaret instinctively wanted to comfort him.
"Don't think about it. It wasn't your fault."

"Of course it was my fault! I should have known not
to marry your mother. She was a pretty child with her
head stuffed full of romantic nonsense, and I was a middle-aged fool who should have known better."

"But if you hadn't married her, I wouldn't be here."

Hendricks frowned, as if that thought had never occurred to him. "Quite true, my dear. And not only do I
have you, but hopefully in a few years I'll have grand-
children to brighten my old age."

Margaret felt her heart contract at the thought of children. Philip's children. After what had happened between
her and Philip, she could well be increasing. And then
what? How could she manage with a child?

Worry about one thing at a time, she told herself. She
had enough on her plate at the moment without thinking
up new things to worry about. Things that might never
happen.

Hendricks drew his own conclusions from her abstracted expression, and from the width of his grin they
must have been happy ones.

"I thought we might visit some bookstores today," he said.

"Bookstores?" Margaret felt the first flash of uncomplicated pleasure she'd felt in weeks. "How many are there?"

"According to my secretary, there are twenty dealers in choice or rare books in London. "That particular volume is from one of the French booksellers."

"Twenty!" Margaret's eyes gleamed with enthusiasm. She loved going through old bookshops, and to have the opportunity to do so without having to worry about how she was going to pay for it . . . It was as close to her idea of Heaven as she was likely to get this side of Judgment Day. For a brief moment the remembrance of how she'd felt when Philip had first started to caress her welled out of the depths of her mind. That, too, was intensely pleasurable. But brief. Far too brief to justify the pain that followed it.

No, the Church was right. The pleasures of the flesh were fleeting indeed. Far better to indulge the mind.

"When can we go?" Margaret asked.

Hendricks beamed at her eagerness. "Right now." He patted his waistcoat pocket. "I have the addresses with me."

Margaret rang for her pelisse and, once they were safely inside Hendricks's carriage, she decided to try to find out some more about the Mainwaring family.

"Papa, Drusilla Mainwaring and her mother came to call earlier."

"There can be no harm in acknowledging the connection," Hendricks said. "Mainwaring is perfectly respectable—now."

No, he was not respectable, Margaret thought bitterly. Nothing would ever wipe away the enormity of the sin he had committed against her mother.

"Drusilla is so pretty and sweet-natured. Is she pledged to anyone?" Margaret said.

"Not that Mainwaring's said. Of course, she's very young yet to be thinking of marriage. Barely out of the schoolroom. Better that she acquire a little town bronze this season and then make a choice next year."

"Is Mainwaring so modern that he will allow her to fix her interest where she will?"

"It isn't so much that he's modern, as it is that he dotes on the child."

"Goodness! She will find herself the target of every fortune hunter in London."

"Mainwaring might dote on Drusilla, but he isn't a fool. He'll never countenance her marrying some half-pay officer.

"But enough of our boring relatives," he said, as the carriage stopped in front of a shop. "We've reached the first bookstore on my list. Shall we investigate?"

Margaret eagerly jumped out of the carriage and, taking Hendricks's arm, followed him into the shop. She was looking forward to this. It promised to be a solitary bright spot in a confusing sea of problems that seemed to have defined her life ever since she'd met Philip.

The day turned out to be as enjoyable as Margaret had hoped. She rummaged through seemingly endless stacks of books, rare ones as well as simply old ones. She tried to be frugal, knowing that not only had she no right to spend Hendricks's money, but she wouldn't be able to carry many books with her when she left. But even so, she wound up with an impressive pile of volumes.

"Thank you so much, Papa," Margaret said when Hendricks finally delivered her back home. "I can hardly wait to examine them more closely."

"When you've finished with that French Book of Hours, I'd like to examine it."

"Here." Margaret promptly held it out to him. "I intend to start with that critique of logic by Plato we discovered at our second stop."

"If you're sure?" Hendricks traced over the elaborate drawing of the Virgin on the cover.

Margaret nodded, watching the reverent movement of his fingers. He really did love books, just as she did. They may have been only distantly related, but in all aspects that counted, Hendricks was far more like her than her natural father had ever been. What would her life have been like if Hendricks actually had been her father? she wondered. *You'd be long dead and buried in a graveyard in France.* She pulled her wistful thoughts up short.

"Would you like to come in for tea, Papa?"

Hendricks shot a quick, speculative glance at the over-sized windows which fronted the salon and shook his head. "No, my dear. Mrs. Arbuthnot will be home. Good-bye for now."

He placed a gentle kiss on her cheek and stepped back, waiting on the flagstones as she mounted the front steps. The door opened before Margaret could knock and with one last wave at Hendricks she went inside, only to come to a precipitous stop when she saw who had opened the door.

Philip! Her stomach did a sudden dive at the unexpected sight of his lean features. She studied his face searching for a clue to his mood. His lips were tightly compressed and the muscles in his jaw were corded with the pressure he was exerting on them. Not good, she decided. Philip was angry about something. But then, when *wasn't* he angry? She mocked her thoughts and immediately felt a flash of warmth shoot through her at the memory of him bending over her. His face had been taut then, too, but taut with the desire he'd felt.

It was safer for her if he were angry, she assured herself.

"Good afternoon," she said when he continued to stare at her.

"That, madam wife, is open to debate!"

Margaret blinked, not sure what kind of response his comment called for. Finally she decided not to say anything. Philip didn't care what she thought, and it was apparent he wasn't in the mood to exchange social pleasantries. Not that she had ever seen him in such a mood. Which was probably why he needed Hendricks's help with his bill. Philip was not a diplomat. He was used to ordering people about, not persuading them.

"What are those?" Philip nodded toward her stack of books.

Margaret blinked as his movement caught the late-afternoon sunlight streaming in through the fanlight above the door, adding a golden aura to his inky-black hair.

He looked like the painting of the drawing of Lucifer in the Book of Hours she'd just given Hendricks. He acted like him at times, too, she thought as he took the top book off the stack she was holding.

"Plato?" He frowned at the thin volume. "In Greek?"

"If that information is supposed to be news to me, I already know!" Margaret said, stung at the incredulous note in his voice.

"Where did you get these?"

"Lord Hendricks bought them for me. He also said that he had convinced two peers to vote for your bill," Margaret said, in the hope of distracting him. It worked. Philip immediately lost interest in the book. He took the whole stack from her and handed it to the hovering footman with orders to take them to the library.

"Which peers?" Philip demanded.

Margaret tried to remember and couldn't. "I don't recall."

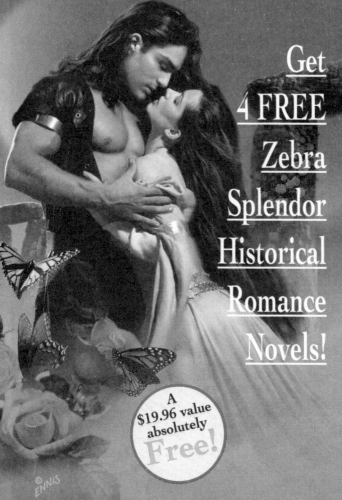

Take advantage of this offer to enjoy Zebra's newest line of historical romance novels....Splendor Romances (formerly Lovegrams Historical Romances)- Take our introductory shipment of 4 romance novels -Absolutely Free! (a $19.96 value)

Now you'll be able to savor today's best romance novels without even leaving your home with our convenient and inexpensive home subscription service. Here's what you get for joining:

- 4 BRAND NEW bestselling Splendor Romances delivered to your doorstep every month

- 20% off every title (or almost $4.00 off) with your home subscription

- FREE home delivery

- A FREE monthly newsletter, *Zebra/Pinnacle Romance News* filled with author interviews, member benefits, book previews and more!

- No risks or obligations...you're free to cancel whenever you wish...no questions asked

To get started with your own home subscription, simply complete and return the card provided. You'll receive your FREE introductory shipment of 4 Splendor Romances and then you'll begin to receive monthly shipments of new Zebra Splendor titles. Each shipment will be yours to examine for 10 days and then if you decide to keep the books, you'll pay the preferred home subscriber's price of just $4.00 per title. That's $16 for all 4 books with FREE home delivery! And if you want us to stop sending books, just say the word...it's that simple.

4 Free BOOKS are waiting for you!
Just mail in the certificate below!

If the certificate is missing below, write to: Splendor Romances, Zebra Home Subscription Service, Inc., P.O. Box 5214, Clifton, New Jersey 07015-5214

FREE BOOK CERTIFICATE

Yes! Please send me 4 Splendor Romances (formerly Zebra Lovegram Historical Romances), ABSOLUTELY FREE! After my introductory shipment, I will be able to preview 4 new Splendor Romances each month FREE for 10 days. Then if I decide to keep them, I will pay the money-saving preferred publisher's price of just $4.00 each... a total of $16.00. That's 20% off the regular publisher's price and there's never any additional charge for shipping and handling. I may return any shipment within 10 days and owe nothing, and I may cancel my subscription at any time. The 4 FREE books will be mine to keep in any case.

Name _____

Address _____ Apt. _____

City _____ State _____ Zip _____

Telephone ( ) _____

Signature _____ SP0199
(If under 18, parent or guardian must sign.)

Terms and prices subject to change. Orders subject to acceptance by Zebra Home Subscription Service, Inc. . Zebra Home Subscription Service, Inc. reserves the right to reject or cancel any subscription.

AFFIX
STAMP
HERE

SPLENDOR ROMANCES
ZEBRA HOME SUBSCRIPTION SERVICE, INC.
120 BRIGHTON ROAD
P.O. BOX 5214
CLIFTON, NEW JERSEY 07015-5214

Philip frowned. "Did he say if he would be at the Levingtons' ball this evening?"

Margaret shook her head.

"Come into the drawing room, and you can try to remember while we have tea. If they've already agreed, I don't want to waste any more time on them."

She'd stand a far better chance of remembering if she were out of his unsettling presence, Margaret thought, but she obediently followed him into the salon.

"Ah, there you are, Margaret." Estelle greeted her with a disgruntled expression that Margaret instinctively mistrusted. "I wondered where you had gotten to."

"Papa and I were out." Margaret sat down and accepted the cup of tea Estelle handed her.

"Oh?" Estelle gave an angry little titter of laughter. "I was that sure that you had gone to meet the author of your letter. So much more romantic."

"Make-believe usually is." Margaret bent her head and sipped her tea to hide the sudden tension which gripped her. Drat Estelle! She was purposefully trying to make trouble because Margaret hadn't invited her along on her outings with Hendricks.

Margaret shot a quick glance at Philip, her heart sinking at his carefully blank expression. There was a tiny muscle twitching along his jawline that spoke of clamped-down fury.

"Oh, dear, wasn't I supposed to mention the letter?" Estelle glanced avidly from Margaret to Philip. "Now, I don't want you to think me an interfering old lady, Margaret, but I feel it is my duty to tell you how to go on. I mean it isn't as if you are used to all this. And——"

"How did you spend your afternoon, madam?" Philip abruptly changed the subject.

Estelle, with a calculating glance at Philip's taut features, decided not to pursue the matter. Instead she launched into a boring monologue of all the latest on-sits she'd heard while visiting, leaving Margaret free to drink her tea. And to worry about what Philip might do in response to Estelle's meddling. That he would do something, Margaret never doubted for a moment.

Ten minutes later, when Estelle finally paused for breath, Margaret hastily got to her feet.

"Please excuse me, but I really must dress if I'm not to be late for this evening's entertainments."

Carefully not looking at Philip, Margaret gave Estelle a totally false smile and made her escape. To her relief Philip made no attempt to follow her. Maybe he would put her letter on a list of things to yell about later, and forget about it, she told herself, not believing it for a moment. If she were to die, he'd probably follow her to Heaven with a lecture about how she hadn't fulfilled her part of the bargain yet.

Margaret giggled as she climbed the stairs, imagining Saint Peter's expression when Philip refused to release her from her obligations. Although she probably wouldn't be going to Heaven if she died anytime soon. The depressing thought weighed on her. Not with her deception of Hendricks on her soul, to say nothing of her determination to avenge her mother's death. And then there was the matter of her affair with Philip. . . .

Don't think about it, she ordered herself. *What's done is done. Concentrate on the future which you have a hope of changing.* She winced at the memory of that twitching muscle in Philip's jaw. Probably not much of a chance, but still, any chance was better than none.

Margaret rang for her bathwater, hoping she would be granted an hour's peace from the inhabitants of this house. All of whom seemed to have as their main goal in life, the destruction of her peace of mind.

Who had written to Margaret? Philip wondered as he watched Margaret leave the room.

Estelle gave an irritating titter of laughter. "You'd best be careful, Chadwick, or people will think you are unfashionably besotted with your wife."

Philip bit back fury. He wasn't besotted with Margaret. Not with any woman. Never again. He only paid such close attention to Margaret because she was pivotal to his plans. And because he didn't understand her motivation, which meant that he couldn't trust her to fulfill her end of the bargain. And that letter was proof that he'd been right not to trust her.

Who could be writing to her? And why? Was the letter from that old roué, Gilroy? Or was she involved with someone else? To what purpose? The question worried him.

"If you will excuse me." Philip got to his feet and left the room, not noticing Estelle's self-satisfied expression at his scowl.

Philip took the stairs two at a time, ignoring Compton's scandalized expression. Outside Margaret's door, he was about to knock when it suddenly opened to reveal Daisy and two footmen, each carrying a large copper bucket.

Daisy gasped. "Oh, my lord! What a turn you gave me."

"Unintentional, I assure you," Philip said, his eyes lingering on the empty pots the men were carrying. Bathwater, he realized in sudden excitement. Margaret was taking a bath.

He could almost feel his temperature rising as he contemplated the delectable scene. Without another word to the curiously watching Daisy, he hurried into his own room.

Dismissing his valet, he yanked off his neckcloth and then shrugged out of his coat, carelessly flinging them on the bed. Instinctively his eyes turned to the door which led to their connecting sitting room. He shouldn't go in now, he told himself. Not when he knew how he'd find her. The temptation to make love to her would be overwhelming, and he'd already decided that he wouldn't do that for a while.

Sitting down on his bed, he yanked off his boots. Stripping off the rest of his clothes, he pulled on his dressing gown. He'd ring for his own bath and, afterward, when they were both dressed, he'd go into her room and demand an explanation of that letter.

Although . . . His hand paused halfway to the bell pull. Maybe he should see her now. If she were in her bath she couldn't walk out on him as she'd done downstairs. She'd have to stay and answer him. Because if she did get up . . . He swallowed uneasily as an image of her naked body glistening with water filled his mind.

This had nothing to do with sex, he assured himself as he opened the door that led to the connecting sitting room. It had to do with that letter she'd received, and as her husband he had a right to know whom it was from and what kind of danger it might represent to his plans.

Twelve

Philip eased open the door to Margaret's bedroom and slipped inside. He looked around the room, immediately finding her sitting in a copper hip bath. Mesmerized, Philip watched as the flickering light from the fire danced over her bare skin, caressing first one spot and then another.

Philip quietly closed the door behind him and moved farther into the room, his eyes never leaving her. Her skin seemed to glow with the luminescence of pearl, luring him closer and closer.

He swallowed hard as she raised one arm and lathered it. Tiny droplets of soapy water ran down her arm and over her small breast, slowly dripping off the rosy pink nipple as if reluctant to leave.

Philip's fingers clutched spasmodically as he envisioned following the path of that water. First with his hand and then with his mouth and then with his tongue. He wanted to taste every inch of her. He wanted to . . .

No! He made a valiant effort to cut off his imagination. He absolutely couldn't allow himself to lose his head over a woman again. But he wasn't about to lose his head, he argued with himself. He wasn't fool enough this time to believe that Margaret was the embodiment of all the feminine ideals. He knew that she was nothing more than . . .

Than what? The perplexing question returned to nag at

him. What was Margaret? She'd been a virgin until he'd bedded her. And he still didn't know why. Or what her relationship with Gilroy was. Or why she sometimes sounded like one of his tutors at Oxford. Nor did he know how she had managed to beat him at chess. She'd either been incredibly lucky or she had had a great deal of practice. But if it was practice, where had she gotten it, and from whom?

And . . . His line of thought suffered a dislocating blow when Margaret suddenly stood up, and he got a clear view of her naked body. His entire body clenched as if a giant fist had just connected with the side of his head, driving out every thought but one. The need to possess her. Now. All his carefully reasoned arguments about why he should wait became just so many meaningless words. Nothing mattered but that he satisfy his compulsion to bury himself deep in her body.

Margaret carefully poured the clear water in the pitcher that Daisy had left beside the tub over herself, rinsing away the soap. Setting down the empty jug, she stepped out of her bath, freezing when she saw Philip standing just inside the door.

She grabbed for her towel and clumsily wrapped it around her body, trying to cover as much of her nakedness as possible.

She stared nervously at Philip, searching for a clue as to his mood. His features appeared to have been carved in marble. The only thing about him that even looked real were his eyes. And they glittered with a light that both frightened and attracted her.

"What do you want?" Margaret tried to use words to build a barrier between them.

Her breath caught in her lungs as he walked slowly toward her, his eyes never leaving her barely covered breasts. She was afraid. She had no trouble identifying the emotion swirling through her. Afraid that he might decide to make love to her again. Afraid of the pain that would inevitably follow. Afraid that his lovemaking would result in a child. But most of all, she was afraid of how his caresses made her feel. Wanton, like the bastard she was and not like the moral woman she wanted to be.

"I want to know about that letter you received." Philip struggled to concentrate on something other than the sight of her half-naked body or his own reaction to it.

Margaret never even heard the words. She was too busy noticing his bare feet sticking out from beneath his maroon robe. Was he naked under that dressing gown? Her heart gave a sudden leap, threatening to choke her.

"Answer me, madam!" Philip's voice sounded odd to her, thick and slightly muffled, not decisive the way it usually did.

A fugitive draft blew over her wet skin, and Margaret shivered convulsively.

"Dry yourself before you catch an inflammation of the lungs."

"I will as soon as you leave my room." Margaret tried to sound more confident than she felt.

"This is my house and everything in it awaits my pleasure, including you!"

Margaret shuddered at his dogmatic pronouncement.

Seeming to lose patience, Philip strode across the room and, jerking the towel out of her fingers, began to briskly rub it over her wet body.

Margaret felt his fingers pressing into her flesh as they moved. The pressure made her feel hot. Hot enough to steam the water off her skin without having to bother with the towel. Her breath became suspended as his hands began to move slower and slower when the towel reached her breasts. Her skin felt tight and tingling. There was a strange sense of urgency wrapping itself around her mind and slowly strangling her common sense.

She had to get him out of her room, she thought desperately. Because if this went on for much longer, she'd be fighting both him and herself with no hope of winning either battle. She didn't understand how her body could be reveling in his touch when her mind knew very well what the outcome of his possession would be, pain. And yet somehow that knowledge had become muted. As if it didn't really apply to her.

"I'm dry." Her words came out as a frightened gasp, but she didn't care. The most important thing was to get rid of him. Now.

Lowering his head, he pressed his lips against her left breast. "There's a tiny bit of moisture right about here."

He kissed the spot.

Margaret tried to squirm away from him, then forced herself to meet his burning black gaze. She couldn't match him for strength, but she refused to let him see how intimidated she felt.

"Who was your letter from?" Philip's unexpected question echoed meaninglessly in her ears.

Letter? Margaret struggled to process the word through her spinning emotions with a singular lack of success.

"Tell me!" Philip's imperious tone unexpectedly helped her to regain a small amount of control. "I am your husband. I have a right to know."

Jailer would be a more accurate description of his relationship to her, Margaret thought, but she had better sense than to say it aloud. She was far too vulnerable at the moment to purposefully anger him.

"It was from George," she mumbled.

"Why would Gilroy be writing to you?"

"Because George loves me," Margaret shot back. "And because he knows I worry about him."

Philip stared down at her flushed face and tried to think. She had claimed Gilroy loved her before, and that she loved him. At the time he'd assumed that she meant physical love, but that wasn't true. What other kind of love could they share that would be strong enough to have convinced her to marry him to save that old roué?

Margaret wiggled slightly, trying to take advantage of his abstraction to escape. It was a futile effort. He instinctively pressed his body against hers to hold her in place. It was almost his undoing because his body reacted by hardening to the point where he found it difficult to think of anything but the need to finish what he had started.

Think, he tried to rally his mind. She had said that Gilroy was her cousin. Could it be true? Could her love for him be nothing more than familial love?

Unconsciously he lowered his head so that he could nuzzle the soft skin of her neck while he considered the idea. It was possible, of course, but he found it highly improbable. In his experience, relatives didn't give, they took—took anything they could get their hands on and then usually complained because it wasn't enough.

The knowledge bothered him even though it never had before. Before, he'd simply accepted his relatives' avarice as a fact of life and tried to avoid them whenever possible.

Impatiently he shoved the idea aside, to be considered later. For the moment all he wanted to do was to sate himself on Margaret's delectable charms. That, and show her that the experience didn't have to be painful. That there were pleasures to be found in bed for women as well as men.

The fear and revulsion he'd seen in her eyes after he'd taken her that first time, grated on his pride. He wanted to show her that he wasn't totally insensitive.

Lowering his head, he set about the delightful task.

Margaret quivered as he began to kiss her, but to her surprise, Philip didn't rush to claim her. He continued to caress her until she ceased to think about anything but how she felt. About the pleasure he was giving her. Pleasure that grew and grew until when he finally did take her she was thrown into a paroxysm of pleasure so intense that she thought she would faint.

When her whirling mind finally slowed enough for her to be aware of her surroundings again, she opened her eyes to find herself staring into his dark eyes.

"How now, wife?" he asked, and Margaret felt humiliated at his smug expression.

How could she have responded so wantonly? Her skin burned with shame, and she wanted to turn her head into the down pillow and sob out all her fears and uncertainties. She knew she couldn't stop him from making love to her, but in her mind, as long as she didn't enjoy it, it didn't seem so great a sin. But now she didn't even have that consolation, and for him to taunt her with it . . .

Her lower lip began to tremble in spite of her best efforts to contain her feelings. A tear of shame trickled out of her eye, running over her temple and dripping into her hair. She watched Philip's lips tighten in anger, and he jerked himself off her.

"You enjoyed that, madam, and don't try to deny it," he bit out.

Margaret made no attempt to deny it; she was too busy trying not to burst into tears.

"Women!" he muttered in frustration and, grabbing his robe, stalked naked from her room.

What the hell was the matter with her? he asked himself. Why did she cry? She'd enjoyed what they'd shared. The signs had been unmistakable. So why was she sniveling now?

He vented his frustration by slamming his bedroom door closed. Margaret Abney was the most contrary woman he had ever run across. Nothing she did or said was what he expected.

No, not Margaret Abney, he thought. Margaret Moresby. And she might be a bundle of contradictions, but she was his bundle of contradictions, and sooner or later he'd figure out the puzzle she represented. The thought gave him a great deal of satisfaction and he was able to ring for his bath with a feeling of vague anticipation.

Margaret shared neither his sense of satisfaction nor his anticipation. She felt as if she'd been pitchforked into a world that she couldn't control and couldn't even understand. Not any of it. Not why Philip behaved the way he did and most certainly not why she reacted to him the way she did.

Tiredly she got out of bed, not looking forward to the evening ahead. At the moment all she wanted to do was to crawl between the lavender-scented sheets and go to sleep. To forget all her problems.

But she couldn't. Philip wouldn't let her. She glanced at the door through which he'd disappeared, and shivered. If she didn't hurry, he might come back and . . .

She gulped, refusing to admit even to herself that a small part of her wanted him to do just that. To come back and take her back in his arms and kiss her again.

Determinedly she reached for her shift to cover her nakedness before she called for the maid to help her dress.

"You look that lovely, milady." Daisy sighed in admiration as she studied Margaret's ballgown. "And when you move, them diamonds sewed on it sparkle just like they was on fire."

"Not diamonds, just paste imitations." Margaret shuddered to think what the gown would have cost if they had been real. Its price had been outrageous enough. She and George could have lived for years on what this gown had cost.

"These, however, are not paste." Philip's unexpected voice from the connecting door made Daisy squeak in surprise while Margaret stiffened. She felt rather like a rabbit she'd once seen in a park in Paris who had frozen into immobility at the approach of a dog. At the time she'd thought it was a singularly inappropriate response to danger, but now she understood only too well the feeling of fear and confusion that had gripped the rabbit, holding it captive to indecision.

"Oh, milady, ain't they lovely!"

Margaret almost shuddered as she looked at the glittering rope of diamonds which hung from Philip's tanned fingers. Coming so soon after his lovemaking she felt as if she were being offered a bauble for her favors.

Which was nonsense, she told herself. In the first place, that glittering string of diamonds was no bauble. It represented a king's ransom, and, secondly, Philip had shown no tendency to placate her to date. It was highly unlikely that he meant to start now.

"Turn around," Philip ordered, and Margaret, under Daisy's interested gaze, had no option but to obey.

She felt the coldness of the necklace settle heavily against her skin, encircling her throat and making her feel trapped. As if the diamonds were a badge of ownership. Put there by Philip for all the world to see.

She trembled when his warm fingertips brushed against the fine hairs on the back of her neck as he fumbled with the fastener. Sharp little tremors spread from the contact, racing over her skin and dislodging memories that she would have preferred to remain buried. Memories of his fingers stroking sensuously over her skin. Memories of his fingertips gently tugging at her breasts until they tingled with desire.

Margaret bent her head and was horrified to see that her nipples were hard and pushing tightly against the thin silk of her gown.

What was the matter with her? she wondered in despair. How could her body operate so independently of her mind?

"That necklace looks a fair treat." Daisy threw into the silence. "Shaped like a bow on a present, it is."

"Yes." Margaret absently touched the center of the bow which contained the largest diamond she'd ever seen.

"That will be all, Daisy." Philip dismissed the maid, and Margaret watched her go, wishing she could escape as easily.

"You don't like the necklace, madam?" Philip's voice had an edge to it.

Margaret absently pushed back one of the curls that had escaped her Psyche knot as she tried to decide what to say.

Philip watched the movement of her slim fingers and felt his body stir as he remembered the intoxicating sensation of those soft fingers holding him during their wild ride to fulfillment.

His eyes dropped to the scant bodice of her dress, and he felt an urge to tug it down. It wouldn't take much to free her breasts. To expose them to his eyes and his hands.

He swallowed, forcing his gaze upward. He couldn't give in to the impulse. Not only was it necessary that they lobby for his bill at the Levangers' ball tonight, but he'd already committed a tactical error by bedding her earlier this evening. If he were to touch her again so soon, she might begin to suspect just how much he craved her. And she'd undoubtedly try to use the fact against him.

Not that she could win a battle between them, he assured himself, but the necessity of reasserting his superiority would take precious time and energy, which at the moment he didn't have.

"It's very pretty," Margaret finally said, in a tone of voice that made him want to shake her until her teeth rattled. What the hell *did* she get enthusiastic about? Besides that old fool Gilroy.

And books—he suddenly remembered the sparkle of anticipation she'd had in her eyes when she'd returned home carrying that stack of dusty volumes. Had her enthusiasm been feigned or had it been real? But if she'd just been acting, what could have been her purpose? The answer eluded him as did so many things about her, increasing his sense of unease and frustration.

"But?" he demanded when she fell silent.

"Well, it's just that . . . Like this dress—" She gestured down at the silvery gown and Philip's eyes followed the movement of her hand, falling no farther than the deeply cut bodice.

"It cost so much money." Margaret tried to make him understand. "A whole family could live a year on what this dress cost."

"And what of the dressmaker?"

"What dressmaker?"

"The one who makes a living selling it to you. And what of the seamstresses who sewed it and the merchants who provided the thread and those . . . things." He gestured toward the glittering spangles. "And what of the importer who brings in the silk and the sailors who sail his ships.

"If no one buys their goods, how are they to survive? Or pay taxes which help to feed the poor?"

Margaret opened her mouth and then closed it when she realized that she didn't have a ready answer for his argument. It was too unexpected. She'd never before thought of buying things in those terms.

"Shall we go, madam?" He held out his arm for her.

Reluctantly Margaret put her hand on his arm, shivering slightly at the feel of his hard muscles beneath the smooth cloth of his black jacket.

"I'm hoping that Morris will be at the ball so I can discuss my bill with him," Philip said.

Margaret stopped as she caught a glimpse of movement through the railings on the stairs to the nursery, and she suddenly remembered her own childhood. How she'd lain awake waiting for her mother to come in and show her finery whenever she had gone out in the evening. Perhaps Annabelle would like to see her dress.

Margaret decided to try. "Let's say good night to Annabelle before we must leave."

"Why?"

Because she's your daughter. Because you should be concerned about her. Because even if you aren't, you should at least pretend to be for the look of things. No, that argument wouldn't work; Margaret immediately dismissed her last thought. From what she'd observed, Philip was not a man who cared overly much what anyone else thought. Which was a very good thing because there were going to be a lot of raised eyebrows when his bill passed and he suddenly announced to the polite world that he wasn't really married after all.

"I want to show her my dress," Margaret finally said.

"Five minutes, no more." To her relief, Philip agreed. She didn't know why he had capitulated, nor did she much care. It was enough that he had.

By the time they reached the nursery Annabelle had retreated to the windowseat. She scowled when she saw them.

Margaret refused to be discouraged. She suspected that Annabelle's usual response to anyone was a scowl, as if she felt the need to reject people before they had a chance to reject her.

"Good evening, Annabelle. I came to show you my gown." Margaret held out her arms and twirled around to show off the dress.

"It doesn't have any ruffles like Grandmama's," Annabelle said, and then added, "I practiced on my chess."

"How did you do?" Margaret asked.

Annabelle made a face. "Grandmama said it wasn't a proper game for a lady, so I had to play myself and when you know what you're going to do, it's hard to win. Would you play me a game?"

"We are on our way out." Philip's immediate veto of the idea annoyed Margaret. Work on his precious bill could wait ten minutes.

"But we have time to start a game," Margaret said. She knew Philip would express his displeasure later, but it hardly mattered. He always seemed to be taking her to task about something or other. At least this time it would be for something worthwhile.

"I have the board set up." Annabelle hurried over to the small table set in front of the nursery fire.

"Philip, why don't you provide the opposition, and Annabelle can help me."

"As if you needed help!" Philip gave her a rueful grin that just for a moment made him look like someone else. Someone young and carefree. Someone she'd very much like to be better acquainted with. An illusion, she hastily reminded herself. And like all illusions, dangerous.

Margaret watched as Philip tried to fit himself into the child-sized chair.

"I like the knights best," Annabelle said. "Can I move one of them first?"

"A good rule of thumb for a beginner is to move several pawns before you bring the knights into the game," Margaret said.

"Why?" Philip asked. "You didn't when you played me."

Margaret gave him a bland smile. "But then I'm not a beginner."

"The only thing more ungentlemanly than a bad loser is a bad winner," Philip grumbled.

"And I'm not a gentleman!"

"No." Philip's eyes lingered on the creamy expanse of bosom that rose above her gown. "You most certainly aren't a gentleman."

A prickly sensation danced over Margaret's skin as she felt her breasts tightening in reaction. Quickly she bent over the board, trying to hide her instinctive reaction to him. He absolutely must not suspect just how unsettling she found him. It would only reinforce his view of her as being no better than a prostitute.

"Are we going to play?" Annabelle's aggrieved voice broke into Margaret's confused thoughts, and she latched on to the chess game as a lifeline.

"Yes. Before you make a move you should have a rough idea of what your next four moves will be," Margaret said.

"Why?" Annabelle demanded.

"Chess is a lot like war. You can't just blunder into the middle of a battle and hope to win," Margaret said.

"I know a lot of politicians who believe otherwise," Philip muttered.

Margaret ignored him. "You need to have a plan, Annabelle."

"That doesn't sound like much fun." Annabelle sounded doubtful.

"The fun comes in winning. In matching your wits against an opponent and trouncing him," Margaret said. "Now, why don't you try moving this pawn to here?"

Annabelle did.

Seven minutes later, Margaret announced victory. "We have him. It will take about six more moves, but his loss is inevitable."

"Really?" Annabelle looked closer at the board.

"No," Philip insisted. "I can still win."

"Only if I were to let you," Margaret said, "and I have too much respect for your intellect to do that."

"Grandmama says that a woman should never beat a man," Annabelle quoted.

"Since women are the weaker sex, they rarely have the opportunity," Philip said.

" 'Weaker' refers to strength of body, not mind." Margaret took exception to his comment. "I have seen no evidence that women are not as intelligent as men."

"Then you haven't been observing society much," Philip said.

"Society proves my point! Women have very little protection under the law so they manipulate men to make their lives a little more bearable."

As Roxanne had manipulated him? Philip wondered. No, he instinctively rejected the idea. She had had his protection. She hadn't had to worry about her position before the law. He'd even accepted . . . His mind shied away from the painful thought.

"I don't understand what you two are talking about," Annabelle complained.

"It doesn't matter." Philip got to his feet. "Your stepmother is wrong."

"Dogmatic statements are not an adequate substitute for reasoned argument," Margaret said.

"The subject is closed. We are due at the Levangers'."

Margaret stifled an urge to throw something at him. Something hard. How dare he announce that the subject was closed simply because he was losing the argument? Philip Moresby was the most aggravating man she had ever met. She turned to sweep out of the room and tripped over a toy on the floor.

Philip grabbed her arm and yanked her up against himself, steadying her. "What is the old saying about pride going before a fall?"

Margaret ignored him. "Good night, Annabelle. If you like, we can try another game of chess tomorrow."

"Maybe," Annabelle said cautiously, but Margaret was encouraged. Annabelle could have rejected her overture outright and she hadn't. She was definitely making progress with the child.

Thirteen

"Mrs. Smith said you talked to Ned this morning," Philip said, once they were in the carriage.

Margaret carefully examined his tone of voice for a clue to his reason for making the comment. She couldn't find one. His voice had sounded neutral. At least as neutral as Philip ever did when talking to her. Mostly he just seemed to be permanently annoyed with her. A faint feeling of regret feathered through her which she didn't understand. Why should she care if Philip viewed her as a thorn in his side to be endured? She wasn't going to be masquerading as his wife long enough for it to matter.

"Well?" His voice sharpened.

" 'Well' what?" Margaret asked. "You stated a fact. Are you asking me to comment on it?"

Margaret watched as Philip's lean features hardened in annoyance. "I'm asking you for the reason why you visited Ned."

"Because I'd already seen his wife."

"That may make sense to the female mind, but I find it a nonsequitur."

Margaret bit back a sharp comment. *A soft answer turneth away wrath,* she reminded herself. Not that she'd seen much evidence of it working with Philip, but she would prefer not to have him furious at the moment. Not with the Levangers' ball to be gotten through.

"Surely my question doesn't require so much thought? Or is it that you don't understand what 'nonsequitur' means?"

"No, sir." Margaret gave him an innocent look. "I was simply surprised that you did."

"What!" Philip howled, wincing when the surprised coachman jerked the horses' reins and the carriage rocked.

"As for your question, when I talked to Lorraine, she was worried about her husband, and I wanted to talk to him myself."

"She has no need to worry. I told her that I will take care of them."

"Tell me, Philip, how would you feel if you were to suddenly lose all your money and Lord Hendricks said, 'Don't worry about it, I'll make you my pensioner.' " Margaret nodded as she watched his eyes narrow in instant rejection of the idea. "Charity really is cold comfort."

"We aren't talking about me, we're talking about Ned."

"And, of course, since Ned is only a member of the lower classes, his feelings can't be compared to those of an earl's."

Philip frowned. "That is not at all to the point! Ned needs—"

"To regain his self-respect," Margaret said, wondering why she even bothered to argue with Philip. He wouldn't change. The aristocracy never did, even if this particular member of the aristocracy did have some concept of charity. But without the realization that the objects of his charity were real people with hopes and dreams similar to his own, Philip's charity was fatally flawed.

"Am I to understand that you are advocating allowing him to make his own way?"

"You don't understand a thing! I'm suggesting that you give him an opportunity to provide for his family by giving him a job that he can actually do."

"And what job might that be?"

His pseudoreasonable tone, as if he were humoring an idiot, made her furious. But even so, she was forced to admit that while his question might be couched in patronizing tones, it was a valid one.

What could Ned do to provide for his family? she wondered. He couldn't soldier, and he couldn't farm, the only two occupations that he knew anything about.

"I'm still waiting for an answer to my question."

"Manufacturing," Margaret finally said. "He could work in a factory that makes things."

"And where is he supposed to find a factory to employee him? With the high unemployment levels, a factory owner can hire able-bodied men. Why should he hire a cripple?"

"Then you'll just have to start up your own factory."

"*Factory!*" Philip repeated the word as if it were an obscenity. "I am an earl. I own land, not manufactories."

" 'The future is in factories,' " Margaret quoted an article she'd read in the *Times*.

"Balderdash!"

"Ned's future is in a factory."

"I don't know the first thing about factories."

"Go into partnership with someone who does."

"That is a simplistic solution to a complicated problem."

"No, that's a practical solution to Ned's problem, and, I would venture to say, a lot of other returning soldiers' as well."

How like a woman to ignore all the problems inherent in such an outrageous scheme, Philip thought sourly. *"Find a partner,"* she said. And where was he supposed to find this partner? He certainly didn't number factory owners among his acquaintances.

Although his man of business might know of someone. Old Blandings was as shrewd as could hold together. But even so . . . Philip winced at the thought of what his father would have said about his son allowing the Moresby name to be associated with trade.

The carriage came to a halt in front of the Levangers' mansion, and Philip allowed his thoughts to fade away. He'd worry about Margaret's idea later. For now he had to concentrate on lobbying for his bill.

Although first he should dance with Margaret, he decided. Just for appearances' sake. Just to make sure that the gossips didn't think that he was a complacent husband. Or a blind one. A shard of pain shot through him at the memory of Roxanne and his incredibe gullibility. *Never again,* he promised himself as he took Margaret's arm in a possessive grip and started toward the front door.

Margaret winced as his fingers closed tightly around her upper arm. She shot him a quick look, but his closed expression discouraged comment. It didn't bode well for an evening that she hadn't been looking forward to anyway.

At least George seemed happy enough in France. She reminded herself of the silver lining of her particular prison. And in the meantime she'd lobby just as hard as she could to get Philip's bill passed, because once it was, she could go back to her old life. Back to where everything was simpler and she understood the rules.

Squaring her shoulders she entered the mansion and prepared to endure the evening.

"Will there be anything else this morning, my lord?" Philip's valet asked.

"No, you may go," Philip said, his attention centered on the door that led to his wife's bedroom. His eyes flicked to the clock on his mantel. It was only nine o'clock, and they hadn't returned from the Levangers' ball until after two. Was Margaret still asleep?

A surge of warmth spiraled through him as his mind

obligingly pictured her lying in the middle of her bed, her golden hair tumbled across the white pillowcase and the flush of sleep adding a light pink gloss to her cheeks.

His breathing became constricted beneath the flood of memories that engulfed him. He could go into her room. After all, he'd resisted the impulse to do so last night when they'd gotten home. Despite the fact that he'd wanted to; no, not wanted—he faced the unpalatable truth—he'd craved her body. Craved it with a hunger that worried him.

But he'd managed to stifle his impulses. He took comfort in the fact. He'd turned his back on her and gone to his own room. He'd proved to himself that he was the one in control. And since he had proved it, he could safely go into her room this morning to find out what she had done last night to further his bill.

Hurrying through the connecting parlor, he quietly pushed open the door and stepped inside. Margaret was standing in front of the wardrobe, her arms twisted around behind her back and a peevish expression on her face.

"What are you doing?" Philip asked.

Margaret jerked at the unexpected sound of his voice. She viewed him nervously, wondering what he wanted. A sudden flush burned across her cheekbones as she remembered the last time he'd been in her room and what had happened. But that had been just last night. Surely it was too soon for him to repeat the act.

How often did a man make love to a woman, anyway? she wondered. She had absolutely no idea, and it was hardly the kind of question she could ask someone.

"It would appear, madam wife, that you should still be in bed since you clearly aren't awake yet."

Margaret's flush deepened at the word "bed," and she rushed into speech to try to divert him.

"I am indeed awake. Your sudden appearance simply startled me.

"Where is your maid?"

"I don't need a maid to get dressed." Margaret surreptitiously tried to reach the buttons at the back of her gown.

"You weren't doing very well when I came in. Turn around."

"Around?"

"I'll fasten your gown for you."

"That isn't necessary, I can—"

"Turn around."

For a brief moment, Margaret debated saying no, but her innate good sense quickly pointed out the futility of refusing. Her best course of action would be to let him fasten the dress and hope that he'd go.

Reluctantly she turned around, shivering as she felt his fingers brush against her back. Tiny rivulets of sensation skated over her skin, raising goose bumps as he pulled the two edges of her gown together. The material stretched tightly over her breasts, rubbing across their sensitive tips.

To her relief, he was quick and she hurriedly stepped back.

Philip felt a surge of anger at her haste to escape. As if there was something wrong with his touch.

He turned slightly, and his gaze lit on the letter lying on her bedside table.

Gilroy's letter. He suddenly remembered that while he might have gone into her room last night to talk about it, they certainly hadn't finished that discussion.

"You are not to have any correspondence with Gilroy. I will write and tell him that you are well," he added, on the off chance that Gilroy really was her cousin.

"Even God doesn't get blind obedience to His dictates!" Margaret said, knowing that it was imperative that she write to George. If she didn't, he would worry, and if he started to worry he might take it in his head to escape and come looking for her. She barely repressed a shudder at the thought of the scandal that would result if George were to find her masquerading as Philip's wife.

"You are not to write to anyone without my permission! Do you hear me?"

"Yes, and no doubt the entire household can, too." Margaret wanted to thump him hard enough to dent his unfailing belief that his was the only viewpoint that mattered.

"It's my house and if I want to yell, I will! And you are my wife and will do what I say."

Crumpling the letter in his hand, he flung it into the fireplace and stalked out of the room.

Wearily Margaret rubbed her forehead, which was beginning to ache. A fight on top of last night's late hours was the final straw. Not that she could precisely call their encounter a fight, she thought wryly. A fight suggested that both parties were able to inflict damage and the only damage she'd inflicted, was to Philip's temper and it was so uncertain that it was hardly an accomplishment.

"Is he gone?"

Margaret looked up to see Annabelle nervously posed in the open hall doorway as if she were trying to decide whether to come or go.

"If you mean your father, yes, he's gone."

"He sounded mad at you."

"Did he?" Margaret said, not sure what she should say. Annabelle might be a child, but she was certainly old enough to recognize anger when she heard it.

Annabelle edged a little farther into the room. "Uh-huh. He yells at me all the time. Why did he yell at you?"

"We had a slight difference of opinion."

"Grandmama says that only men are allowed to have opinions. Women are supposed to agree. But I don't see why only boys should get to have an opinion. I'm just as good as any old boy," Annabelle burst out.

"You're preaching to the converted."

"What?" Annabelle looked blankly at her.

"I mean you don't have to convince me. I already believe you."

"Oh." Annabelle allowed her gaze to roam around the bedroom. "This room gives me the dismals. Grandmama says that no one has done a thing in here since my other grandmama came here as a bride."

"Other grandmama?" Margaret asked, not sure what Annabelle meant. Hadn't this room been the beauteous Roxanne's?

"You know. Papa's mama. She died when I was little. This was her room. Grandmama says that my mama and papa and me lived in a smaller house when Grandmama was still alive. Grandmama says that it wasn't right. That papa was the earl, and he should have demanded that his mother move out of this house, but he wouldn't."

Margaret sorted through the various grandmamas, her spirits rising as she realized what Annabelle was saying. The incomparable Roxanne had never lived in this house. But why? If Philip had been as besotted with Roxanne as everyone kept telling her, then why hadn't he moved his mother out so that his bride could have the bigger home? Unless it had been Estelle who had wanted her daughter to live here, and Roxanne had been content to follow Philip's wishes?

"Why don't you change things?" Annabelle asked. "Grandmama says that Papa's rich as Croesus and that whatever else he is, he isn't mean. I could help you."

"And I would appreciate your help, but I think I'd better wait until your papa is in a better mood to ask. Although you could help me decide what kind of governess to hire."

Annabelle scowled. "They's all the same, and what does it matter, 'cause they never stay very long."

"I hope the one we hire stays long enough to teach you to read so that you'll be able to read the poetry the young men will no doubt write to you."

"Did your beaux write poetry to you?"

"No, but I was not an earl's daughter like you."

"Yes, I am," Annabelle said with a smug satisfaction, before she turned and raced back up the stairs to the nursery.

Margaret watched her go, trying to understand their encounter. It would appear that misery really did love company, since the fact that the earl yelled at his wife, too, made the daughter sympathetic. No, not precisely *sympathetic,* Margaret amended. Simply less antagonistic. But that was a distinct improvement over being the object of the child's temper tantrums. Now if she could just find a good governess who could continue her work once she was gone.

Thoughtfully Margaret made her way downstairs to the breakfast room.

"Ah, so there you are. Tell me, was Chadwick very angry over my mentioning your letter last night?" Estelle demanded from behind the remains of her meal.

"Not at all. Just coffee, please," Margaret addressed the footman who was standing by the sideboard.

"Really? But Philip was furious when he left the house just a few minutes ago. Why, the expression on his face made me shiver."

Margaret bit back the urge to say something very rude. It was bad enough that she had to deal with Philip and his unfathomable moods, but having to listen to them replayed by Estelle was outside of enough.

"Which newspaper should I use to place an advertisement for a governess?" Margaret determinedly changed the subject.

"Governess!"

"I fail to understand why the mention of what is an unexceptional occupation should elicit such a response." Margaret added sugar to her coffee and took a revving sip.

"We had a governess," Estelle insisted.

"The past tense being the operative word."

"Huh?" Estelle peered at her.

Margaret swallowed a sigh. There were times in this household when she felt as if she were speaking a foreign language. The only one who understood her was Philip, and his understanding went no deeper than the words she used.

"I meant that Annabelle needs a governess now. Are you aware that the child can't read."

Estelle bristled, sensing criticism of herself. "Annabelle isn't clever like some people, and it isn't kind to tease her about what she can't change."

"Miss Mainwaring has arrived and is in the sitting room." Compton's announcement that Drusilla had come for their rendezvous with Mr. Daniels came as a welcome relief to Margaret.

Today, after a lifetime of being able to do nothing more than dream about revenge against Mainwaring, she was finally going to be able to take the first step toward her goal.

"Thank you, Compton. Would you know which paper I should use to place an advertisement for a governess for Lady Annabelle?"

"I venture to say that you might find some likely candidates from the employment agency which Mrs. Smith uses."

"Fine." Margaret ignored Estelle's snort of annoyance. "If you would please inform the agency of our need."

"Certainly, my lady." Compton nodded and withdrew.

Margaret hurriedly drank her coffee and then got to her feet, eager to set her plan in motion.

"What is the Mainwaring chit doing visiting at this hour?" Estelle said.

"I mentioned to her that I sorely missed the chance to

take exercise in London, and Miss Mainwaring very kindly offered to show me a place to walk in the park."

"Walk!" Estelle stared at Margaret.

"A most unexceptional pastime," Margaret said, wondering if walking was on the seemingly endless list of proscribed activities for women.

"But you might . . ." Estelle glanced toward the door to make sure no servant was close enough to overhear and then whispered, "Perspire!"

Margaret stared at her in confusion. What did Estelle think the housemaids did when they cleaned up the messes she created, or the cook who stood over a hot stove all day long? Or was it only the ton who weren't suppose to descend to human reactions?

"I will bear the danger in mind." Margaret dropped her napkin on the table and made her escape.

"Oh, Cousin Margaret." Drusilla jumped to her feet, her slender face aglow with eagerness as Margaret entered the salon. "I am here as I said I would be. And I didn't have to bring my maid. I told Papa that I was going to go walking in Hyde Park with you, and he said in that case you would be chaperone enough. Papa worries so about me."

Margaret glanced down to hide the spark of anger she felt at the reminder of just how differently Mainwaring had treated his two daughters.

"Mama says that it is because my poor brother Andrew is such a worry."

"Andrew?" The question popped out even though Margaret hadn't meant to ask it. She didn't want to know about what problems Andrew might have. She had enough of her own. And she'd never be likely to meet him anyway. Children rarely appeared in society, and she would be gone long before he was old enough to be out. Margaret squashed the faint frisson of something unsettling that flittered through her mind at the thought.

"Poor dear Andrew. He is the very best of brothers, but he is so frail. Mama says that she despaired of him when he was a baby. It's his lungs, you see." Drusilla's soft face looked pained at the thought.

"He has so much trouble breathing. Sometimes he just gasps for breath, and it is so frightening." Drusilla shivered. "He turns blue and sometimes he passes out. Mama says that she had an older brother just like that, but that he died when he was still a boy."

"How frightful," Margaret said. It would appear that along with a respectable dowry and an impeccable name, Hendricks's choice of bride had also brought a tendency to illness. The thought immediately faded, leaving her feeling thoroughly ashamed of herself. It was one thing to plot revenge against a man who deserved every indignity she could heap upon his head, and quite another to take satisfaction in the sufferings of a young boy who had no more choice about his father than she had had.

"My groom is waiting outside to drive us to the park," Drusilla said. "We don't want to be late because I told Mr. Daniels to meet us there on the walkway. That way it will seem as if our meeting is accidental."

"Then we must leave." Margaret rang for her pelisse and bonnet and when they came, followed Drusilla out of the house.

Drusilla's groom was sitting in the carriage in front of the house, shivering in the brisk wind that blew down the street.

"He looks chilled." Margaret murmured her thoughts aloud as she pulled her pelisse a little closer around her shoulders.

Drusilla looked around the empty square. "Who does?"

"Your groom."

"I doubt he is cold," Drusilla said, as the footman leapt down from the back of the carriage to lower the steps for them. "Papa says that the lower orders aren't as sensitive as we are."

Margaret bit back an angry comment on what she thought of Mainwaring's opinion. She knew from bitter experience just how cold the so-called lower orders could get. But she wasn't about to change Drusilla's way of thinking, and to try to might put her on her guard and thus make it impossible for Margaret to gain her ends.

Margaret climbed into the luxurious carriage and leaned back against the soft, leather squabs, allowing Drusilla's peon of praise about the incomparable Mr. Daniels to flow over her head as she tried to imagine what Drusilla would be like if she had been the one born a bastard. Her imagination failed her. There wasn't enough substance to Drusilla to imagine her in any other role than that of a cherished, indulged daughter.

Margaret shuddered at the memory of the slum that she and her mother had been living in when George miraculously appeared to rescue them. The damp and the cold and the scarcity of food probably would have killed poor Andrew. But then, if Andrew had been born a bastard, Mainwaring wouldn't have cared if he had lived or died; he certainly hadn't cared if she and her mother had.

Margaret frowned as she remembered the viciousness in his voice when he'd told her mother that he'd supported her for thirteen years, and he wasn't going to support her one second longer. It had almost seemed to Margaret that he'd wanted them to die.

"There! There he is!"

Drusilla's excited voice cut into Margaret's tangled thoughts, and she obediently looked where Drusilla was pointing.

She saw a tall, well-proportioned man wearing a forester green double-breasted coat over lilac pantaloons.

"Isn't he the most fashionable man you have ever seen? I vow he quite puts all other men into the shade. And his person . . ." Drusilla sighed in pleasure. "My particular friend, Emily, says that he is the handsomest man she has ever seen, and that if he didn't already love me she would try to attach him herself!"

Margaret stared at the man, automatically comparing him to Philip. Where Philip exuded a quiet elegance, Mr. Daniels's choice of colors seemed to assault the eye. And his mincing steps as he made his way toward their carriage made her want to giggle. He walked as if his pants were too tight to allow him to take a normal step.

But just because Mr. Daniels subscribed to a more flamboyant style of fashion didn't make him less of a man for it, Margaret told herself as she allowed the footman to help her out of the carriage. Simply because she found him laughable didn't mean that he was. And the fact that Philip fitted her ideal of masculinity didn't mean that his behavior did.

"Cousin Margaret, allow me to make known to you Mr. Daniels. Mr. Daniels, this is my cousin, the Countess of Chadwick, who I'm sure will stand our friend."

"Charmed." Mr. Daniels gave her a wide smile that displayed his perfect white teeth to advantage. "The whole world is agog with curiosity over Chadwick's new bride.

"That you would play friend to Drusilla and me is more than I could have hoped for."

Margaret felt a moment's unease when her gaze encountered his flat brown eyes. They were hard. Hard and calculating, as if he were sizing her up and trying to decide how she could best be used to his advantage.

You're imagining things, she told herself. *Simply because you are indulging in subterfuge and intrigue doesn't mean that everyone else is.*

Margaret tugged her fingers free of his grip and gave him a vague smile. "Ah, but how could I not be Drusilla's friend when she told me how Gothic her father was being!

Why, I must be the happiest woman in London since my marriage, and I would have every woman know such happiness."

"How true." Mr. Daniels gave an arm to each lady. "I shall be the envy of every man who sees me escorting two such exquisite flowers of femininity."

Drusilla blushed enchantingly, but Daniels's fulsome compliment left Margaret unmoved. Much as she disliked aspects of Philip's behavior, at least he didn't insult her with meaningless flattery.

Cautiously she glanced around Mr. Daniels's surprisingly broad chest to look at Drusilla. She was staring at him as if he were the font of all wisdom. Clearly Drusilla found his type of conversation enthralling. But then, she already knew that Drusilla liked Mr. Daniels—it was her father who didn't.

Why? Margaret wondered. Because Daniels didn't have enough money? Or did Mainwaring also look in Daniels's eyes and see the calculation there? Margaret hastily dismissed the thought. She didn't want to have anything in common with her natural father, not even a conclusion. And what Daniels was really like, didn't matter in the slightest to her plans. All that mattered was that Mainwaring didn't want him for Drusilla, and that thwarting Mainwaring would be the biggest blow to his pride Margaret could ever hope to deliver.

Fourteen

They had finished their walk along the deserted park pathway and were almost back to Drusilla's carriage when Drusilla came to a sudden halt.

"Oh, dear, look there, Cousin Margaret," Drusilla said.

Margaret looked, to find Lord Hendricks sitting in his curricle beside Drusilla's parked carriage, talking to her groom.

"I must not monopolize your time, Miss Mainwaring, for I have not the right, although I pray that that will soon change," Daniels said to Drusilla, in a caressing tone that made Margaret want to giggle. The man sounded as if he'd been plucked whole from the pages of one of Maria Edgeworth's novels.

Margaret tried to imagine Philip using that sort of unctuous voice and failed miserably. Or sharing Daniels's sentiment. A reluctant smile curved her lips. If Philip wanted to monopolize someone's time, he'd do it and rights be damned.

"Until this evening, Miss Mainwaring, my heart will count the very seconds that I am apart from you," Daniels said.

Margaret glanced at Drusilla to find her staring at Mr. Daniels with a soulful look that would not have been out of place on a faithful hound. The more Margaret became acquainted with Drusilla, the harder she found it to believe that she was Drusilla's half-sister. They were nothing alike. Even when she was Drusilla's age she never would have believed the drivel Daniels was spouting.

But what would she have been like if her mother really had been married to Mainwaring, and they had come to London with him after he'd inherited the title? Margaret wondered. Would she have grown up to be like Drusilla? It was a sobering thought to which Margaret didn't have an answer. But one thing she did know was that she never would have been allowed to continue her studies which meant so much to her. It had been obvious to her even when she was a child, that scholarship was not only something Mainwaring didn't value, it was something he positively mistrusted. No, if she and her mother had gone to London with Mainwaring, she would have been forced into the mold of a society miss. She probably would have been married off to someone chosen by Mainwaring to fit his narrow definition of an acceptable son-in-law. One who had both money and social position.

"Oh, Cousin Margaret!" Drusilla said, as she watched Daniels walk away. "Is he not everything I claimed? Every night when I say my prayers I thank the good Lord for my incredible luck that Mr. Daniels should return my regard. I don't know what I have done to deserve such happiness."

What indeed? Margaret wondered with a nagging sense of unease.

"Good morning, Margaret. Miss Mainwaring." Lord Hendricks greeted them.

Margaret smiled at him, finding to her surprise that she didn't have to force it.

"Good morning, Papa. What brings you to the park so early?"

"Happy chance, as it turns out. May I offer you both a turn in my carriage?"

"Thank you, Lord Hendricks, but it is getting late and

I must be returning home," Drusilla said. "We only descended the carriage to . . . to take the air. But now I must hurry home because the dressmaker is coming to give me a fitting for my presentation dress, and she becomes out-of-reason cross if she is kept waiting.

"She's French, you know," Drusilla added by way of an explanation. "Papa says that foreigners never know their place."

Firmly beneath his heel, no doubt! Margaret thought.

"In that case allow me to convey Lady Chadwick home," Hendricks said.

"That's fine, we've already seen . . . I mean . . ." Drusilla faltered to a stop, her cheeks a brilliant pink.

". . . That our delightful outing is already at an end," Margaret rescued her. "Good day, Cousin Drusilla. I trust I shall see you this evening at the Carringtons' ball."

"Oh yes." Drusilla sighed, and her features took on a beatific expression, reminding Margaret of a Botticelli angel. "Till tonight." She clamored into her carriage without so much as a smile at the patiently waiting groom.

"Can you climb up yourself, my dear?" Hendricks asked. "If I get down to help you, this pair might bolt. They are very fresh."

"Certainly." Margaret nimbly climbed into the seat. "Just between the two of us, it is a myth that the female of the species is helpless."

Hendricks chuckled, tightening the reins as Margaret settled her skirts around her. "That, my dear, must be the most badly kept secret in the world. Although . . ." He glanced thoughtfully at Drusilla's disappearing carriage. "I would venture to say that not all women are competent. Young Miss Mainwaring, for example."

"Oh?" Margaret tried to keep her tone neutral. She most definitely did not want Hendricks curious about her association with Drusilla. He was far too shrewd. "She is very young," Margaret said. "I doubt that she has had much opportunity to develop competence in any area. But that is not to say that she won't in the future."

"She'll need to, if she continues to encourage Daniels. Tell me, was the meeting with him today prearranged?"

"I doubt it, since going for a walk in the park was my idea." Margaret stretched the truth to the breaking point.

"I see." Hendricks checked the heavy traffic and then sent the carriage out of the park into the street. "I feel I must warn you about Mr. Daniels, my dear, since you don't have a great deal of experience with London society, and you have a kind heart which might lead you into difficulties."

Margaret mentally squirmed at his description. Kind heart! If only he knew just how very unkind she could be. How unkind she was already being to him. And how she was planning to use Drusilla to revenge herself on her natural father.

But she was only giving Drusilla what she wanted, and as for Hendricks, she hadn't had any choice. Not really. It was him or George, and, much as she was coming to like and respect Hendricks, she loved George. Loved him and owed him more than she could ever repay.

"If Miss Mainwaring imagines herself in love with Daniels, don't let her draw you into her schemes," Hendricks continued. "Mainwaring will never countenance his daughter's marriage with a penniless provincial. No respectable father would."

She was reminded of how his narrow viewpoint had been the indirect cause of her mother's fall from what she had thought was a respectable marriage, and her abrupt descent into abject poverty, which effectively banished Margaret's feelings of remorse. Acceptable husbands in the eyes of the ton were those who had the twin blessings of birth and fortune. Nothing else mattered. Daniels had to have birthright or he wouldn't be invited anywhere, which meant that what he lacked was money—the cardinal sin to men like Mainwaring and Hendricks.

"Tell me what brings you to the park this morning." Margaret deliberately changed the subject.

"I was escaping from the bombast in the House of Lords. One thing I had forgotten during the years I spent at my estate is the ability of so many of the members to speak at such great length and say absolutely nothing. I was hoping that a brisk run in the fresh air would help me to regain my equanimity.

"Ah, here we are." Hendricks pulled up in front of Philip's house.

"Would you care to come in for tea?" Margaret asked. "The footman can drive your team around to the stables while you're here."

"Thank you, my dear, but I have an appointment with Norfolk shortly, and it wouldn't do to be late. Not when I'm the one seeking support."

"Good-bye." Margaret climbed down from the carriage seat, being careful not to catch her skirt on the wheel. "Will I see you at the Carringtons' affair tonight?"

"Yes."

Margaret suddenly shivered as a gust of wind slithered up her skirts.

"In you go, and take care to have a warm cup of tea," Hendricks said. "You don't want to come down with a chill."

Margaret waved as she watched him drive away, warmed by his concern even though she knew full well that it wasn't her he was worried about; it was the woman he thought she was—Mary Hendricks.

"Good morning, my lady," Compton greeted her as he opened the door. "As you requested, I sent a message to the employment agency Mrs. Smith favors, about a governess, and they say that they have two likely candidates on their books at the moment who will present themselves for interviews at your convenience."

Margaret blinked in surprise. "They are very prompt."

"They would be eager to place a governess in the Earl of Chadwick's household," Compton said. "They would hope that by giving satisfaction, your ladyship would mention them favorably to women of your acquaintance."

Margaret nodded. That seemed reasonable to her.

"Please tell the agency that I would like to interview the applicants late tomorrow morning."

"Certainly, my lady. Also, the earl is at home."

Margaret felt the sudden tightening of her nerves.

They tensed still further when she heard Philip's voice behind her.

"There you are," Philip said.

Margaret turned to find him standing in the study door. Her eyes skimmed over his lean body to linger on the lines of his face, looking for a clue to his mood. She couldn't find one.

"Come into the study." Philip stepped aside.

Margaret hurried into the room, and Philip shut the door behind her.

"I have been considering your idea that I go into trade," he said.

Margaret braced herself, expecting to get a lecture on the dignity of being a peer, and never mind that the vast majority of English peers behaved in the most undignified manner.

The thought struck her, that although Philip might resort to blackmail, he wasn't undignified. The thought brought her no comfort. Undignified would be a whole lot easier to deal with than Philip's ruthlessness.

"I discussed the idea with my man-of-business on my way home from trying to talk sense into that beef-witted fool." His voice unconsciously hardened.

"And which beef-witted fool might that be?"

A sudden smile curved his mouth, and Margaret felt her stomach lurch at the glint of humor reflected in his eyes. He looked so different when he smiled. Younger and carefree. As if . . .

As if she were indulging in a fantasy. She yanked her imagination up short. Smiling or not, Philip was the same person, and that person had goals diametrically opposed to hers.

"The beef-witted fool in question is Salferton," Philip said. "Sometimes I feel as if I could get more response talking to my mother's collection of jade animals. They, at least, are pleasing to look at."

Margaret bit her lip at his frustrated expression. Knowing that nothing she could say would ease his frustration, she decided to try distracting him from his problems for a while.

"I will be interviewing candidates for the position of Annabelle's governess tomorrow morning," Margaret said.

Philip frowned. "I pay her grandmother handsomely to take care of details like that."

"Simply because you pay someone, doesn't mean that they are doing a good job. Are you aware of the fact that Annabelle is functionally illiterate? And that Estelle is content to ignore the situation?"

"Estelle is her grandmother," Philip said.

"And you are her father."

Philip stared at her for a seemingly endless moment and then said, "No."

The flatly uttered word seemed to hang in the air between them. *No?* Margaret examined it, not understanding what he was referring to.

"No, I am not her father," Philip elaborated.

Margaret blinked, completely taken aback. Did he really mean he wasn't Annabelle's father? Or did he mean . . .

Mean what? She'd seen no evidence that he ever indulged in philosophical flights of fancy.

Margaret stared uncertainly at him. His lean face appeared sharply etched, as if every muscle in it were clenched. His lips were pressed together, and there was a tiny muscle twitching along his jawline, as if there were violent emotions seething just beneath the surface struggling desperately to get out. And his eyes . . .

Instinctively she took a step back, shocked at the bleakness in his dark eyes. He looked as if he were dealing with a pain so intense it threatened to rip him apart. None of this made any sense. Why would Philip believe that Annabelle wasn't his?

"Why do you say that?" She voiced the question. Much as she would have preferred to simply ignore his unexpected revelation, she couldn't, for Annabelle's sake. No one knew better than she the results of being denied by your father. She wouldn't wish that on any child.

"Because it's true, dammit!"

Margaret focused on the bridge of his straight nose, trying not to see the pain in his eyes or the tension in his face. They were too distracting, raising emotions she didn't quite understand.

No, she amended honestly, she understood them perfectly. She wanted to put her arms around him and comfort him. She wanted to erase his pain. What she didn't understand was why she should feel that way. After the way he had treated her, she shouldn't care how he felt. In fact, she should be happy that he felt so miserable. It served him right for forcing her into a bogus marriage.

Worry about it later, she told herself. *For now, find out as much as you can about the situation.*

"Your saying something doesn't make it true," she finally said.

Philip gave her smile that owed nothing to humor. "Truth? What would any woman know of truth?"

"You have already beaten that horse to death! Try another line of reasoning. One that contains a few facts."

Philip turned and walked across the room to the window. Grabbing the curtain, he yanked it aside and stared down blindly at the street below.

Why wouldn't she just accept what he said? Why did she have to keep digging and digging until she had the whole sordid story out of him? Why wasn't she like most women, who were happy to ignore the unpleasant things in life as long as they were given a plentiful supply of money?

He rubbed his fingers over his forehead, feeling the headache which had been nibbling at his composure all day, intensifying under the strength of his emotions.

Making up his mind, Philip swung around to face her.

"You want facts. How about this one? Annabelle was born on April eighteenth, but I was in France on a mission during the entire months of June, July, and August the previous year."

Which meant . . . Margaret mentally counted back from April, feeling a chill course over her.

"But Annabelle could have come early." She instinctively rejected his conclusion. "Lots of babies are early."

"She weighted almost nine pounds."

"But . . ." Margaret struggled to integrate his shocking revelation with what she thought she had known. Everyone had been at such pains to tell her how besotted with Roxanne Philip had been. Although, simply because Philip had loved Roxanne didn't mean that she had reciprocated his feelings.

"Have I finally managed to reduce you to silence?"

"But why would Roxanne have had an affair at a time when, if she were to become enceinte, it would be obvious that you couldn't be the father?"

"Not all women are as devious as you."

"I'm not talking about deviousness. I'm talking about common sense. Or self-protection, if you prefer."

"No, I don't prefer! I prefer to forget the whole thing!"

"And if wishes were horses, then beggars would ride," Margaret quoted.

"Spare me the platitudes!"

"All right, no platitudes. Just facts. You believe Annabelle is not your daughter."

"I know Annabelle is not my daughter. I hadn't touched Roxanne since the day I returned to England and discovered that the woman I trusted had made a cuckold of me."

Margaret winced at the echo of the torment she could hear in his voice. Roxanne's infidelity must have been a terrible blow to his pride. And to have Annabelle as a constant reminder around his home . . .

Margaret sighed. It really was ironic. She was Mainwaring's daughter, but he refused to acknowledge her because she was illegitimate, while Annabelle wasn't Philip's daughter and yet he had to acknowledge her because he'd been married to her mother.

"But why did Roxanne have an affair?" Margaret asked.

"You think I haven't asked myself that question time and time again?" His hands clenched into fists. "Besides, what difference does it make? She did it."

"Yes." Margaret said slowly, inexplicably feeling a sense of sadness for the unknown Roxanne. She had had everything a woman could want—a husband who adored her, social position, more money than she could ever spend—and she had thrown it all away. All that remained of her was a small daughter left in the unwilling care of the man she had rejected so humiliatingly.

Margaret took a deep breath preparing to fight for that child. "Roxanne's sins don't justify your behavior to Annabelle."

"Justify! I do not have to justify myself to anyone."

"More's the pity! Think, Philip. A great deal of Roxanne's . . ." Margaret groped for a word. ". . . problem, must have been due to the way Estelle raised her, and yet you've given the rearing of Annabelle to her, guaranteeing that she will visit her mistakes on yet another generation. As far as the world is concerned, Annabelle is your daughter. So be a father to her."

"A father . . ." Philip sputtered to an outraged stop.

"Why not?" Margaret refused to back down. "I could understand your reluctance if she were a boy and would inherit your title, but she isn't. She's a girl. In time she'll marry and leave you. Why should she spend her whole life looking back on the man she thinks is her father, with hate and loathing?" Margaret's voice rose with the suppressed memory of her own bitterness, but Philip was too caught up in his own emotions to notice.

"It's impossible!"

"It seems to me that you're willing to make all kinds of sacrifices for the soldiers, and yet you won't make any for a defenseless child. Or is it that what Roxanne really injured was your pride, and that Annabelle is a living reminder that you aren't omnipotent? That you can't control everyone?"

Margaret instinctively took a step backward as Philip raised his hand. His face was set in hard, unyielding lines. There was a deep flush high on his cheekbones and his eyes glittered with the force of his rage. Margaret held her breath, praying he'd regain control of his temper before he did something she'd regret.

To her relief, he suddenly turned and stalked to the door wrenching it open with a squeak of its protesting hinges.

Margaret collapsed into a chair as he slammed the door behind him with enough force to make the windowpanes rattle. She leaned her head back and took a deep breath, trying to still her racing heart. She hoped she never saw a man so angry again. For one scary moment she feared that he would actually strike her.

But why was he so angry? Roxanne had been dead for years. Why was he still so affected emotionally by what had happened? Could it be that despite what Roxanne had done, he still loved her?

Margaret found it a disquieting thought.

Fifteen

Philip stifled a curse as the carriage wheel lurched into a hole as it approached the Carringtons' mansion. He pressed his forefinger against his temple, trying to ease his growing headache. It didn't help. It continued to throb with a relentless pressure.

He couldn't be ill, he told himself. He had far too much to do to take to his bed. Even if it did seem like an attractive proposition at the moment.

And it would be an even more attractive proposition if he were to take Margaret along for company. He glanced across the carriage at her. She was staring out the carriage window at the dark streets. His eyes slowly traced over a single curl which had escaped the knot on top of her head to nestle against the slight hollow beneath her ear.

An unexpected spurt of desire filled him as he remembered the delicious scent of roses which clung to her skin when he'd nuzzled that same ear. He tensed, trying to control the growing heaviness that filled him at the provocative memory.

Yes, he'd be more than willing to take to his bed if he could be sure of having Margaret there with him to while away the time.

First, he'd pull her into his arms and then he'd . . . His eyes drifted down over her body with the same intensity with which he'd studied the dessert course when he was young. She seemed to be composed of hundreds of delectable parts, each created expressly for his enjoyment.

A momentary sense of satisfaction filled him as he remembered the intense pleasure he'd felt as he drove himself into her soft body only to find that it had never yielded to a man's passion before. But just because she hadn't taken a lover before, didn't mean that she might not in the future.

The pain in his head intensified as he remembered his shock and horror when he'd returned to London to find that his bride had cuckolded him. Remembered Roxanne's insouciant expression when he'd finally found the courage to tax her with her perfidy after Annabelle had been born. Remembered how she'd allowed the green silk negligee she'd been wearing to slip provocatively off her lush shoulders. Remembered how she'd smiled at him and told him that it was all his fault for leaving her alone while he had harried off to France to fight some stupid little war. Remembered how she'd claimed that it didn't matter anyway because it wasn't as if Annabelle were a male who would inherent his title.

And Margaret had said much the same thing when she'd urged him to embrace Roxanne's bastard as his own. Was that the way all women thought?

"Does no woman have a sense of honor?" Philip only realized that he'd spoken aloud when Margaret answered him.

"Is that a rhetorical question?" she asked, trying to read his expression in the dim light of the carriage lamp. What she saw wasn't promising. His face was taut and pinched-looking, as if he were laboring under some kind of strong emotion. Or illness. She frowned, remembering how flushed he'd been at dinner. Short-tempered, too, although at the time, she'd assumed that his snappishness was a remnant of their earlier argument. But now she wasn't so sure.

"Never mind," Philip said.

"Are you ill?" Margaret asked.

"I am never ill." He spoiled his dogmatic pronouncement with a violent sneeze.

Margaret wisely held her tongue. She knew from nursing George that even the kindest of men became irritable when they were ill. And she would hardly describe Philip as kind. Her eyes narrowed as she remembered poor Annabelle. A kind man would take the child to his heart. Especially after Roxanne was safely dead. But he hadn't.

And yet he had brought Ned and his wife into his own home, refusing either to leave them on the street or to give them a few coins and forget them. And, from what Lorraine had told her earlier that evening, Philip was sending them to his estate the following morning in his own carriage when he simply could have bought them tickets on the stage—behavior that could on the surface at least be called kind.

Philip must be the most complex person she had ever encountered. His behavior defied easy explanation.

Their carriage came to a stop when it finally reached the Carringtons' front door and, after making their way through the receiving line, they were free to go into the ballroom.

Margaret glanced around the crowded room, searching for Drusilla.

"Who are you looking for?" Philip asked.

"Someone to talk to about your bill," Margaret lied.

Philip grimaced. "I doubt that it will do much good. I've been talking for months now, and I swear I haven't changed a single mind."

Margaret felt a flash of disquiet at his discouraged expression. Admitting the possibility of defeat wasn't like Philip. Usually he was positive about everything. Even when he was positively wrong. Perhaps he really was sickening for something? Uncertainly she studied the hectic flush coloring his lean cheekbones. Was it deeper than it had been at dinner?

How Philip felt wasn't any concern of hers, she told herself. It wouldn't be long before she would be gone from his life, and she didn't have the slightest doubt that once she was gone he would forget her within the week.

The thought unexpectedly chilled her, and she wanted a few minutes alone to regain her composure, something she seemed to be continually losing around Philip.

"I need to visit the ladies' retiring room," she said, choosing the one place where she could be sure he wouldn't follow her.

To her relief he merely nodded and she rushed away.

"Lady Chadwick, how good to see you again!" A pudgy middle-aged woman with an improbable purple turban accosted her outside the retiring room.

Margaret gave her a polite smile as she scrambled to put a name to the woman. She couldn't. Which was hardly surprising. She excused her lapse. She had met hundreds of people since she'd come to London and with a few exceptions there had been little to distinguish one from another.

"I saw you come in and wondered where dear Estelle is?" the woman gushed.

Mrs. Wooster. Margaret was finally was able to identify the woman with the added clue. This was the woman who had been taking tea with Estelle the afternoon of her arrival in London.

"She will be here later," Margaret said. "She wanted to put in an appearance at a friend's musicale first."

"The Fanshaws'. The music will be uninspired."

"It can hardly matter," Margaret said, "since at the one musicale I attended, the guests talked throughout the entire performance."

"And the refreshment will be insipid." Mrs. Wooster ignored the interruption. "The Fanshaws are all-to-pieces.

One more bad run at the faro tables, and they'll have the bailiffs in the house. Poor Fanshaw is so unlucky."

"That being so, I should think the prudent course of behavior for him would be not to gamble." Margaret furtively glanced past the woman, trying to figure how to escape without giving offense.

"Oh, but he can't help it. It's in his blood, don't you know. All the Fanshaws gamble. Tell me, is your father here this evening?"

Margaret blinked at the abrupt change of subject. Was Mrs. Wooster a rival of Estelle's for the privilege of sharing her father's name and, far more importantly, his fortune?

"I haven't seen him yet," Margaret hedged.

"He's such a dear man." Mrs. Wooster heaved a theatrical sigh, and Margaret was hard-pressed not to giggle as an image of her father being pursued through London by a pack of purple-turbaned, overweight women flitted through her mind.

No—Hendricks wasn't her father! Margaret hastily corrected herself. Mainwaring was her father. Hendricks was simply a distant cousin who was also a nice old man. A nice old man who was going to be devastated when he found out that she wasn't his daughter; that Mary Hendricks was truly dead.

Margaret swallowed on the metallic taste of guilt.

"One wonders why he never remarried." Mrs. Wooster's avid voice broke into Margaret's unhappy thoughts.

"Well, for one thing he didn't know until recently that Mama was dead and that he was free to remarry." Margaret groped for a plausible explanation. To her surprise, her words seemed to electrify Mrs. Wooster.

"How true! I never thought . . . Tell me," Mrs. Wooster grabbed Margaret's wrist, "has he said anything about wanting to remarry?"

Margaret tentatively tried to pull away, but Mrs. Wooster's grip tightened, leaving Margaret with the option of demanding that the woman release her and risk causing a scene, or submitting to the inquisition. Or . . .

Margaret had an idea. Leaning forward as if she were about to impart a secret, Margaret lowered her voice and said, "Strange that you should ask, Mrs. Wooster, but just this morning Papa was saying that he wished he had a son to inherent his estates. From some other things he has said about this year's crop of debs, I do believe that he intends to wed one."

"What!" Mrs. Wooster dropped Margaret's arm and jerked back as if stung.

"Ah, there you are. I wondered what was keeping you. Come, the music is starting. Mrs. Wooster." Philip's nod to the woman was a masterpiece of chilly politeness.

Margaret was as pleased to see him now as she had been eager to escape him earlier. Philip might be aggravating at times, but he knew how to protect himself and her, too, from the bores of the ton.

"I'm sorry to have kept you waiting, but I stopped to greet Mrs. Wooster. It was so nice talking to you, ma'am."

"I . . . Yes." Mrs. Wooster gave Margaret a frustrated look as Philip hustled her away.

"You need to be more assertive," Philip said.

"What?"

"I saw your hunted expression when Mrs. Wooster trapped you. You need to be more assertive."

Margaret studied him for a long moment and then said, "Go away."

"I'm not finished talking to you!"

"Strange, that was Mrs. Wooster's reaction when I tried to escape her, too."

"I am not Mrs. Wooster!"

He certainly wasn't, Margaret thought, her gaze lingering on his broad shoulders. The tight fit of his inky-black evening jacket seemed to emphasize their width, and Margaret swallowed as she remembered what they had looked like without the trappings of clothes. How his firmly muscled flesh had felt beneath her fingers as she'd clutched them. How the heat had poured off them when his body had covered hers. How . . .

Stop it! Margaret pulled her wayward imagination up short. That was one of her problems in dealing with Philip, she suddenly realized. For some reason she had developed the nasty habit of drifting off into airdreams around him.

"You might not resemble Mrs. Wooster, but you certainly act like her," Margaret said. "You both refuse to listen to me. So, how can I assert myself?"

Philip stared down into her soft blue eyes and felt a flash of heat drop through his chest, coming to rest deep in the pit of his stomach. Did she really not know how easily a beautiful woman like her could influence a man? All she had to do was to lift those luscious pink lips of hers in an inviting smile and lean closer to him. Close enough that he could see the promise of her soft white breasts.

His eyes followed his thoughts downward, and he felt his heart begin to pound as his eyes traced over the curves of her breasts, visible above the deep-cut bodice of her gown.

"Well?" Margaret's voice recalled him to the conversation at hand.

"It's a skill you'll learn in time," he muttered. "For now . . ." Philip absently rubbed the middle of his forehead with his forefinger, trying to push back the pain.

"You do have the headache. You *are* sickening for something."

"I do not have the headache, and I am not sick!"

"Au contraire, I fear your common sense has sickened to the point of death."

Her use of a French expression caught Philip by surprise. As did the perfection of her accent. Where had she learned to speak French? But maybe she didn't, he told himself. Simply because she knew a phrase didn't mean she could speak a language.

Although . . . Where had she been living before he'd met her in Vienna? he wondered. Virtually everyone there had come specifically for the Congress. So where had she come from? He'd assumed England, but maybe she hadn't. Maybe she'd already been living somewhere on the Continent. Before he could ask her, a tall, thin man approached them, making private conversation impossible.

"Ah, Lady Chadwick. I am desolate to think that I have not seen you for days," the man said. "Ah, Chadwick." Gaunt nodded to Philip. "I heard your speech on the floor today. Can't say that I agree with it. All this talk of handing out pensions will be giving the lower classes ideas above their stations. Although . . ." Gaunt turned back to Margaret. "You must dance with me and tell me why I should support your husband's bill, my lady."

Margaret tried to tell herself that the greedy expression in Gaunt's protuberant eyes was a product of her imagination. The man probably was simply trying to find a mutual topic of conversation.

To her surprise, Philip came to her rescue.

"Since you are interested, I would be more than happy to discuss the bill with you, Gaunt. My wife not only knows little about politics but she was about to visit the ladies' retiring room."

Margaret gave Philip a smile that she hoped didn't look as relieved as she felt. Or as puzzled. Philip had brought her to London only to help promote his bill, so why was he missing an opportunity to do so now? Unless he thought that he had a better chance of changing Gaunt's mind than she did? But whatever Philip's reason, she was grateful not to have to stand up with Gaunt.

Margaret hurried back to the ladies' retiring room and this time made it inside. She spent twenty minutes hiding there before she decided that it would be safe to come out.

The first person she saw when she emerged was Drusilla.

Drusilla's face lit up as she caught sight of Margaret, and Margaret was caught off guard by the flood of guilt she felt.

She wasn't doing anything wrong by helping Drusilla's romance with Daniels. Margaret tried to deny the feeling. Simply because Daniels didn't have any money and was determined to remedy his lack by marriage didn't mean he would be a bad husband. Roxanne had done the same thing with her marriage to Philip and society had applauded her common sense. So why should that same society condemn Mr. Daniels?

And Drusilla loved Mr. Daniels, Margaret reminded herself. Drusilla didn't find his frivolous conversation or lack of purpose in life annoying.

But what about when Drusilla matured? The troubling thought intruded. Would she still love Mr. Daniels next year? Or five years from now?

"Cousin Margaret, I have been looking everywhere for you. I was afraid that you might have decided not to attend."

"As you can see, I did. Why don't we sit down so we can talk in comfort?" Margaret said.

Drusilla frowned uncertainly. "Oh, but I can't do that. Mama most specifically said I wasn't to."

"Why would your mother forbid you the comfort of sitting down?"

"Because only chaperones and antidotes sit on the sidelines. Because it is important that everyone see that I am in demand. Because nothing is more damaging to a young girl's chances of making a good marriage than to be thought to hold no interest for the gentlemen." Drusilla rattled off the words as if she'd long since committed them to memory.

"Allow me to expand your knowledge, Cousin. With very few exceptions, the unfortunate young women sitting on the sidelines are girls whose parents are unable to provide them with a dowry that the ton considers acceptable. Since your father's pockets are deep, you need have no fear that the gentlemen will somehow misinterpret your desire to sit as anything more than tired feet."

Drusilla blinked at Margaret's acerbic tone before she slowly turned and stared at the unfortunate girls occupying the seats in question as if she were seeing them for the first time.

"But marriage doesn't always depend on a large dowry," she finally said.

"True, if a young woman is beautiful enough, there will usually be a gentleman or two willing to overlook her lack of dowry." Such as Philip had done with Roxanne, and look where that led to, Margaret thought.

"Good evening, Miss Mainwaring, my lady." Daniels seemed to materialize behind Margaret. He gave Drusilla a cloying smile and then favored Margaret with a conspiratorial look that inexplicably annoyed her. But why shouldn't he think she was conspiring with him to fool Mainwaring? she told herself. It was true. That she was doing it for her own reasons and not his, was irrelevant.

"Why, good evening, Mr. Daniels." Drusilla gave him a glowing smile.

Daniels took a quick look around to make sure no one was near enough to overhear and then whispered to Margaret, "I cannot tell you how much we appreciate your serving as our friend in this matter, Lady Chadwick. It is too cruel that such a sordid thing as money should tear us apart."

Margaret kept her smile in place with an effort. Daniels

sounded more like a character out of the Minerva Press every time she talked to him.

"We thought that I would dance with you and then afterward you could present me to Drusilla as an acceptable partner. That way her father would not dare to object, since you are a kinswoman of his."

"A distant kinswoman." Margaret instinctively tried to distance herself from Mainwaring. "But I see nothing wrong with your plan."

Daniels hand felt soft and very slightly damp as he led her into the dance, and Margaret found herself comparing his touch with Philip's.

Philip's hands were warm, dry, and slightly callused. She glanced down at Daniels's immaculately clean fingernails as he swung her into the movements of the waltz. Both men appeared to be fastidious about their personal habits, although Daniels favored a lavender scent which she found overpowering. Both men were about the same height, although she would be willing to wager a considerable sum that Philip was far stronger.

Daniels reminded her of the bread dough she used to make whenever George and she were lucky enough to be living in accommodations that included a kitchen. With a little pushing and prodding, the dough could be molded into any shape she'd wanted, much as she suspected Daniels could rearrange his personality to become whatever his audience demanded.

Philip leaned up against the marble pillar at the edge of the ballroom floor and watched through narrowed eyes as some popinjay whirled Margaret around the ballroom floor. He watched with an increasing sense of wrath as the man pulled her close as he maneuvered them around a particularly clumsy pair of waltzers. Why was she letting him hold her so close? And who was he?

Philip rubbed his forehead, trying to ease the headache that was making it increasingly hard to think.

"There was a picture in my old nursery of an avenging angel that my nanny used to claim was just waiting for me to be a naughty boy before he whisked me off to hell." Lucien's voice broke into Philip's thoughts. "And allow me to inform you, my friend, that with that scowl on your face you bear a remarkable resemblance to him."

"Good evening, Lucien." Philip muttered, his eyes never leaving Margaret.

"Who are you . . ." Lucien followed the direction of Philip's gaze. "Ah, your bride. I see. It isn't the dark angel you're impersonating; it's the brooding Byron. Tell me, am I to anticipate you penning lines of bad poetry next?"

Philip ignored the question. "Who's the man she's dancing with?"

Lucien looked closer, his eyebrows rising as he recognized Daniels. "So he's back. But then it's been what—two years?"

"I don't know. I can't remember ever seeing him before."

"No. It would have happened one of the times you were in . . . away," Lucien amended. "And the whole affair was hushed up. Fact is, I wouldn't have known anything about it, or cared for that matter, if it hadn't happened at the inn I was staying at."

"Quit speaking in conundrums."

Lucien frowned off into the middle distance. "All right, I'll tell you about it since the young woman in question is now safely married and has disappeared from the London scene.

"The man is Daniels. He eloped with a spotty little squab from Yorkshire whose singularly stupid mother had brought her to London to make a brilliant match. Not that the girl might not have done reasonably well for herself."

"Family well-to-grass?" Philip said.

"Exceedingly plump in the pocket from all accounts. The mother set an enviable table.

"Anyway, I was on my way up to Argyll's place in the Highlands for a little grouse-hunting and had stopped for the night at an inn on the Great North Road. I was in the common room eating my dinner when first Daniels and his heiress arrived."

A reluctant smile teased Philip's lips. "Knowing your insatiable curiosity, I'm surprised you didn't immediately join them."

Lucien shook his head. "Absolutely not. The young lady was carriage-sick. Or perhaps being alone in the carriage with Daniels had been enough to give her second thoughts about his desirability as a husband and she was shamming sickness. At any rate, Daniels kept telling her they had to continue the journey and she kept whining that she didn't feel well. I tell you, Philip, it was better than a play.

"And then Mama and her man-of-business arrived, and the girl went off into strong hysterics. The end of it was that Mama hustled the girl away, and Daniels retired to an upstairs room with a raw beefsteak to put on his eye."

"The man-of-business struck him?" Philip turned and watched as Daniels smiled at Margaret. The idea of Daniels with a black eye appealed to him.

"No." Lucien coughed deprecatingly. "I did."

"I thought you were just an onlooker."

"I was until Daniels started to impugn the lady's virtue. Not at all the thing." Lucien shook his head. "Besides, I didn't think it was possible. I mean, can you really imagine trying to make love to a woman in a moving carriage?"

Instinctively Philip's gaze returned to Margaret. He certainly could imagine it. And it wouldn't be that hard to accomplish. All he'd have to do was to slip his hands beneath her skirt and push it up to bare her exquisite body. Then he'd pull her onto his lap and . . . He swallowed as he felt himself react to his provocative thoughts.

"Daniels is an ugly customer," Lucien continued. "Al-

though perhaps we misjudge him. Perhaps he was so overcome by love of his provincial miss that he couldn't contain his impetuosity."

Daniels had better contain his impetuosity where Margaret was concerned, Philip thought grimly, or Philip
would do more to him than merely blacken his daylights.

Philip froze as Margaret misstepped and landed against
Daniels's chest. Had she done that on purpose, or because
she still wasn't quite comfortable with the dance? Before
he could decide how to interrupt them, the music stopped
and Daniels began to escort her to the sidelines.

Philip sagged back against the marble post in relief.

"Damn uncomfortable, isn't it?" Lucien gave him a
commiserating look.

"What?" Philip turned to his friend.

Lucien gave him a wicked grin. "Why, if you don't
know, I'll leave you to discover it yourself."

Philip watched Lucien walk away in puzzlement. What
the hell was Lucien talking about? He seemed to take
great delight in wrapping the simplest statement up in a
riddle.

Sixteen

"Please excuse me," Margaret mumbled, unable to tear her horrified gaze away from the thin, balding man she'd just spied across the ballroom.

"Not at all, my lady. The ball is such a sad squeeze it's impossible to find space to perform the waltz adequately," Daniels said.

To her relief, the music finally ended and she was able to give up the increasingly difficult task of trying to remember the dance steps. She absolutely had to have a few minutes to herself to think. Her gaze returned with a horrified fascination to the man in the rusty black suit. Although, what good thinking was going to do . . .

Daniels escorted her to the sidelines where Drusilla was eagerly waiting their return.

Margaret automatically went through the motions of presenting Daniels as a desirable partner to her half-sister, barely noticing when they left to take the dance floor. Her mind was too taken up with her growing fears.

What was she going to do?

Margaret stared down at the intricate pattern of the parquet floor to keep her gaze from returning to the man and inadvertently attracting his attention. No, the question wasn't what would she do. The question was what *could* she do?

Margaret slipped into a vacant chair and then furtively

glanced across the room at the man. His attention appeared to be focused on the elderly woman beside him. What was his name?

She tried to remember and couldn't, finally giving up the effort as irrelevant. It didn't matter what he had called himself when he'd been pretending to be a minister in Vienna, because he was probably using another name now.

Her worried gaze swept the crowded dance floor, looking for Hendricks and at the same time hoping she wouldn't find him. She'd always known that sooner or later he would find out that she wasn't his daughter, but she didn't want him to make that discovery in front of a room full of avidly watching people. He didn't deserve that. He didn't deserve any of this.

To her dismay Margaret located him across the room talking to Lady Jersey. Nervously she chewed her lower lip as Hendricks caught sight of her and with a final word to Lady Jersey, started toward her.

Unless . . . She frowned as another explanation for the man's presence occurred to her. Was it possible that he had deliberately followed them to England in order to blackmail Philip?

Could his appearance at the ball be meant as nothing more than a nonverbal threat? If so, it was working, Margaret thought. She was frightened out of her wits, and he hadn't even approached her yet.

"There you are, my dear." Hendricks sat down beside her.

Margaret surreptitiously studied him, looking for some sign that the man had already approached him. There was nothing to be seen in his face but tiredness.

"Why aren't you dancing, my dear?" Hendricks asked.

Margaret forced a smile, trying to appear normal. "Dancing is a rather tiring exercise. Both physically and mentally."

Hendricks bushy white eyebrows rose questioningly. "Mentally?"

Margaret nodded. "It is very wearing trying to think of something to say while trying to keep track of the steps."

"Practice will take care of the necessity of minding your steps," Hendricks comforted her.

Unconsciously Margaret's eyes strayed back to the fake minister. He was still talking to the elderly woman. She doubted she was going to get much more practice. Her days masquerading as Philip's wife were numbered. And that was a good thing, she assured herself. She would be able to go back to George and the life she was used to. She refused even to acknowledge the uncertainty that tumbled through her.

"Who are you looking at?" Hendricks's curious voice broke into her confused thoughts. "Surely not that prosy old bore?"

"Which prosy old bore?" Margaret stalled.

Hendricks nodded toward Margaret's nemesis. "The withered old stick in the suit that looks as if he slept in it."

"I think I've met him before," Margaret said.

"I can't imagine where it might have been. Preston isn't the type of man who is on any hostess's guest list. He's only here because he's Mrs. Carrington's personal chaplain and no doubt feels that it's his duty to make sure that her guests don't have too much fun."

Chaplain! The word hit Margaret with the force of a blow. If he was really a chaplain . . . A confusing flood of emotion poured through her, leeching the color from of her cheeks. It couldn't be true! Philip couldn't really have married her. He was an earl, and she was Mainwaring's bastard daughter.

Earls married for gain and there was nothing Philip could gain from marrying her. Nothing that he couldn't have acquired by pretending to be married to her. So why had he—

"Are you feeling indisposed, my dear? You've gone quite pale."

Margaret blinked, scrambling to collect her scattered wits. "I'm fine. It's just a little close in here."

"It certainly is." To her relief, Hendricks didn't question her explanation. "Should I find Chadwick and ask him to take you home? Or I could take you myself. I certainly wouldn't mind leaving," Hendricks assured her. "The older I get, the more tedious I find these events. And for some reason this evening has been worse than usual. Do you know that I've been accosted by four matrons, each with a marriageable daughter in tow? All of them young enough to be my granddaughter! I cannot understand it."

Margaret caught her lower lip between her lips and stared at him, torn between laughter and chagrin at the unexpected consequences of her impulsive words to Mrs. Wooster.

Hendricks's pale blue eyes began to twinkle as he noticed her expression. "Tell me, my dear, why do I have the feeling that you are not as surprised by my news as I expected?"

"I might as well make a full confession. Not that I intended it to happen. I simply wanted to get rid of the woman."

"And which woman would that be?"

"Mrs. Wooster."

He nodded in commiseration. "A sensible reaction."

"Yes, well . . . She cornered me, and I was afraid she would stick like a burr in order to get to talk to you, so to escape I impulsively gave her the impression that you were . . ."

" 'Were?' "

"Desirous of remarrying a young woman to get a son to inherit your estates." Margaret blurted out the worst.

Hendricks stared at her in shock for a moment, and then he chuckled. "So that's it," he said.

Margaret smiled back weakly, wondering how his wife could have been such a goosecap as to have preferred another man to him. Not only was he a thoroughly nice man, but he had a lively sense of the ridiculous.

But maybe his wife had felt the same sense of mindless longing for her lover that she felt every time Philip took her in his arms, Margaret thought uneasily. That feeling had nothing to do with common sense, or even right and wrong. It seemed to have a separate existence all its own.

"Good evening, Hendricks. What could you possibly find humorous about this gathering?"

Philip's dark voice poured through her, stirring her already skitterish nerves.

"Good evening, Chadwick," Hendricks said. "My approaching nuptials to one of this season's young buds."

Margaret watched Philip's dark eyebrows shoot up. In surprise or dismay? she wondered. Could Philip's reason for marrying her have been to get his hands on Hendricks's fortune through her? She studied the hard lines of Philip's face. It was possible. From her own personal observation, members of the aristocracy valued money above all things. And if Hendricks believed her to be his daughter, then he would naturally leave the bulk of his fortune to her, and since Philip was her husband, he would have control of it.

But somehow she couldn't quite believe that was his motivation. From what she'd seen so far, money didn't seem to be all that important to him. If it were, he would have long ago put a rein on Estelle's lavish spending.

"I can't decide if I should be offering congratulations or condolences," Philip said.

Hendricks chuckled. "Definitely condolences. Although in this case, the announcement of the demise of my bachelorhood is premature."

"I said something that gave Mrs. Wooster the impression that Papa was seeking a son to inherit his fortune," Margaret explained, at Philip's confused look. "And he has been waylaid by hopeful mamas ever since."

"Being of sound mind, I intend to wait for a grandson. Your second son, I think, my dear, since your first will inherit the earldom," Hendricks said.

Margaret stole a quick glance at Philip, trying to judge his reaction to Hendricks's words. His face was impassive. If he was disappointed that she would not be Hendricks's heiress, he was keeping the emotion well hidden.

"Ah, Lord Chadwick, I thought I saw you." Preston's unctuous voice broke into Margaret's thoughts. "Lord Hendricks." Preston nodded deferentially to him. "I hear that you are about to take the plunge into matrimony again."

Margaret choked. How could her impulsive words have spread so quickly? She knew the ton thrived on gossip, but this was ridiculous!

"You've been listening to wicked gossip, Preston," Hendricks said. "I have no intention of remarrying."

Preston made a clucking sound that reminded Margaret of a chicken. "Scandalous, the way rumors get started."

Philip's lips twitched ever so slightly, and he glanced down at Margaret. She stared up at him, mesmerized by the sparkling little lights she could see dancing in his dark eyes. If only he looked like that more often. If only . . . If only *what?* She mocked the thought. Philip might look like a different person when he was amused, but that didn't mean he was. He was still the same impatient man who'd thought she was George's mistress.

"And even more scandalous, the way people listen to those rumors and repeat them," Philip said.

Preston nodded emphatically, totally missing any personal message in the words. "Indeed, my lord, women must be constantly reminded that they must not indulge in gossip."

"Women!" Margaret said.

"Oh, yes." Preston smiled condescendingly at her. "It is as the Bible tells us. Women are frail beings, and must be constantly guided lest they fall into sin."

"And yet it was Judas Iscariot who betrayed the Lord!" Margaret shot back. "And the Sanhedrin who accused him, and Pontius Pilate who condemned him, and the soldiers who crucified him. *Men* to the last one. It seems to me that it's men who should be hanging their heads in shame."

Preston gulped, his Adam's apple bobbing at her unexpected attack.

Margaret watched his eyes widen in disbelief as he finally recognized her.

"Miss . . . um . . . My lady," he gasped. "I didn't realize that . . . I mean . . ." He glanced around the room as if seeking help.

"Is that Mrs. Carrington looking for you?" Philip unexpectedly provided it.

"Oh, I must go." Preston hurried away.

"That—" Margaret choked on her indignation. "That looby! To stand there and repeat the gossip he's just heard, and then to have the effrontery to try to somehow shift the blame to women."

"Well you must admit that gossip is normally a woman's trait," Philip said.

Margaret's eyes darkened in annoyance. "mh krinete inx yh k riute."

Philip blinked, taken aback by her quote. She really did speak Greek. She hadn't been pretending to be interested in Hendricks's abiding hobby.

". . . night." The very end of Hendricks's sentence penetrated Philip's thoughts.

"Yes, it is getting late." Margaret's agreement gave Philip a clue as to what had been said.

"And I've talked to all the peers who attended. We might as well go home," Philip said. He took Margaret's arm.

Margaret suppressed a smile at Philip's words. Clearly he did not look upon a ball as a time to have fun. Not that she didn't agree with him. Dancing with the same people, listening to the same boring gossip, and fending off the same flirtatious men night after night, was not her idea of enjoyment, either.

Surreptitiously Margaret glanced around the crowded ballroom as she left with Philip, looking for either Drusilla or Daniels. She didn't see Daniels, but Drusilla was standing with her father near the door. With them was a stout young man who was gazing at her with a worshipful expression.

From the blank look on Drusilla's face, it was clear that whatever the young man was saying, he was not impressing her. Could he be Mainwaring's choice for a son-in-law? If so, he was clearly no competition for Mr. Daniels.

Margaret followed Philip out of the mansion and toward their waiting carriage. The feel of his fingers pressing against her waist as he handed her up into their carriage effectively drove all thoughts of Drusilla and her unknown suitor from her mind.

Philip sat down across from her and peered at her through the darkness. Her pale skin had an almost ethereal luminosity about it. As if she didn't really exist at all. As if she were a ghost sent to haunt him.

And she was doing a damn good job of it, too! he thought. Her advent into his life had turned it upside down.

In a strange way the situation was very similar to when he'd made the appalling discovery of Roxanne's infidelities. Suddenly everything he'd thought he'd known about women had seemed wrong. They weren't gentle beings who needed a man's care and guidance. They were conscienceless schemers who cared nothing for honor and the vows they'd taken.

And now Margaret had upset his thinking yet again. All of the lessons he'd thought he'd learned from Roxanne didn't seem to apply to Margaret.

She shifted slightly, and he caught a glimpse of the swell of her breasts as her movement separated her pelisse. Desire swept over him as he stared at her delectable cleavage.

He clenched his fingers in a fist to negate the desire to caress her soft skin.

But why should he resist? he thought. Margaret was his wife. He had every right to touch her. And no one could see into the carriage in the dark. It was as private as if they were in her bedroom. Moreover, since she hadn't known that he'd been trying to ration his sexual contact with her, she wouldn't know that he'd failed. Again.

Not giving himself time to consider the wisdom of his actions, he moved across the seat and sat beside her.

Margaret jumped, surprised by his unexpected action. "What's the matter?" she asked.

"Nothing," he muttered, finding it beyond him at the moment to come up with a plausible explanation for his actions. His mind was too taken up with other things. Such as her tantalizingly feminine scent which his every breath pulled deeper and deeper into his lungs, feeding his craving for her.

Giving in to his overwhelming need, Philip dipped his hand into her bodice. Her heated flesh seemed to scorch his fingers, and he closed his eyes in order to more fully savor the sensations rocketing through him. His fingers inched lower, tightening around the soft mound of her breast, and the feel of her nipple hardening against his palm dissolved the last vestiges of his control.

He tugged her bodice down to expose her breasts, but in the darkness he couldn't see them clearly. It didn't matter, Philip decided. Touch was far more satisfactory than sight anyway.

He could feel the frantic beating of her heart against his hand, and he dimly wondered what she was feeling. Did she find pleasure in this? Wives weren't supposed to, but then, in no way could Margaret be called a normal wife. She was very different from any other woman he'd ever met. Her grasp of scholarship and her unrelenting logic, in some ways made her more masculine than feminine.

But her body . . . A shudder ripped through him at the thought of her body. It was the most feminine thing he'd ever seen. A constantly changing storehouse of sensual delights. He felt as if he could spend his entire life delving into its secrets and never learn everything there was to learn.

Margaret bit her lower lip to keep from moaning as his fingers caressed her. His touch felt incredible, slightly rough against her hypersensitive skin.

A gasp escaped her as he leaned over and she felt his warm breath against her cheek. Her heart was pounding in her chest, threatening to choke her. Her eyelids felt heavy, much too heavy to keep open without a great deal of effort—effort she couldn't spare because her whole concentration was focused on trying to hide how wanton his touch made her feel.

It was becoming harder and harder. It was all she could do not to grab his head and pull his mouth down on hers. And why shouldn't she? she told herself. As incomprehensible as she found the fact, she was married to him. Surely married women had a right to derive enjoyment from the marital act.

Doubt shimmered through her growing sense of urgency as she remembered her mother's and her friends' unceasing complaints about the marriage bed, but she brushed it aside. Making love to her husband couldn't be wrong. It was a wife's duty to submit to his advances and, if in this case, duty followed inclination, so much the better.

Her thoughts scattered into a thousand tiny fragments as she felt the roughened texture of Philip's cheek against the swell of her breasts. She trembled beneath the tumbling flood of emotions that engulfed her as his mouth closed hotly over her nipple and he suckled it. Rivulets of sensation shot through her body, collecting in her abdomen and making her feel slightly frantic.

Instinctively she threaded her fingers through his crisp hair to hold him close. His hair was soft and cool beneath her fingers in direct contrast to the blazing heat of his devouring mouth.

A moan bubbled in her throat and try as she might, Margaret couldn't stop it from escaping. The yearning sound echoed in the dark carriage.

A massive sense of depravation filled her when Philip moved back slightly. But instead of retreating to his own side of the carriage as she'd thought he'd do, his mouth found hers in the dark.

Eagerly she parted her lips, welcoming the sensuous feel of his tongue moving against her. She pressed her body closer to him. The fact that they were in a closed carriage driving through London no longer had any meaning for her. All that mattered was that he not stop.

She clutched frantically at his coat when he moved back, but instead of leaving her as she'd feared, he grabbed the hem of her gown and yanked it up over her slender thighs.

The chill of the night air on her overheated skin provided a momentary break on her mounting passion, and she shook her head, trying to focus on something other than her growing need.

He didn't answer her in words but with action. Circling her waist with his hands, he lifted her off the seat and set her on his lap.

She gulped as she could feel his swollen manhood pressing intimately against her. The heat burned away the natural inhibitions, leaving her filled with a devouring need that craved satisfaction.

She could feel the trembling in his fingers as he roughly pushed her shift aside, and the knowledge that he was as affected as she was filled her with a wild sense of exhilaration.

And then she ceased to think at all as he positioned himself.

Margaret gasped in disbelief at the feelings which tore through her as he filled her. The urgency which had been building in her suddenly spiraled out of control at the incredible sensation.

Margaret arched her body back against his strong arms, trying to draw him even deeper into her. She wanted to experience him in ever fiber of her being. She wanted . . .

Her thoughts became hopelessly tangled when his movements finally drove her into a sensual realm of enchantment that bore no relationship to the real world. She was so caught up in her own pleasure that she was only dimly aware when he found his own release.

It was the sound of the watch calling out something in the street which finally recalled Margaret to her senses, and she lifted her head from Philip's chest, mortified at her abandoned behavior.

Her sense of embarrassment escalated to shame when Philip lifted her off his lap, set her down on the seat, and then retreated to his own seat.

How could she have responded so wantonly to his shocking liberties? Her mind didn't offer an answer, and she bit her lip to fight the urge to burst into tears.

Philip peered uncertainly across the seat at Margaret as

a feeling of dread grew in him. How could he have treated her like a lightskirt? He winced as he watched her pull her cloak tighter around her slender body. How could he have behaved in such a barbaric manner? Self-disgust rolled through him, making him feel sick. Somehow he was going to have to make her forget what he'd done. Maybe if he were very careful not to touch her for a while, the memory of his appalling behavior would fade from her mind.

Was there that much time left in his life? he wondered.

Margaret's fingers stilled in their task of fastening her morning dress, and she frowned at the sound of coughing in the hallway as Philip passed by her bedroom door.

She frowned. He should have stayed in bed this morning with a hot brick at his feet and a mustard plaster for his chest. Instead he'd undoubtedly go out into the freezing air and make his cold even worse. Her pointing it out would only serve to make his temper as uncertain as his health was at the moment. And that being so, she'd do well to keep her opinions to herself, she decided.

Leaving her room, she made her way downstairs to the breakfast room.

"Ah, my lady." Compton greeted her at the bottom of the stairs. "The employment agency will be sending the candidates for Lady Annabelle's governess over later this morning."

"Thank you for reminding me, Compton," Margaret said, wondering if she should ask Philip to attend the interviews. Since she'd already told Annabelle that she could be there, it would be an excellent chance for them to be together.

Just because his initial response to her idea that he treat Annabelle as his daughter had been negative, it didn't mean he might not change his mind in time, she told herself. And she had time. A sense of confused wonder flooded her. She really was married to Philip. She wasn't going to be sent back to France as soon as he got his bill passed.

Although . . . Margaret frowned, as an unexpected complication occurred to her. What was George going to say when she told him that she was married to his arch-nemesis.

"Is there a problem, my lady?" Compton asked.

It would be easier to list the things in her life that weren't a problem at the moment, Margaret thought wryly, but she merely shook her head and headed into the break-fast room. Maybe a hot cup of coffee would help to restore her equilibrium.

Then again, maybe it wouldn't, she thought as she paused on the threshold of the morning room, her eyes instinctively homing in on Philip's dark head.

He looked up from the coffee cup he'd been staring into, and she felt her gaze captured by his knowing eyes.

Margaret felt her face flush as she remembered what had happened last night in the carriage. Determinedly she raised her chin and stared back at him, refusing to be intimidated. He was the one who'd taken her in his arms last night. She couldn't have stopped him if she'd tried.

"Good morning." To her annoyance her words sounded tentative in her own ears.

"Not so far," Philip said. "Eat something, so we can leave."

"Leave where?"

Margaret jumped at the sound of Estelle's voice coming from near the sideboard. She had been so taken up with Philip that she hadn't even realized Estelle was in the room.

"I have an appointment with a Mr. Whitman."

"I don't remember numbering a Mr. Whitman among our acquaintances," Estelle said.

"Probably because he isn't." Philip frowned at the lone muffin Margaret had chosen. Getting up, he took a second plate, piled an assortment of food on it and set it down in front of her.

Margaret ignored it. The thought of trying to eat that much so early in the morning made her feel positively bilious.

"My man-of-business set the meeting up. Mr. Whitman is in manufacturing."

"Manufacturing!" Estelle pressed her hand against her plump breast in a theatrical gesture worthy of Mrs. Siddons. "Say you aren't going to—to actually go into trade. Think of your good name. Think of your daughter's prospects."

Margaret watched Philip's face darken with anger at Estelle's ill-advised strictures. Afraid that in his anger he might blurt out something about Annabelle's real parentage, Margaret jumped to her feet. She had to get him out of here before Estelle goaded him into saying something that could never be recalled; something that would preclude there ever being any kind of relationship between him and poor Annabelle.

"I'm ready," she said. "Let's go."

"You haven't . . ." Philip began, and then started to cough.

"Really, Philip," Estelle sniffed. "In my day, men had the courtesy not to come to the table when they were ill."

"It is my table and my home, and I'll damn well go anywhere in it I like!"

Margaret stifled a sigh. Could Estelle really not understand just how aggravating her words were to someone with Philip's forceful personality, or was she purposefully trying to infuriate him? But toward what end? Philip was Estelle's sole source of support.

"I should be back before the governesses arrive,

Estelle," Margaret threw into the strained silence. "But if I'm not, please give them tea and ask them to wait."

"Governesses?" Estelle said.

"Yes, for their interviews. I would appreciate your help in choosing one since you know Annabelle so much better than I."

"I should think so," Estelle muttered, only partially mollified by Margaret's acknowledgment of her skills. But to Margaret's relief, Estelle did hold her tongue as she and Philip left.

Seventeen

Margaret hunched her shoulders against the cold. The wind was trying to blow her off the seat of the high-perched phaeton as she studied the two bright splotches of red on Philip's pale cheeks.

Philip deftly steered around a young man who was having trouble controlling his horses in the heavy traffic, and frowned irritably at Margaret.

"Why are you staring at me?"

"I'm trying to decide whether illness makes men behave like fools or whether they behave like fools because they're men and the illness is secondary."

Philip looked down his nose at her. "I am not ill!"

"At least you're honest enough not to deny being a fool!" she shot back, forgetting the cold in the exhilaration of arguing with him. And it did exhilarate her, she admitted with a vague feeling of surprise. She couldn't begin to understand why it should be so, but it was.

All her life, she had prided herself on being a rational person who responded to events with logic and not emotion, and yet for some reason that all had changed when she met Philip Moresby. Her husband. She examined the word, still not comfortable with the idea that she really was married to him; that he wasn't going to disappear from her life the minute his bill passed. Although she could disappear from his, she conceded. He could be planning to banish her to one of his estates when he no longer had a use for her.

"Life's too short to pamper oneself," Philip said.

"And from the way you're behaving, it's getting shorter by the minute. I wouldn't be surprised if you were to come down with an inflammation of the lungs from being out in an open carriage in this wind."

"I never get sick!" Philip punctuated his disclaimer with a cough.

Margaret winced at the deep rasping sound that seemed to echo in his broad chest. She studied him out of the corner of her eye. She wasn't quite sure why she wanted to protect him. More often than not, Philip infuriated her. Except when he took her in his arms. Margaret swallowed against the unsettling tangle of emotions which tore through her at the disquieting thought. Not wanting to think about the implications of her wanton reaction to him, she forced herself to concentrate on the streets through which they were passing. It was a part of London she hadn't seen before.

Philip pulled up in front of a black-painted door which bore a copper plate engraved with the name Jacob Blandings.

Jumping down, he tossed the reins to the groom and walked around the horses' heads to help Margaret down. His hands closed around her waist, and he swung her down onto the street as if she weighed no more than Annabelle.

Margaret stole a quick look at him as he escorted her across the freshly-swept flagway, her eyes lingering on the width of his shoulders beneath the multicaped gray coat he wore.

Curious, she turned her attention to the house when they reached the front door. It was narrow, with one sparkling window on either side of the door, and much smaller than the buildings on either side of it. But despite its diminutive size it exuded a feeling of solidarity, of permanence. Anyone seeking financial advice would find it reassuring.

Before Philip could knock, the door was swung open by a well-scrubbed, round-faced boy of about twelve.

"Good morning, your lordship, sir. And . . ." The boy stared at Margaret as if he had never seen a woman before.

And he probably hadn't, Margaret thought. At least not in this particular establishment. From what she had observed, the women of the ton were appallingly ignorant of all things financial. But whether that was indolence on their part, or a deliberate ploy by their husbands to maintain power by keeping a death grip on the finances, she didn't know. Or perhaps neither explanation was true. Perhaps it was simply a matter of custom. So much of the ton's life seemed to be ordered by a custom that defied logic or even common sense.

"I'm Lady Chadwick," Margaret said. "And you are?"

"Thomas Crofton, if you please, my lady."

"I am pleased to meet you, Thomas," Margaret said.

"Um . . ." Thomas glanced over his shoulder as if seeking help to deal with this unexpected development. He couldn't ever remember any of Mr. Blandings' clients professing themselves pleased to meet him.

"If you will announce us to Mr. Blandings." Philip came to his rescue, and Thomas scurried off.

A small man with thinning brown hair and thick glasses emerged from his office a second after Thomas had announced their arrival.

"Good morning, your lordship. And Lady Chadwick?" His voice seemed to echo Thomas's uncertainty at her presence.

Margaret decided to ignore it. Whether Mr. Blandings wanted her here was irrelevant, as was whether she wanted to be here. The only one whose opinion mattered was

Philip's, and he had demanded her presence. Presumably, she would discover why shortly.

"If you will come in." Mr. Blandings ushered them into his office.

"This is Mr. Whitman." Mr. Blandings gestured to the man who had hauled himself out of one of the chairs in front of his desk.

Everything about him seemed to be oversized, from his belly, straining against his green-and-yellow-striped waistcoat, to the huge diamond stickpin decorating his elaborately arranged neckcloth.

"I see you've noticed my little bauble, my lady." Mr. Whitman chuckled richly, rubbing his pudgy fingers together. "Trust a female to notice the gewgaws first thing."

Margaret felt Philip stiffen beside her, and she hurried into speech. "It would be hard not to notice it, Mr. Whitman. I've never seen a diamond quite that big."

"Why I thank you, my lady, but all the world and his wife knows that Chadwick's grandfather brought back far bigger gems from India," Whitman said.

Margaret blinked in surprise. Philip's grandfather had been in India?

"And I heard tell he brought back colored ones, too. Like to get my hands on a really fine ruby, my lord. If'n you ever decide to sell, I'd appreciate you thinking of me first. Give you a good price, I will."

"I have no need to sell the family jewels." Philip's voice was one degree above freezing.

"I know you have no need." Whitman didn't seem to take offense at Philip's tone. "Although I do admit, when Blandings first approached me about this idea of yours, I wondered if it might be low tide with you and you was looking for me to haul you out of the River Tick, but my sources tell me you're rich as Croesus. Which makes me wonder why you'd be wanting to go into trade. I mean, in the normal way, it ain't the kind of thing earls do."

"I'm not sure that I do," Philip replied. "The idea was my wife's."

Whitman's bushy gray eyebrows shot up. "Never met a woman before who was interested in making money. Only in spending it."

"Perhaps you ought to enlarge your acquaintanceship!" Margaret shot back.

"No offense intended, my lady, but that still doesn't answer my question. Why should you want me for a partner for this venture of yours?"

"Because I plan to set up a factory which would hire the soldiers who have been mustered-out, and I need your expertise to make it work," Philip said. "I don't know how closely you follow events in Parliament, but I have been attempting to pass a relief bill for the returning soldiers."

Whitman shook his head. "Cork-brained notion. It'll raise taxes and high taxes are bad for business."

Margaret stared at Whitman's disgruntled expression with a feeling of disorientation. He was a member of her own class, and yet he seemed totally indifferent to the desperate plight of the returning soldiers.

"Without those soldiers we'd have lost the war to the French. That would have been much worse for your business," Philip said.

Margaret glanced from Philip's fever-flushed cheeks to Whitman's clamped jowls. It seemed to her they were about evenly matched when it came to stubbornness. If they started arguing, it could last for hours.

"Mr. Whitman, if you didn't feel this venture offered opportunity for profit, you wouldn't be here," Margaret reminded him.

Whitman stroked his beefy fingers over his chin.

"Well now, my lady, there's profit and there's *profit*. Personally I'm not so sure that your husband's idea will make money," Whitman said. "Especially not if he involves himself too deeply in the day-to-day running of it."

Whitman held up his hand when Philip opened his mouth, no doubt knowing what Philip intended to say. "Now, I don't mean no disrespect in that, my lord, but you must allow each man his trade and the truth is, manufacturing ain't yours."

"Mr. Whitman"—Mr. Blandings entered the conversation—"perhaps it would facilitate matters if you were to explain to his lordship exactly why you agreed to discuss the matter?"

Whitman shifted in his chair as if reluctant to come to the point. Finally he said, "The facts of the matter are these, my lord. I have a daughter. The apple of my eye, Nellie is."

His voice softened and so did Margaret's aggravation with him. Any man who could smile like that when talking about his daughter couldn't be entirely unfeeling.

"Her poor mother has long since gone on to her reward. Not but what it might not be for the best, you understand, for my Beth was a good, honest Yorkshire lass, but there's no denying that she wasn't the least bit social."

Margaret blinked at such plain speaking.

"At any rate that was long ago, and now my daughter is nineteen and of an age to marry."

Margaret nodded, fearing where this conversation was going. Surely he didn't think that she was capable of launching his daughter into society? Her own standing in the ton wasn't any too secure, and once it came out that she wasn't really Hendricks's daughter, she very much doubted that being married to Philip would be enough to salvage her position.

"Now, I've tried to find her a suitable husband myself, but it's come to naught. Last spring I hired a woman who said that she had entry into the ton. Fair bled me dry, she did, too." His voice rose in remembered grievance. "But it was all a hum. All she was able to get my Nellie invitations to, was a few routs given by cits. I need someone who really is the tip of the ton like yourself, my lady, to sponsor my gel."

Margaret stared at him, scrambling for something to say. She didn't want to make promises that she couldn't keep, but then she'd been doing all kind of things that she didn't want to do since she'd met Philip.

"So that's my offer." Whitman threw the words at Philip when Margaret remained silent. "If your lady wife will undertake to find my Nellie a husband during the Spring Season, I'll be your partner in this factory, hire your soldiers and do my best to make a success of it."

"But Mr. Whitman," Margaret said before Philip could accept on her behalf, "have you considered that your daughter might be more comfortable marrying among her own class?"

"I promised her dear, sainted mother on her deathbed that I'd see her daughter married to a lord. And you needn't think that I mean to be clutch-fisted about her dowry. I intend to settle a plum on her."

Margaret hadn't as yet heard that particular expression, but from Mr. Blandings's quickly indrawn breath, she assumed it would be substantial.

"A hundred thousand pounds," Philip enlightened her, and Margaret felt like echoing Blandings's gasp.

"But what kind of man would allow himself to be bought?" Margaret tried a different tact.

"Ain't buying him," Whitman said. "It's a business deal. A fair trade. My money for his title. Besides, you women can natter all you want about romance, but we men know that it's money that makes the world go round. Ain't that so, my lord?"

Philip stared at Margaret's troubled features. Money certainly hadn't been the impetus that had driven his own marriage. But then, neither had love. His eyes lingered on her soft lips. The knowledge unexpectedly grated on his already ragged nerves.

"Well, my lord, what's it to be?" Whitman looked from Philip's impassive features to Margaret's troubled ones.

Margaret bit her lip, wondering at Philip's continued silence. Was he waiting for her to say something? Probably not. She immediately rejected the idea. He hadn't shown the slightest interest in what she wanted so far, so it was highly unlikely that he should start now.

The taut silence was finally broken by Philip's coughing.

Mr. Blandings hurriedly got to his feet and, opening the cabinet to the right of his desk, took out a crystal decanter of wine. Filling a glass, he handed it to Philip.

Philip drained the wine with one swallow and handed the empty glass back to Mr. Blandings.

Getting to his feet, Philip turned to Whitman. "I will discuss your proposal with my wife and let you know my decision within a few days. Mr. Blandings."

If he did, it would be the first thing he ever had discussed with her, Margaret thought.

Curious, she glanced at Philip's expressionless face as he escorted her out of the office, wondering why he hadn't accepted Whitman's proposal at once. Could it be that he was worried about the propriety of her launching a country girl into London society under his auspices?

Margaret stumbled on the uneven flagstones as an idea suddenly exploded into her mind.

"Be careful," Philip said.

A prophetic order, Margaret thought. What she was contemplating was not a plan for a careful woman, or even a prudent one, but if it worked . . .

Margaret hurriedly scrambled into the seat of the high-perched phaeton by herself, not wanting to have to deal with the added distraction that Philip's touch always caused. She needed to keep her wits about her if she was to have a chance to bring her plan off.

Philip jumped into the seat beside her, tossed a coin to the groom and said, "Get yourself a pint to warm you up, Jennings. I won't need you for the rest of the morning."

"Thank you, milord!" The man gave him a wide smile and, whistling happily, headed toward the alehouse across the street.

Had Philip done that because he was a considerate master, or because he wanted to give her her orders about Miss Whitman without the risk of the groom overhearing him?

"What did you think of Whitman's offer?" Philip asked, answering her question.

Margaret ignored her surprise at being asked her opinion and said, "Bear-leading a young girl through the pitfalls of a season is not a skill that I have. Not only that, but what will the ton say about my sponsoring a cit's daughter?"

"Those with marriageable daughters will deplore it, while those with expensive sons will applaud."

"And what happens if Hendricks finds out that I'm not really his daughter before the season is over? The scandal could make it impossible for me to find Miss Whitman a husband."

Philip shrugged his broad shoulders as if he were trying to redistribute a weight that was becoming increasingly heavy.

Could he feel guilty about what he'd done to Hendricks? Margaret wondered. Originally she would have said no, but living with him had convinced her that he was a far more complicated man than she'd first thought. He might act like Machiavelli at times, but she was coming to believe that it was circumstance that had dictated his actions, rather than inclination.

"The news will be a nine-day wonder," Philip said.

"And as for your lack of experience, Estelle can help you pop off Whitman's daughter."

"Estelle! Condescend to sponsor a cit's daughter?"

"If Estelle expects me to continue to foot her bills, she will study to please me."

Margaret grimaced. If Philip really thought that threats would bring about Estelle's wholehearted cooperation, he was sicker than she'd thought.

"Well?" Philip demanded.

Margaret took a deep breath, trying to figure out the best way to put her idea to him so that it didn't sound like blackmail—even if it was. But it was for Annabelle's sake, not her own, and the child's needs were more important than how she secured Philip's cooperation, Margaret told herself, and then winced when she remembered that Philip had used a variant of that same argument to justify his appalling use of Hendricks.

This wasn't the time to get bogged down in a philosophical dilemma. This was the time to act. "I will do what Mr. Whitman wants, if you will . . ."

Her voice failed her as she watched the muscles in Philip's jaw suddenly tauten. *Don't think about what he might do to you. Think about poor Annabelle and what she needs.* Margaret rallied her dwindling courage.

"Yes." His silky voice sent a shiver of apprehension through her. "Do go on. You were about to tell me the cost of your cooperation, I believe."

"I want you to make an effort to get to know Annabelle."

"I told you, she isn't my daughter," Philip said, caught completely off guard by her request.

"That's the past. Nothing will ever change that. I'm talking about the future."

"Roxanne—"

"—Is dead and has nothing to do with Annabelle anymore. As far as the world is concerned, Annabelle is your daughter. All I'm asking you, is to make an effort to become acquainted with her as a normal father would."

"All?" Philip thought incredulously. Did she have any idea just how hard a man would find it to be forced to embrace his wife's bastard as his own?

"It isn't that I don't like the child," Philip said. "It's just that every time I look at her I remember what happened."

"I wonder what she thinks of, every time she looks at you?"

"What?"

"Annabelle. I wonder what she thinks she's done wrong to make you hate her so."

"I told you. I don't hate her. I just don't want . . ."

"To have to deal with her because it would demand that you stop wallowing in self-pity!" Margaret decided she had nothing to lose by being brutally honest.

"Self-pity!"

Margaret nodded. "That's what it looks like to me. You married a beautiful face and then found out that the woman behind the face wasn't at all what you had expected."

"I suppose that the next step is to blame me because my wife took lovers!"

She couldn't think of a single reason why Roxanne would have taken a lover, but she could hardly tell Philip that. It would be far too revealing.

"Roxanne made the decision, and hers is the blame," Margaret finally said. "Although from what people have said about her, I doubt that there was any premeditation in her decision. She sounded like a spoiled, vain young woman who acted on the impulse of the moment. I doubt that she even considered the consequences of her actions until she found herself enceinte."

Philip frowned at her. "Is that supposed to make me feel better?"

"I'm not trying to make you feel better." Margaret forced herself to ignore the pain she saw in his eyes. "I'm trying to make sure that Annabelle doesn't become another Roxanne."

Why was she so determined to involve herself in Annabelle's future? Philip wondered. He couldn't think of a single reason, but simply because he didn't see her motivation didn't mean it didn't exist; and that it might not come back to haunt him at a future date.

"You can start by attending the interviews for Annabelle's governess this morning," Margaret gently pushed.

"Damnation, woman, don't nag."

"I'm not nagging! I'm outlining the price of my cooperation."

Philip rubbed his forehead, trying to banish the nagging ache that made thinking difficult. "Gilroy is still in my hands," he muttered halfheartedly.

"George is part of another deal we have. Or are you a man who doesn't honor his word?"

Her scathing voice made him wince. He knew she was right; but she was wrong about one thing: He didn't hate Annabelle. He didn't love her, but neither did he hate her.

"All right," he said. "I'll try for one month."

"For one month," Margaret echoed, wondering how she was going to manage to make him see Annabelle as an individual separate from Roxanne in one month when eight years hadn't accomplished it.

Eighteen

"Good morning, my lord, my lady." Compton greeted them when they returned from their meeting with Whitman. "The post has arrived. It is on the hall table."

Margaret handed her pelisse and bonnet to the waiting footman, not particularly interested in the post. She couldn't expect an answer from her letter to George for weeks yet. Months if he set it aside to be dealt with later. She smiled at the memory of George's habit of procrastinating in the hope that something would happen and he wouldn't have to deal with whatever the task was.

"The two applicants for the position of governess arrived while you were out, my lady," Compton added. "They are waiting in the salon."

Margaret turned to Philip, frowning slightly as she noted the rigid set of his broad shoulders beneath his bottle-green jacket. He was staring at the battered letter he was holding as though it were capable of biting him.

Philip looked up, his taut features sending a shiver of apprehension down her spine. Now what? she wondered. Philip in this mood would convince even the most desperate governess that unemployment might have its advantages.

"If you would come into the study, madam," Philip said.

Margaret followed him, mentally reviewing what she

might have done to have caused his abrupt change of mood. She wasn't left in doubt for long.

Compton had barely closed the thick mahogany door behind them before Philip gestured angrily with the letter he was carrying. "I told you that you were to have no private correspondence with Gilroy!"

"George?" Margaret looked more closely at the crumpled sheet. That letter was from George? A wave of fear shot through her, leeching the color from her cheeks. What had happened to make him write so soon after his last letter? Before he could have possibly received her answer?

"You told me not to write to him. So far as I know, you said nothing to him about writing to me!" Fear for George drove all thoughts of placating Philip out of her mind. "May I have my letter?" Margaret held out her hand for the precious missive.

"You are my wife. Your mail belongs to me. It is the law."

"It is also the law that mustered-out soldiers are to be left to starve in the street, and yet I don't see you accepting that."

Philip ground his teeth in exasperation. Arguing with Margaret was like arguing with a man. She used a relentless logic that defied easy answers.

"It isn't the same thing at all," he said. "Women need the guidance of their husbands."

Margaret sniffed disparagingly. "The laws that reduce women to little more than some man's chattel, have nothing to do with guidance. They have to do with power, and reserving it for the men who are in control."

Philip opened his mouth to refute her statements, and then closed it. He couldn't effectively argue with what she was saying. Not when he knew it was the truth.

Reluctantly he handed her the letter, wincing at the eagerness with which she grabbed it.

Hurriedly Margaret broke the seal, unfolded the sheet and read the crabbed handwriting.

And then reread it when she couldn't believe what it said. Surely George couldn't mean it? Could it be some sort of trick to confuse Philip? But that didn't make any sense, because George didn't know that she was in Philip's clutches. He thought she was still working as a governess.

"What did he say?" Philip demanded when she continued to stare blankly at the letter.

"That he's getting married." The words didn't sound any more probable spoken aloud than when she'd read them. "To the housekeeper at your villa."

"Madame Gireau? Why would she do a daft thing like that?"

"George is a very nice man." Margaret instinctively defended him. "Although I can't say that I think he'd make a very conformable husband," honesty made her add.

Philip studied her, trying to understand her reaction. She didn't seem so much upset by Gilroy's news as confused. As if his marrying were something that she had never expected to happen, but now that it had she wasn't so sure that it might not be a good idea. Which had to mean that the attachment between them really was familial, as he'd hoped, and not romantic, as he'd feared.

He barely suppressed a sigh at the relief he felt that he wasn't going to have to deal with Gilroy in the future.

"George says that Madame Gireau has a brother who operates a prosperous inn south of Paris, and Madame Gireau is going to invest her savings with him and they are going to help the brother run it," Margaret offered, further reinforcing his conclusion that she didn't mind Gilroy's marriage. Or that he had written anything which had to be kept secret.

Before Philip could respond, the study door was shoved open without so much as a knock, and Annabelle burst into the room, coming to a sudden stop as she saw Philip.

"Hasn't anyone ever told you to knock before entering a room?" Philip said, frustrated at being interrupted.

Annabelle screwed up her slender face in thought and then said, "No."

"Well, consider yourself told," Margaret said. "But since you're here, were you looking for me?"

Annabelle nodded her head vigorously, sending silky wisps of black hair flying around her face.

"Uh-huh. I saw those governesses arrive from the top of the stairs, and I don't like the looks of either of them."

"Don't judge a book by its cover," Margaret automatically responded.

"A cliché, yet!" Philip said.

"Things become clichés precisely because they are true," Margaret said.

"What does the book-cover thing mean?" Annabelle asked.

"It means that you can't tell what someone is like on the inside by looking at them. But you are right to remind me that they are waiting," Margaret said slipping George's astonishing letter into her pocket to be reread later.

"Please ask Compton to inform your grandmother that we are ready to talk to them now, and then have him show the one who arrived first in here."

"Is Papa going to stay?" Annabelle stared doubtfully at him.

A doubt Philip shared. He knew nothing about selecting a governess. Children were the wife's domain.

"Your papa is very interested in your welfare," Margaret said, hoping that by constantly repeating it she could make it true.

"He is?" Annabelle said, and Philip felt a frisson of shame at her patent disbelief.

"Go tell your grandmama we're going to start, Annabelle," Margaret said.

Philip walked over to the fireplace and kicked the blazing log, sending a shower of sparks up the chimney. Could Annabelle really think that he disliked her, as Margaret had claimed? Surely not. He'd never been actively unkind to the child and very few fathers of the ton paid much attention to their young children. Even if she had been his, he doubted that he'd find much about an eight-year-old child to interest him.

Margaret watched the play of emotions across his face as she sat down at one of the two couches flanking the enormous fireplace. Was he already regretting his promise? she wondered. But even if he was, she was sure that he'd keep his word.

Philip had plenty of faults, but he also had the kind of bone-deep integrity that was rare anywhere, let alone in the aristocracy.

"Really, Margaret, this is most irregular!" Estelle's complaining words preceded her plump body into the room. "Your upbringing in France among the nuns has poorly suited—"

"Cut line, woman," Philip said. "If you don't wish to stay, then go away. But cease your complaining."

"Well!" Estelle's formidable bosom swelled at her outrage, and Margaret watched in fascination, wondering if the seams of the thin silk gown Estelle was wearing would prove equal to the strain.

"That I should live to see the day when my own dear Roxanne's husband should accuse me of complaining, after all I've done for him."

"Miss Edgerton." Compton's announcement cut off Estelle's reproaches, and with a disdainful sniff she flounced over to the sofa beside Margaret and plopped down.

Estelle was correct about one thing, Margaret thought. Her upbringing certainly had not prepared her to interview governesses. But simply because she hadn't been bred to the job didn't mean she couldn't learn, she told herself, trying hard to believe it.

A tall, thin woman of indeterminate middle age strode purposefully into the room. She appeared to be made up of various shades of brown—from her gray-streaked brown hair which had been ruthlessly scraped back into a chignon, to her biscuit colored dress which covered her from neck to toe.

"Good morning, Miss Edgerton," Margaret began, and then paused when Annabelle rushed into the room, cautiously skirted Miss Edgerton, and threw herself onto the couch between her and Estelle.

"Please be seated." Margaret nodded to the opposite couch. "Allow me to make known to you the Earl of Chadwick," Margaret gestured toward Philip who straightened up long enough to sketch a bow before he leaned back against the fireplace mantel.

"Lady Annabelle and Mrs. Arbuthnot, her grand-mama."

"Ah yes, the young lady in need of instruction." Miss Edgerton peered at Annabelle rather as if she were a bug who had wandered across her path and she wasn't sure whether she wanted to brush it aside or step on it.

"I think, my lady," Miss Edgerton said, "that you will find my references without parallel. I have worked for the dear Duchess of Warwick these past twenty-five years."

When no one had the temerity to challenge the statement, she continued. "And where is Lady Annabelle in her studies?"

"I can't read!" Annabelle blurted out.

"Can't read!" Miss Edgerton repeated as if she must have somehow misunderstood her.

Annabelle shook her head. "Going to, though," she said. "So's I can read my dance cards."

Margaret ignored Philip's snort.

"Lady Annabelle's education has been rather neglected to date," Margaret began.

"And I suppose I'm to blame for it!" Estelle broke in.

Margaret took a deep breath, reminding herself that Estelle was Annabelle's grandmother and, indolent though she might be, she did love the child.

"I am sure that you did the best you were able to under trying circumstances, Estelle," Margaret said.

"What's a trying circumstance?" Annabelle looked from her grandmother's furious face to her father's sardonic expression.

"Children should be seen and not heard," Miss Edgerton stated in a tone that effectively silenced Annabelle.

"What are you qualified to teach?" Margaret tried again.

"English, literature, poetry, letter writing, arithmetic, penmanship, geography, French, Italian, popular science, religion, watercoloring, deportment, and needlework," Miss Edgerton rattled off.

"Popular science! It is hardly necessary to teach a young lady that," Estelle said.

"Young women are quite capable of learning the most rigorous subjects. And as the dear Duchess says, young ladies must be educated or how else can they effectively raise their sons to be responsible citizens?"

Margaret thoroughly agreed with the Duchess, but not for the same reason. Women should be educated for their own benefit, not simply to serve as more intelligent mothers.

"I presume that Annabelle can speak French and Italian?" Miss Edgerton asked.

"She lives in London," Estelle answered. "Everyone here speaks English. If a foreigner wants to speak to her, they can learn English."

"Now there's an incentive," Philip said, and Margaret frowned at him, her sense of exasperation growing at the devilment she could see dancing in his dark eyes. He was enjoying her discomfort, the wretch!

"But now that that monster has been defeated, one may safely travel on the Continent," Miss Edgerton said. "And, as the dear Duchess is wont to say, in order to partake of a culture, one must at least have the rudiments of its language."

Margaret found herself nodding in agreement.

"I can foresee no difficulty in teaching Lady Annabelle," Miss Edgerton said. "You may reach me through the agency."

She got to her feet, effectively terminating the interview. "There is a family who have requested my services, but as tempting as their offer is, it is not quite what I am used to. They are in trade." Her features wrinkled in distaste. "Good day."

Miss Edgerton nodded regally at Margaret, curtsied to Philip and, ignoring both Estelle and Annabelle, sailed out of the room.

Margaret let out her breath as the door closed behind the woman. She felt as if she was the one who'd just been interviewed, and been found sadly lacking in the bargain.

"I don't like her," Annabelle announced to no one's surprise.

"But she did work for a duchess." Estelle was torn between the social cachet of having a former ducal governess teaching Annabelle, and her complete disagreement with the woman's philosophy of education.

"And I doubt that we'll ever be allowed to forget it," Philip said.

"Miss Murchin." Compton announced the second applicant, and a petite, fairylike creature seemed to float into the room. Her jet-black hair was arranged in a riot of curls which caressed her flawless ivory skin. Margaret's eyes widened when she saw that Miss Murchin had violet eyes. Incredibly beautiful violet eyes.

"Good morning, Miss Murchin," Margaret said. "I would make known to you the Earl of Chadwick."

Miss Murchin gave Philip a slow smile in which admiration, interest, and bravery seemed to be about equally mixed.

How dare she smile at Philip like that? Margaret thought angrily. Philip belonged to *her*. No, Margaret struggled to contain her growing indignation. Philip belonged to himself. He might have actually married her, but he'd made no promises about fidelity.

"And this is Lady Annabelle," Margaret continued.

Miss Murchin spared Annabelle a quick smile and then turned back to Philip.

"She looks very much like you, my lord," Miss Murchin said.

Margaret glanced at Philip to find him studying Miss Murchin with a curiously intent look, and she felt her heart sink. Surely Philip wouldn't dally with his own daughter's governess, would he?

"And this is Annabelle's grandmother, Mrs. Arbuthnot." Margaret finished the introductions, trying to keep her growing sense of impending disaster under control.

Estelle gave Miss Murchin a tight-lipped nod.

"You are so beautiful," Annabelle breathed reverently, and Miss Murchin laughed, a musical sound as perfect as her features.

"Thank you, Lady Annabelle. But I must admit that being beautiful is a great trial for someone in my position in life." She gave Philip a wistful smile that hinted at all kinds of pathos. "So many women simply don't wish to have me join their household. It is so unjust." She dabbed her eyes with a wisp of lawn handkerchief. "Why, I was dismissed from my last job simply because my employer told his wife that she should ask my opinion on a gown she had bought."

Margaret felt her instinctive dislike of Miss Murchin

growing with every word she uttered, and knew she should feel ashamed of herself. The problem was, she didn't. "What are you qualified to teach, Miss Murchin?" Margaret broke the silence.

"Why, anything that a young lady might need to know. Watercolor and globe reading and deportment. My father was a baronet before . . ." The handkerchief came out again to dab her eyes. "Before he succumbed to his fondness for gambling and lost the family fortune. So I am more than qualified to instruct Lady Annabelle in how to go on in society."

"Can you instruct her in any foreign languages?" Margaret asked.

"My last employer employed a Frenchman to instruct his children in the language," Miss Murchin said, "because there is no one like a native speaker to master the accent. Certainly not we poor English. Although I have never understood the necessity of instructing children in a foreign tongue. If foreigners wish to speak to us, they should learn English."

Margaret glanced at Estelle, expecting her to applaud the sentiment. To her surprise, Estelle merely stared at Miss Murchin with a sour expression.

The clock on the mantel chimed the half hour and Philip suddenly straightened up. "Sorry, my dear"—he gave Margaret a smile that she instinctively mistrusted—"but I am promised to the House of Lords shortly, so I must take my leave."

"It is so admirable to find such an important man making time to interview his child's governess. Having a father who is interested in her progress will make it so much easier to teach Lady Annabelle." Miss Murchin smiled approvingly at him.

Philip didn't answer. Instead he fixed an imperious eye on Margaret and said, "I would speak to you before I leave. If you would step into the hall with me?"

Margaret got to her feet and obediently followed him out of the room, since she could hardly refuse under everyone's watchful eye. No doubt he was going to demand that she hire the gorgeous Miss Murchin. Which would be her punishment for having demanded that he be present in the first place.

Philip urged Margaret through the study door with a gentle push between her shoulder blades. She could feel the warmth of his fingers through the thin material of her morning dress, making it hard for her to concentrate on marshaling arguments against hiring Miss Murchin.

Philip led her into the library away from the footman's curious eyes, and closed the door behind them.

"You will not hire that woman," he said.

"That woman?" Margaret repeated, caught off guard.

"Miss Murchin." He gestured toward the closed door and Margaret followed the movement of his hand, becoming hopelessly distracted. He had such intriguing hands. Hands that could induce the most delightful responses from her body by doing no more than touching her. She swallowed uneasily as she felt a sudden tightening deep in her abdomen.

"Pay attention!" Philip's sharp voice cut into her thoughts.

"I am. Her name is Miss Murchin, and she has the most beautiful violet eyes," Margaret inadvertently spoke her thoughts aloud.

Margaret's eyes were far prettier, Philip thought as he stared into the unreadable depths of her bright blue eyes. And far more appealing to him because there was intelligence behind them. Margaret might infuriate him beyond words at times, but she certainly didn't bore him.

"I don't care if she's the reincarnation of Helen of Troy," Philip said. "You are not to hire her."

"As you wish." Margaret was only too happy to agree. "Then you prefer Miss Edgerton?"

Philip scowled. "Not really, although at least she understands that a governess's role is to impart information."

Margaret gave an gurgle of laughter that shivered through Philip, making him forget that he was due at the House of Lords. He wanted to take her in his arms and press his lips against her delectable mouth. He wanted to absorb that enchanting sound into his own body and let it soothe him.

"I think the information Miss Edgerton will impart at depressingly regular intervals is just how her previous employer, the dear Duchess, did things—and it's all your fault!"

"My fault?" Philip watched the laughter sparkle though her eyes with fascination.

"Most certainly. If you would have had the foresight to have been born a duke, Miss Edgerton would have no grounds to compare."

"How remiss of me not to have considered that point in time. Remember that we are promised to the Charletons this evening."

"Yes, sir." Margaret automatically responded to his abrupt change of subject.

"And don't call me sir!" Philip's control suddenly snapped and he succumbed to his growing need for her.

Grabbing her, he yanked her slender body against his solid frame. His arms instinctively tightened around her, binding her against him. Cupping the back of her head, he held her immobile as he captured her mouth.

Just a short kiss, he appeased the part of his mind that was horrified at his lack of control. Just one kiss to quiet his need for her which had been growing all morning.

He took a deep breath as his lips closed over hers, letting the light floral scent that always seemed to cling to her body fill his nostrils. The tantalizing aroma drifted down into his lungs where it seemed to intensify.

Hungrily he pushed his tongue against her soft lips. To

his pleasure her mouth opened, allowing him the freedom to explore the soft moistness. It was the very intensity of his own reaction that gave him the strength to withdraw.

Releasing her as abruptly as he'd taken her in his arms, he stepped back.

He watched as Margaret slowly ran the tip of her pink tongue over her lower lip, and it was all he could do not to yank her back into his arms.

Go, he urged himself. *Leave now before she realizes just how badly you want her and uses that knowledge against you.*

Philip turned and left the room.

Automatically accepting his hat and gloves from the footman, he ordered his carriage to be brought round and then he stepped outside, breathing in great gulps of the cold air in an attempt to clear the lingering effects of that kiss from of his mind.

He looked up as he heard the sound of a carriage approaching. He recognized it as Hendricks' as the groom came to a halt in front of him.

"Good morning, sir," Philip said when Hendricks emerged from the closed carriage. "What brings you here this morning?"

"I wanted to give this to Margaret." Hendricks reached back into the carriage and pulled out a painting. "I was going to hang it in my study, but I was able to convince Lawrence to start a portrait of her next week so I decided to wait and hang that one instead."

"I'm sure that . . ." Philip's voice trailed off in shock as he got a good look at the painting Hendricks was holding.

Hendricks chuckled at Philip's reaction. "It gave me quite a turn, too, when I first saw it."

Philip's eyes narrowed as he studied the portrait closely. It was Margaret, and yet it wasn't. Or were the faint differences he could see due to a lack of skill on the part of the artist? But if that were the case, when had it been painted?

"And why is she wearing such an old-fashioned dress?" Philip unconsciously voiced his thoughts aloud.

"Because that was in style when she lived," Hendricks explained, clearly enjoying Philip's confusion. "This is a portrait of Jane Hendricks, who is a grandmother several times removed of mine, and thus Margaret's. Uncanny resemblance, don't you think?"

Frightening would be more descriptive, Philip thought grimly. Especially since he knew full well that Margaret wasn't Hendricks's daughter. But if she wasn't his daughter, how could she so closely resemble an ancestor of his?

"It makes me wonder if I might not have a grandson who looks like me." Hendricks gave Philip a hopeful look that Philip didn't even notice. He was too busy trying to figure out the implications behind that astounding portrait.

"I won't detain you," Hendricks said. "I imagine you're off to the House of Lords to listen to Northumberland's speech."

"Yes." Philip looked up to find that his carriage was approaching from the stables.

"Good day, sir," Philip said, when what he wanted to do was to accompany Hendricks back into the house and demand an explanation of Margaret.

Philip climbed into his carriage and rubbed his forehead as he tried to reconcile what he'd just seen with what he knew. He couldn't. Clearly he was missing something. Something important, but what?

How could Hendricks have a portrait of an ancestress of his that was the living image of Margaret?

No, that wasn't the question. Philip corrected himself. That was a fact. Hendricks had the portrait—had had the portrait all his life. So it couldn't be a forgery. Besides he himself was the only one who would have had reason to try to place a fake painting of Margaret in Hendricks's possession, and he hadn't done it. Not only had the idea never occurred to him, but there hadn't been time.

The explanation that made the most sense was that Margaret really *was* Hendricks's daughter, but he didn't see how that could be. Not only was she two years too old, but his informant had been quite clear: Hendricks's wife and his daughter had died at the convent.

Could Hendricks's wife have passed off another child as her daughter while leaving her real daughter with . . . With whom? Philip wondered. And for what purpose? From everything that had been said about her she had been a bird-witted woman who lived to indulge herself. Certainly not the kind of woman to involve herself in murky plots.

No, Margaret couldn't be Hendricks's daughter. He was sure of that.

He stared blindly at the brown leather seat opposite him and tried to figure out what else he was sure of when it came to Margaret Abney. He had learned lots of assorted bits and pieces about her, ranging from the incredible way her naked body felt beneath him, to her surprising education, the full extent of which he had the lowering feeling, might well exceed his own. But her background was still a closed book.

Could she be Hendricks's *natural* daughter? The idea suddenly occurred to him. It would explain her uncanny resemblance to the portrait. But how could he find out? He could hardly ask Hendricks if he happened to have sired a bastard about thirty years ago and if he had, what had he done with the child?

And why hadn't Margaret mentioned that portrait to him? Because she knew why she resembled the woman in it? A shaft of excitement shot through him at the probable explanation.

Just as soon as he concluded his business in Parliament

today, he'd send a courier to his operatives in France and tell them to find out everything they could about her. And they could start by interrogating Gilroy.

Since it appeared that Gilroy really was her cousin, he would know her background. He might even be able to throw some light on the puzzle of Hendricks's portrait.

Philip frowned. There were too many loose ends connected with Margaret, and loose ends had a nasty habit of strangling the unwary.

Nineteen

"And your eyes rival the stars for brilliance, Lady Chadwick," Daniels said as he waltzed her around the dance floor.

Margaret kept her smile pasted firmly on her face and tried not to yawn.

Why was he spouting such fustian? she wondered. Because he believed that all women wanted to hear compliments and the more outrageous, the better? Or could his compliments have another purpose? Could he feel that, if he emptied the butter-boat on her every time they met, she would continue to help him in his pursuit of Drusilla?

Margaret didn't know. In fact, about the only thing she could state with any certainty about Daniels was that he wanted to marry Drusilla. And that he had no money. At least, no money by the ton's standards. But he must have some. He was always dressed very fashionably and, while she found his style too flamboyant for her own taste, she knew that such excesses of fashion did not come cheaply.

Not only that, but he had rooms at the Albany, which was a gentleman's establishment and couldn't be cheap.

"Your white dress makes one believe you are a Greek goddess." Daniels delivered the words as if they were a gift.

"I certainly hope not!" Margaret's instinctive response surprised him, and he missed a step in his confusion.

"The Greek goddesses were not renowned for their faithfulness," she explained once they had regained the dance's rhythm.

"Ah, but what about Penelope? She waited years for her husband to return."

"Twenty years—and she wasn't a goddess. She was simply the poor, neglected wife of a man who didn't have the sense to stay home where he belonged!"

Daniels's eyes widened at her tart tone. "Ah, my lady Chadwick, you are indeed an original." His laugh sounded forced to her critical ears.

If only he knew just how much of an original she was, Margaret thought uneasily. She must be the only bastard countess in the whole of England.

"You have earned my lifelong gratitude for your incredible kindness to Drusilla and me. Without your help I fear we would have been torn apart and our love would have been left to wither into dust."

Margaret smiled weakly, wondering if he would continue to talk like that after he and Drusilla were married. Surely he had other interests to discuss? Philip did.

To Margaret's relief the dance finally ended and she was able to step out of his arms.

"Thank you for the dance, Lady Chadwick." Daniels gave her a wistful smile that was not reflected in his hard brown eyes, which were watching her carefully. To judge the effect of his words?

What was the matter with her tonight? Margaret wondered uncertainly. Why was she being so critical of Daniels all of a sudden? If Drusilla didn't mind his lack of conversation, why should she? In fact, she should be glad that Daniels was so shallow, because the less there was to him, the more his presence would grate on Mainwaring's nerves over the years, and the richer would be her revenge.

Catching sight of Drusilla on the sidelines, Margaret started toward her.

Drusilla's face lit up with pleasure at the sight of Daniels, and Margaret felt the nagging feeling of unease that had been growing on her over the past week.

"Cousin Margaret. Mr. Daniels." Drusilla gave him a shy smile that made Margaret feel old. Old and culpable. But it shouldn't, she argued with herself. She wasn't forcing Daniels on Drusilla. Drusilla had picked him out before she'd ever arrived in London.

"Miss Mainwaring." Daniels gave her a conspiratorial smile. "What a surprise to find you without your usual crowd of admirers."

He forgot to tell her that she was beautiful, Margaret thought, and then choked on a hastily suppressed giggle when Daniels, as if in answer to her unspoken criticism, added, "You are such a vision of loveliness that you quite take my breath away."

"Are you all right, Cousin Margaret?" Drusilla asked uncertainly. "Would you like Mr. Daniels to get you a glass of punch?"

"No, no, I'm fine," Margaret said. "Why don't you and Mr. Daniels dance?"

"Mama said that I was to wait for her here." Drusilla was clearly torn between what she wanted to do and what her mother had ordered her to do.

"I'll wait here for your mother to return and tell her that I insisted you dance," Margaret said.

"Oh, thank you. It will be all right, then." With a grateful smile at Margaret, Drusilla eagerly followed Daniels out onto the floor.

Margaret watched as they joined one of the country sets forming. Drusilla really was a nice young woman. And she deserved better than Daniels. But what could be better than a man who adored you? Margaret argued with herself.

What would it be like to have a husband who loved you? Margaret wondered. To have him hang on your every word? To have him constantly striving to please you?

She tried to imagine Philip gazing at her in blind adoration and begging her to tell him how he could please her, and failed abysmally.

On the other hand, she had no trouble imagining him telling her what she could do to please him. A rueful smile tugged at the corners of her lips at the thought.

Philip gritted his teeth as he watched the play of expression on Margaret's face as she watched Daniels dancing. What could she possibly find to admire in that fop? Was that the kind of man she admired? Wastrels who gambled their inheritance away? Like Roxanne's last infatuation with Grimshaw's youngest son. She . . .

No. Philip made a valiant effort to control the anger building in him. Margaret wasn't Roxanne. Roxanne had taken numerous lovers and cuckolded him in the eyes of the polite world. Margaret hadn't done that. Yet. He swallowed uneasily as he watched her continue to watch Daniels.

Margaret was Margaret, he repeated to himself. She was very different from Roxanne. Different in almost every respect. Margaret had unexpected depths to her personality. And it was those depths that worried him. He scowled forbiddingly as he remembered Hendricks's startling portrait. An elderly matron who'd been about to approach him suddenly changed her mind and headed in the other direction. He was finding it increasingly difficult to wait for his operatives to report on her. It would be weeks, maybe as long as a month before he could even hope to hear something.

Simply asking Margaret about that portrait certainly hadn't enlightened him any. She'd shrugged and disclaimed all knowledge of how she could look like Hendricks's ancestress. And when he'd persisted, she'd tried to distract him in some improbably philosophical discussion about dopplegängers.

Philip relaxed slightly when Mainwaring's wife approached Margaret, claiming her attention. Margaret couldn't get into trouble with her. In fact, he strongly suspected that Satan himself would perish of boredom if forced to endure more than a few minutes of Lady Mainwaring's company.

Momentarily satisfied, Philip went looking for a peer with whom to discuss his bill.

"Good evening, Cousin Margaret," Lady Mainwaring said, and then glanced around, clearly looking for her daughter.

"Drusilla was talking to me and when she was asked to dance I told her to go and I would wait until you got back and tell you where she was."

"That was kind of you, Cousin Margaret." Lady Mainwaring scanned the dance floor.

Margaret could tell the exact moment Lady Mainwaring caught sight of Drusilla because her eyes narrowed and her lips compressed in annoyance.

"Is something wrong?" Margaret asked.

"No!" Lady Mainwaring tried to soften the harshness of the word with a forced smile. "It is simply so vexing. Drusilla will dance with Mr. Daniels when she knows full well that he is not an eligible connection."

"But he must be of good family or he wouldn't have gotten an invitation." Margaret automatically defended him.

Lady Mainwaring snorted inelegantly. "You haven't been in society long, Cousin Margaret, and, while your charitable outlook does credit to the nuns who sheltered you, I'm afraid that in the real world things are often not what they seem."

Of that, Margaret had not the slightest doubt.

"Mr. Daniels might look a fashionable, young man, but in truth he hasn't a feather to fly with. No, he is hanging out for a rich wife. And Drusilla is too innocent to see it, despite her father telling her again and again. And what he's going to say when he finds out about her necklace . . ." Lady Mainwaring clicked her tongue in exasperation.

"He?" Margaret asked beginning to get slightly confused.

"Mainwaring. He's going to be so upset. He just gave her those pearls a few months ago to mark her come-out and for her to have lost them . . .

"Of course, he's given her jewelry since she was born," Lady Mainwaring continued, "but they were mere baubles compared to the value of those pearls."

Since Drusilla was born. Margaret examined her words. As far as she could remember, her natural father had never given her anything. In the end, it turned out that he hadn't even given her his name.

"Now I ask you, Cousin Margaret," Lady Mainwaring continued with her complaints, "how could anyone have a necklace slip off their neck while walking in the park and not notice it? You didn't happen to notice it, did you?"

Margaret frowned uncertainly. "Me?"

"Drusilla said it happened while you were walking with her yesterday. She said the only reason that she was wearing her pearls was that you had admired them, and she wanted to please you."

"No, I didn't notice them," Margaret said, trying to think. She was almost positive that Drusilla hadn't been wearing her pearls yesterday, but not positive enough to say so.

But why would Drusilla claim she had been wearing them, if she hadn't?

"I tell you, I have been frantic. I've had our footmen

and the stablehands scouring the park looking for the necklace, but they haven't found a thing. Which is hardly to be wondered at. There are so many unsavory people in London now that the war is over."

"Hungry ones too," Margaret added.

Lady Mainwaring sniffed. "Then let them go to the poorhouses! We certainly pay enough taxes to support them."

Margaret didn't even waste her breath trying to argue. Nothing she could say would ever change Lady Mainwaring's opinion. Lady Mainwaring was the product of centuries of privilege. She had never wanted for anything in her life and probably never would.

"Ah, here is Drusilla now." Lady Mainwaring looked over Margaret's shoulder.

Margaret turned and watched as Drusilla, a flush of pleasure still lighting her face, walked toward them beside Mr. Daniels.

"There you are, Drusilla." Lady Mainwaring's voice was an accusation.

"Good evening, Lady Mainwaring," Mr. Daniels said.

Lady Mainwaring ignored him. "Come, Drusilla, your godmama was asking after you. Cousin Margaret." Lady Mainwaring nodded to Margaret and, still ignoring Daniels, left, trailed by the dejected-looking Drusilla.

Chilled by Lady Mainwaring's snub, Margaret turned to Daniels and was shocked by the malevolent expression on his face. It was gone so quickly that she couldn't be sure that she actually saw it. Not that she blamed him for being angry. Lady Mainwaring had been appallingly rude, but even so . . .

For one brief instant, Margaret had felt as if she had caught a glimpse of a totally different personality from the one Daniels normally presented to the world.

"I hope you don't mean to drop my acquaintance, too,

Lady Chadwick, simply because my father was imprudent with the family fortune," Daniels said.

"No, of course not," Margaret said. "But I also don't intend to spend the evening in your pocket. I certainly wouldn't want to give Drusilla cause for jealousy." She tried to make light of her impulse to get away from him.

"Drusilla knows that she has my heart forever and that no woman, even one as beautiful as you are, can ever replace her. But, since Lady Mainwaring will be guarding Drusilla for the rest of the evening and you won't favor me with another dance, I might as well retire to the card room. Even though they only play for chicken stakes.

"Until tomorrow, Lady Chadwick. I can't tell you how much Drusilla and I appreciate your efforts on our behalf. Especially since we know how society would censure you for your kindness to us if it were to become known."

With a graceful bow, he left.

Margaret watched him go, his final words ringing in her ears. Had there really been a threat in them? A threat to expose her involvement in his and Drusilla's clandestine affair if she didn't continue to help them? Or was she simply imagining things?

She didn't know. There seemed to be so many things in her life lately that she just wasn't sure of.

Margaret looked up and caught sight of Philip talking to a portly man near the refreshment tables. Critically she studied him, searching for signs of the cold that had dogged him all week. His face didn't appear to be flushed, and she hadn't heard him cough once tonight.

As if the intentness of her stare had drawn his attention, Philip looked up and saw her. Margaret felt light-headed as her gaze became entangled in his.

He had the most beautiful eyes, she thought. Eyes she would never tire of looking into—because she loved him. The shocking fact erupted in her mind with the force of a blow.

No! She instinctively rejected the appalling idea. She couldn't be in love with Philip Moresby. Love was a gentle emotion, and there was nothing gentle about her reaction to Philip. He seemed to raise effortlessly the most violent emotions in her. Emotions that ran the gamut from a strong desire to do him an injury, to a compulsion to protect him from the pain he still felt at Roxanne's betrayal.

Not only that, but love left a woman vulnerable. Love had held her mother captive to her father's wicked deception and, when Mainwaring finally threw her love back in her face, he destroyed her very reason for living.

Margaret felt the blood drain from her cheeks at the memory of her mother's wasted form lying in her coffin. In a very real sense her mother's love for Mainwaring had killed her. But she wasn't her mother, Margaret tried to reassure herself. Her mother had been a frail, gentle woman who hadn't had the slightest inkling of how to deal with adversity. She, on the other hand, had the mental fortitude to tackle all kinds of problems, from living on a pittance to coping with unexpected husbands.

"Are you ill?" Philip's dark voice flowed enticingly over her agitated nerves, adding to her sense of disorientation.

Margaret ran the tip of her tongue over her dry lips and tried to force her muddled thoughts into something approaching their normal order.

"Margaret?" Philip's voice took on an all-too-familiar impatient edge when she simply stared at him in bewilderment.

She stifled a sigh. Clearly he didn't hold any tender emotion for her or he'd never bark at her like that. He'd be supportive and sympathetic and gentle and . . . And totally unlike the man she had come to know, she conceded.

He grasped her slender shoulder. "What is the matter with you?"

"Nothing." *Other than the fact I have committed the monumental folly of falling in love with you,* she thought, wondering what he would say if she were to tell him.

He might pity her. The appalling thought helped to steady her. She could live with his impatience, even with his anger, but not with his pity. Pity would corrode her soul and destroyed her self-respect.

"I have the headache." She gave the first excuse that came to mind.

"Then I'll take you home and go on to my clubs since I can't accomplish anything more for my bill this evening. This rout is too thin of company."

Margaret was only too glad to leave. She wanted to think about her self-discovery in the privacy of her own room.

After an almost sleepless night of examining her problem from all angles, Margaret came to the conclusion that the fact that she had fallen in love with Philip needn't make any difference so long as Philip never found out. She still wasn't happy at her wayward heart's idiocy, but she felt she could cope with the situation.

Her resolve was put to the test as soon as she stepped out of her bedroom and saw Philip striding down the hall toward her.

Her breath caught in her throat as a complex flood of emotions cascaded through her. She wanted to grab him and press her mouth against his lips. She wanted to feel the hard warmth of his body against her much-softer one. And, paradoxically, she wanted to yell at him for making her feel that way.

Remember your plan of action. She dragged her gaze up over his broad chest to his beloved features. Annabelle was her first priority. She was going to get him to see Annabelle as a person in her own right and not as a living reminder of Roxanne's infidelities, if it was the last thing she ever did.

"Good morning," Margaret said. "I was just about to go up to the nursery to say good morning to Annabelle."

"Don't let me detain you."

"You won't, because you are going to come with me." Margaret tried to sound more sure of herself than she was.

Philip looked down his nose at her as if she were a worm he'd just found in his apple, infuriating as well as confusing her.

How could she be in love with Philip and yet want to thump him? She remembered her earlier doubts. Drusilla was in love with Daniels, and Margaret was as certain as she could be that Drusilla had never entertained an uncivil thought about the man. So did that mean that she wasn't in love with Philip, or did it mean that Drusilla wasn't really in love with Daniels?

"Would you care to take odds on that?" Philip's voice broke into her confused thoughts.

"You gave me your word. For one month you promised to try."

Philip grimaced. "I must have been mad to have agreed to that."

"As the recipient of your promise, I am not required to verify your state of mind."

"Tell me, since you seem to have all the answers, what am I supposed to say to Annabelle once we reach the nursery?"

Margaret shrugged. "I have no more knowledge of children than you do. Less, in fact, because I've never even shared a house with one."

"No brothers and sisters?" Philip slipped the question in.

"No," she said, for the first time wondering if her mother's failure to have had a son had been a factor in her father's rejection of her. No, she finally decided. Even if her mother had a son, he still would have been a bastard and unable to inherit the barony.

"When does Miss Edgerton start?" Philip asked.

"Not for two more weeks because—"

"The dear Duchess still needs her?"

Margaret's lips twitched at his wry tone as she started up the back stairs to the nursery floor. She'd felt the same sense of disbelief when Miss Edgerton had told her that.

Philip followed her, his eyes lingering on the gentle sway of her slender hips beneath the thin woolen morning dress she was wearing. He could feel the now-familiar tightness begin to spiral through his loins. He wanted to grab her and pull her back against him. He wanted to gather her up and carry her off to his bed. He wanted to hold her captive while he kissed and caressed her and claimed her body.

His breathing shortened at the rush of emotions that surged through him, at the exquisite thought of his man-hood being encased in her silkiness. At the indescribable delight he felt when he spilled his seed deep within her.

"What do you want?" Annabelle's truculent tone was like a dash of icy water on his overheated emotions.

"I came to say good morning and to see how your chess game was progressing." Margaret refused to take offense.

"Then what's he here for?" Annabelle gestured toward Philip. "He can't play chess."

"Shakespeare was right," Philip muttered.

"Who?" Annabelle demanded.

"The man who said that an ungrateful child is sharper than a serpent's tooth," Philip said.

Annabelle frowned. "Does that mean I should lie and say you're good at chess?"

"Your father is not a bad chess player." Margaret tried to rescue the deteriorating conversation. Annabelle might not be Philip's daughter, but she certainly shared his blunt-ness.

"But you beat him and you're only a woman."

"I beat him because I happen to be an excellent chess player. Would you like to have a lesson?" Margaret asked.

"I guess so." Annabelle hurried over to the chess board with a speed that belied her indifferent words. "What do I do first?"

Margaret waited until Philip had folded his body into the child-sized chair.

"Nod gracefully to your opponent. Chess is a game played by gentlemen." Margaret repeated the first instructions she'd ever been given.

"I am not a gentleman," Annabelle said.

"A mere bagatelle. Follow the instructions."

Annabelle nodded awkwardly at Philip and then looked down at the pieces. "I want white so's I can go first."

"It seems to me that I should have white since it's two against one," Philip said.

"That doesn't matter," Annabelle said. " 'Cause Margaret could beat you by herself."

To Margaret's relief, Philip merely shook his head at such plain speaking.

"Let's try a center opening with *d*-pawn," Margaret said.

"Huh?" Annabelle looked blankly at Margaret.

"Each of the squares on the board is named," Margaret explained. "The bottom of the board is *a* through *h* starting from the left, and the side is one through eight starting on the bottom. So *d*-pawn would be your fourth pawn from the left."

"You mean this one?" Annabelle moved the correct pawn one place forward."

"Very good," Margaret approved, waiting to see what Philip would do. His response was cautious and as a result it took Margaret almost half an hour to put his king in checkmate.

"I won," Annabelle crowed, "but I still don't see why I can't take his king. I won it."

"A king is never captured. The game ends before that."

"Why?" Annabelle persisted.

Margaret shrugged. "It's just the rules. Perhaps because it's a very old game, and kings thought they were so important that no one ever dared suggest that they might be captured. Even in a game."

"Kings still think they're omnipotent," Philip said as he got to his feet. "Next time I get to be white."

"But I like white, and it doesn't make any difference, does it, Margaret?"

"Yes, it does. White gets to move first and that means that white is automatically the aggressor while black must defend. At least until black can wrest control from white."

"Excuse me, my lady," Compton's voice interrupted them, "but Miss Mainwaring is here. She said that you were expecting her?" The very slight narrowing of his nostrils showed what Compton thought of such early callers.

"Thank you. I'll be right down," Margaret said, remembering Daniels's parting comment about seeing her today. Probably he and Drusilla had planned to meet here during their dance together.

Margaret fought down her sense of distaste, knowing it was unreasonable since helping their romance along had been her goal from the beginning. No, she corrected herself, not helping their romance. Helping Drusilla to humble their mutual father was her goal. Helping Drusilla's romance along was merely a means to an end.

"Don't go, Margaret." Annabelle ordered, sounding like Philip at his most imperious. "I want to play another game."

"Not me." Philip headed toward the door. "I intend to quit while I'm only one game down."

"And I have to see my visitor," Margaret told the glowering child. "Why don't you visit with your grandmama?"

"Don't want to! I want to play another game!" Annabelle shouted at her.

"That is your decision," Margaret said, and left the nursery, ignoring Annabelle's screams that she come back.

Margaret sighed, trying not to feel discouraged at the child's tantrum.

To Margaret's disappointment, Philip had already disappeared down the nursery stairs when she reached them. She shot a quick look around the salon as she entered, refusing to admit even to herself that she was disappointed not to find Philip there.

"I'm so sorry to come calling at such an unfashionable hour, Cousin Margaret, but Mama has forbidden me to go to the park and, if I came later your salon would be full of visitors and someone might notice Mr. Daniels was here, too, and tell Mama."

Drusilla heaved a dismal sigh. "I vow it's just like Mr. Daniels says."

"What's that?"

"That we are just like Romeo and Juliet."

"No!" Margaret said, not liking the analogy. Drusilla was impressionable enough without wallowing in a Shakespearean tragedy.

"But we are," Drusilla insisted with a stubbornness that seemed totally at variance to her normal reticence.

"I meant that Juliet was only thirteen years old," Margaret said.

"Thirteen! But that can't be!"

"Read the play. But enough of Shakespeare. Tell me about your necklace. Your mother was up in the boughs about it last night. She seemed to feel I was somehow partially responsible."

"Oh, that." Drusilla flushed a bright pink. "I am so sorry to have involved you, Cousin Margaret, but I didn't know what to do. If I said that I lost it at home, Mama would blame the servants."

Margaret didn't understand. "Did you lose it at home?"

Drusilla shook her head unhappily. "I didn't lose it at all. It was just that saying I had was the only way I could think of to explain it being gone. "You see . . ." Drusilla fixed a pleading eye on Margaret. "I gave it to Mr. Daniels because it wasn't his fault that he had such a run of bad luck. And the pearls were mine. Papa gave them to me."

"Bad luck?" Margaret repeated uneasily.

"It wasn't his fault," Drusilla repeated. "He was only trying to win enough so that we could be married and his luck turned and he found that he was losing."

"He should have stopped playing!"

"Oh no," Drusilla said with an innocence that Margaret found chilling. "He explained to me that luck always turns, and he forced himself to continue playing because he was desperate to win the money to establish himself. But when the game was over, he found he owed more than he could pay and he was going to have to rusticate and then I wouldn't have been able to see him, so I gave him my pearls. Of what worth are pearls when weighed against true love?"

Margaret was unable to believe that anyone even remotely related to her could mouth such nonsense. Had Drusilla no common sense? Or was it that she had been so protected her entire life that she'd never had a chance to develop any? And what kind of man would accept such an expensive gift from a young girl?

"You agree with me, don't you, Cousin Margaret?"

Margaret stared at Drusilla, seeing not Mainwaring's legitimate daughter, but a naive young woman who was teetering on the brink of disaster. If she continued to help Drusilla, she would elope with Daniels, and Margaret would have her revenge on Mainwaring. But the cost to Drusilla would be far greater than she'd originally thought.

Margaret took a deep breath. Much as she hated Mainwaring, she couldn't go through with it. She couldn't go through with it because she herself knew what it was to love a man. If Drusilla married Daniels, she'd never have a chance to find a man who was worthy of her love. A man she could respect.

"No, I don't agree with you," Margaret said. "I thought the only impediment to your marriage to Daniels was that he had no fortune, but any man who gambles with money he doesn't have and then wheedles jewelry out of a young woman who trusts him to pay his debts is no gentleman. He is a scoundrel."

Drusilla stared at Margaret in shock, two bright pink patches stained her cheeks and her lower lip trembled. "How can you say such things about the man I love?"

"Perhaps it's because I'm not emotionally involved that I'm able to see the situation more clearly. You must see—"

"No!" Drusilla jumped to her feet. "All I can see is that everyone is trying to tear us apart. And I thought you were my friend!" Drusilla burst into tears and rushed from the house.

Margaret swallowed on the sour taste in her throat, feeling as if she'd just struck a defenseless child. She might know in her heart that she'd done the right thing, but at the moment she found it cold comfort.

Twenty

Margaret studied the creased, faded marriage license that her mother had always carried with her, even after she found out that it was a forgery, and felt all her old feelings of impotent grief and anger welling up inside her.

Jerkily she walked across her bedroom and, twitching aside the heavy curtains, looked out into a gray morning that exactly matched her mood. All her grandiose plans to extract revenge from Mainwaring had come to exactly nothing.

She glanced at the document again, her eyes narrowing as she tried to remember specifics from the last horrific scene between her parents that she'd been an unwilling witness to.

She vaguely recalled her mother saying that they had to be married because the ceremony had been performed in church, and her father responding that the man who had pretended to marry them had only been the brother of the real rector.

Which church? Her eyes skimmed the document. St. Agnes Church, Lanham Place, London—and a John Younger was listed as the presiding minister.

It would give her some small consolation to find this John Younger and tell him exactly what she thought of him for allowing his brother to use his church for such a vile purpose. Even if John Younger were no longer the rector at St. Agnes, his successor might be able to give her his direction.

A burst of determination burned away her feelings of frustration. It wasn't much of a revenge, but it was better than nothing.

St. Agnes Church, Lanham Place—she committed the name to memory. She would begin her search immediately after Philip left for Parliament this morning.

At the thought of Philip, her eyes instinctively swung to the door leading to their shared sitting room. Why didn't he visit her room anymore? The question that had nagged at her all week resurfaced to plague her.

Could he be bored with her already? Uncertainly she gnawed on her lower lip. Could he have sought consolation elsewhere? Stark jealousy ripped through her, making her skin tingle. The very thought of Philip taking another woman in his arms made her feel angry and faintly desperate.

Restlessly Margaret began to pace across the snuff-colored carpet. Or could it be that her wanton response to him in the carriage that night had so disgusted him that he didn't want to touch her?

Her stomach twisted painfully at the thought of never again being able to feel his warm supple body covering hers.

"Why are you scowling at the carpet?" Philip's deep voice jerked her out of her tangled thoughts, and she whirled around to find him standing in the sitting-room doorway.

A rush of pleasure at the sight of his lean features flooded her, but she hastily tried to hide the fact beneath a mask of unconcern which matched his brusque manner.

"It hardly seems worth looking at. In fact"—he looked around the room as if seeing it for the first time—"This whole room looks appalling. Why don't you do something to it?"

"Such as?" Margaret asked absently, her mind taken up with the question of why had he come into her room. Not to make love to her, or he wouldn't be fully dressed. She eyed his Spanish-blue coat and fawn trousers.

Philip shrugged. "New furniture? Chinese wallpaper or maybe some light-colored paint?" A pale rose paint, Philip thought. Like her exquisite skin. Or perhaps a dusky pink rose to match her nipples. A quiver in reaction to the image that popped into his mind shafted through him, and he swallowed as he felt his body's instinctive response.

He didn't want to remember what her breasts looked like. He wanted to see them. He wanted to kiss them. He wanted to hear the enchanting little sounds she made deep her in throat when he made love to her.

It was too soon. Ruthlessly he stifled his longings.

First he had to give her time to forget his barbaric behavior in the carriage. Then he'd try to insinuate himself in her bed again.

Uncertainly Margaret waited, wondering at his abstracted expression. Was it because he didn't want to think about changes being made to his mother's room, as Estelle had claimed, or was it because he didn't care much and his mind was elsewhere? Probably he didn't care, she decided. Because Philip being Philip, if he cared, he'd flatly refuse to let her change so much as one threadbare pillow.

"You ought . . ." Philip started, only to be interrupted when there was a loud thump on the hallway door a second before it burst open, and Annabelle rushed into the room.

"Lookee, Margaret! Lookee what I . . ." Annabelle came to a precipitous halt when she saw Philip.

"I knocked first," she told him.

"So you did," Margaret agreed with her, debating whether to add that one usually waited for permission to enter before one opened the door, and decided against it.

Too many new rules all at once would only discourage the child.

Philip stared down at the child's thin face, looking for some sign of Roxanne's beauty. He couldn't find it. The only trace of Roxanne he could see in her daughter was her dark hair, and even that lacked the gloss that had characterized Roxanne's.

Annabelle must have inherited her undistinguished looks from her father. Whoever that might have been. His features hardened at the thought.

"What have you got, Annabelle?" Margaret hastily changed the subject, not liking the expression on Philip's face. If he were to utter something cutting, Annabelle would undoubtedly retaliate, and one more day of the fast-dwindling month would be wasted.

"Marbles. See?" Annabelle held out a scruffy leather bag.

Margaret took it and poured the contents onto the bed.

"I haven't seen those since I was Annabelle's age." Philip picked up a cloudy blue marble and rolled it between his thumb and middle finger. About to tell her that marbles were for boys, Philip suddenly remembered the pleasure he'd felt when he'd discovered old toys in the nursery cupboards. Somehow they'd always seemed better than the toys his doting parents had showered him with. And Annabelle didn't even have doting parents. All she had was a foolish, vain old woman.

And a formidable, if unexpected, champion in her stepmother, Philip reminded himself. Poking among the marbles, he located his favorite shooter and held it up to the scant light coming in through the window to make sure it wasn't cracked.

"Do you play marbles?" Annabelle asked Margaret.

Margaret shook her head. "No, my mother always claimed it was a boys' game."

"I'll show you how," Philip heard himself offer at the disappointed expression on Annabelle's face.

"Show me, too." Margaret hurried to reinforce his offer before Annabelle said something that made him remember an urgent appointment elsewhere. She wasn't sure if his offer was a result of his promise or whether it was simply a nostalgic wish to indulge in a boyish game, but whatever it was, she intended to take advantage of it.

Philip divided the marbles into three groups, handing one pile to Margaret and one to Annabelle.

"That's not fair," Annabelle complained. "You got the prettiest ones."

"They're all the same," Philip said.

"But I like red ones best," Annabelle said, "and I was the one that found them."

"Trade with your father, then," Margaret said. "He won't mind, because he thinks they're all the same."

Philip looked into her dancing eyes and completely forgot about marbles. He wanted to play other games with her. Far more intimate games. He was so wrapped up his thoughts that he didn't even notice when Annabelle substituted half of her marbles for all of his own.

"How does one play?" Margaret asked.

"First we put the smaller ones in a circle." He glanced around, saw her body powder on the dressing table, and used it to mark a circle on the brown carpet.

"We take turns using the bigger marbles to shoot the smaller marbles out of the circle. If you do, you get to keep that marble and you get another turn besides."

"Sounds like gambling to me," Margaret said as she placed her marbles within the circle. "No wonder marbles are the province of males."

Annabelle hopped up and down on one foot in excitement. "I get to go first."

"All right, but let's let your father take a practice shot so we can see how to do it."

Philip obediently got down on his knees and, carefully positioning his marble, shot it, knocking one of Annabelle's pieces outside the circle.

Replacing the marble, he nodded to Annabelle who squatted down and, with an absorbed expression that Margaret found enchanting, shot. She missed.

"I get another turn," Annabelle said.

"No," Philip said. "If you're old enough to play, you're old enough to play by the rules."

"Margaret . . ." Annabelle turned to her.

"Sounds fair to me," Margaret said. "Now it's my turn." Getting down on her knees, she tried to position her marble as Philip had done. The marble wouldn't stay put.

"Here, let me help," Philip said. Leaning over her, he positioned the marble between her thumb and forefinger.

Margaret took a deep breath trying to banish the prickly feeling that danced over her skin at his touch.

"Try now," he ordered.

She obediently shot her marble and managed to hit one of his, but not with enough force to get it out of the circle.

"My turn." Philip positioned his marble and then shot. He not only got one marble, but that one knocked out a second one. "And I get another turn because I—"

"What is going on in here?" Estelle's outraged voice sounded from the open doorway. "Chadwick, are you playing . . . *marbles* with my granddaughter?"

"No!" Philip snapped, embarrassed at having been caught on his knees playing such a childish game and annoyed at Estelle's melodramatics. "I was playing marbles with my daughter and my wife."

Margaret ducked her head, not wanting Philip to see her feeling of triumph at his calling Annabelle his daughter. She was sure his words were simply an unconscious reaction to Estelle's ill-chosen words, but it was a beginning. If she could just get him to continue thinking of

Annabelle as his, sooner or later he'd accept her in his heart, too.

"Marbles are not a suitable occupation for a young lady," Estelle insisted.

"In that case I'll take myself off to Parliament which is where I should have been in the first place." Getting to his feet, Philip stalked out of the room.

Margaret watched him go with regret, still no wiser as to why he had sought her out in the first place.

"Well! What rag manners!" Estelle glared at his departing back.

"Aw, Grandmama! You spoiled everything. I was going to win!" Annabelle scooped up the marbles and raced from the room.

"Practice and we'll try again later," Margaret called after her.

"Really, Margaret, I am disappointed in you," Estelle said. "And you raised in a convent, too. What would the good sisters think of your leading a child astray?"

Margaret blinked. Astray? With a child's game? Unless there was a lot more to marbles than Philip had mentioned she couldn't see any harm to it. Although . . .

Her breathing developed a sudden hitch as she remembered the deliciously suffocating feeling which had gripped her when Philip had bent over to help her. Maybe Estelle was right. Maybe marbles was a game best practiced by adults. She'd definitely have to challenge Philip to a game one evening. She could lure him into her bedroom and—

"Margaret, are you listening to me?"

"Yes, and I'm so struck by the force of your argument that I'm going to go to church and pray."

Estelle's mouth fell open. "What?"

"I'm going to go to church and pray for forgiveness for my sins," Margaret repeated, hard-pressed not to giggle at Estelle's dumbfounded expression.

"But—"

"I must hurry. There's not a moment to lose." Margaret pulled her pelisse out of her wardrobe, grabbed a bonnet at random, and left before Estelle could think of a way to stop her. Or, even worse, offer to accompany her. She certainly wouldn't be able to say what she wanted to the Reverend Younger with Estelle there.

St. Agnes Church turned out to be a small limestone structure sandwiched in between two much-larger buildings. The square it fronted had a faintly shabby air about it, as if it had fallen on hard times recently.

Once through the massive oak doors, she paused to give her eyes a chance to adjust to the dim light inside the church.

"May I help you?" a thin voice to her right asked, and Margaret jumped in surprise.

"I'm so sorry to have startled you, madam, but you looked a little . . . lost?"

Margaret turned to find a thin, elderly man wearing a clerical collar. A wispy fringe of white hair circled his head just above his ears and his eyes were bright blue and full of kindness.

Margaret instinctively knew that this man would never have knowingly assisted in the ruin of a naive young woman.

"I'm the Reverend Mr. Havergal. How may I be of service to you, Miss—" He glanced down at her hands, caught the bump of her wedding band through her gloves and corrected himself. "Mrs. . . . ?"

"Marsh," Margaret used the name she'd decided on. She didn't want to say anything that might link her to Philip. Not that Mr. Havergal looked as of he were very much aware of the doings of the ton.

"I've been living on the Continent for the past fifteen

years, and now that I've returned to London, I promised my mother that I would visit the church where she was married. You see, my mother still lives on the Continent, although my father is dead," Margaret lied.

Mr. Havergal murmured sympathetically.

"Mama asked me to come to the church and obtain a copy of her marriage lines because during the unsettling events in Europe, she lost hers. It would mean so much to her if I were to talk to the minister who married her and have him write out a copy." Margaret smiled hopefully at Mr. Havergal.

"Well, Mrs. Marsh, we must do our very best for your poor mama, but it might not be so easy."

"Why not?" Margaret asked, knowing full well why he wouldn't find a record of her parents' marriage, but curious as to how he could know there'd be a problem.

"When was your mother married here?"

"August twentieth, 1785."

"Dear me. I feared as much . . . Because of your age, you see," he added at her confused look. "Mr. Younger was the rector here then, God rest his soul." He shook his head as if trying to dislodge painful memories. "A wonderful man of God and an inspiration to us all, but dead now, you know."

Margaret felt a surge of disappointment. There had always been that possibility, of course. Thirty years was a long time. She felt her shoulders droop.

"Now, now," Mr. Havergal murmured at her crestfallen expression. "Even though you can't talk to him, we can still see about getting your mother a copy of her marriage lines. If you'll help me look."

"Through the church records?" Margaret said, foreseeing an morning spent searching for something that wasn't there.

"Unfortunately, no. You see, in 1796 there was a fire in the church and all the records were burned."

"Seventeen ninety-six?" Margaret repeated.

"Yes, June twenty-ninth, to be exact. St. Peter's and Paul's feast day. I'll never forget that day. I was Mr. Younger's curate. He and I were in the rectory going over the Sunday sermon when the verger came running in screaming about a fire. Mr. Younger sent me to fetch the fire brigade, and he went to the church because the verger said he'd seen a man go in shortly before the fire broke out, and we were worried that he might be trapped.

"When I returned with the fire brigade, Mr. Younger was dead. A burning beam had fallen and crushed him. And we never did find a trace of the man the verger had seen."

Mr. Havergal removed his spectacles and polished them on his jacket as if his thoughts were to painful to dwell on. "Death is such a waste."

"Yes," Margaret said bleakly, remembering her mother.

"So you see, we don't have the records here. You would have to go to Canterbury."

"Canterbury?"

"Yes. Every year the rector of a church is charged with copying out all the births and deaths and marriages and baptisms and sending them to the cathedral in Canterbury for safekeeping."

"I see," Margaret murmured, her mind still focused on the date of the fire. The church records had burned exactly three days after her father had abandoned her and her mother.

"Unless . . ." Mr. Havergal's eyes suddenly lit up as he remembered something. "Perhaps Mr. Younger recorded your parents' marriage in his journals. I can't promise, of course, but he was normally a very meticulous journalist. He always said that writing things down at the end of the day helped to put the workings of the church into perspective for him."

"They weren't burned in the fire?" Margaret asked.

"Oh, no. He kept those in the study in the rectory. Come along. Since you know the date, it should be an easy matter to check."

Margaret meekly followed along behind him, even though she knew that he wouldn't find an entry. But she could hardly tell him she'd suddenly changed her mind without giving rise to exactly the sort of speculation she wanted to avoid.

Mr. Havergal ushered her into a large study that had to be the nightmare of his poor wife's housewifely instincts. Books lined every wall and had spilled out onto the floor where they fought for space with piles of papers.

"It's a little messy," Mr. Havergal muttered absently as he searched through a stack of thin black books in the glass-fronted bookcase beside the door.

"Aha!" He pulled out one and held it aloft. "This is the journal for 'eighty-five. Now what day did you say they were married?"

"August twentieth."

Mr. Havergal flipped through the pages, finally coming to a stop. "Here we are. Mr. Younger says that it was a fair day made all the fairer by the loveliness of the bride he married."

Mr. Havergal beamed at her, and Margaret smiled back weakly. Had Mr. Younger married someone else that day, and Mr. Havergal was assuming it was her parents?

"He says that Miss Abney was so nervous that he could barely hear her responses, but that Mr. Mainwaring's heartiness more than made up for it."

A wave of dizziness swept over Margaret, chilling her skin and confusing her thoughts. How could Mr. Younger have her parents' names right? It didn't make any sense.

"Mr. Younger goes on to say that your mother wore a lovely blue gown that made him think of the delphiniums his mother used to grow in her garden, and that your father was wearing his regimentals and looked very handsome.

He also said that they didn't have any witnesses with them so he had to press the housekeeper and the verger into service. He feared that perhaps their families were not in favor of the marriage, especially since they had a special license instead of having had the banns announced."

Mr. Havergal peered over the top of his spectacles at her. "I do hope that wasn't true?"

"Oh, no," Margaret said, feeling terrible at lying to this dear old soul. But what could she do? Tell him the truth and shock him to the depths of his unworldly soul? What was the truth anyway? And what about that fire?

Her feeling of disorientation grew. She rubbed her fingers over her forehead, trying to banish the strange ringing sensation in her ears.

"Oh, my dear!" Mr. Havergal suddenly noticed her pallor. "The excitement has been too much for you. Sit down, do." He hastily swept a pile of books off a leather chair and urged her into it.

Margaret sank down, concentrating on breathing. She absolutely couldn't do anything so appallingly missish as faint.

"I'm all right. It's just that . . ." Her voice sounded faint and far away in her own ears.

"I know, my dear." He awkwardly patted her trembling fingers. "Perhaps I should ask my housekeeper to show you to a guest room where you can lie down."

"No." Margaret took a deep breath, willed the feeling away and got to her feet. "I must go home now."

She had to get away so she could think; so she could try to make sense of what she'd learned. She felt as if the facts forming the basis for her life had suddenly shifted and she was now looking at the world from an entirely different perspective.

Margaret allowed Mr. Havergal to help her into the hackney coach he had hailed for her. It required a huge effort on her part to respond with something approaching normalcy to his announcement that he would write to the Cathedral for a copy of her mother's marriage lines, and that she should call for it before she left London. Her thoughts kept whirling through her mind in disjointed fragments, making it difficult to concentrate.

As the hackney pulled away from St. Agnes, Margaret closed her eyes and struggled to think with something approaching her normal levelheadedness.

One fact seemed to rise above the others: Mr. Younger really was an ordained minister of the Church of England, and he really had married her parents. Which meant that she wasn't illegitimate. She was Charles Mainwaring's legitimate daughter. And her mother had really been his wife. But even though he must have known that, he had abandoned her and her mother without a qualm. He also must have known that her gentle, ineffective mother wouldn't have had the means or will to fight him. That she would believe his lies and . . .

And what? Margaret stared blankly at the passing London scenery. Why had he done it?

Because of Hendricks's ultimatum, the answer was immediately obvious: Mainwaring had wanted the money that went with the title, and he had been afraid that if he admitted already being married to a merchant's daughter, Hendricks wouldn't give it to him.

And all those years, when her mother had faded away under the crushing shame of thinking that she'd been living in sin with Mainwaring and had given birth to a bastard . . . Margaret swallowed a sense of outrage so intense it threatened to choke her.

That despicable excuse for a man! Margaret blinked as she suddenly realized something else. Her mother hadn't died until years later. Almost six years later. And Mainwaring had married the present Lady Mainwaring almost immediately after he'd abandoned her and her mother.

Margaret's breath caught in her throat as she suddenly realized the full implications of those two facts.

Not only was his second marriage invalid, but he was a bigamist. Or had been. Did one stop being a bigamist when one of the wives died? She didn't know, but of one thing she was certain, Mainwaring's second marriage wasn't valid. Which meant that Drusilla and her young brother were bastards.

Margaret chewed her lower lip as she considered the shocking thought. Being a bastard was a curse that had haunted her her entire life. Society did not deal kindly with children born on the wrong side of the blanket.

How was Lady Mainwaring going to feel when she discovered the truth? Would her spirit be as crushed as her own mother's had been? At least she wouldn't have to worry about being cast out to starve, Margaret realized. According to Hendricks, she had private means. But even though she and her children wouldn't lack for material things, they would be effectively barred from society.

Margaret felt a fierce surge of satisfaction as she contemplated Mainwaring's reaction when he realized that his precious children would become social pariahs. That his daughter would never be able to make a respectable marriage, and his son could never attend his old school or inherit his title or . . .

Margaret shifted uncomfortably as she remembered what Hendricks had said about the boy's health being frail. Would the blow worsen it? And what of Drusilla? How would she react to losing everything she'd always thought was her birthright?

It would destroy her. Margaret answered her own question. Drusilla didn't have the inner resources to face adversity. In many ways Drusilla was more like Margaret's mother than Margaret herself was.

Margaret frowned. The sweetness of extracting a truly fitting revenge on Mainwaring would be tainted by the fact that three innocent people would have their lives totally destroyed. And that destruction would be on her hands.

She would be doing to them what her own father had done to her and her mother all those years ago. The fact that she had right and the law on her side didn't mean that her father's second family would suffer any less. And they *would* suffer. Margaret had no illusions about how narrow-minded English society could be.

"This be the address ya give me." The hackney driver cut into her muddled thoughts. "Has ya changed yer mind?"

"No. No, thank you." Margaret reached into her reticule and, finding a crown, handed it to him.

Not even hearing his profuse thanks at the size of the coin, Margaret climbed out of the carriage, picking up a dirty smear on her skirt as she did so.

As she crossed the flagstones toward her front door, a small boy who smelled strongly of the stables darted out from behind the iron railings next door and rushed up to her. " 'Scuse me, mum, but be ya Lady . . ." He paused as if trying to remember, and then blurted out, "Chadwick?"

Margaret nodded, wondering who this urchin was. Despite the fact that he smelled as if he hadn't had a bath in months, he looked well-fed and his clothes, while dirty, were neither tattered nor ill-fitting.

"Good. Miss Mainwaring, she told me t'give ya this note, but no one else." He held a grimy, folded square of paper out to Margaret.

Startled Margaret simply stared at it, wondering why Drusilla would be writing to her.

"Please, mum." He gestured with the sheet. "I gots t'get back t'the stable."

"Sorry," Margaret muttered. Digging into her purse,

she found a shilling which she handed to the boy in exchange for the note.

The boy's eyes widened at such largess, and he gave her a shy grin before taking off at a run, rather as if he were afraid she might change her mind and demand her money back.

Margaret gingerly opened the note and frowned at the almost illegible writing she found. Whatever other skills Drusilla had acquired, penmanship wasn't among them. It took Margaret three tries to translate the scrawls and then when she had, she wished she hadn't. Crumbling the sheet in frustration, she hurried up the stairs to her front door.

"Is the earl at home, Compton?" Margaret asked the minute he opened the door.

"No, my lady. He has not yet returned from Whitehall."

She was glad, Margaret told herself. It would be far better if she were to handle Drusilla's latest start herself—without Philip finding out about it, or about her own part in it.

Slipping into the quiet of Philip's study, she reread Drusilla's letter in the hope that she might have misunderstood it. She hadn't. Drusilla's letter rambled on and on about how her parents were determined to ruin her life by separating her from the only man she could ever love and since Margaret was no longer willing to stand their friend, Drusilla had taken the only course open to her and had eloped with her own true love.

"Damnation!" Margaret muttered, sinking into the chair behind Philip's desk.

What was the old saying about being careful what you wish for because you may get it? Well, she had. Her initial plan had come to fruition. And the only emotion she felt was anger. Anger at Drusilla for being such a feather-brained ninnyhammer as to elope, anger at Daniels for being so unprincipled as to have taken advantage of Drusilla's naiveté, and underlying it all was anger at herself, she admitted. Because she had also taken advantage of Drusilla's naiveté to urge her into a rash act. The fact that in the end she'd found she couldn't go through with it, didn't absolve her own guilt. If she hadn't encouraged Drusilla in the first place, Drusilla never would have found the courage to do it.

Margaret winced under the lash of her conscience. She was no better than Mainwaring, willing to destroy another for her own ends—although maybe it wasn't too late to make amends. Margaret glanced at the clock on the mantel.

If they were to elope, they must be going to Scotland. And to get to Scotland they would have to go by way of the Great North Road.

Margaret jumped to her feet. She very much doubted that Daniels owned a closed carriage, which meant that he'd have to hire one and the obvious place to do so would be at a staging inn north of London.

With luck she might be able to intercept them before they left London. Failing that, she would have to go after them. Somehow she had to stop them. If she didn't, she'd have Drusilla's unhappy marriage on her conscience for the rest of her life.

But how could she go chasing after them? The practical side of her nature immediately saw the difficulties. She would need money to hire horses and pay for tolls. And she didn't have any money. At least not more than a few coins. Credit with various merchants, yes. But as for cash . . .

Margaret found her gaze fixed on the middle desk drawer. She had once seen Philip take a box full of bills from that drawer. Was the box still there? And if it was, how much money was in it? Enough to pay for the hire of a carriage and horses?

Not giving herself time to consider the wisdom of what

she was about to do, Margaret yanked open the drawer and pulled out the box. To her dismay it was locked. Briefly she weighed the ethics of breaking it open against the disaster Drusilla faced, and decided to sacrifice the lock.

She shivered at the thought of what Philip would say when he found out. He wasn't going to be the least bit happy about any of this. But he'd be even more unhappy if Drusilla did manage to elope and Margaret's own part in the scandal became known.

Grabbing the silver letter opener off the desktop, Margaret shoved the slender tip beneath the lock and twisted. The beautiful mahogany splintered. To her relief there was a roll of paper money inside, which to Margaret's untutored eyes looked large enough to finance half a dozen elopements and their subsequent rescues.

Briefly she debated writing a note to Philip to explain, but she couldn't figure out what to say. *Please forgive me for stealing your money, but I needed it to stop a naive young girl from eloping which she never would have done it if I hadn't put the idea in her head in the first place?* Or, *Have gone to Scotland, will return later?* Or, perhaps, *I've realized I love you, and I've gone to make sure that my half sister doesn't marry the wrong man and never be able to marry a man she loves?*

Margaret grimaced. She could just imagine his reaction to a declaration of love on her part. No, the best thing for her to do would be simply to tell Compton that she was going to visit the Mainwarings and would return later. Hopefully she would be back before anyone missed her. And as for how she was going to explain the shattered box . . . Perhaps something would occur to her.

She shoved the ruined box back into the drawer and grabbed for her reticule. In her haste she managed to spill its contents on the floor. Hurriedly she stuffed the wad of bills, along with her scattered paraphernalia, back into her reticule before rushing out of the study, intent on finding Drusilla and returning her to her mother as soon as possible.

Twenty-one

"Just a moment, Chadwick. I want to talk to you."

Philip clamped down on his raging sense of impatience to be gone, and waited for Petersham to reach him. Despite the fact that Petersham had flatly refused to vote for his relief bill, he was an old friend of his father's and deserved respect.

"Let's go over here where we can be private." Petersham led the way through the milling crowd outside the Parliament chambers and into a tiny antechamber.

Once they were finally alone, however, Petersham seemed in no hurry to begin. He cleared his throat several times and then tugged on his left ear as if waiting for inspiration.

Philip mentally willed him to get to the point. It had been a long day. He wanted to get home and see Margaret. To talk to her and let her sane observations add some balance to the petty frustrations of his day.

"Now, I don't want you taking this amiss, Chadwick. Fact is I've known you since you were breached. So if I can't give you a word of advice, then who can?"

Philip bit back his urge to give the question the answer it so richly deserved, and waited for Petersham to deliver his all-too-familiar harangue about taxes already being too high and how Philip's ill-conceived relief bill was going to drive the country into bankruptcy.

Philip eyes widened as Petersham began to talk, and he realized what was bothering him had nothing to do with his bill.

"Exactly what is it you are claiming, Lord Petersham?"

"I am not claiming anything, Chadwick. I'm simply telling you what I saw with my own eyes. And I wouldn't even be doing that if your father hadn't been one of my greatest friends. But the fact is, I saw your wife at the Feather and Dove on the Great North Road hiring a traveling carriage not two hours ago."

Petersham must be mistaken. Philip instinctively denied it. It couldn't have been Margaret he'd seen. Not only would she have no reason be hire a carriage, but she had no money to pay for it. Unless . . .

An icy trickle of fear slithered down his spine as he suddenly remembered the money he normally kept in the strongbox in his study. She knew about it. She'd seen him take money out of it.

"You must be mistaken," Philip said.

"Had quite an eye for the ladies in my day," Petersham said. "Might be too old to do much about it now, but a man's never too old to look. And Lady Chadwick is well worth looking at. Not another woman in London to match her for looks. If your tastes run to blondes.

"Women take the strangest notions at times," Petersham said. "Not at all logical like us men."

Margaret was. Philip mentally contradicted him. Margaret was one of the most logical people he knew—man or woman. She acted for very good reasons. At least, good reasons as far as she was concerned. The problem was, Would he think what she was doing was reasonable?

A sinking feeling twisted through him, making his insides churn painfully. Could she have been so disgusted with his uncivilized lovemaking that she felt she had to run away from him? Or had she run away with someone?

It couldn't be Gilroy, because Philip knew where he

was—in France, safely married to Madame Gireau by this time. And there was no one else . . .

A sudden image of Daniels's smoothly smiling face filled his mind. Margaret had stood up with him at every ball they'd attended. Could it signify more than just politeness? Could she have been taken in by that coxcomb's polished manners?

A murderous rage gripped Philip at the thought of Margaret in Daniels's arms. She belonged to Philip. Because he loved her. The shocking realization burst full-blown into his mind, freezing it.

"It's probably nothing," Petersham offered when Philip didn't respond. "But I thought that 'a word to the wise' and all that . . ." Petersham cleared his throat and hurried away.

Philip barely noticed his leaving. His mind was far too taken up by this unexpected and totally unwanted discovery.

Maybe he wasn't really in love with Margaret. He clung to the hope. His feelings for her had very little in common with what he'd felt for Roxanne. He didn't have the slightest desire to place Margaret on a pedestal and worship her; he wanted to yank her into his bed and make love to her. Nor was he content to merely gaze at her beauty as he was with Roxanne.

Not that she wasn't every bit as beautiful, but somehow Margaret's beauty was a very minor part of who she was. Her sharp mind intrigued him far more. He could talk to her about things other than fashion or the latest gossip and be reasonably certain of getting an intelligent response. Not that he always agreed with her analysis of a situation, but at least he could understand her reasoning. Which was far more than he could with the vast majority of people he knew, be they men or women.

And Margaret was kind—not the type of ineffectual kindness that wrung its hands at misfortune and wept.

Her kindness was practical. He remembered her efforts to find Ned a way to support his family and how she'd championed Annabelle.

Uncertainly Philip rubbed his forehead, finally deciding that how he felt about Margaret didn't matter at the moment. What was important now was that he find out if Petersham was right; if it really had been Margaret renting a carriage at the Dove and Feather. Because if it was, he had to find her and tell her . . . what?

That she should come back to him because he loved her? She'd never believe him. Not after the way he'd forced her into marriage. Not after the way he'd all but attacked her in the carriage. He was finding it hard to believe himself.

Never mind, he told himself. First he had to find her and then he'd worry about what to say to her.

Rushing out of the building, Philip hailed a hackney. Perhaps he could suggest they begin again? That they try to fashion something out of their unconventional marriage?

"Here ya is, milord."

The hackney driver pulled up in front of Philip's house, and Philip tossed him a coin as he vaulted out of the carriage. Racing up the stairs, he pushed open the door, ignoring Compton's pained expression at such a breach of etiquette.

"Is Lady Chadwick here?" Philip demanded.

"She left the house about three hours ago, my lord."

Philip felt a sense of dread plummet through him. It looked as if Petersham had been right.

"She said she was going to visit the Mainwarings," Compton added.

"Tell Jennings I want to see him." Philip started for his study, but Compton's next words stopped him.

"Her ladyship didn't use one of your lordship's carriages. She took a hackney," Compton aimed the information to a point over Philip's left shoulder.

Because she didn't want his groom to know where she was going. Philip reached the obvious conclusion. And if it hadn't been for Petersham being at that inn, he wouldn't have known.

Philip stalked into his study and gave vent to his fear and frustration by slamming the door shut. The impact rattled the china ornaments on the mantel, but it didn't help his feelings at all.

Hurrying over to his desk, Philip jerked open the middle drawer and pulled out the box he kept his ready cash in. His lips tightened when he saw the splintered wood around the lock. Margaret had opened it, and not very neatly. As if she didn't care he knew. Because she had no intention of ever coming back. The wave of pain that swept through him left him dizzy.

He slammed the broken box down on the desktop in impotent frustration. Her suddenly running off didn't make any sense. Margaret had been so adamant about how he had to be a father to Annabelle. She'd even started to teach her to play chess. Why would she go to the trouble of not only befriending the child, but involving him, if she were planning on leaving? And what about her promise to launch Whitman's daughter next season? How could she have left with all those obligations?

Because they didn't balance her dislike of him? He sagged down into his leather chair, feeling crushed beneath the weight of the obvious conclusion. Could she dislike him that much?

His features unconsciously softened as he remembered the sparkle of devilment in her eyes when she'd looked at him over the chessboard after she'd beaten him.

She hadn't seemed to dislike him then.

He was wasting time. There was no way he could understand why she'd left until he somehow managed to catch up with her and ask.

He jumped to his feet and knocked over the chair which fell to the floor with a thump.

The door opened immediately and Compton asked, "Did you call, my lord?"

"No, I . . . Yes," Philip said. "Tell Jennings to hitch up my curricle and have it out front as soon as he can."

"Of course, my lord." Compton closed the door behind him with maddening calm.

First, money. Philip planned. He hurried across the room and shoved aside the Constable landscape that hid the safe. Opening it, he stuffed the money in his pockets.

He had started toward the door when a piece of folded paper under the desk caught his eye. Curious, he picked it up and opened it.

What were the marriage lines of a Mary Abney doing in his study? He'd never heard of anyone named Mary Abney. Could Margaret have dropped it when she'd been rifling his moneybox?

He checked the date on the marriage license? It could be Margaret's mother's. But if it was, then why did Margaret call herself Abney instead of . . .

He checked the license again for the name of the groom. Charles Mainwaring? His sense of confusion grew. Could the Charles Mainwaring in the license be the Charles Mainwaring *he* knew? Could Mainwaring have been married before?

He refolded the license and shoved it into his vest pocket. He might not understand its significance, but one thing he did know. It had to be important to Margaret or she wouldn't have brought it from Vienna. Nor would she have been carrying it with her.

He grimaced. It was just one more thing to add to the list of things that he would ask her about when he finally found her. And he would find her if he had to take Scotland apart rock by godforsaken rock.

But to do that, he'd need help. Help from someone he could trust to remain silent. His friend Lucien immediately came to mind. Lucien would help. Philip would stop by his lodgings and take Lucien with him.

Margaret winced as her ill-sprung hired carriage hit yet another pothole, jarring her already aching body. She sniffed disconsolately. Philip never would have allowed himself to have been fobbed off with a musty smelling yellow bounder and a team who had been in their prime during the last century.

The only consolation she could find in the whole situation was that she was relatively sure that Daniels hadn't been able to afford any livelier horseflesh, so he shouldn't be too far in front of her—provided the young couple the ostler at the Feather and Dove had described to her really was Drusilla and Daniels. Margaret tried to ignore her doubts, which seemed to grow with each weary mile she traveled.

"We's comin' on the Bird-in-Hand, miss," the postboy called down to her. "Got good horseflesh, they do. Good food, too. We usually change horses there when we's goin' north, and get us a bite to eat."

He paused to allow Margaret to comment and when she didn't, added, "Next place is the Fox and Hound and it's another fifteen miles, and it got bad horses."

Rather like the ones your employer rented me, Margaret thought. *Although . . .*

She straightened up as something occurred to her. If it was normal practice to change horses at the Bird-in-Hand, then Daniels and Drusilla might have stopped, too. In fact, they could still be there. From what she'd been told by the innkeeper, the young couple who matched their description hadn't left that long before her.

"All right," she called up to the postboy. "Stop to change horses, although whether we stay to eat or not depends."

"Depends?" The postboy sounded crestfallen. "On what?"

"Just depends." Margaret had no intention of advertising the reason behind her wild dash north. "However, even if we don't stop, you may ask the kitchen to fix you a hamper of food to take with us."

"Thank'ee." He urged the lethargic horses to greater efforts.

Margaret studied the busy innyard as the postboy drove in, looking for a carriage that matched the description of the one that had been rented to Daniels. She saw several possibilities, and she decided to go inside and cautiously inquire after them.

She climbed awkwardly out of the carriage, her cold, stiff muscles protesting every inch of the way. "I'll be back shortly," she told the postboy.

He nodded disinterestedly as he started to unfasten the horses' harnesses.

Sending up a silent prayer for success, Margaret walked into the inn and looked around the common room. That late in the evening it contained mostly local tradesmen and farmers sitting around the roaring fire, nursing mugs of ale.

There was a sudden break in the conversation when they caught sight of Margaret standing in the entrance by herself.

Margaret ignored them and turned toward a portly man wearing a clean white apron wrapped around his ample stomach, who had just emerged from a private parlor. The frown on his face wavered slightly when he got close enough to see the quality of her clothing.

Margaret had no trouble understanding his uncertainty. Her clothing proclaimed her a member of the aristocracy, but her being in his inn alone raised serious doubts.

Margaret briefly debated the advantages of playing the helpless female over behaving imperiously, and opted for imperiousness. She'd always found it hard to maintain the role of featherbrained female for more than a few minutes at a time.

Copying the haughty look which seemed to be a permanent fixture on the countess Lieven, Margaret said, "You are the proprietor of this establishment, my good man?"

"Yes, ma'am. Jed Heathrow, I be, ma'am."

"I require information. I was to meet my cousins at the Feather and Dove in London and travel home to Scotland with them, but unfortunately, when I was late, they must have assumed I had changed my mind and left without me. I am hoping that they have stopped here to change horses and partake of refreshments."

"Cousins?" he repeated with a quick glance over his shoulder at the closed door of the private parlor.

"I certainly hope my cousins are here," Margaret continued, trying not to let show her sudden sense of excitement at his betraying motion. "It is not at all the thing for me to be traveling by myself."

"No, it ain't." The innkeeper seemed to relax slightly. "They shouldn't have left ya there by yourself. Not but what ya don't seem like a capable young lady. Not at all like young miss in the private parlor. Given to strong hysterics, she is," he confided. "And the young man, he's out back seeing about a new team of horses."

"Thank you, then, I need not trouble you any further." With a dismissive nod, Margaret hurried toward the door, hoping that it really was Drusilla. If it wasn't, she'd simply repeat her story, apologize for disturbing whoever it really was, and withdraw to continue chasing after Daniels and

Drusilla. Her muscles gave an involuntary twitch of protest at the thought.

Deciding not to knock and give Drusilla warning of her presence, Margaret quietly opened the door and peered inside. An overwhelming sense of relief poured through her, loosening her tense muscles and making her want to collapse. It really was Drusilla! She'd found her!

"Margaret!" Drusilla jumped to her feet. "What are you doing here?"

Margaret hurriedly stepped inside and closed the door.

"I came after you, of course! Did you think I wouldn't, after you sent me a letter telling me what you were about to do?"

Drusilla's lower lip trembled pathetically. "I guess I didn't think what you'd do."

" 'Didn't think about' describes this whole mess!" Margaret's sorely tried patience slipped.

"But I love Mr. Daniels, and he loves me—but it isn't at all like I thought it'd be!" Drusilla's voice rose on a wail.

"Reality is a lot like that."

"It all cost so much more than Mr. Daniels thought it would," Drusilla continued as if she hadn't heard Margaret. "But I do think Mr. Daniels could have borrowed enough money to pay our expenses, and I don't care what he says, I'm not going to give him my grandmother's locket."

For a moment Drusilla sounded eerily like Mainwaring himself. "It's all I got left of Grandmama, and Mama would never forgive me if I was to let Mr. Daniels pawn it like he did with my pearls."

Drusilla suddenly burst into noisy tears that Margaret suspected were caused as much by frustration as by grief over having her elopement interrupted.

"You are coming back with me to London." Margaret tried to put all the authority she could into the words.

"It's too late for that, Lady Chadwick. Drusilla is going to Scotland with me."

Margaret spun around at the sound of a hard male voice. Daniels stood in the doorway. Behind him were the avid features of the innkeeper, obviously scenting scandal and determined not to miss an instant of it.

"Close that door!" Margaret said, trying not to let Daniels see that she found his demeanor intimidating.

All she could think about was George's old saying about a cornered animal being dangerous. That was exactly what Daniels looked like to her at the moment. A cornered rat who was about to lose what he'd thought was his ticket to a life of ease. And from his expression, he wasn't about to give in easily.

A trickle of fear seeped through her. What could she do if he used physical violence against her? Would the innkeeper come to her rescue if she screamed?

But if she screamed, the whole mess would become public knowledge. And while she hoped that they were far enough out of London that news wouldn't get back, she couldn't be sure. Gossip had a nasty way of spreading and, if word of this did get out, Drusilla would be doomed to spinsterhood.

"I've arranged for new horses, Drusilla. Come." Daniels started for the shrinking Drusilla and Margaret hurriedly stepped between them.

Infuriated by her interference, Daniels reacted by roughly shoving her aside. Caught off balance, Margaret tripped and fell, striking her head with a painful thump on the edge of the fireplace. Brilliant sparks of light exploded like Catherine wheels in front of her eyes seconds before everything faded to gray, and she slid into oblivion, accompanied by the sound of Drusilla's shrieks.

"You know, Philip, I don't believe that I've ever ridden *ventre à terre* after someone before." Lucien hastily clutched the side of the curricle as Philip recklessly rounded a corner. "And if I have anything to say about it, I never will again. Has it occurred to you that if you lame the horses, you'll never catch up with her?"

"There's a full moon." Philip dismissed his fears. "And from the sound of the horses that charlatan of an innkeeper rented her, we should overtake them shortly.

"And according to what the ostler at the Dove and Feather told me, the Bird-in-Hand is the most likely place for her to stop to change horses. It can't be too much farther."

It wasn't. The Bird-in-Hand came into view as they rounded the next corner.

"A thriving establishment," Lucien said as Philip drove into the innyard. "There must be a dozen carriages here."

Philip tossed the reins to the ostler who rushed out to meet them. "Change them, and I want fast ones." Philip's demand was met with a respectful nod.

Philip vaulted out of the curricle and, followed by Lucien, hurried into the inn.

His impatient gaze swept the assortment of people in the common room, feeling a bitter sense of disappointment when he didn't see Margaret, even though he hadn't really expected to find her there. With the amount of money she'd taken from his cashbox, she would have rented a private parlor.

"Yes, your worships?" The landlord, recognizing quality when he saw it, approached them. "How may I be of service?"

"I am trying to catch up with my sister." Philip offered the lie he'd decided on. "She's traveling with—"

"Her cousins, no doubt!" The proprietor's tart tone caught Philip by surprise. How many people had she included on her escapade?

"In there." The man jerked his thumb toward the door behind him. "But I'm warning ya, quality or no, I got me reputation to think of. Won't be having no carryings-on here."

"Why do I have the feeling we are providing the climax to a farce?" Lucien said, as the landlord waddled back toward the common room.

"The climax will come if I find she's traveling with Daniels."

Philip ripped off his gloves and stalked toward the parlor door.

"Philip, I absolutely forbid you to kill him." Lucien hurried after him.

"I don't intend to kill him! I'm merely going to beat him senseless."

"You'd do better to let him beat you." Lucien tried to moderate Philip's temper. "Women always side with a vanquished hero."

Philip snorted. He didn't care about what women usually did. All he cared about was Margaret, and that she came back to him. He shoved open the parlor door, and it slammed against the wall with a bang.

"Really, old man." Lucien clicked his tongue in exasperation. "Bad ton, don't you know."

Philip ignored him. His sight was riveted on the blonde woman who was peering fearfully at him from the circle of Daniels's arms. It wasn't Margaret.

Relief poured through him like an icy shower, washing away his fear and allowing him to think clearly for the first time since he'd started this mad chase.

It was Mainwaring's chit, with Daniels. Surely he hadn't come all this way chasing after her?

No. The innkeeper at the Feather and Dove had described Margaret exactly. She had to be with them, but where?

As if in answer to his unspoken question he heard a soft moan to his left. He turned to find Margaret lying on a plain wooden settee which had been shoved against the wall. Her skin was the shade of well-bleached linen which highlighted the ugly purple bruise on her left temple.

"What the hell is going on here?" Philip's acerbic tone seemed to breathe life into the room's occupants.

Daniels immediately launched into a self-exculpatory monologue punctuated by Drusilla's sobs.

Philip ignored the pair of them, his attention focused on Margaret's pale face. He covered the distance between them in three long strides and gingerly ran the tip of his forefinger over her discolored skin, sucking in his breath as he felt the extent of the swelling.

"Nasty." Lucien peered over his shoulder. "Must hurt like the very devil."

"That's not the only thing that's going to hurt!" Philip turned, focusing his anger on Daniels.

"I didn't hit her," Daniels bleated, having no trouble interpreting the murderous glare in Philip's night-dark eyes.

"Truly he didn't, Lord Chadwick," Drusilla said. "Cousin Margaret fell and hit her head on the fireplace."

"I can sympathize with your wish to hit someone, old man." Lucien grabbed Philip's arm. "But I fail to see how drawing Daniels's claret is going to help Lady Chadwick. Nor will creating a scandal for the locals to gawk at help the situation."

Before Philip could tell Lucien that hitting Daniels might not make Margaret feel better, but it would do a lot to relieve his own feelings, Margaret made a sound and he hurriedly turned back to her. He gripped her hand, watching as her eyelids fluttered, fanning her dark golden lashes against her pale cheeks.

Margaret felt the warmth and strength from his hand flow into her chilled skin, nudging her to consciousness. She struggled through the gray wisps clogging her mind. With a monumental effort she opened her eyes, wincing at the shaft of pain that pierced her head as the light stuck her eyes.

"Philip." With difficulty she identified the face hovering over her. He looked different, somehow. His swarthy skin was set in harsh lines, and his eyes seemed to glow with the force of his emotions. Anger, most likely. The knowledge returned her to full consciousness with a thump.

"Margaret!" His harsh voice reverberated painfully in her head. "Are you injured?"

"My head hurts," she muttered.

"That's hardly to be wondered at, my lady. You have a nasty lump on your temple," Lucien observed.

Margaret struggled to bring into focus the man leaning over Philip's shoulder. He was Philip's friend; she finally recognized him even if his name escaped her at the moment. But why was he here? she wondered fretfully. For an out-of-the-way inn, this place certainly drew a great many of the ton.

"Would you mind telling me what the hell is going on here?" Philip's hard voice sliced through her muddled thoughts.

"Don't yell at Cousin Margaret," Drusilla worked up sufficient courage to say. "Can't you see that she has the headache? And you aren't the least bit romantic, either! Poor Cousin Margaret."

"Save your pity, Drusilla." Margaret instinctively defended Philip who was staring at Drusilla as if she were mad. "I don't want a romantic for a husband. I much prefer a man who knows how to go on. Philip would never set out on a journey without sufficient funds to pay for it. Would you?"

"No," Philip muttered, having the growing feeling that Lucien had been right. This was a farce. But on the other hand, Margaret had said she preferred him to a romantic man. Did she really mean it? Could she possibly harbor some small affection for him, despite the mess he'd made of everything?

A sudden spark of hope warmed his heart. But before he could explore her words, first he had to get her alone, and to do that he had to sort out this mess.

"What are you doing in this inn, Miss Mainwaring?" Philip homed in on the girl as the weakest of the personalities present.

"Well . . . I . . . I was eloping with Mr. Daniels," Drusilla blurted out.

Philip's eyebrows shot up, driven by the force of the relief that shot through him. Margaret hadn't been taken in by Daniels.

"Not at all the thing, Miss Mainwaring," Lucien said.

"Never mind that, Lucien. Why did you drag my wife into your scandal, Miss Mainwaring?" Philip demanded.

"She didn't drag me; I came of my own freewill." Margaret tried to shield Drusilla, who looked ready to start crying again. "Or rather, I followed after them.

"Well, someone had to stop her and bring her home," she added defensively at Philip's incredulous look.

"Seems to me that should have been her father's task," Philip said.

"You can't tell my father! He'll be so angry." Drusilla began to sob noisily.

"Philip, you are not helping the situation," Margaret reproved him.

"I don't want to help the situation. I want to get you home and call a doctor to look at your head."

"I am feeling much more the thing now." With a determined effort, Margaret swung her legs over the edge of the settee and sat up.

For a second, the world swam alarmingly and she was afraid she would faint again, but fortunately her vision settled almost immediately. There was no time for her to be sick. They had to get Drusilla home before the servants noticed just how long she had been gone.

"Drusilla, quit crying. You know full well that your father will have to be told. There's no excuse that would serve to explain why you are arriving home so late."

When Drusilla didn't answer, Margaret turned to Daniels. "Mr. Daniels, I think you will agree that your presence here is de trop."

Daniels cast a frustrated look at the sniveling Drusilla and then shrugged. "I would concede that I misjudged the depths of Miss Mainwaring's affection for me and retire from the field, but, unfortunately, I find myself somewhat short of funds."

"When haven't you been short of funds?" Lucien asked, as if the answer really interested him.

Daniels ignored the question as did Margaret. Reaching into her reticule, she pulled out the remainder of the bills she'd taken from Philip's strongbox. She didn't like Daniels, and she most emphatically didn't like the way he'd tried to take advantage of Drusilla's naiveté, but her basic honesty made her admit that she was responsible for a great deal of what had happened. Not only that, but she knew the terror of being stranded without money in a strange place.

"I'm not going to give that paltroon money!" Philip said when he realized what she was doing.

"No, I am." Margaret shoved the wad of bills at Daniels, who grabbed them before Philip could stop him. With an unrepentant grin at Margaret, Daniels hurriedly left the room.

"Of all the idiotic . . ." Philip sputtered to a stop as his outraged feelings got the better of him.

"I think she's right." To Margaret's surprise, Lucien defended her action. "Much as it goes against the grain to pay him off, if we leave him stranded here, who knows what he might do to raise the wind? And if he were to get caught doing it, this elopement could become general knowledge, and we certainly don't want that."

"We certainly don't!" Margaret got to her feet, wavering slightly. Philip immediately grabbed her arm, steadying her trembling body against his lean strength.

"Can you make it out to the carriage?" he asked.

"Yes," Margaret assured him.

Drusilla stopped crying long enough to say. "I have to visit the necessary room."

Philip gave her a suspicious glance, his eyes going to the door through which Daniels had exited a minute before.

"Certainly, Miss Mainwaring," Philip said. "Mr. Raeburn will accompany you to make sure that you are not accosted by the disreputable characters which seem to frequent this inn."

Lucien, drawing on a lifetime of training in good manners, smiled at the weeping girl and said, "It will be my pleasure, Miss Mainwaring."

The door had barely closed behind them when Philip said, "And now, madam wife, I'd like a few answers while we're waiting."

But I don't like, Margaret thought. *I don't like any of this. Not Drusilla's elopement, not my own part in it and, most definitely not the idea of trying to explain it.*

Twenty-two

"Well!" Philip demanded.

" 'Well' what?" Margaret stalled, not wanting to give him a comprehensive explanation in case he hadn't as yet figured out the full scope of what she'd done.

"Suppose we start with an explanation for this." Philip pulled a folded yellowish sheet out of the pocket of his gray coat.

Margaret stared at it uncertainly. How had he gotten hold of her mother's marriage lines? It had been in her reticule and . . . She'd dropped its contents in the study in her haste to get away, and obviously failed to pick everything up.

A feeling of frustration choked her, and her lower lip trembled despite her efforts to control it. She was so tired, and her head felt as if it might fall off at any minute. She did something she almost never did, and burst into tears.

"Margaret!" Philip's horrified voice echoed around the room. "Don't cry!"

His order was harsh, but the arms which enfolded her were exquisitely gentle. He gathered her to his broad chest, and she nuzzled her face into the crisp folds of his neckcloth and cried all the harder.

"Margaret?" Philip's voice sounded strangled, as if he were having trouble breathing properly.

Raising her head, she peered up at him. He looked tormented. Because she was crying or because of the scandal she'd involved him in? she wondered.

Making a valiant effort, she gulped back her tears and stepped away from him, hoping to clear her thoughts enough to make him understand. "That is my mother's marriage lines." Margaret nodded toward the paper he held. "I kept it because it was important to her. I think because she saw it as proof that she hadn't knowingly done anything immoral."

"I've heard marriage called many things, but never immoral."

"Yes, well, it's a bit complicated, you see. For over ten years my mother thought she was a legally wedded wife. Then one day my father came home and said that they weren't really married. That the minister who had supposedly married them was nothing more than a university friend who had only been pretending to be a minister for a lark. He told my mother that he'd just inherited the barony and he intended to marry into his own class, and Mama and I were to go away. . . ."

"And?" Philip prodded when Margaret fell silent, lost in the unhappy memories.

"We went, but with almost no money we didn't get far. Just to a Bath slum."

Philip watched the expressions play across her face and felt a burning anger grow in him at Mainwaring's cruelty. How could any man discard a mistress who had borne his child without making financial provisions for her and that child?"

"That was where Mama's cousin, George, found us." A fond smile curved her lips. "George might just seem like a foolish old man to you, but to me he will always be the embodiment of a knight in shining armor. He swept us off to France, and while we didn't have much, at least we had enough to eat and a roof over our head."

"What happened?"

"Mama died a few years after that. She'd never been very strong, and my father's revelation seemed to kill something vital in her. She simply gave up."

Margaret took a deep breath. "After we buried her, George continued to make a chancy living playing cards, and I kept house for us."

"So revenge was why you took up with Miss Mainwaring?" Philip had no trouble following her reasoning, because in her place he'd have done exactly the same thing. Try to avenge his mother.

"Yes." Margaret stared down at her hands, feeling thoroughly ashamed of herself. "That was why I fostered the acquaintance originally, but it all got so confused. Miss Mainwaring is . . ."

"An unworthy opponent?"

Margaret nodded. "But it was more than that. She hasn't done me any harm. And yet I was going to use her to hurt our father. Once I got to know Drusilla, I just couldn't do it, but by that time I'd already set events in motion I couldn't control."

"Daniels," Philip muttered on a flash of anger, wishing he'd called him out when he'd had the chance and to hell with the scandal.

"Yes, but I found out today that everything is far more complicated than I thought," Margaret said. "When I decided that I couldn't go through with encouraging Drusilla to marry Daniels, I went to the church listed on Mama's marriage license to see if I could find out anything about the man who had pretended to be the vicar. "But he really was the vicar, and he really did marry them, and that license is real," she blurted out.

"What!"

"Not only that, but three days after Mainwaring told Mama that she wasn't really his wife, there was a fire in the church where they were wed and all their records were burned."

"Mainwaring covering his tracks." Philip immediately reached the conclusion it took Margaret hours to deduce.

"Probably, but what he didn't know was that not only did the vicar keep a journal in which he listed every birth, death, baptism, and sermon he ever officiated at, but that the Church keeps copies of all its records at the Cathedral."

"I didn't know it, either, but it makes sense," Philip said, his mind still taken up with the implications of her revelation. "But why would Mainwaring cast off his legal wife and legitimate daughter?"

"I think because Hendricks was the executor of the late Baron Mainwaring's personal fortune, and he could give it to Mainwaring or withhold it as he wished. Hendricks told me he told Mainwaring that he had to marry the present Lady Mainwaring in the hopes that a suitable marriage would steady him.

"I can only guess that Mainwaring was afraid to tell Hendricks that he was already married, for fear of losing the money."

"When did your mother die?"

"Five years after Mainwaring married his worthy heiress."

"Good God!" Philip stared at the door through which Drusilla had gone. "That means Miss Mainwaring and her brother are bastards."

Margaret winced at the word. "The only bastard, as far as I'm concerned, is our mutual father and yet he's considered perfectly respectable."

"He won't be when this comes out."

"No!" Margaret surprised both herself and him by the strength of her protest. "Much as I want to tell everyone that my mother really was his wife and Mainwaring is an unprincipled villain, don't you see, if I do that, Drusilla, her brother, and her mother will be effectively cut off from any level of society. The scandal will follow them no matter where they go."

Philip reached out and pulled her to him on a wave of love so intense it threatened to choke him. He couldn't think of anyone else who would be willing to forgo such a richly deserved revenge for the sake of the children who had supplanted her. Margaret was the most incredible woman he'd ever met and she was his. All his.

Margaret blinked, uncertain as to why he was holding her so tightly, but not wanting to ask, for fear he might stop. "Not only that, but if Hendricks finds out that he was the unwitting cause of my mother's death, on top of finding out that I'm not really his daughter . . ."

"Yes, Hendricks." Philip winced as the guilt about how he'd used Hendricks erupted with a jab of pain.

"He probably won't help you with your bill anymore," Margaret said.

Tucking her head beneath his chin, Philip rested his cheek on the top of her head, drawing comfort from the floral fragrance which clung to her. "I very much doubt that Hendricks's help is going to make much difference to my bill in the end." Philip finally faced the facts he'd been trying to ignore. "Too many of the peers refuse to see beyond their pocketbooks."

"I'm sorry," Margaret said, really meaning it. Somehow, Philip's cause had become important to her also.

"I am, too. At least your idea of the manufactories will help ease some of the suffering. But it still seems hard to let Mainwaring get away with such infamous behavior."

There was a brisk rasp on the door a second before it was pushed open to reveal Lucien.

"There you are." He fixed an accusing eye on Philip. "I have been listening to Miss Mainwaring cry for the last ten minutes and only my sense of obligation to our longstanding friendship has kept me from throttling the wench. I loathe watering-pots!"

"We're coming," Philip said, trying to contain his impatience at being interrupted. Although perhaps it was better this way, he told himself. A shabby inn was hardly the right setting to tell her how sorry he was for the way he'd treated her; to tell her that he loved her, and to ask her to give their marriage a second chance.

He glanced down at Margaret's pale features as he escorted her out of the inn. He'd tell her later. After they'd taken Drusilla home. He'd assure her that his ungentlemanly attack in the carriage had been a momentary aberration, and that he'd never do anything so unseemly again. And he'd keep a close guard on himself to make sure he didn't.

Margaret allowed Philip to hand her into her rented carriage beside Drusilla, waiting while he conversed outside with Lucien in low whispers.

Finally Lucien got into Philip's curricle and drove away.

Philip watched him go and then climbed up beside the postboy.

Margaret bit back a sigh of regret that he didn't intend to ride inside. Not that she blamed him. He must be thoroughly disgusted with her and with Drusilla at the moment.

Although he hadn't seemed to care overly much about her revelations concerning her background, she decided. Even her startling announcement that she was Mainwaring's legitimate daughter hadn't brought the kind of amazed incredulity from him that she had expected.

Why not? she wondered. Surely a wealthy, powerful earl would be overjoyed to find that his wife was his social equal and had a right to her father's name? But the only emotion he'd displayed that she could clearly remember was anger at Mainwaring's duplicity. Could he not care that she was legitimate because he didn't care all that much about her? Was he already bored with her and planning to banish her to one of his remoter estates once the season was over? Was that why he hadn't been near her bed in the last week? It was a depressing thought, and one that Margaret didn't want to consider, but no matter how hard she tried to dismiss the disquieting idea, it wouldn't go away. It nagged at her already-ragged nerves, making her feel faintly frantic.

"Papa will be so upset." Drusilla stopped her crying long enough to say when the carriage finally reached London.

"He'd have been more upset if you had accomplished your elopement," Margaret said.

Drusilla sniffed. "I never was more deceived in a man! Imagine Mr. Daniels treating me like that!"

Margaret started to ask which particular treatment Drusilla objected to, and immediately thought better of the question.

"But then, you were deceived by Mr. Daniels, too, weren't you, Cousin Margaret?"

"Yes," Margaret lied, since there was no way she could tell only a part of the truth.

"And you are much older than I am," Drusilla observed with a total lack of malice. "So it is hardly any wonder that I was taken in."

"Hardly any wonder," Margaret promptly agreed, ignoring the slight on her age. Right at this moment she felt every one of her years.

Drusilla fell silent as the carriage came to a halt in front of Mainwaring's town residence.

"We've arrived," Philip announced unnecessarily, as he opened the door and pulled down the steps.

Drusilla climbed out of the carriage, reluctance in every line of her young body. "Cousin Margaret, would you please come in with me? Just for a moment."

"Yes, we'll go in with you." Philip's prompt agreement caught Margaret by surprise.

She searched his lean face for a hint as to his reason,

but it was impossible to read his expression in the darkness. Perhaps his sense of duty was such that he felt he had to deliver Drusilla directly into her parents' hands. Especially since his wife had been the instigator behind Drusilla's mad start in the first place.

Margaret took the arm Philip offered and climbed the steps to the Mainwarings' home every bit as reluctantly as Drusilla did. She didn't want to see Mainwaring. He was even more of a villain than she'd always thought, and she was going to find it hard to keep her tongue between her teeth in his presence.

Philip rapped sharply on the ram-headed knocker, and the door opened immediately.

"Miss Drusilla!" A middle-aged man Margaret assumed was the butler exclaimed.

"Drusilla, my dear!" Lady Mainwaring rushed into the hallway clearly torn between a desire to take her daughter into her arms and the need to present as normal a front as possible in front of the servants.

"Pray forgive us for being so late in bringing Drusilla home," Margaret tried to help Lady Mainwaring's efforts. "We had intended to return much sooner, but I fell and injured my head and your daughter wouldn't hear of leaving until I felt more the thing," Margaret said.

"Gracious me!" Lady Mainwaring's eyes widened as she caught sight of the livid bruise on Margaret's temple. Her eyes quickly swung to Drusilla's unblemished features, and she relaxed slightly.

"Who is it?" Mainwaring emerged from a room farther down the hallway. His pudgy features relaxed in a smile when he saw Drusilla.

"Chadwick and his lady have brought Drusilla back from her visit." Lady Mainwaring rushed to fill the silence before he could say anything the servants might repeat.

"And we wish to convey in person our apologies for

being so late, Mainwaring." Philip's tone of voice sent a shiver of foreboding through Margaret.

Nervously she glanced at him. The only sign of life in his face was the glitter in his dark eyes.

Margaret swallowed uneasily, wondering what Philip was planning to do.

"Certainly, my lord," Mainwaring said. "Come into my study. Your lady can have tea with my wife while we talk."

"She will come with me." Philip's voice left no room for argument.

"As you wish." Mainwaring motioned them into the study.

Closing the door on Lady Mainwaring's curious features, Mainwaring said, "I must thank you for bringing my daughter home, Chadwick, although"—a peevish note that Margaret remembered all too well from her childhood crept into his voice—"it would have relieved our minds if you had sent a message to tell us where she was."

"Where she was, was eloping to Scotland with Daniels," Philip said, "and I was too busy trying to track her down to worry about your feelings."

"Eloping . . ." Mainwaring turned back to the door.

"She's fine. We caught up with her when they stopped to change horses," Philip said. "That's not what I wanted to see you about."

Mainwaring collapsed into his study chair as if he'd been struck. "Eloped! How could she do such an underbred thing?"

"I neither know nor care," Philip said. "What I want is an explanation for this." He pulled the folded piece of parchment out of his coat pocket.

Margaret made an instinctive mutter of protest, but Philip just shook his head at her and handed it to Mainwaring.

Why? Margaret wondered in despair. Why was Philip doing this to Drusilla and Andrew?

As if to reassure her, he put his arm around her shoulders and gave her a comforting squeeze before gently pushing her down onto the sofa.

"Where did you get this?" Mainwaring demanded hoarsely. "It's obviously some lightskirt's trick!"

Philip frowned warningly at Margaret when she instinctively opened her mouth to defend her mother. "While tracing Hendricks's daughter on the Continent, I was sidetracked by reports of an Englishwoman named Abney and her blond daughter," Philip said.

The color bled out of Mainwaring's face at Philip's words.

"I discovered that document at the convent where Mrs. Abney took shelter. I found it quite curious."

"It's a forgery!" Mainwaring blustered. "Mary Abney was my mistress, and she didn't like being given her congé. She wanted more than the handsome settlement I gave her."

Margaret stared at Mainwaring through a blind rage that bathed him in a reddish light. She wanted to pick up the poker from the fireplace and smash it over his fat, complacent head. Her poor mother had had three pounds, six shillings, and twopence when he'd thrown her out of their home.

To Margaret's relief, Philip removed the license from Mainwaring's pudgy fingers. That piece of paper had meant respectability to her mother and as such it would always be precious to Margaret.

"I must admit my first thought was that it was a forgery, too. But recently I found myself near the church where it was issued and I stopped by to see the vicar out of curiosity. And do you know what I found, Mainwaring?"

Mainwaring's pink tongue darted out to lick his full lips. "I can't imagine. Nor can I imagine why you would be interested in my family," he added on a burst of bravado.

344   *Judith McWilliams*

Margaret held her breath waiting for Philip to announce who she was.

"Because you are related to my wife through Hendricks as you were so quick to point out to her at your first meeting," Philip said.

Margaret glanced down at her clenched hands to hide her surprise. Apparently Philip intended to keep her real identity a secret from Mainwaring. But what would that accomplish, if the secret of Mainwaring's bigamy came out? Mainwaring's second family still would be ruined. And Hendricks would still suffer an agony of remorse over his unwitting involvement in the whole affair. But one thing she was sure of, Philip's career as a spy had given him a far more devious bent of mind than she was ever likely to have. She'd wait and see what he had in mind.

"That marriage license is undeniably real," Philip continued relentlessly. "You really should have taken the trouble to check Church practice before you burned the records at St. Agnes, Mainwaring. The Church keeps copies of all its records at the Cathedral."

"You don't understand!" Mainwaring said. "I had no choice. Hendricks told me I had to marry Miss Wilcox, and he was right. She is far more suitable a wife than Mary Abney ever was—she was just a merchant's daughter."

"She was your wife!" The words exploded from the depths of Margaret's anger.

"She was nothing but a cit!" Mainwaring defended himself. "Why, she didn't even have a son. Nothing but a daughter who didn't even know her place."

Margaret closed her eyes trying to wall off her anger; it was making her head pound and the pain made her feel faint.

"Mary used her beauty to get me to offer marriage. It wasn't my fault!" Mainwaring appealed to Philip. "You are a man of the world, my lord. You know how some women are."

"The question in point is not how some women are, but how some men are," Philip said. "You committed bigamy. Both your daughter and your son are bastards!"

"Andrew is my heir," Mainwaring whispered, his cheeks a pale shadow of their normal ruddy color.

"Not once this comes out." Philip drove the knife a little deeper. "I wonder which distant cousin will inherit?"

"Chadwick, for the love of God, have pity on my children. They are innocent."

"As was your daughter! Your legitimate daughter." Philip relentlessly tightened the noose.

"She wasn't like Drusilla. She was nothing but a vulgar cit. Always telling a man what to do. Always knowing things she shouldn't."

Tentatively Margaret probed Mainwaring's hurtful words seeking pain, but there wasn't any. She really didn't care what he thought of her, she realized with some surprise. In fact, if she could somehow change herself into the kind of woman he admired, she wouldn't.

Mainwaring's desertion had killed her mother, but Margaret had thrived under George's benign neglect. She had taken advantage of her unusual freedom to explore all kinds of scholarly subjects usually closed to a woman. In a very real sense she was the person she was today because Mainwaring had disowned her.

"Please, my lady." Mainwaring turned to her. "Tell Chadwick that he can't hurt the innocent."

Mainwaring's whining voice filled Margaret with a deep feeling of disgust. She wanted to get away from him, wanted never to see him again. She looked at Philip, not sure what he intended to do.

"You don't think we should expose his villainy to the polite world?" Philip asked.

"I don't want Drusilla hurt," Margaret said.

"And she would be," Mainwaring rushed to point out.

"But what of your legitimate daughter?" Philip said.

"But she's dead! She must be, after all this time!"

"Oh no. I had no trouble finding her on the Continent. She is living, as you might well imagine, in rather reduced circumstances."

Mainwaring's small eyes darted around the room, rather as if he expected to find his eldest child secreted beneath the furniture. "She can't come here!"

"At the moment she doesn't know that her mother really was your wife," Philip said.

"You could not tell her," Mainwaring said. "What difference could her birth make to someone like that?"

"Money makes all the difference in the world," Philip said. "And as your daughter, she is entitled to one-third of your fortune."

"One third!" Mainwaring gasped. "But—"

Margaret shook her head in revulsion. She didn't want anything from Mainwaring. Not his name and certainly not his money.

But Philip ignored her instinctive denial. "That is the price of my silence. That you make amends to your only legitimate child. I'll have my man-of-business call on you tomorrow to go over your assets and to value your properties."

"But . . . What will I tell my wife?" Mainwaring whispered.

"You could try the truth!" Philip bit off. "It certainly should have some novelty value.

"Come, my dear." Philip held out a hand for Margaret. "I feel the need for fresh air."

Leaving Mainwaring slumped in his chair, Philip took Margaret's arm and escorted her out of the house. He handed her into the carriage, and after a quick word to the postboy, climbed in beside her.

Margaret rubbed her throbbing head.

"Is your head hurting?" Philip's voice sounded odd to her and, much as Margaret wanted to believe that it was caused by worry about her, she knew more than likely it was impatience with her physical weakness.

"It's not too bad," she said. "And I won't touch a farthing of that man's money. I'd sooner accept Judas' thirty pieces of silver."

"You're entitled to it. In fact, as his only legitimate heir, you're entitled to the whole estate."

"Maybe legally, but not morally. I won't take it."

"Hurting him financially is the only way we have of making him pay for what he did to you and your mother."

"Then take the money and give some of it to George for his care of Mama, and use the rest to help the soldiers," Margaret said.

"You're sure?"

"Positive. Although I'm not so sure that you haven't devised a far more eloquent revenge than I ever could," Margaret said. "In the back of his mind will always be the fear that we might tell. He'll never be completely comfortable again."

"Is that enough of a revenge for you?" Philip asked.

Margaret considered it for a moment and then nodded. "Yes. I still hate him, but mixed up in my hate is a strange kind of pity. He is such a weak, self-centered man."

"That he is. In fact, one wonders how he ever fathered you."

Margaret blinked, not certain whether he was complimenting her or not. Most men preferred weak, clinging women like Drusilla. But then Philip wasn't most men.

"So we can consider the subject of your parentage closed?" Philip asked.

"Yes," Margaret said, rather surprised to find it was true. After their confrontation this evening, she would be able to consign Mainwaring to the past and, while she'd never forget what he'd done, she wouldn't constantly dwell on it, either.

"That brings me to another subject," Philip said, and Margaret froze at the tension she heard in his voice. Was he about to tell her that their marriage had served its purpose and it was time to end the charade? Had his real goal in forcing her father to make a settlement been so that he could send her away with a clear conscience?

Margaret swallowed against the sudden fear that swept through her. She wouldn't cry and plead with him, she told herself. She would accept his terms and leave with her pride intact, as if she didn't care. As if her heart weren't breaking into a million tiny fragments. If she couldn't have his love, she would settle for his respect.

"I . . . I must apologize," he finally said.

Margaret blinked at the totally unexpected words. She waited for him to elaborate on the bald words, and when he didn't, cautiously asked, "For what?"

Philip cleared his throat and muttered, "For my unforgivable behavior in the carriage the other night. I can't offer any suitable explanation for allowing my animal lusts to overcome my gentlemanly instincts, but . . ." His voice trailed away into silence.

"Animal lusts?" Margaret whispered, feeling chilled by his description. What she had found so enchanting—if admittedly unconventional—he viewed as disgusting?

"A gentleman is supposed to remember at all times that a gently nurtured female—"

"I am not a gently nurtured female!"

"But you must have found my conduct objectionable?"

Margaret swallowed and cursed her unruly tongue. Why couldn't she just have accepted his apology? Now she either had to admit finding his lovemaking enthralling, which she suspected no respectable woman would ever do, or she had to lie and say she *did* object, in which case he would probably never do it again.

"Margaret?"

"Your behavior might have been impetuous and unex-pected, but . . . I didn't find it disgusting," she finished in a rush.

"You didn't?" His voice took on a note that she couldn't quite identify.

"No, I didn't."

He let his breath out on a long sigh. "Thank God for that. I was afraid that you'd demand that I never touch you again, and I don't think I would have been able to keep my promise."

"Why not?"

"Because I love you, dammit!"

Margaret's breath caught in her lungs at his astounding words.

When she didn't say anything, he rushed on. "Margaret, don't reject me out of hand. I know that we married under unusual circumstances—"

"That's one way to describe it," she mumbled, her mind still trying to absorb his amazing declaration. Could he possibly mean it? It seemed impossible to her that a so-phisticated, worldly man like Philip would fall in love with someone like her, but if he hadn't meant it, why would he lie about it?

"Maybe you could learn to hold me in some affection?"

"I don't have to learn to. I already love you," she blurted out.

"Margaret!" He grabbed for her and awkwardly pulled her to him, his lips closing roughly over hers. It seemed as if he was trying to vent all his pent-up hunger in the ferocity of his kiss.

Just as suddenly as he'd instigated the kiss, he lifted his head. "No," Philip said, staring down at her softened features. "Not until we get home, and I can have you to myself all night long."

Margaret shivered longingly at the deep note in his

voice. "Just because I love you doesn't mean that I think you're always right," she felt compelled to add. "Nor do I promise to be a conformable wife."

"I certainly hope not!" Philip was unable to resist nuzzling the soft skin beneath her ear.

Margaret's fingers clutched his suit jacket as the most delicious sensations tore through her. To think that she was now free to enjoy his caresses, free to . . .

Her escalating sense of pleasure evaporated as she suddenly remembered Hendricks.

"What's the matter?" Philip caught her sudden tension.

"I was just thinking about Hendricks. He is going to be devastated."

"Yes, and that's why I don't think we ought to tell him."

"Not tell him? But we lied to him."

"And it's a lie that I deeply regret the necessity of, even though I'm not sure I wouldn't do it again, given the same circumstances," Philip said. "Not only that, but what would it gain us to tell him?"

"We'd have cleared our consciences," she said.

"Yes, at the price of forever destroying his peace of mind."

"But—"

"Think, Margaret. His daughter is dead. If we destroy his belief in you, there is nothing and no one that we can offer him to replace you. We will have effectively sentenced him to being alone for the rest of his life. Which I very much fear might not be too long after he finds out."

"Yes." Her single word dropped like a stone into the heavy silence. "And he is a fine father, too. If I could have chosen my ideal father, he would have been it."

"But you can choose him. In fact, you could argue that I made the choice for you, months ago in Vienna."

"I am exceedingly fond of him," Margaret said.

"And you are his closest relative other than Mainwaring."

"True. There really is a blood tie between us, so maybe it wouldn't be totally wrong to continue the fiction."

"Not wrong at all. In fact, I think we ought to embellish it." Philip went back to nuzzling her ear.

"Oh?" Margaret shivered as she squirmed in his arms to try to fit herself more closely against his hard body.

"He was hinting just the other day, that he was really looking forward to being a grandfather. I think we ought to present him with a grandchild or two. It's the least we can do to try to make amends."

Margaret trembled with the force of the emotions that tore through her at the thought of bearing Philip's child.

"And what, my dearest, is the *most* we could do?" she asked.

"Wait until we get home," Philip promised as his lips met hers, "and I'll show you."